Judy Hansen

The HAMPTON HERITAGE

BY

Julie Ellis

Simon and Schuster   New York

PUBLISHED BY SIMON AND SCHUSTER
A DIVISION OF GULF & WESTERN CORPORATION
SIMON & SCHUSTER BUILDING
ROCKEFELLER CENTER
1230 AVENUE OF THE AMERICAS
NEW YORK, NEW YORK 10020
DESIGNED BY IRVING PERKINS
MANUFACTURED IN THE UNITED STATES OF AMERICA
1 2 3 4 5 6 7 8 9 10

LIBRARY OF CONGRESS CATALOGING IN PUBLICATION DATA

Ellis, Julie.
    The Hampton heritage.

    I. Title.
PZ4.E46623Ham [PS3555.L597] 813'.5'4
78-17050

For Pat Myrer

PART I

Atlanta

Chapter One

JUNE 22, 1897 looked gray and foreboding, but all of London was aware only that this was Jubilee Day, the ultimate tribute to Victoria's sixty-year reign. Yesterday the magnificently refurnished royal train brought Her Majesty to Paddington. This morning, while the Queen still slept at Buckingham Palace after a hot night, millions of her subjects left their homes to seek advantageous positions to observe the Jubilee procession. The roofs and balconies were crowded with viewers. Every inch of ground along the procession route was occupied.

Londoners had spent a quarter of a million pounds on flags and street decorations, some of which mingled thousands of tiny gas jets with the new marvel of electric bulbs. In Whitehall a stand, built at the cost of 25,000 pounds, illustrated the material progress of the longest royal reign, for here were ladies' rooms and lavatories, so sadly missing at Victoria's Coronation, and telephones, which had not then been invented.

In the immense but orderly throng that waited before the darkly imposing Christopher Wren masterpiece that is St. Paul's Cathedral, where an outdoor thanksgiving service was to be held, stood small, slim Caroline Hampton, born eighteen years ago today. Even in the excitement of the occasion Caroline's loveliness attracted uncommon attention. Her hair was the color of a spring sunset, her blue eyes luminous. Her smile—in eclipse these past few days since her mother's sudden illness and death—was dazzling. Caroline, who had been carefully cloistered by her mother, glowed with a beguiling innocence, yet simultaneously she radiated a potent physical appeal.

Caroline stood with rigid intensity, seeing no one about her at

9

this moment, remembering how her mother had anticipated this occasion, only to be cheated of participation. Three days ago she had stood with elderly Mr. Lonsdale, the family attorney, and watched while her mother's body was lowered into the grave beside that of her father's, where he had lain for almost nine years.

SHe was alone, *completely alone* in the world, she reminded herself fearfully. She refused to consider that her father's parents, her grandparents, were alive in far-off Atlanta, Georgia. They were not even aware of her existence. They refused to be aware. When she was born, her father had joyously written to them of this event. The letter was returned unopened, as all previous letters had been returned.

"They're coming now!" a small wiry man in front of Caroline cried out jubilantly as a shout went up a hundred yards beyond them.

On the broad steps of St. Paul's, where waiting church dignitaries included the Archbishops of Canterbury and York and the Bishop of London, along with the enormous choir prepared to participate in the *Te Deum*, there was a rustle of anticipation. A cheer went up as Captain Ozzy Ames of the Second Life Guards, at six feet eight the tallest man in the British Army, appeared astride a gigantic horse. Proudly he led the Escort, Indian Cavalry Lancers.

Behind the Escort came colorfully uniformed representatives from all the armed forces of the Empire. Mounted Rifles from Victoria and New South Wales, from Natal and the Cape, from "Our Lady of the Snows." Hausas from the Gold Coast and Niger, Chinese from Hong Kong, Dyaks from North Borneo, brown-skinned soldiers from the West India regiments as well as Imperial Service troops sent by the native princes of India. English, Scotch, Welsh and Irish paraded in honor of their Queen. Gilded carriages carried Prime Ministers from all the colonies and representatives of nations throughout the world.

"Now that's a strange sight!" a woman behind Caroline chortled.

"What would that be?" her companion inquired.

"The gentleman in the carriage there with the French and Spanish ambassadors. They're all so dressed up for the occasion in their fine uniforms and he's in black evening dress! Now who would that be?"

"That's Mr. Whitelaw Reid," Caroline turned to explain. "He's representing President McKinley of the United States."

"Is he in mourning?" the woman asked curiously. "Only the Queen and he are wearing black in this beautiful procession."

"It's the custom of the American envoys to wear black evening dress on such occasions," Caroline explained politely.

Caroline remembered her father telling her about the famous "dress circular" of Secretary of State Marcy, in the Pierce Administration, which set the precedent of Americans wearing their customary evening dress in the monarchial ceremonies. Like the Secretary of State, Papa had felt this was more fitting to a Democratic nation.

Unmindful of time Caroline watched the seemingly endless procession. Then all at once an ominous rumble sounded in the distance. The guns in Hyde Park were announcing that Victoria had left Buckingham Palace to join the celebration. Simultaneously, as though waiting for this moment, the sun burst through the clouds. Despite her grief over the recent death of her mother Caroline was caught up in the excitement of the moment.

Patiently the crowds before St. Paul's waited until at last a tidal wave of cheers told them Victoria's carriage was approaching.

"She's a grand old lady, she is!" a man in front of Caroline said exuberantly.

"But it don't seem decent, somehow," his woman companion objected, "to thank God in the street!"

"Would you be havin' the poor lame old lady climbin' down from the carriage and into the church?" the man chided.

Immediately in front of Victoria's open State landau rode Lord Wolseley, V.C., the Commander-in-Chief. Her Majesty's carriage was drawn by eight fine, cream-colored horses marching proudly beneath their golden harnesses, blue reins held by grooms wearing scarlet coats encrusted with gold.

"Go it, old girl!" an affectionately admiring masculine voice yelled from the crowd, but nobody seemed perturbed by this irreverence.

Caroline's gaze rested on the round, lined face of Queen Victoria, sitting beneath a parasol of black Chantilly lace. When the carriage pulled to a halt before the steps of St. Paul's, the Princess of Wales, who sat opposite the Queen along with Princess Christian, leaned forward to press Her Majesty's hand.

Mama, Caroline remembered, had adored the Queen. Papa had a charming affection for the old lady, but to him Democratic government was the only government for which he had respect. However, from the age of nineteen Papa never saw his homeland. Anger welled in her when she recalled his anguish in his long exile. For that she hated her grandfather, Josiah Hampton, as Mama had hated him.

Even now, almost nine years after Papa's death, while she stood here witnessing the *Te Deum*, her eyes filled with tears as she remembered the pain in his voice, in his eyes, when he told her—on her eighth birthday—about how he had fled from the United States at the outbreak of the War Between the States.

For that Papa's father had disowned him. When Papa wrote home after the War, his letters were returned by Josiah Hampton unopened. He wrote a cousin in Columbus, who made it clear he also wished no further communication from Francis Hampton; but the cousin told him that his two younger brothers had both died on the battlefield, that his mother was bereft of reason from the shock.

Miraculously Hampton Court had escaped the devastation of Sherman's March through Georgia, but the operation of a huge plantation without slaves as field hands was impossible. After the War Josiah Hampton had convinced himself the South would survive only with industrialization. He had borrowed from Northern cousins, enlisted the support of many small investors to construct the Hampton Mill and the adjoining mill village of Hamptonville. When the mill prospered, he built a mansion at the edge of Atlanta, only a brief walk to Hamptonville.

Caroline's father had followed his family's activities after the War by reading the *Atlanta Constitution*. Francis Hampton ordered the newspapers sent to London in bulk every six months. He neatly cut out every mention of Josiah Hampton, who had entered the War as a Major and emerged a Major General, by which title he was known even all these years later.

Caroline withdrew herself from retrospection as the brief thanksgiving service was finished and the bells pealed out from St. Paul's. Cheers welled from the watching throngs. The Jubilee procession moved along its route. Suddenly restless, Caroline abandoned her intention of remaining at St. Paul's to witness the rest of the procession.

She walked away from the crowds, unwilling to return yet to the overwhelming loneliness of the modest little flat she had shared with her mother for almost nine years. She sought the streets that would take her to Kensington Gardens.

Tears welled in her eyes as she entered the Gardens, splashed with glorious color this time of year. She could visualize herself lying in the grass, nibbling three-penny worth of Fry's chocolates while she listened to her mother talk of Hampton Court, second-hand, of course. As though she were ten again, Caroline lowered herself onto the grass.

She was alone, she reminded herself again. Tomorrow she must go to Mr. Lonsdale's office to discuss how she would earn her living. When her father died, her mother had gone out to tutor to support the two of them. For years Caroline had spent hours each day seated beside the daughters of Lord Englewood in the library of their Belgravia mansion, after which her mother and she returned to their flat to continue her own studies until it was time to prepare supper.

Lord Englewood's daughters spent their afternoons at garden parties and flower shows, played tennis or had their bicycles brought by carriage to Battersea Park so that they might ride, with the coachman and footman in attendance. In the evenings they saw Sir Henry Irving at the Lyceum or the Gilbert and Sullivan operas at the Savoy Theatre. Sometimes they went to see the plays of Pinero and Oscar Wilde. Soon they would "come out," to be wooed by the proper young men of English society.

Daily Caroline had been exposed to the luxury of their lives, but she had not shared. When her father was alive, they had roamed Europe each summer for three weeks, though with extreme modesty; but since her father had died there was little money for travel. Her mother and she had kept no carriage. They seldom rode in a cab. On the rare occasions when they traveled by rail, it was always third class. Her mother had made all their clothes. She had scrimped so that twice a year they might see the D'Oyly Carte. But Caroline's grandfather, General Josiah Hampton, was one of the richest men in the state of Georgia.

Caroline's face tensed as she stared unseeingly at the exquisite blue of the sky. She was hearing her father's low, melodic voice talking to her mother.

"Elizabeth, when Caroline is eighteen, I'm taking the two of you to see Atlanta and Hampton Court. We'll hire a carriage and ride out to the plantation. But we won't go calling," Papa had exhorted sternly. He was too proud to grovel. Yet his longing to see home and family was so intense that young Caroline could feel this as a personal pain. "We'll arrive in Georgia in the spring, when I know Mama and Papa will be living at the Atlanta house. They only go to Hampton Court now for the summers and at Thanksgiving, Christmas and Easter. We'll ride up that quarter-mile curving driveway lined with pecan trees and flowering dogwoods, and we'll pause at the great circle in front of the house. I can almost smell the camellias and jasmine. Then before the servants come out to inquire who's calling, we'll ride away as though we had made a mistake and come to the wrong house. But at least Caroline will see Hampton Court," he insisted triumphantly. "And she will see Atlanta."

How many times had she heard her parents play this small charade? Papa would describe the house in such detail that she would feel she was sitting in the carriage at that flower-banked circle before the tall white house with eight massive, round white columns on the porch that reached beyond the second floor to support the roof. She could visualize the iron filigreed balcony over the entrance.

A few weeks after her father's death her mother had stunned her with the confidence that Hampton Court would, in truth, belong to her at her grandmother's death.

"But don't you ever believe that evil old man will allow you to inherit what is rightfully yours," Mama warned bitterly. "Whichever of them dies first—and the poor old lady has no mind at all now, so she can make no decision—Josiah Hampton will make sure his son's child will never own Hampton Court."

"Mama, why should it belong to me?" she had asked bewilderedly.

"Because you are Francis Hampton's child," her mother said with pride. "Hampton Court was built as a wedding gift for your grandmother, Louisa Hampton. Her parents were furious when she insisted on marrying a penniless young lawyer, the son of a Presbyterian minister, so they arranged for Hampton Court to be entailed by deed to Louisa's heirs by blood. You're the sole remaining heir, Caroline." Her eyes had glowed with pleasure despite her conviction that her daughter would never claim her inheritance. "Hampton Court will belong to you." And now Caroline rebelled at the prospect of a dull future as a tutor, which seemed the only livelihood open to her, when Hampton Court should someday be hers.

At last Caroline returned to the flat she had shared with her mother, steeling herself as she climbed the dreary dank stairs to her door to face the emptiness that awaited her within. She paused before the door, key in hand, trembling with the knowledge that never again would she walk into the tiny sitting room that Mama had determinedly made so cheerful and see her mother fussing over the flowerpots she tended with such affection.

Inside the flat Caroline dropped her slender frame into the small worn chair by the window. She was alone in the world, as Mama had been alone when Papa met and married her. How different their lives could have been if Josiah Hampton were not such an arrogant, heartless man! How it used to exasperate Mama to hear Papa try to make alibis for his father's treatment of him! How could he persist in loving a father who treated him so shabbily?

"Elizabeth, you must understand the Southern thinking to understand Papa," he would reiterate gently. "Honor is revered above all else. To Papa I dishonored the Hampton name. That was unforgivable."

"I won't let you say that!" Mama would lash back indignantly. "You say it yourself. The War Between the States was fratricidal."

"It was a war that never should have happened," Papa acknowledged, his face angry. "The South expected Europe to intervene on its behalf. It expected Europe to break the blockade and impose peace. Europe failed the South."

Subconsciously Caroline reached out for the slender volume of poems by Sidney Lanier that her father had bought for her just weeks before he died. She opened the book to Papa's favorite, *Song of the Chattahoochee*. From his bedroom window at Hampton Court Papa could look out upon the muddy Chattahoochee River.

IN THE morning, as she was about to leave the flat to call on Mr. Lonsdale, Caroline collided headlong with her loquacious, pot-bellied landlord, breathing heavily from the efforts of carting a huge parcel to her door.

"One of them boxes came again," he panted, eyeing the carton respectfully. Caroline realized instantly that it was the semiannual delivery of back issues of the *Atlanta Constitution*. Despite the cost, Mama had doggedly kept this up even after Papa died. Atlanta had become an obsession for both Mama and her.

"Thank you, Mr. Williams." She pushed open the door so that he could deposit the carton inside.

With the errand accomplished, he hesitated.

"Beggin' your pardon, Miss Caroline, but I'm a business man and I hafta be askin' these questions. Will you be stayin' on in the flat?"

"I'll let you know by the end of the week," Caroline promised, her throat tightening.

She closed the door behind Mr. Williams and went for a knife with which to open the carton. Her heart pounded as she worked to free the newspapers. It was always this way when the carton came from across the Atlantic. But this time she was alone.

It would be all right if she delayed an hour in calling on Mr. Lonsdale. He would not notice if she appeared at his flat an hour later than she had planned. His days were spent sitting by a window gazing out upon the street. Not for a dozen years had he practiced his profession, but his mind was still sharp.

She dropped to her knees before the opened carton, eager to read everything at once. The oldest newspaper first, she ordered herself, the way Papa and Mama had always done. Her eyes skimmed the pages, searching for the Hampton name. There was rarely social news, though two years ago, at the time of the Cotton States and International Exposition, the General had entertained lavishly. Note was taken that the General's wife was indisposed and unable to serve as hostess.

Caroline put aside the first newspaper and reached for the next. All at once she froze in shock. She read the large black type that headed a front-page three-column article:

LOUISA HAMPTON, WIFE OF GENERAL HAMPTON, IS DEAD

Though she had never known her grandmother, Caroline felt a poignant sense of loss. Despite her anger at her grandfather, instilled by Mama's resentment of him, she had always harbored a secret hope that one day she might know her grandmother. Papa had loved her so deeply. He had grieved about her mental state. But most of all he remembered how beautiful she had been, how devoted to her children. The oldest, her firstborn, Papa had been especially close to her.

"Caroline, your grandmother is a beautiful lady," Papa would say with reminiscent pride. "When I was a little boy, I would force myself to stay awake in my bed when I knew there was to be a ball or a dinner that night. I would sneak out of my room and from the top of the stairs watch Mama receive her guests in the foyer below. Honey," he would chuckle, "that foyer is almost as big as our whole cottage, and your grandmother was a sight to see when she stood there, so lovely and gracious, welcoming the guests."

According to the date of the *Atlanta Constitution* issue that Caroline held in her hands, Louisa Hampton had died almost five months ago. Only her grandfather and she remained of their bloodline of the Hamptons, she realized with desolation. They bore no relationship to the Hamptons of South Carolina, Papa had always pointed out.

There were distant cousins, she recalled, both in Georgia and the North; but Papa's brothers—her two uncles—died on the battlefield, too young to have enlarged the close family circle. The

General lived, she thought acridly, unaware that she existed.

Carefully Caroline cut out the report of her grandmother's death, folded it into a neat square and placed it inside the tea caddy. She must leave now for Mr. Lonsdale's flat. She had told him she would be there this morning.

Leaving the house she walked with compulsive swiftness. How ironic that Mama had died only four days before word came from Atlanta that Louisa Hampton was dead. Mama would have gloried in the knowledge that Hampton Court belonged to her, despite the conviction that Josiah Hampton would never allow her to take possession of what was rightfully hers.

Why must it be that way? her mind suddenly challenged. Excitement welled in her as she walked. High color stained the porcelain fairness of her face. Mama said Hampton Court was to be hers when her grandmother died. Her great-grandparents had provided for that in the deed. Then she must claim what legally belonged to her!

No, she would not be staying at the flat. *She was going to Atlanta to fight Josiah Hampton for Hampton Court.*

Chapter Two

C AROLINE sat with Mr. Lonsdale in his tiny sitting room, cluttered with the memorabilia of three generations. Anxiously she inspected his lean, lined face as he poured tea into the pair of hand-painted bone china cups that were all that remained of a service that once belonged to his mother. Caroline knew he was turning over in his still keen, analytical mind her announcement that she intended to go to Atlanta to fight for her inheritance.

"Mr. Lonsdale, I have enough money to pay for the trip to Atlanta," Caroline reassured him with a confidence she did not feel. The cost of the transatlantic voyage and the long journey by train from New York to Atlanta would almost exhaust her mother's small savings, hoarded for an emergency. "If my grandfather refuses to receive me in his home, then I must immediately look for a job. I'm young and strong and willing," she said resolutely. "I can provide for myself while I fight for Hampton Court."

"Caroline, you must not make an impetuous move," Mr. Lonsdale cautioned, handing her a cup of tea. "You can't claim an inheritance when you have no papers in your possession to substantiate this."

"My mother told me Hampton Court is entailed to me," Caroline said stubbornly. "My father had told her. There must be records in Atlanta that'll prove that Hampton Court belongs to me. I'll find them, Mr. Lonsdale," she said zealously.

Mr. Lonsdale sighed. He knew she would not be dissuaded.

"Before you leave London, we must ascertain your legal position," he stipulated. "I'll write to the courts in Georgia. There must be records on file." Yet he seemed uneasy. "I fear, though, that your grandfather may have arranged for alterations that deny your ownership. You tell me he's a wealthy, influential man." He smiled faintly, his eyes compassionate but cynical. "Such men know how to manipulate legal matters to accommodate their own requirements."

"Mr. Lonsdale, it'll take weeks for you to receive a reply from Atlanta," Caroline rejected apologetically. "I can't afford to wait. What funds I have must be used to take me to Atlanta." But even as she recoiled from delay, she realized that Mr. Lonsdale spoke with logic. She must confront her grandfather with proof in her hands that Hampton Court was legally hers.

"I'm aware of your financial situation, Caroline," Mr. Lonsdale soothed. "And I believe I have a solution. I spoke just yesterday with the two maiden lady daughters of a former client. They wish to leave their mother, who's a recluse in their London house, to go to Wiesbaden to the baths; but they've been reluctant to leave her without a suitable companion. There are servants in the house, but Mrs. Middleton likes to be read to for several hours each day. The servants are inept at this. You would have your food and lodging plus a very modest stipend. You would be required only to read to Mrs. Middleton for two hours in the afternoon and again in the evening. And even if she dozes off, which she's apt to do," he admitted, "you must continue to read. She would be upset to awaken and realize you knew she had dropped off," he explained with an indulgent smile.

"How long will they be gone?" Caroline hedged. How long before Mr. Lonsdale had a reply from Atlanta?

"As soon as you're ready to leave for the States," Mr. Lonsdale said, "I'll wire the Misses Middleton in Wiesbaden and they'll return immediately."

"When would I go to the Middletons?" she asked, still indecisive.

"I'll send a boy with the note immediately," Mr. Lonsdale promised. "By morning the arrangements will be confirmed. You should present yourself to the ladies by Saturday."

"I can manage that." Caroline strived to sound matter-of-fact.

She walked back to her flat with new awareness of her surroundings. In a few weeks she would leave London behind her, perhaps forever. It was simultaneously terrifying and exciting.

Before going up to her flat she paused to talk to the dealer of a nearby shop, who would come up to make an offer on what she planned to sell. How unreal this was, she thought with a fresh surge of grief. To see Mama's possessions in a shop.

With the dealer scheduled to come up late in the afternoon, Caroline went directly to the flat. Not until the arrangements for her to become Mrs. Middleton's companion were definite would she tell Mr. Williams that she was leaving.

In the sitting room Caroline settled herself in Mama's chair to resume reading the old newspapers from Atlanta. Now everything she read held special meaning for her. *She was going to live in Atlanta.* No matter what reception she received from General Josiah Hampton, she would make Atlanta her home.

For most of his life Papa lived in exile, convinced he was disgraced in the eyes of all who had known him. She would change that, Caroline vowed. Somehow, in the years ahead, she would make all of Atlanta respect Papa's memory.

As HE had promised, Mr. Lonsdale told her in the morning that she was to report to the Misses Middleton on Saturday. They would leave the next day for Wiesbaden, content that Mr. Lonsdale had recommended her. On Saturday the dealer would come to remove from the flat what he had purchased for a shockingly small amount of money. Mama's pots of pansies would be cared for by Mrs. Williams, who had long admired them.

Caroline moved about the tiny bedroom she had shared with her mother, choosing what would go with her first to the Middleton house and then to Atlanta. The miniature of Mama which Papa had so cherished. The photograph of the three of them taken eleven summers ago in the Tuileries Gardens on their trip to Paris. The volume of poems by Sidney Lanier. Mama's watch, all she had from her own mother, and her enamel *étui*.

On Saturday Caroline was installed as Mrs. Middleton's companion. Each day in the ensuing weeks she read for long hours in her light, lilting voice, delighting Mrs. Middleton with her lack of reproach when the hours extended far beyond the periods stipulated in the arrangements. She masked the mounting impatience that welled in her while Mr. Lonsdale and she waited for word from Atlanta. When word came, it was disappointing.

"The County Clerk's office in Atlanta was unable to give me any information," Mr. Lonsdale reported. "We must give them the specific location of Hampton Court, and you know only that it's a few miles from Atlanta and situated along the Chattahoochee River."

"But wouldn't they know it by name?" Caroline asked in astonishment. "Papa said it was one of the finest plantations in Georgia."

"Perhaps the name has been changed?" Mr. Lonsdale suggested gently.

"No," Caroline rejected. "My grandfather would never have considered that."

"It's quite possible the records were destroyed during the War," Mr. Lonsdale suggested. "Still, I would think that the family would have re-recorded the deed after the War. This must have been common procedure." He frowned in thought for a moment. "I'll write again. Perhaps my letter was handled by an inefficient clerk. We'll explore further," he promised with a conciliatory smile.

"Mr. Lonsdale, I'm going to Atlanta now." *She could wait no longer.*

"Caroline, that's unwise," Mr. Lonsdale remonstrated. "You mustn't go to Atlanta so ill-prepared."

"I'll introduce myself to my grandfather." Her voice deepened with excitement. She would hide from her grandfather the anger she felt toward him. Outwardly she would be polite, respectful. "If he refuses to take me in, then I'll find work. I'll search for proof that Hampton Court belongs to me. I'll fight until it's mine. I know I mustn't make unsupported claims," Caroline conceded realistically. "But the time will come when I can approach Josiah Hampton and say, 'Hampton Court is mine.' But I won't say that," Caroline promised convincingly, "until I have the law on my side."

It was late August before Caroline said good-bye to Mr. Lonsdale at Euston Station and climbed aboard the train that was to take her to Liverpool. She was not going to the United States as an immigrant but as the child of an American citizen. Mr. Lonsdale had insisted on clarifying her position, though passports were not necessary in the United States. Caroline knew he concealed grave misgivings about this venture, yet he nurtured a wistful hope that Josiah Hampton's Southern upbringing would not allow him to turn aside a granddaughter—his only grandchild—who wished to place herself under his protection.

In Liverpool she left the railway station for the dock, where she was to board the American steamship that was to transport her to New York. She would travel for the first time in her life in first-class accommodations. Mr. Lonsdale had insisted upon this.

"I've heard unpleasant tales of travel across the Atlantic," he said sternly. "I owe it to Francis to see that his daughter travels with a degree of safety." And despite her protests he had insisted on paying the difference between third- and first-class fares.

At the dock Caroline stood motionless for a few moments in the midst of the frenzied activities about her. Her mouth parted slightly, her eyes shining, she viewed the long, broad-decked, three-funneled ship that she was about to board.

" 'Tis a beauty of a ship," a woman was saying with admiration as she moved past Caroline with a companion. "With the hull of the giant clippers that my father used to talk about. And though the three masts carry no sails, this one has the grace of the old sailing ships."

Settling herself in her stateroom, Caroline wondered if Mr. Lonsdale was responsible for her sharing this with an elderly member of the Society of Friends, going to join her family in Pennsylvania. Her companion confided that she, too, was traveling first-class because her family felt this was advisable for a lady traveling alone. Remembering Mr. Lonsdale's instructions, Caroline left her cabin to seek out the purser to learn where she was to sit in the dining room.

The purser, whose admiration for her was flatteringly obvious, not only assigned her to her seat in the dining room but introduced her to Congressman and Mrs. Bolton, going home after a six-week tour of Europe. Caroline radiated delight as she listened to the melodic softness of their speech, which was so like her father's.

"Are you from the South?" Caroline inquired eagerly.

"From Georgia," the Congressman confirmed with a courtly smile that suddenly broadened. "Are you related to the Hamptons of Georgia?"

"General Josiah Hampton of Atlanta is my grandfather." All at once she was trembling. "Do you know him?"

"We've met on occasion," Congressman Bolton said. "Everyone knows the General, of course."

"My father was Francis Hampton," she said after a moment, watching for some signal of displeasure. "He lived in London for many years." If the Congressman remembered the old scandal, he gave no inkling, Caroline noted with relief. "I was born there. I've never been home." How easily she said that! But Atlanta *was* home. She had shared Papa's exile.

"I hope we're at the same table," Mrs. Bolton said warmly, and turned inquiringly to the purser.

"Yes ma'am," he assured her. "I was hoping you would keep an eye on a young lady traveling alone."

"We will, indeed," Mrs. Bolton promised with approval.

Caroline was enchanted with the floating palace that was to be her home for the next seven or eight days. Her stateroom was bright and cheery, its polished solid oak door three inches thick. The grand saloon—glass-domed like the Crystal Palace, its walls adorned with pictures wrought in tapestry—seated four hundred twenty people. Table stewards saw to it that endless delicacies were brought to the tables at every meal. An organ in an overhead niche played soothing melodies throughout dinner.

Caroline spent much time each day in the company of Congressman and Mrs. Bolton and their shipboard friend, an American correspondent returning to New York briefly before going on assignment to Cuba. Like Mrs. Bolton, Caroline was eager to question the journalist about beautiful Evangelina Cisneros, the young Cuban girl whose imprisonment had aroused women throughout the world.

"I've read that she's imprisoned with criminals of the worst kind!" Caroline said indignantly. A tenderly reared young girl exactly her age. "That she scrubs floors and is subjected to unspeakable indignities. And that she's been sentenced to twenty years in Ceuta."

"How would they dare to send her to that dreadful penal colony in Africa?" Mrs. Bolton demanded. "She was guilty only of protecting her chastity. That awful Colonel Berriz, who declared she was plotting sedition, ought to be executed."

"I'm looking forward to searching for the truth," the American correspondent said guardedly.

"Do you believe she's guilty of sedition?" Caroline asked in astonishment.

"Miss Hampton," he said with a quizzical smile, "when you've been a newspaperman as long as I have, you don't believe everything you read."

"But even President McKinley's mother and Clara Barton have come to her defense!" Caroline protested.

"You ladies have been active," Congressman Bolton agreed.

But Congressman Bolton regarded the efforts of the ladies with indulgent amusement rather than respect, Caroline thought in frustration. Even Victoria, who should be sympathetic, displayed implacable hostility toward the women's movement.

ON THEIR final morning aboard ship Caroline arose at six, eager for her first sight of New York, but it was almost nine o'clock when the ship passed Sandy Hook. She was disappointed that rain obscured the view of New York Harbor.

"That's Lafayette Island there on the left." Congressman Bolton appeared at her side as the ship moved in. "That's where Southern prinoners were held during the War Between the States."

"Papa called the War fratricide," Caroline said. "He feared that the North and the South would never be truly reunited."

"We've had our bad times, Caroline," the Congressman said heavily. "And there are many among us who still refuse to allow the past to be buried. Until that happens the South won't be entirely healed."

"Is my grandfather like that?" she asked.

"I don't rightfully know," Congressman Bolton acknowledged. "I pray that he isn't."

Yet from the guarded glint in the Congressman's eyes Caroline suspected her grandfather was still General Josiah Hampton of the Confederate Army. Why else had he refused to forgive Papa?

The ship moved into the inner harbor. The paddle steamers were moving across to New Brighton and New Jersey, Congressman Bolton explained. Yachts were at anchor. Ships were being towed into port. Caroline felt a surge of excitement as they spied the Liberty Statue holding aloft its torch.

"That's the city there on the right," the Congressman said in a little while. "The green garden there—that's the Battery."

"It doesn't look very warlike," Caroline laughed.

"See those tall buildings there? Some of them are sixteen stories high. That's Wall Street."

The Customs-house officer boarded the ship at the Quarantine Station and distributed blanks on which passengers were to declare any items on which duty was to be paid. Their luggage was examined in a covered hall that adjoined the wharf. The Congressman and his wife remained protectively with Caroline, though their own luggage was examined before hers since this was done alphabetically.

The Congressman summoned a carriage to take them to a hotel, insisting that Caroline was their guest. She would stay in their suite overnight and tomorrow they would put her on the train that would take her to Atlanta. The Congressman and his wife, Caroline knew, were going to Boston to visit Mrs. Bolton's sister for a week.

The hotel chosen by the Boltons was quiet and comfortable, situated in an area exactly between the residential and business districts.

"Many of the diplomats I've met in Washington tell me they

always stay here when they're in New York," the Congressman said with satisfaction as they alighted from the carriage.

Later the Congressman escorted his wife and Caroline into the quiet elegance of Delmonico's for dinner, and afterwards they attended the theater. Caroline found it difficult to sleep that night and blamed this on the excitement of having dined at Delmonico's and attended the theater her only evening in New York. In the morning, however, Mrs. Bolton gently complained about the oppressive heat within the hotel rooms.

"Though I must admire the clean outdoor air," she said conscientiously. "It's far superior to the air in any other great city we've visited."

Caroline was grateful that the Boltons were so knowledgeable about traveling arrangements. In mid-afternoon they took her by ferry from West Twenty-third Street to the Exchange Place terminal in Jersey City and put her aboard the Southern Railway's *The Great Limited*, which went all the way from New York City to New Orleans, via Atlanta. Caroline paid spasmodic attention to the newspapers Congressman Bolton had bought for her before she boarded the train. Her eyes turned recurrently to the panorama of America rolling past her window. Her father's country. *Her* country.

Not until after ten in the evening did they approach Washington. Ignoring the sleep-inducing monotony of the rolling train, Caroline determined to stay awake, resolved to see whatever was possible of the national capital. She was disappointed that the dense fog of the night shrouded the view of Washington. Despite her expectation of falling asleep immediately after the train left the Washington station, she lay awake far into the night, speculating now on the approaching confrontation with her grandfather.

She awoke early, to discover the train was leaving Danville, Virginia. The next stop would be at Charlotte in North Carolina. They were truly in the South now. Close to four in the afternoon a white-jacketed porter moved through the train to announce that they would soon be pulling into Atlanta.

"Union Depot not far ahead, young lady," he paused to tell Caroline. "Make sure you don't leave nothin' on the train."

Caroline clung to the window as the train moved right through the city, her eyes straining to encompass everything within sight. This was not the Atlanta Papa had known. When he had left, there were little more than 11,000 people here. Now Atlanta was a city of over 110,000.

The train slowed to a crawl, pulled to a stop beneath a somber iron and brick shed with two steeples at either end and one in the center. An unpretentious depot for the Gate City of the South, though Papa had said it was quite the showplace of Atlanta when it was built back in 1871.

Despite the warmth of the mid-September day, Caroline was cold with excitement as the conductor helped her down the steps. *She was here. She was in Atlanta.* A good-natured black station porter, her luggage in tow, escorted her to a waiting carriage.

"The Kimball House, please," she instructed the driver. Back in London she had promised herself she would go to a hotel before calling on her grandfather. She recoiled from the prospect of dashing from train to house with her luggage clutched in each hand. Her arrival must be properly timed. This was the most important encounter of her life.

The Kimball House was next to the depot; but Mrs. Bolton said she was to take a carriage around to the ladies' entrance, on Decatur Street, where ladies traveling alone could register in privacy. She leaned toward the carriage window to inspect the hotel of elegant pressed brick, adorned with terra-cotta and granite trimmings. Seven stories, she tabulated, and with the air of the old Dutch Renaissance buildings Mama had admired in Holland and Germany. She saw the fine, small shops that occupied the street façades.

A porter met her as she alighted from the carriage, took her luggage and led her into the private office where she was to register. Such luxury here! The ground-floor lobby was a charming garden open through seven floors to the skylight and with galleries surrounding it on each floor. Caroline admired the polished oak wainscoting, carved woodwork, tiled fireplace openings and marbled stairways.

She could not afford to stay here more than two days, she reminded herself as the porter ushered her into her room. If her grandfather refused to receive her in his house, then she must at once seek out an inexpensive room and find a job.

"The bathroom is in heah," the porter said with a touch of pride, opening a door to the right. She realized it was for her sole use. "There's hot and cold runnin' water." He pointed to the stationary basin with two faucets.

"Thank you." Caroline smiled and reached into her bag for a coin for the porter.

When the door closed behind her, she darted to a window to gaze upon the bustling thoroughfare below. *Atlanta.* But why was she behaving in this lightheaded fashion? She was not a carefree tourist like those eager Americans who came to London each summer in such droves. She was here on serious business. She could not afford to waste a day. Not even this day, she admonished herself.

She reached into her bag for her mother's enamel-cased watch. For a poignant moment, holding the watch in her hand, she could almost feel her mother's presence. Her grandfather would be coming home from his office at the mill within two or three hours, she calculated. Not to Hampton Court, she reminded herself. To his fine mansion near the mill. She would be waiting there to introduce herself to him when he arrived. She would leave here in an hour; it would not do to arrive too early.

With a need to avoid dwelling on the imminent confrontation with her grandfather, Caroline unpacked and put away her modest wardrobe. She paused to dab at her moist forehead with a dainty handkerchief and to brush damp tendrils of her hair away from her face. How hot it was in Atlanta in September! But then her blue serge traveling dress was hardly appropriate for this southern climate.

She would have a bath and change into the flowered silk that Mama had made for her in the spring. All at once a devastating sense of loss swept over her. No! She must not give in to this. Mama would be impatient with such self-pity.

An hour later, her mouth parted faintly, her eyes betraying her inner excitement, Caroline left her room and descended in the elevator, as the lift was called in the States. Downstairs she walked with quick, small steps through the sumptuous public

29

area to the street, conscious of the admiring male glances that followed her.

She acquired a carriage and gave the driver her destination. The horses carried her smoothly through the city traffic. Her grandfather's house was far out at the edge of town she reminded herself; it would be an expensive drive. But she refused to arrive by way of the streetcars that ran out of the city in every direction.

She was impressed by the wide boulevards, the handsome business structures, the beautiful homes. Soon they were leaving the heavily populated area behind them. They traveled now along a broad avenue planted with graceful shade trees, live oaks predominating. Most of the houses were Victorian, set far back on landscaped acres.

They must have traveled two miles when the carriage at last turned off the avenue and the houses became far apart. They were driving along a high plateau overlooking the city on one side, with exquisite amethyst views of valleys and hills stretched on the other. Dusk was beginning to descend on the city.

Caroline's heartbeat quickened. Instinctively she guessed they were approaching her destination. A tall, white house reminiscent of what she knew of Hampton Court appeared in view. A colonnade extended around three sides, with columns rising to above the second floor. To the rear of the house was a large stable with quarters above, which Caroline guessed were for the servants. This was as splendid a home as Lord Englewood's mansion in Belgravia.

Perhaps a thousand feet beyond the house, where the plateau dropped to a lower level, stood a drab, rectangular brick building with opaque windows, night-dark except for one small area. The Hampton Mill, Caroline guessed. In the stillness she could hear the lulling flow of water over the dam that supplied power for the mill. The cluster of humble, low houses huddled timorously in a tree-barren clearing along the river must be Hamptonville, the company-owned town where the millworkers lived.

The driver turned off the road into the driveway which curved before the house, where every room on the lower floor seemed to be lighted. Servants were discreetly drawing the draperies tight at the tall, narrow windows.

Papa had never even seen this house, Caroline thought bitterly as she walked up the steps and across the wide porch to the massive front door and lifted the knocker. Papa had been exiled to a small cottage with a tiny patch of earth.

She waited, cold despite the warmth of the evening, hearing the sounds of footsteps coming in answer to her summons. A tall, elderly black man with a cap of tight white hair opened the door to her, and she had a swift impression of gilt and brocade and burnished mahogany. Had this man been a slave at Hampton Court? *Had he known Papa?*

"Yes, Miss?" he asked with puzzled politeness.

"I'm Caroline Hampton," she said with a dazzling smile that masked the tumultuous emotions that assaulted her. "I've come to call on my grandfather, General Josiah Hampton."

Chapter Three

THE man at the door stared at Caroline, too stunned to reply for a moment.

"Yes, ma'am," he stammered, prodding himself into speech, and pulled the door wide. His dark brown eyes clung to her face; he seemed afraid to trust his own vision. Caroline could hear Papa saying, *Honey, you're the spitting image of your Grandma.* "The General be home any time now."

"Thank you," she said gently, and walked into the immense high-ceilinged reception hall. An exquisite, intricately designed Kirman carpet dominated the entrance area, over which hung a gilt chandelier in the Classic Revival style. The walls on either side were adorned with gilt-framed prints depicting Confederate soldiers in action.

"This way, please, Miss Caroline." The man's low, melodic voice was unsteady, his eyes troubled. "I'll show you to the parlor."

Caroline followed him across the magnificently polished dark floor. Papa had told her the house slaves at Hampton Court spent hours every day rubbing cornmeal on the floors to make them gleam this way.

"Have you been with my grandfather for a long time?" Caroline asked as he paused to open the huge silver-hinged mahogany folding door to the parlor.

"I'm sixty-seven years old, Miss Caroline. I been with the General sixty of them years. Except when the General was away fightin'," he added with a tender pride that astonished Caroline. "I wanted to go with him to the War, but he say, 'You stay here and take care of Miss Louisa.' "

"Then you knew my father." Caroline's face was incandescent. "You're Seth!" she guessed, pulling the name from Papa's reminiscences of Hampton Court.

"Yes, ma'am. I'm Seth." His eyes were bright with unasked, fearful questions.

"Seth, Mr. Francis was my father," Caroline said softly.

"We—I didn't know Mr. Francis had a family, Miss Caroline." Seth's eyes clouded with remembered anguish. "I didn't know what happened to him."

But Josiah Hampton knew, Caroline thought with recurrent anger. When the black-edged letter came from Mama, he must have known Papa was dead. *The letter he returned unopened.*

"Papa died nine years ago, Seth," Caroline explained, and saw him flinch. "But Papa always talked about Hampton Court. He talked about you. He told me how you used to take him fishing with you when he was a little boy, and how you would fry a pair of catfish over a fire for your breakfasts. He loved to talk about those days."

"I loved that boy, Miss Caroline. I grieved when he—he went away." He was distraught now. "Please sit down, Miss Caroline. The General, he be home directly."

"Thank you, Seth."

She was glad that Seth was the first person she met in this house. For a few moments the love Seth and she shared for Papa had brought him almost unbearably close.

Seth left the parlor, shutting the door behind him. Caroline was conscious of the pounding of her heart. Very soon now Josiah Hampton would be arriving from the mill. He would open the door there, and she would come face to face with her grandfather. They were the last of their line. All at once she wished desperately to be accepted by him. She wished to be accepted with love.

She gazed about the large, square parlor, admiring the massive pier mirror that hung between a pair of velvet-draped windows, the handsome six-octave piano in one corner, the fine French antiques. And then her gaze focused on the painting that hung above the Carrara marble mantel.

She walked across the Aubusson rug to stand before the portrait of a young woman in a ballgown. All at once she was trembling, yet exhilarated. She recognized the woman in the painting, though they had never met. This was Louisa Hampton, wearing the emerald and diamond necklace Papa had described in minute detail. The necklace she wore to every important social event in Atlanta. The portrait had hung at Hampton Court. Every feature of Louisa Hampton was familiar to her. It might have been she in a ballgown of an earlier period. Papa's mother. *Her grandmother.*

Caroline stiffened as an authoritative thump of the knocker on the front door shattered this meeting with Louisa Hampton. She spun about to face the door. She stood motionless, listening to the voices in the reception hall. Seth was talking agitatedly to Josiah Hampton about his unexpected guest.

Moments later the door was flung wide. A tall, erect, ruddy-faced man with white hair and a commanding presence strode into the room. At seventy-seven he still bore the vestige of impressive handsomeness.

"Seth told me a young lady had arrived to see me," he said with calculated brusqueness.

"I'm Caroline," she said with charming guilelessness, and saw his eyes sweep involuntarily from her to the portrait of his wife. He was clearly shaken by the resemblance, yet hostility emanated from him. "My father was Francis Hampton." She waited for a reaction. He only tightened his mouth; his eyes remained hostile. "Papa died almost nine years ago." For an instant she thought she saw pain in his guarded dark eyes, but he said nothing. "Mama died in June. Papa told me if ever I should be left alone in the world, I was to go to my grandfather in Atlanta." She smiled uncertainly, watching wrath darken his eyes.

"You walk in here and expect me to believe you're my granddaughter?" he demanded contemptuously.

"I suspected you would not. I have papers here to prove I'm Francis Hampton's daughter." He couldn't bear to hear his son's name spoken aloud, she thought, fighting rage as she opened her bag and pulled forth her parents' marriage records along with proof of her birth. Wordlessly, her eyes challenging his, Caroline extended the papers.

34

Josiah took them from her and walked to a rosewood commode with floral marquetry at one side of the room. From a drawer he drew out a pair of spectacles, settled them on his face. The papers fluttered in his hands as he read them.

"What is this supposed to mean?" he asked impatiently after a few moments. "A man named Francis Hampton married a woman named Elizabeth Heath. There are many Hamptons in England. How can you presume to believe that your father was my son?"

"Because he told me so!" Color stained her porcelain cheeks. "He always talked about Atlanta! About Hampton Court!" Caution silenced her for an instant. Did he suspect she was here to claim her inheritance? She must pretend she knew nothing until she was properly equipped to fight him. "Papa knew that his brothers died in the war. He—he knew about his mother."

"My wife is dead," he said tersely. "I don't care to discuss her with you. Where did you find the impertinence to come here with this absurd claim? It isn't difficult to understand your motives," he said scathingly. "No doubt you're very clever—"

"I am your granddaughter!" Caroline interrupted furiously. "Can you look at that painting of Louisa Hampton and deny this?"

Her eyes held his without wavering. He uttered a low sound of irritation, withdrew his eyes from hers, and stalked to the door.

"Sophie!" he yelled. "Sophie, come in here immediately."

Caroline remained at the mantel, conscious of the drama of her appearance beside the portrait of her grandmother. How dare he deny the papers she had brought to prove her identity!

"Sit down," he ordered, waving her to the French Empire sofa. The amazing resemblance between her grandmother and her was upsetting him. He had not denied her challenge, neither had he accepted it. "When did you arrive in Atlanta?" he demanded when she was seated.

"Two hours ago," she said quietly.

"You didn't waste any time." His eyes were cold with suspicion.

"I registered at the Kimball House and came directly here to pay my respects. As Papa would have wished," she added quietly.

A tall woman, somewhere in her late forties, with severely dressed gray-blond hair and beautiful gray eyes walked into the room with surprising grace for a woman of her girth.

"Josiah, if you're angry that dinner is delayed, it's not Mattie's fault," she began reproachfully.

"I'm not worried about dinner," he interrupted. "Sophie, this young woman claims to be my granddaughter." His mouth pressed into a stern line of rejection, he handed the papers Caroline had given him to her.

"I am Francis Hampton's daughter," Caroline explained softly.

"You don't seem to understand that is a common name in England," he said irascibly. Why did he avoid calling Papa by name? Was it never mentioned in this house? "I don't know who put you up to this."

"My father told me his family home was Hampton Court, near Atlanta." Despite her resolution to play the sweet, respectful granddaughter, she was allowing a faint defiance to seep into her voice. "Papa was the most truthful man that ever lived. He could not lie if he wished." Instinct warned this was a crucial moment. Gamble. Show the General a trace of Hampton pride. "But if you refuse to recognize your son," she rose to her feet, head high, "then I'll return to my hotel without further conversation."

"Sit down, Caroline," Sophie commanded. "Josiah, we must look into this matter more deeply." Sophie lowered herself into an amply fashioned damask-covered chair. "I'm Sophie Anderson. I manage the household and I help the General at the mill." Plainly she was more than a housekeeper and assistant at the mill. She was very close to Josiah Hampton, Caroline assessed. "Where are you staying, Caroline?"

"At the Kimball House." She saw Josiah's eyes fasten with ferocious intensity on the portrait of Louisa.

"After dinner Zeke will drive you to the Kimball House," Sophie said matter-of-factly. "Patience will go along to pack for you." Josiah's eyes swung to her with imminent rebellion, but Sophie ignored this. "You'll stay here, of course."

This was no indication that she was being accepted into the

family, Caroline cautioned herself. Her grandfather and Sophie would argue heatedly about the authenticity of her claims. Now that Sophie was accepting her, Caroline appraised the situation; but Sophie was of a less explosive disposition than the General. Sophie would carefully consider the documents that she pointedly did not return.

With polite impersonality, Sophie questioned her about her journey. Caroline was grateful for this effort to put her at ease, yet she was uncomfortably aware of the General's simmering resentment of her invasion. But she was to stay here. If he became convinced she was his grandchild, he would feel a certain responsibility. Southern chivalry would insist on this.

Within a few minutes Seth came into the parlor to announce that dinner was ready to be served.

"Tell Mattie we'll come right to the table," Sophie told him.

"Yes, ma'am." Seth's eyes rested affectionately on Caroline for a moment, and she responded with an effervescent smile. She had one friend in this house.

Sophie rose to her feet. Self-consciously Caroline joined her. Dinner would be a trial, she was warning herself when her thoughts were derailed. A tall, handsome young man with sardonic hazel eyes and unruly dark hair appeared in the doorway, pausing there with a touch of drama. How tall he was! She would just reach his shoulders. He carried himself with a rakish air, yet Caroline sensed a blend of strength and rebellion in him. Before he spoke, Caroline felt the impact of his magnetism.

"Seth said you had not gone in to dinner yet." His voice was deep and warm, evoking unfamiliar emotions in Caroline.

Sophie's face lighted.

"Tonight you're in time." Reproach lurked in her emphasis. He lived here, Caroline realized. Was he Sophie's son? She seemed to adore him.

Eric's eyes settled on Caroline with an air of approving appraisal. He lifted one eyebrow in inquiry as neither Sophie nor Josiah made a move to introduce her.

"This is my grandson, Eric," Josiah introduced him irritably. Caroline struggled to conceal her astonishment. *How could this be?* Papa's two brothers had died in their teens, during the War Between the States. If either had a child, the grandson would be far older than Eric. "Eric, this is Caroline." The General turned to her with mock graciousness. "I believe you said your name was Caroline?"

"Yes, sir." Her smile was charmingly guileless. "I was named for your mother." Her eyes clashed with his.

"You're from England, aren't you, Caroline?" Eric sought to dispel the tense moment, though he was at a loss to understand. "I was there a few months ago."

"I'm Francis' daughter," Caroline explained. From the startled glint in his eyes she was sure he knew about Papa. "I was born in London."

"The young lady has presented herself as my granddaughter," Josiah said with deliberate sarcasm. "I've tried to make her understand that there are many Hamptons in England."

"But I know of only two Hampton Courts," Caroline retaliated swiftly. "One outside of London and the other outside of Atlanta. Papa was born at Hampton Court near Atlanta." Again, her eyes locked with her grandfather's, daring him to make further denials.

"Isn't Tina coming down to dinner?" Sophie intervened with a covert exchange between Eric and herself. Sophie and the General would discuss her presence here privately with Eric.

"Lucinda called downstairs as I came in to say that Tina had just arrived from a UDC meeting. She's changing for dinner." Eric turned to Caroline again. "Were you in London for Jubilee Day?" he asked.

"Oh, yes!" Tina must be Eric's wife, Caroline thought.

"It must have been quite an occasion."

"Every Londoner will remember it forever." Caroline's face glowed with recall. "That evening every British city was lighted up. Twenty-five hundred beacons shone from the hills in England, Wales and Scotland."

"We'd better go in to dinner or Mattie is going to be upset," Sophie said briskly. "We're having trout. It should be eaten as soon as it's done."

"We can't upset Mattie," Eric said good-humoredly. "Come along, Caroline." He smiled reassuringly at her. Again she asked herself, how could Eric be Josiah Hampton's grandson? If Eric were Louisa's grandson, then he should inherit Hampton Court rather than she because he was the older. A new fear was disconcerting her.

They left the parlor to cross the hall to the French Victorian dining room, where Seth and a small uniformed maid were bringing platters of food to the table. A gilt-framed mirror hung over the fireplace, reflecting the image of the delicately wrought iron chandelier that illuminated the room. In grim silence Josiah seated himself at the head of the table, laid for five. Seth must have automatically assumed she would stay at the house. Sophie sat at the other end of the table.

"Sit between Eric and me," Sophie told Caroline with a tense smile. "I want to hear about your trip across the Atlantic. I've never been beyond Charleston."

"It was an exciting trip." Caroline sought for details that might interest Sophie, while Seth and the maid moved about the table serving asparagus soup in white bone china bowls. How unreal to sit here talking about her trip from London as though she were a casual tourist! "I met an Atlanta couple on board," she finished breathlessly.

"Atlantans love to make the 'Grand Tour,' " Eric drawled.

"Tina and Eric were in Europe on their honeymoon," Sophie told her. Eric's face seemed to tense at this. "Who were the couple from Atlanta?" Sophie pursued.

"Congressman and Mrs. Bolton. They were delightful to me. I stayed overnight at their hotel suite in New York, and they put me on the train the next day." All at once she was aware of her grandfather's intense scrutiny.

"I voted for Bolton," Josiah said abruptly. "I'm not sure I should have."

"You voted for a Democratic Congressman but for a Republican President," Eric twitted.

"You're damn right, and I had plenty of company," Josiah retorted. "I contributed plenty to the campaign to put McKinley in the White House. How many Southern manufacturers voted for Bryan?" he challenged. "Not until McKinley got into office did this country start to pull out of the Depression."

"I'm sure President McKinley is going to do wonderful things for this country," a sweetly Southern, feminine voice said confidently from the doorway. Caroline turned her head toward the tall, spectacularly beautiful young woman, perhaps a year or two older than she, who was joining them at the table. She wore a porcelain blue gown splashed with small roses that displayed a splendid figure. The gown, Caroline thought admiringly, surely had been made by one of the fine French costumers, such as M. Félix of Paris. "You did right in supporting him, Grandpa," she said with a charming, deferential smile. This was Tina, Eric's wife. Lustrous black hair, shimmering green eyes, cameo features.

"Tina, this is Caroline Hampton from London," Sophie introduced her. "Caroline will be staying with us."

"How nice," Tina said with an air of pleasure, as she seated herself across the table from Eric, in a chair flanking Josiah. "I just adore the way the English talk." Her friendliness was reassuring. If Tina was curious about Caroline's relationship to the family, she gave no indication.

"Eric said you were at a UDC meeting." Josiah unbent slightly now that Tina was at the table. "Are you ladies beginning to make plans for the Reunion next July?"

"Oh, yes, sir! The committees are being set up already. Everybody's so pleased that it's to be held in Atlanta next year."

"I'm not sure that the United Daughters of the Confederacy isn't doing more harm than good," Eric said bluntly.

"Because we're making plans for the Reunion?" Tina asked with wide-eyed astonishment. "Oh, honey, how can you say that?"

"I'm not talking about the Confederate Veterans Convention," he brushed this aside. "I don't like the way the UDC is making a religious cult of the Confederacy. This is a New South. Let the past stay buried."

"You can't bury what happened to us in those four years!"

Josiah rejected, a vein distended on his forehead. "The rest of the country has never stopped trying to humiliate us."

"This is 1897, Grandpa," Eric objected. "The South has made tremendous strides. Not that we don't have problems," he acknowledged. "But so has the rest of the country."

"And what do you do about it?" Josiah challenged, ignoring the food he had piled on his plate. Caroline sensed this was a subject of much strife between Eric and him. "You waste your time with that piddling newspaper of Jim Russell's."

"Jim Russell is one of the brightest minds in the country," Eric said vigorously.

"Damn it, Eric, the South desperately needs new politicians!" Josiah exploded. Tina was listening intently. "Men to carry on in Henry Grady's trail. You talk a lot about the South's problems. When are you going to move into politics and do something about them?"

"Grady was a journalist," Eric reminded. "He always refused to enter politics."

"Henry Grady was the finest politician the South ever had!" Josiah blustered. "He happened to act in the role of a newspaper editor."

"No man ever did more to bring the North and South together," Eric agreed with deceptive calm. "No one worked harder to create a New South."

"Grady saw Atlanta's future." Josiah was ruffled by Eric's reference to a New South but pretended to ignore it. "He prodded this city into industrialization. Without him we never would have had the International Cotton Exposition back in '81!"

"And he used the *Constitution* to do all this," Eric pounced triumphantly.

"Don't compare the *Constitution* to Russell's rag," Josiah said with contempt. "It's never going to amount to anything. The Populist newspapers are dying off fast. Tom Watson is in virtual political retirement."

"For which we can all thank God," Sophie sighed. "Why couldn't Watson have stayed in the Democratic Party and fought for his reforms?"

"Eric, when are you going to settle down and take on some re-sponsibilities?" Josiah interrupted. "First you leave Princeton to work on that magazine in New York that nobody ever heard of, then you go chasing up to the Arctic Circle with that man Peary—"

"Peary is making important scientific discoveries," Eric em-phasized.

"You're not a scientist!" Josiah flashed back. "What the devil did you get out of freezing to death up there?"

"It was a great experience." Eric refused to be annoyed.

"Like that wild-goose chase down in Panama?" Josiah chal-lenged.

"I organized that syndicate to go down there to try to buy the franchise from the French—who're doing nothing about it—because I'm convinced that a canal linking the Atlantic and the Pacific will be as important to the world as the Suez." He spoke with a calculated calm that Josiah found more irritating than anger.

Sophie turned to Caroline.

"Twenty-three years old and Eric persuaded a group of men two and three times his age to consider an investment of millions of dollars." Her smile mirrored her affection.

"But the deal fell through," Josiah pounced.

"The men were heavy investors in the railroads." Contempt glowed in Eric's eyes. "The railroad chiefs convinced them they would be cutting their own throats if they tried to finish building the canal. Too much competition from the shipping lines."

"How long were you in Panama?" Caroline asked.

"For five months," Eric acknowledged and chuckled. "From freezing in the Arctic to sweltering in Panama. Then I came home and went to work for Jim Russell."

"Eric, I was talking this morning with Cyrus Madison." Josiah's tone was ingratiating. "You have to admit his law firm is one of the most prestigious in the state. Cyrus is willing to have you come in and read law with him. You'd be—"

"Grandpa, I don't want to be a lawyer," Eric interrupted. His eyes battled with Josiah's. "That's why I refused to go to law school."

The General was accustomed to manipulating lives, Caroline

42

thought. Eric would not permit this. Her father had not permitted it, Caroline remembered with pride.

"Eric, you ought to consider what Grandpa says," Tina coaxed appealingly. "Why can't you at least talk with Mr. Madison?"

Ignoring Tina, Eric turned to Caroline.

"Are the English as incensed as we Americans about the Evangelina Cisneros case?"

"Oh, yes!" Caroline was warmed by the compassion she felt in him for the young Spanish prisoner, yet she was shocked and embarrassed by his cavalier treatment of his wife. "Everyone talks about it."

"That's the fault of yellow journalism," Josiah said disdainfully. "Those New York publishers will do anything to sell papers."

"I met an American correspondent on board ship," Caroline said soberly. "He was going to Cuba shortly. He said—" She frowned in an effort to recall his exact words. "He said he was looking forward to searching for the truth. But how could he believe the Spanish might be right in imprisoning her so shamefully?"

"Spain has outrageously mismanaged her West Indian colonies," Eric said heatedly. "All those atrocity stories can't be wrong. Cuba should be independent."

"That's the kind of talk that will throw us into war with Spain," Josiah warned. "Despite McKinley's efforts to keep us out. We need peace if this country's going to prosper. We're just coming out of four years of Depression. We've got to maintain our trade with Cuba and Spain."

"You mean Wall Street is against war," Eric pinpointed with bitter humor.

"Enough of this," Sophie decreed. "Can't we ever sit down to dinner in this house without its becoming a political tirade?" She turned to Caroline. "How do you find this Atlanta heat? Does it bother you?"

"It's different from England," Caroline conceded, "but it doesn't bother me." She paused. "Sometimes I think Papa used to miss it."

"Did your father ride much in England?" Josiah asked with

strained politeness. Until this moment he had ignored her presence at the table. "He was a fine horseman."

"We didn't keep a horse, but there were horses at his disposal. He rode often." They could not afford to keep a horse, Caroline thought with recurrent resentment, because of their modest means.

"He used to enjoy the fox hunts at Hampton Court," Josiah said reminiscently.

"Not Papa," Caroline refuted softly. *He was testing her.* "Papa never hunted. He would never kill any animal." Her smile was sweet and unaffected, but her guard was up.

Josiah cleared his throat.

"Of course," he retreated. "I'm an old man. My memory plays tricks on me sometimes." He was as sharp as he was forty years ago, Caroline judged. Why couldn't he accept the truth?

"Papa used to wonder if Mr. Woodridge was still living," Caroline said ingenuously. Mr. Woodridge had been the attorney who handled Louisa Hampton's business affairs. "I suppose he would be quite old."

"He's alive. He must be eighty-six if he's a day." Josiah scrutinized her warily. She tensed. She must be more cautious in her prying. If Mr. Woodridge was still living in Atlanta, she would find him. *Yet if Eric was Louisa Hampton's grandson, she had no claim on Hampton Court.* "I was never aware of my son's fondness for Woodridge." Still he could not bring himself to say "Francis."

"Papa talked about everybody back home," she said innocently. "He so missed Hampton Court and Atlanta. He thought Atlanta the finest city in the world." She refused to allow herself to feel compassion for the sudden look of anguish that seemed to age Josiah a dozen years.

While they lingered at the dinner table over tall glasses of iced tea, Sophie sent for Patience and told her to have Zeke bring around the carriage.

"You'll go with Miss Caroline to the Kimball House and pack for her," Sophie ordered.

"Yes, ma'am." Small, ebony, delicately fashioned Patience

smiled good-naturedly and darted from the room.

"I'll see you to the Kimball House," Eric told Caroline, and Tina looked stricken. "I have to go to the city anyway." He pointedly avoided looking at his wife.

"They'll be coming right back with the carriage," Josiah reminded testily. He was irritated that Eric was leaving the house.

"Grandpa, I'll get home all right," Eric promised indulgently.

In a few minutes pretty, young Patience, obviously delighted with this evening's excursion, hurried into the dining room to announce that Zeke was out front with the carriage.

Tall, lean, pleasant-faced Zeke greeted them with a broad grin. "Evenin', Mist' Eric." He gazed shyly at Caroline. "Miss Caroline."

"I'm working on our project, Zeke," Eric said encouragingly, as Zeke helped Patience up to the perch.

"Thank you, sir."

Caroline was touched by Zeke's obvious idolization of Eric.

"What project were you talking about?" she asked impulsively when they were settled in the carriage.

"I've promised to make sure he's able to vote in the coming election. We've got a contemptible situation here in the South." Eric's eyes darkened with distaste. "The purpose of the Fourteenth Amendment was to assure Negroes the right to vote. It's not working out quite that way."

"Why not?" Caroline asked. It was the law.

"Southern reformers have concocted a variety of means to keep the Negroes from voting. In Georgia a Democratic registration committee has the power to draw up lists of so-called qualified voters. I mean to make sure Zeke's name is on that list. He's twenty-three and eager to vote." Eric chuckled. "I suspect Seth is worried that his grandson is becoming an aggressive Negro."

"But why should Zeke be deprived of his rights?" Caroline protested.

"Seth's thinking about last year." Eric frowned in recall. "A crowd of five thousand whites attacked Negroes, broke windows and turned over wagons at Decatur, Pryor and Five Points. All over town people stood in front of their houses with loaded guns."

45

"Were many people hurt?"

"A few, but no one was killed and things quieted down, fortunately. But Seth worries."

Like the General, Seth was mentally living in prewar days, Caroline thought. This was a new Atlanta. A city that vibrated with promises of exciting change. Eric felt that, too.

"At dinner you seemed interested in the Evangelina Cisneros case," Caroline probed. "Do you think she'll be saved?"

"There's no way of knowing, Caroline. The whole Cuban situation disturbs me." He hesitated. "I've been debating for weeks about going down to join the rebels."

"Eric, it's so dangerous!" Caroline was cold with alarm.

"Being alive is dangerous," he derided. "I was two when a tornado hit Americus and killed both my parents. There they were, safely tucked away on their small plantation—but they died in that tornado. The General is actually my third cousin. He took me in and raised me as his grandson." Eric's eyes lit with laughter. "You were wondering where he had acquired a grandson?"

"I was," she confessed.

"When Tina and I were married, he insisted we come and live with him. Tina was delighted." All at once his voice was harsh. "I couldn't afford to build a house at Inman Park, which she had expected." With chameleon swiftness his mood lightened again. "Don't say anything to Grandpa about my possibly joining the Cuban rebels. Not that I'll let him run my life for me," Eric said, his face tensing. "The decision will be mine. I'm in contact now with the Junta in New York."

"I'm sure you won't let the General influence your decision." She hoped Eric would decide against going to Cuba. Despite the intensity of her sympathy with the rebel cause, she recoiled from the prospect of Eric's being in the kind of danger that was part of their daily lives.

"You won't let Grandpa run your life, either," Eric guessed.

"No," she acknowledged. "Not that he'd care to at this point. He won't allow himself to believe I'm his granddaughter."

"Inside he believes you are," Eric assured, "or he would have tossed you right out of the house."

"My father always said his father was the most stubborn man alive." Caroline managed a wry smile.

"Your coming into his life this way, with no warning, was a colossal shock to him. It's been the tragedy of his later years that he had no direct heirs—or so he thought. He felt he was cheated of immortality."

"He cut my father out of his life," Caroline reminded defensively.

"He's a stubborn old man and too proud to admit he made a mistake. Now he's presented with a granddaughter. Give him time to digest that."

"I'm willing."

"Your resemblance to Aunt Louisa is uncanny. The General was always Grandpa to me and his wife was Aunt Louisa," Eric explained. "Though sometimes she would misplace relationships." His eyes were tender in recall. "Sometimes she would call me Francis."

Even with her poor mind in such a state, Louisa Hampton remembered her firstborn; Caroline clung to this realization.

At the Kimball House Eric went upstairs with Caroline and Patience. He stood at the door regaling her with stories about the hotel while Patience packed. When she stopped at the office to pay her bill, Eric offhandedly told the clerk in charge to send the bill to Josiah Hampton.

"You don't expect your grandfather to allow you to pay?" he chided, a glint of laughter in his eyes at her start of astonishment.

"I did," Caroline acknowledged high-spiritedly. "But I'm happy this way."

In truth she felt uneasy. Hampton Court belonged to her; beyond that she wanted nothing of her grandfather. Except his love, and that hardly seemed forthcoming.

A hand protectively at her elbow, Eric guided her to the street, where Zeke waited with the carriage. Atlanta, Caroline thought respectfully, must surely be the most illuminated city in the country.

"Be patient with the old man," Eric coaxed as he helped Caroline into the carriage. Zeke was teasing a delighted Patience while he gave her a boost up to the perch. "He'll come around. And welcome to the family, Caroline." With an insouciant smile he leaned forward to kiss her lightly on the cheek. She felt a strange excitement at the touch of his mouth. "Drive carefully, Zeke," he ordered. "You're carrying precious cargo."

Caroline watched through the carriage window as Eric disappeared into the night. She remembered the way Sophie had greeted him on his arrival. It was his custom to spend many evenings away from his bride.

She felt as though she had been waiting all her life to meet Eric. He evoked in her emotions that were unfamiliar, terrifying—and yet exhilarating. But he was her cousin, Caroline admitted ruefully. And he was married.

Chapter Four

J OSIAH sat in his favorite gold velvet and needlepoint wing chair with his eyes deliberately shut while Tina played a Schubert sonata with passable skill. The inference was that he enjoyed the music more thoroughly in this fashion. In truth it was Josiah's way of isolating himself from the others in the parlor.

What the devil was the matter with Sophie, bringing the girl into the house this way? He had expected her to handle the matter with her usual cool-headed efficiency, to tell the girl off and send her packing. What greedy charlatan had contrived this diabolical charade? Unbelievable, her resemblance to Louisa! Of course, that was the basis of the whole scheme.

Francis must have known the girl, remarked on the astonishing resemblance to his mother. A whole campaign had been cunningly devised to ship her here to pose as the granddaughter he never knew about so that she would inherit his estate. Damn it, he had not slaved all these years to build Louisa's inheritance into one of the most respected fortunes in the South so that some conniving stranger might enjoy it! And he had no intention of dying for a good twenty years.

This girl, who had the impudence to give herself his mother's name, had been shrewdly coached by someone who must have been an intimate of Francis. She even knew about Francis' obsession against killing. His face tightened as he visualized that January evening in 1861 when Francis came to him to say he was running away to London. Georgia had just become the fifth state to secede from the Union. The whole country knew that war was inevitable . . .

49

"I'm sorry, Papa. I can't stay here and become part of killing."

"Francis, have you lost your mind? Our survival is at stake! Are you so cowardly that you'll run to protect your own hide?"

"Papa, I won't take up arms against our own people," he insisted, his eyes tortured.

"Your people are here in the South!" How could Francis align himself with the North? "With Lincoln going into the White House our very existence is threatened!"

"Lincoln may go into the White House," Francis said with that quiet air of rationality that, somehow, always enraged him, "but the Republicans control neither the Senate nor the House of Representatives. The Supreme Court is dominated by pro-Southern judges."

"But that's no guarantee that Northern Democrats will vote for the preservation of slavery," he retaliated. "My mistake was in sending you North to Princeton! You acquired traitorous ideas!"

Josiah stirred restlessly in his chair. How could Francis have disgraced the Hampton name that way? He should have been here fighting along with his father. The two younger boys went into uniform as soon as they reached sixteen. They couldn't wait for that day.

Fresh anger surged through Josiah. How could Francis have put his mother through such shame? If he had not run away, if he had performed his duty as a Southerner, his mother would have had that to help her fight against her breakdown. He was always her favorite. There was a closeness between Louisa and Francis that sometimes irritated him; it seemed to shut him out on occasion. With Francis home Louisa could have borne the deaths of the two younger boys.

Tina stopped playing. Abruptly Josiah rose from his chair.

"I'm going up to my room." Sophie and he were at the mill by 6:00 A.M. each day.

"We'll all go up in a few minutes," Sophie said calmly. "It's cooler now. We shouldn't have any trouble sleeping tonight."

"Good-night, Grandpa." Tina came over to kiss him in that slightly flirtatious, girlish manner that he found so appealing. What the devil was the matter with Eric, leaving her alone so much? He didn't believe those cock-and-bull stories Eric handed

50

out regularly about meeting with Jim Russell. When he had a beauty like Tina at home, why did he have to run around after other women?

He pulled himself out of his chair and left the parlor, his mind involved with Eric. When was Eric going to settle down and face reality? He was bright; he knew the whole Populist movement was dead. Why wouldn't he go into Cyrus' office and read law? He had the mind, the personality for politics.

Everything had been too easy for Eric. He had taken Princeton for granted. God, the way *he* had worked, along with Papa, to be able to go to Princeton! A minister's son never forgot the stinting and scraping, the doing without. But he had graduated from Princeton and gone into a Congressman's office immediately. He had dreams in those days. He had vowed to himself that he would be in the Legislature by thirty, Congress by forty. Even the White House had not seemed beyond his grasp.

Louisa's parents had deliberately saddled him with Hampton Court. They took malicious pleasure in driving him away from a political career. Till the day they died they never forgave him for marrying Louisa. And his dream was dead until Louisa gave him his first son. He held his firstborn in his arms and told himself Francis would fulfill his dream. But Francis turned on his own people, and Yankee soldiers killed the two younger boys.

Josiah sighed, the familiar frustrations taunting him again. With Eric growing up, so brilliant in school and college, he had promised himself that at last the dream would come true. He would mold Eric in the image he had plotted for himself. He didn't care how much money was required to push Eric up the political ladder. Mark Hanna had bought the Presidency for McKinley. He could do the same for Eric. He had enormous power in the Party. Eric was aware of that. He owned half a dozen Congressmen, and three Senators and a Governor were beholden to him. It didn't matter that he was seventy-seven. He came from hearty stock. *Before he died, he wanted to see Eric in the White House.*

He climbed upstairs to his room, feeling the weight of his years tonight. More irascible than usual, he dismissed Seth without a word. But Seth understood. He changed into nightshirt and dressing gown and settled himself in a chair by the window, where the slight breeze that stirred in the night alleviated the heat and brought in the heavily sweet fragrance of the Cherokee roses climbing the trellis beneath his window.

He reached for the book on the table beside his chair, knowing it would be long before he slept tonight. Minutes later he heard the others coming up to their rooms. God knows when Eric would be home. Spoiled rotten, that was his trouble. Sophie had spoiled him all his life. Every woman wanted to spoil Eric.

What was going wrong between Eric and Tina? They came back from their fancy European honeymoon that had cost him a fortune, and right away they were in separate bedrooms. Louisa and he had shared a bedroom from the day of their marriage until her breakdown.

They had twenty good years together, Louisa and he. She was not a passionate woman, but she had loved him. He had worshipped her. Was Tina cold in bed? Beautiful but cold? That could have sent Eric chasing. Women had been after him since he was sixteen. But Tina had got him hot enough to propose. He was twenty-five. Time he settled down.

Sophie had been passionate, he remembered nostalgically. She had made his life bearable these last thirty-one years, though it must be a dozen years since he was in her bed. Together they had brought up Eric. She should have married, had children of her own.

He leaned back in his chair, remembering the tall, slim girl who came to work in the mill office when she was barely sixteen. He had known the Anderson family for years. Her father and three brothers killed in the war, her two sisters gone out West with their husbands. Alone with her ailing mother she had been desperately in need of funds, the way many tenderly reared Southern young ladies were in those years right after the War. The flower of Georgia womanhood could be found selling in grubby shops, side by side with "poor white trash." There were a few who succumbed to less than moral existences in order to survive. He had sent word to Mrs. Anderson that he would be proud to have Sophie in his office, not knowing then how indispensable she would quickly prove herself.

Two years after she came into the office her mother had died. She was alone. Louisa was like a small child; he no longer had a wife. He brought Sophie into the house to live and to manage the servants. A few months later he was in her bed. She knew he could never marry her, but it had been enough for her to be with him.

What a revelation Sophie had been! Young, beautiful, and unconcerned about the difference in their ages. He was as strong as a bull then, and as hot as an eighteen-year-old. Where Louisa had been passive, Sophie shared. Hell, why couldn't a man keep on that way till he was in his coffin? Now he could be passionate only in his mind. He closed his eyes. His thoughts hurtled backward through the years. He was re-living the first time with Sophie . . .

IT WAS a cold winter night in 1868. Josiah sat alone in the library at Hampton Court. The roaring fire that Seth had nurtured into being lent spurious warmth. Heavy slanting rain, mixed with hail, pounded at the windows.

Dinner tonight had been a trial. Normally Louisa was sweet and docile, like a child of seven or eight. Tonight she had been depressed, breaking into tears at the table without seeming to know why she cried. Sophie was so tender with her. Thank God for Sophie's presence in this house.

Damn, when was this rain going to stop? Rain aroused him. It was abnormal for a man of his inclinations to be without a woman. All the years of the War he had been celibate. He had come home, full of grief over the tragedies that had beset the family but impatient for reunion with Louisa. But her poor mind had broken. She was a child.

He stirred in his chair, aware of his rising passion. Sitting at the table tonight, watching Sophie, he had unwarily admitted to himself that he was lusting in his mind for her. Hell, he was crazy. He was twenty-nine years older than she. But he looked fifteen years younger than his age and felt like a man just reaching his prime.

With sudden resolution he rose from his chair and walked to

the pull cord. Sophie never objected when he called her down to the library to take a letter that he suddenly felt moved to dictate. Soon after coming to work for him she had shyly talked about learning the system of shorthand introduced by an Englishman named Pitman. It had given him disconcerting pleasure to dictate to her while she leaned forward so earnestly, making strange marks in a notebook. He had become aware of the delicious curve of her breasts beneath her sedate office dresses, her tiny waist, and innocently she looked at him with an adoration that made him tense his thighs in need.

He had become accustomed through the years to the admiration of women. Though he was married, there had been many a pretty, bold woman who let it be known that she would welcome his advances. He was too much the son of the Presbyterian minister to avail himself of such opportunities. But now night after night in his solitary bed he allowed himself guilty fantasies about Sophie and himself.

"Seth, tell Miss Sophie to come down to the library with her notebook," he ordered briskly when Seth appeared, and crossed to the cabinet that held his supply of bourbon. He was not a drinking man but occasionally he allowed himself a glass of fine bourbon.

He sat in the chair, glass in hand, to wait for Sophie to come downstairs and relieve the loneliness that haunted him since his return from the War. He was proud that Hampton Court had miraculously escaped the devastation of surrounding plantations.

The rain continued to pour relentlessly. Claps of thunder resounded through the night. The storm seemed to be gaining momentum. Lightning darted into the room with fleeting artificial brightness. It would be good for the fields, he told himself, even while he was uncomfortable with the arousal the heavy downpour evoked in him.

The door opened. Clutching notebook and pencil, Sophie came into the library. She was slightly flustered at having been summoned at so late an hour. She wore a blue dressing gown of soft material that emphasized her tall slenderness.

"I didn't take time to dress," she stammered, blushing becomingly. "I didn't want to keep you waiting."

"This is your home, Sophie," he said with unintentional brusqueness. "You don't have to dress to come downstairs. I want to dictate a letter to Henderson and Lathrop while the matter's clear in my mind. We've got to get more equipment, somehow, if the mill's to operate." Still, he would manage to retain control. Nobody could tell him how to run his mill. "I'm sorry to bother you at this hour, Sophie," he said.

"No bother," she said with that quick, faintly breathless manner of hers that always set his teeth on edge.

He tried to concentrate on the letter; but tonight, with the storm raging outside, her presence was erotically disturbing.

While he dictated, Seth came noiselessly into the library, moving about the room to close the shutters against the storm.

"Leave one pair of shutters open," he ordered Seth.

"Yessuh." He hesitated. "Will you be wantin' anything else tonight, Mist' Josiah?"

"No, go on to bed," he dismissed Seth.

He was having trouble with the letter. Could Sophie guess why? He prowled about the room, trying to gather his thoughts together. He paused at the window, momentarily fascinated by the exhibition outdoors.

"Come over here, Sophie," he said impulsively. "There's a kind of splendor about a storm like this."

Sophie put aside her notebook and pencil, came to stand at the window. She shivered slightly.

"You're cold," he said solicitously. "Go back to the fire."

"I'm not cold," she denied. "I think storms are exciting to watch." She lifted her face to his. She was almost as tall as he, yet she seemed fragile. An almost unbearable desire welled in him as his eyes moved involuntarily from her face to the curve of her breasts beneath her dressing gown.

A sudden clap of thunder rocked the house. Lightning wrapped them in eerie brightness. A startled sound of alarm escaped her. He reached out a hand to reassure her; and all at once, without his realizing it had happened, she was in his arms. His mouth found hers, clung.

He was forty-seven years old, but no woman had ever responded to his desire as Sophie was responding at this moment.

At last, trembling, he withdrew his mouth from hers.

"Sophie, this is wrong," he said unsteadily, but his hands held her tightly against him.

"No," she denied with sweet defiance. "Who's to be hurt?"

Wordlessly he brought his mouth to hers again. Her hands tightened at his shoulders. Her body strained to him with a passion that matched his own.

"Sophie, do you know what you're doing?" Josiah asked gently.

"Yes," she said clearly, her eyes telling him she loved him and that nothing else mattered.

"Go to the fire," he ordered, and crossed to lock the library door, though he knew there would be no intrusion.

How beautiful, how desirable she was, he thought as he strode across the room to where she waited. He paused en route to turn down the lamps. Her smile was exquisite when he reached to pull her close to him. For a few moments he was satisfied to sway with her before the warmth of the fire, his hands familiarizing themselves with her slenderness.

"You're not cold?" he asked while he tenderly pulled away her dressing gown.

"No, Josiah," she whispered. Not tonight the respectful "Mr. Hampton." With a sudden unexpected gesture she reached with both hands to pull her nightdress above her body and over her head. She stood before him, her nightdress at her feet, her eyes glowing. How many times had he imagined this moment?

"I knew you would be beautiful." His voice was unnaturally hoarse. He was impatient to bury himself within that lovely body, yet he wished to savor every moment of this encounter.

"Josiah, take me." Her voice was a caress.

"I'll show you how to love," he promised. His eyes never left her as he swiftly removed his clothes. His body was still lean and firm, like that of a man half his age, he thought with satisfaction. Sophie would not be disappointed.

"Josiah—" She leaned toward him, mouth parted, as eager as he for this union. She reached a hand to touch him and he could contain himself no longer.

"Sophie!"

He pulled her to the floor beside him, lowered himself above her and probed with a six-year hunger. For a moment Sophie cried out and he was still, cursing himself for his roughness. But then her arms pulled him close and she was moving with him.

At last they lay spent before the orange and purple blaze in the fireplace.

"I dreamed it would be like this." Her eyes were velvet with pleasure.

"No one must know," he reminded.

"No one," she said with conviction.

She lifted herself to lean over him and brought her mouth to his with appealing tenderness. Already he felt desire rising in him again. Tonight he would teach Sophie every nuance of love, because she was a woman who would accept and enjoy what he had never dared to bring to Louisa. Tonight would live forever in his memory . . .

JOSIAH ROSE from his chair with a frown, dismissing reverie. It was the present with which he must contend. These past few hours were unreal. Sophie could not truly believe that girl was Francis' daughter? Sophie was usually so calm, so realistic.

All at once he felt it imperative to talk to Sophie. She was an integral part of his life, though the carnal years were long past. Sophie and he would discuss the situation, and in the morning she would dismiss the sly adventuress who called herself Caroline Hampton.

At Sophie's door, he knocked lightly. She opened the door and beckoned him inside. Tonight, too, she wore a delicate blue dressing gown.

"What took you so long?" she mocked.

"Sophie, what in hell prompted you to invite that girl to stay here?" he demanded with a scowl.

"That's exactly what you expected me to do, Josiah," she said matter-of-factly. "You were manipulating for time to accept her as your granddaughter."

"You don't believe her?" he scoffed. "She's a scheming little fortune hunter."

"I believe her," Sophie refuted. "Those papers were real."

"How can you be so naïve?" Josiah stared belligerently at her, then crossed to the wing chair near the window and sat down. "Whoever engineered this scheme—and you can be damn sure that pretty piece didn't do it all alone—would know exactly how to forge a few documents. There's a fortune at stake. Francis talked too much about his rich old father."

"Looking at her was like looking at Louisa," Sophie said gently, and he felt again the shock that charged through him when he saw her standing there beside Louisa's portrait. "She's Francis' child. Josiah, stop fighting the War Between the States," she pleaded with sudden intensity. Enjoy this gift. *Your grandchild*, Josiah."

"My only grandchild is Eric," Josiah resisted stubbornly. "I love that boy like my own flesh and blood."

"I love him that way, too," Sophie reminded. "But that doesn't mean that you're to throw your granddaughter out of your life. Caroline has spirit. She was ready to walk out when you were be-having so cantankerously."

"She was bluffing." Josiah's eyes narrowed. "She figured you'd be too sentimental to let her walk out at that point."

"If she was, she comes by it naturally. How many times have you bluffed your way into a favorable business deal?" Sophie's eyes held his. She knew how upset he was over this absurd situa-tion, but she wasn't going to give him an inch.

"All right," he said truculently. "I'll let her stay for now, but don't think I'm swallowing that fairy tale. I'm calling in Cyrus tomorrow morning. I want him to send a man to London im-mediately." He paused, his eyes bitter. "Even if she is Francis' child, she's only here because I'm an old man and rich." He would never forgive Francis for robbing Louisa of thirty-one years of her life. He had no room in his heart for Francis' child. "I swear before God, Sophie, she won't see one cent of Hampton money!"

Chapter Five

IN the large square "blue" room, charmingly furnished in the American William-and-Mary style of the mid-eighteenth century, Caroline shuffled restlessly in the four-poster bed. It was surely past midnight. She was physically exhausted from her travels. Why did she lie here staring, fully awake, into the darkness? She had achieved a minor triumph. *She was here in Josiah Hampton's house.*

She could not thrust from her mind the traumatic confrontation with her grandfather. For a moment, when she stood beside her grandmother's portrait and faced her grandfather, all her bitterness toward him, the silent accusations that lay within her, evaporated. *This was Papa's father.*

If he had opened his arms to her, she would have forgiven everything he had done to Papa. If he had taken her into his heart, she would have wept with joy, feeling that part of Papa was with her again.

But Josiah Hampton had made it agonizingly clear that he resented her intrusion into his life. Even when he came to believe she was his granddaughter, as Eric predicted he must, he would resent her. Her presence was an unwelcomed reminder of what he considered a disgraceful blot on the Hampton name. His pride was far more important than love for his son. How could Papa have loved this arrogant, unfeeling man? But she was here in Atlanta; and if she could not have the grandfatherly affection that was due her, she would, one day, have Hampton Court.

Again, her mind replayed the happenings of the evening. When Patience and she returned from the Kimball House, Sophie had instructed Patience to put her belongings here in the "blue" guest room, which was next to Tina's room. Tina was politely puzzled by the General's coldness to her. Had he explained to Tina, in her brief absence, that Caroline Hampton, fresh from London, was his closest living relative?

Sophie had herself escorted her to the bedroom, telling her with such pleasure about the fine ladies and gentlemen who had slept in this room. She would never comprehend the Southern thinking, Caroline thought impatiently, that could put pride above compassion and understanding.

Caroline pushed aside the light coverlet that Patience had placed on the bed in anticipation of a night drop in temperature. She was not sleeping because of the unaccustomed heat, she told herself fretfully. Droplets of moisture gathered on her forehead, along her throat. The scent of roses and late-blooming jasmine was cloyingly sweet. Somewhere in the distance a dog barked. A neighbor was out hunting, Caroline surmised.

She frowned, remembering her grandfather's clumsy effort to trick her. Papa *never* enjoyed fox hunts at Hampton Court. He never hunted in England, though there were always invitations. People were drawn to Papa. The way, she suspected, they were drawn to Eric.

When would she see Hampton Court? She could close her eyes and imagine herself walking into the splendor of the house, each room etched in her memory by Papa's recall. But she must not appear too anxious to visit the plantation, lest the General realize her intent.

He knew Hampton Court belonged to her. Was that why he fought against conceding her identity? Once he accepted her as his granddaughter, would he reveal to her that Hampton Court was her inheritance from her grandmother? No, Caroline mocked herself. Like Mama, she was convinced Josiah Hampton would not release what was hers until the day she took him into a court of law. *And she would do that.*

When at last Caroline fell asleep, the first light of dawn had crept into the sky. She slept soundly, waking to sunlight, instantly aware of her surroundings. She darted from the bed to a window, pushed aside the blue damask drapes. The exquisite aroma of fresh-cut grass assailed her nostrils while her eyes swept the expanse of lawn that surrounded the house. Patience's light laughter echoed through the morning stillness.

"You think you is the greatest shot an' the best horseman anywhere in this state," Patience teased Zeke.

It must be late, Caroline thought guiltily, and hurried to consult Mama's watch, which lay with its chain on the finely crafted mahogany highboy. Almost ten o'clock!

Forty minutes later Caroline left her room striving to conceal her unease, and went down to the lower floor.

"Good mornin', Miss Caroline." In the hall a small, heavily built Negress greeted her. "It's so nice outside. Would you like yo' breakfast out on the verandah? I'm Annie Mae," she added in response to the question in Caroline's eyes. "The housekeeper."

"That would be lovely," Caroline agreed with a smile. All the servants knew her. Seth must have told them about her. "Annie Mae," she asked impulsively, "have you been with the family for a long time?"

"Yes, ma'am," Annie Mae's face softened. "I knew yo' Papa. I was a little girl at Hampton Court when the fightin' started. My Mama and me, we stayed with Miss Louisa. We didn't go runnin' off like some of them crazy niggers. When the General built this house, Mama and me came along. Mama died a long time ago but I kept on workin' for the General. Your Papa was a fine gentleman." Her eyes were richly affectionate. "Nobody finer. And him about the best-looking young man I eveh remember seein'. Welcome home, Miss Caroline."

"Thank you, Annie Mae." Tears welled in her eyes.

"You go set yourself down on the side verandah." Annie Mae waved toward the right of the house. "You can go out through the door in the lib'ary. I'll send Patience out with yo' breakfast directly."

Caroline walked through the spacious, booklined library—noting that many volumes dealt with law and government and history—and onto the verandah. A handsome, mahogany-red Irish setter lay sleeping on the gray-and-white marble floor of the verandah. She sat in a chair at the round pine table and leaned forward to stroke the silken head of the dog. Instantly the setter opened his eyes, inspected her admiring face, then rose on all feet to lay his head in her lap for further fondling. As she supplied this, her eyes were drawn to the ugly building beyond the windows that she was sure was the mill. In the distance rose a mountain that was unlike any Caroline had ever seen. Vast patches of bare stone alternated with patches of green, and a haze of smoke encircled it, lending it an aura of another Vesuvius. The smoke, she guessed, came from nearby factories.

Patience arrived shortly with her breakfast tray.

"Miss Caroline, that dog let you pat him?" Patience's eyes were bright with astonishment. "Nobody go near him exceptin' the General and Mist' Eric."

"Oh, we're friends." Caroline leaned forward to scratch behind his ears. "What's his name?"

"The General, he call him Alex," Patience told her. "That's short for Alexander the Great."

Caroline was conscious of the sudden pounding of her heart. When Papa left home, there had been an Irish setter called Alexander the Great. Probably there was always an Irish setter named Alexander in the household of Josiah Hampton.

"Miss Caroline, you eat that omelet while it's hot," Patience ordered. "Mattie's right proud of her omelets."

"I will," Caroline promised.

"Patience!" Annie Mae's voice rang with authority. "You git upstairs and do Miss Caroline's room."

Accustomed to her light English breakfast, Caroline was astonished at the hearty array of food set before her, but she ate with relish. When she could not consume another bite, she poured herself a second cup of strong, fresh coffee, remembering how Papa used to tease Mama about her incessant cups of tea. While she sipped the second cup, Zeke came out to bring her the morning newspaper.

"When you finish readin' it, Miss Caroline, I'll put it in the lib'ary for the General," he said with a respectful smile.

"Thank you, Zeke."

Caroline tried to focus on the front page of the *Constitution*, but the newspaper in her hands evoked a sudden aching sense of loss. The small flat in London, where she had last sat and read the *Atlanta Constitution*, was poignantly fresh in her memory.

"Good morning, Caroline." Tina's sweet, Southern voice was a welcome sound in the stillness. "I thought I'd have another cup of coffee out here till Zeke finishes up whatever he's doing and can drive me to my mother's house." Her eyes widened as she watched Alex push his head beneath Caroline's hand in a bid for further attention. "My goodness, you've made friends with Alex! Nobody does that."

"We took to each other instantly," Caroline said with a brilliant smile.

"Don't let Grandpa frighten you, Caroline," Tina coaxed, sitting across the table from her. "He's truly a sweet old man. He gave Eric and me a wonderful honeymoon in Europe. That was to make up for our very simple wedding. Aunt Louisa had died only four months earlier, it would have been out of the question to have a big wedding. I was so delighted that, out of all the girls in Atlanta who were dying to marry him, Eric asked me."

"I don't think the other girls had a chance," Caroline laughed. But she remembered how Eric, so soon after the honeymoon, was neglecting his bride. "Where did you go in Europe?" she asked.

"After a week in London, we went to Paris for two weeks, then on to Vienna and Rome. I adore Paris. I've been hearing my brother Chad talk about Paris for years. He ran away from Atlanta when he was twenty—he's eleven years older than me—and lived in Paris for almost a year, until his money ran out and Papa refused to send him any more." She frowned. "Why is Patience taking so long with my coffee? All that girl does is stand around waiting to catch a glimpse of Zeke. I promised Mama I'd be at the house before noon." Her eyes were following an elegant victoria driving past the house in the direction of the mill. "That looks like Mr. Madison's carriage. I'll bet Mr. Madison's going to the mill to talk to Grandpa about Eric's coming into his office, and Eric's being so difficult."

"But Eric isn't interested in law," Caroline reminded.

"He ought to be!" Tina was indignant. "He refuses to go into the mill. All he does is waste his time on that stupid newspaper. Grandpa can do so much for Eric. I don't know how Eric can go on disappointing him this way."

63

"Is that the mill village?" Caroline made an effort to divert this discomforting conversation.

"Yes, that's Hamptonville. Isn't it silly?" Tina laughed. "This is Atlanta, and a thousand feet beyond begins Hamptonville. Grandpa deliberately built the mill beyond the town limits. It has something to do with being out of the jurisdiction of Atlanta. He's so smart about business matters," she said admiringly. "I wish Eric would be more like him."

Patience arrived with Tina's coffee. Her earlier air of ingratiating friendliness had evaporated. She was polite but guarded. Caroline sensed that she disliked Tina.

"Patience, tell Zeke to hurry up whatever he's doing. I have to leave in a few minutes," Tina said sweetly, and turned to Caroline. "If Mama and I weren't going to the doctor I'd invite you to come along into town with me," Tina apologized.

"I'm glad just to sit around the house today," Caroline said quickly. "After all that traveling. But how do you get into town if you don't go by carriage?"

"Honey, there are four carriages here," Tina chided indulgently. "Eric is absolutely out of his mind, of course. He insists on walking all the way over to the streetcar line, and taking that down to Peachtree."

"I like to walk," Caroline said ingenuously. She would have nobody from the house know where she went, lest some word leak back to the General. "How far is it?"

"Grandpa said it's at least a quarter of a mile," Tina said earnestly. "And why should you ride on the dirty old streetcars when we have four carriages?" She looked up inquiringly as Patience hovered, unsmiling, in the doorway.

"Zeke said he's going out to the stable now for the carriage," Patience reported.

"Thank you, Patience." Tina took a final sip of her coffee and rose to her feet. "I left my hat and bag on the foyer table. I'd better get them now. I'll see you at dinner, Caroline."

JOSIAH LEANED across his wide office desk, his face stern.

64

"Don't write off this business about Eric, Cyrus," he ordered. "Give me some time. He's got to come to his senses. But let's get back to the girl—"

"Josiah, the documents appear authentic," Cyrus Madison told him. "I see no reason to question them."

"Damn it, they can be forged!" Josiah insisted. "You know that and I know it. I want you to send a man to London to check out her story. I don't want any doubts to remain about her real identity." He took a deep breath. "Whichever way it turns out." Why did she show up just now, months after Louisa died? She couldn't know about the stupid entailment in the deed. "Find out if her mother did die in June, as she claims."

"This is going to be expensive," Cyrus warned.

"To hell with the costs!" Josiah bellowed. "I want facts." He leaned back in his chair, tired from having slept so little last night. He had shut his mind against the realization that Francis was dead. When the black-edged letter came from the woman who called herself Elizabeth Hampton, he returned it unopened. Up until then he had never given up hope that Francis would come home and beg forgiveness. Not by way of a letter. Francis himself at Hampton Court, admitting he had committed a terrible deed. For his mother he should have done that. "Cyrus, you send a man to London immediately. Find the truth no matter what it costs." He frowned at the light knock on the door. "Come in."

The door opened. Tina walked into the room, stopped dead as she spied Cyrus Madison.

"Grandpa, I didn't mean to interrupt a business conference," she apologized prettily.

"It's all right," he said briskly. "We've finished. Cyrus, you know what to do."

"I'll take care of it, Josiah," Cyrus promised, rising to his feet. "You're looking beautiful as usual, Tina," he said with a courtly bow.

"Thank you, Mr. Madison."

Cyrus Madison left the room. Josiah gestured Tina to a chair. Maybe he was working at Eric in the wrong fashion. For all Eric neglected Tina, she was his wife. There must be nights when Eric made his way into her bed. Use Tina to push Eric into politics. Damn it, it was for his own good.

"I'm going to see Mama and I thought, wouldn't it be nice to sweep up Grandpa and take him off for lunch downtown first. You're always working so hard," she chided with the blend of deference and flirtation that was her approach to the General.

"Why do we have to go to a restaurant for lunch when Mattie serves us perfectly fine meals?" he protested, but she knew he was pleased at this attention.

"I want to show off my distinguished, handsome escort," she teased. Tina smiled with a potent sweetness that was the envy of many an Atlanta belle.

"One of these days we'll have lunch," Josiah hedged. "Today I'm too busy. I'll call the house and have a tray sent over." Tina sighed, wistfully indulgent. "I'm glad you came over, though. We've got to do something about Eric." He pushed back his chair, rose from behind the desk and pulled up another chair close to Tina's. She waited for him to speak. "I can't bear to see Eric waste himself on Jim Russell and that stupid newspaper. Eric has every quality necessary to succeed in government. Brains, more charm than he knows what to do with. Even without a law background, he could win a seat on the City Council. And that's only the beginning. I don't know if you fully realize Eric's potential, Tina. The future that could be yours." He reached for her, searching her eyes. Oh, yes! Tina was already visualizing herself as the wife of the rising young politician.

"Grandpa, I'll do anything to help," she said with little girl breathlessness. "Truly I will. But Eric won't listen to me."

"You'll find a way," Josiah soothed, his eyes holding hers. Quickly she lowered her own, but she knew exactly what he meant. The way to convince Eric was in her bed. "We'll work together, Tina," he encouraged. "One step at a time. The City Council first, then into the Legislature. With Eric's personal qualifications and what I know—and what I'm willing to spend," he emphasized, "Eric can win the Governorship in a dozen

66

years. From there Congress will be a natural step. As a Washington wife you'll have a fascinating life, Tina. Parties, dinners, balls. A fine house where you'll entertain regularly."

Tina's eyes glowed. In a few moments, Josiah congratulated himself, he had transformed Tina into an ambitious wife.

"Grandpa, I'll do anything you tell me," she promised fervently.

"Give him a child, Tina." She stared at him, the color draining from her face. Why the hell had he been so blunt? But why should she be upset that he talked this plainly? She had been married five months. She knew what it was to have a man in her bed. "It'll be the best thing in the world for Eric," Josiah pursued persuasively. "It'll keep him home," he added meaningfully. No pussyfooting at a moment like this.

"You're always right, Grandpa." Tina managed a shaky smile.

"The day you present Eric with a child, I'll call in the finest architect in Atlanta to design the plans for a house for you in Inman Park. To your specifications, Tina," he said expansively. If Tina were cold in bed, this should warm her up. Francis had failed him. He would not accept that from Eric. Eric was his last chance on this earth to make his mark on history. For more than sixty years he had dreamt about the decisions he would help to frame that would lead the country—and especially the South— to fresh greatness. With Eric in politics he could do this. There were no limits to Eric's future. After all the disappointments the prospect of having *his* man in the White House would be impetus enough to keep him alive for the next twenty years. "I'll build you the most splendid house in Inman Park, Tina."

"I would adore that!" Tina smiled radiantly.

"*Your* house," Josiah stipulated cannily. "The deed will be in your name." In the dark crevices of his mind he was aghast. Louisa's parents had done this to him. But a house in Inman Park was not Hampton Court. He could afford to make this gesture. A political candidate with a family was infinitely more appealing to the voters than one without. "Tina, can't you visualize it?" he said zealously. "Together we'll make Eric a leader of the nation. By the time your child is old enough to vote, Eric will be running for the Presidency. You will be the most beautiful First Lady this country has ever known."

WHEN TINA left him to go out to the waiting carriage, Josiah leaned back in exhaustion. She had sworn not to divulge their private conversation either to her mother or to that spoiled, decadent brother of hers. How long before she would come to him and tell him she had conceived? Eric's child would become his great-grandchild. After his father, heir to the Hampton fortune. That conniving girl who called herself Francis' child would grow bored soon enough and take herself back to England where she belonged. He would pay for her journey. But he wished with a staggering intensity that she looked less like Louisa. How long must he gaze at her at the dinner table and remember the thirty-one years of Louisa's life that Francis had stolen? The disgrace that Francis had brought to the Hampton name.

Chapter Six

FROM the side verandah Caroline watched Tina leave the mill and ascend again into the carriage. Tina had been impatient to be on her way to her mother's house, Caroline recalled curiously. Why had she delayed to go to the mill?

The day dragged. Caroline barely touched the luncheon Patience brought to her when she returned from a walk about the spacious grounds. She settled herself in the library, delving into the volumes of history in which the General had inked pithy remarks. Late in the afternoon, unprompted by her, Seth brought her a tray of tea and English biscuits.

At five Caroline heard Tina return and go directly up to her room. Soon the General and Sophie would come home from the mill. Caroline hoped that Eric would be at the table for dinner. Only with him did she feel at ease.

To her disappointment Eric did not appear at dinner. Striving to lighten the mood at the table, Tina flirted with Josiah.

"Grandpa, if you were thirty years younger, I would leave Eric and run off with you," Tina declared.

After dinner they retired to the parlor. Tina went directly to the piano and began to play. The General read the morning's *Constitution* until he had surveyed all that interested him, then sat with eyes closed. Sophie concentrated on her needlepoint.

Caroline sat with a small, fixed smile. She was allowed to eat and sleep in this fine house, but to her grandfather, she did not exist. She stiffened at a sound at the front door. A moment later she heard Seth talking with Eric.

Tina looked up from the piano as Éric appeared at the door, but continued to play. The General opened his eyes in recognition of Eric's presence and closed them again.

"Did you have dinner?" Sophie framed the words silently, and Eric nodded. Now he turned to Caroline.

"Do you play chess, Caro?" She started at the diminutive.

"Not too well," she warned. Still, she was hopeful of a game. She had played nightly with her father until his death. At seven he had seated her before her first chessboard.

Eric crossed to the *secrétaire* and pulled forth an ivory chess set. He removed the center cushion of the green and gold tête-à-tête and, with a flourish, gestured to Caroline to join him.

Caroline focused all her mental capacity on not disgracing herself. Instinctively she knew that Eric would be a canny player.

"You play a fine game," Eric said finally with an air of respect. "I never expected that from such a beautiful young lady." His eyes were gently mocking.

"My father would have no sloppy playing. He taught me the 'Evans Gambit' and Philidor's Defense and—just everything he could cram into my head." She stopped self-consciously. Her grandfather was scrutinizing her. Tina left the piano to cross to the tête-à-tête.

"Caroline, you're so smart," she said admiringly. "Chad's forever trying to teach me some game or other, but I can just never learn."

"What are you doing tomorrow, Tina?" Eric asked, and Tina seemed startled.

"In the morning I'm going with Mama to Chamberlin-Johnson-Du Bose to choose material for her new dresses." She turned to Caroline with an air of confidence. "Everybody says that black silk will be 'the rage' this winter. We're still following Paris, of course."

"What about the afternoon?" Eric pinpointed, and Caroline realized he was intent on arranging for her to be included in Tina's activities.

"Oh, I'll have a boring afternoon!" Tina made a moue of distaste. "Mama insists that I go with her to her reading club."

"I'm going upstairs," Josiah announced. "Sophie and I are at the mill by six A.M.," he said pointedly.

"Grandpa, Andrew could hold the fort if you slept late one morning," Eric joshed. But the inference was that Eric was an idler.

Moments after Josiah had retired to his room, the others left the parlor to go up to their rooms, also. While opening her door, Caroline saw Tina put a hand on Eric's arm. Tina murmured to him. His voice was too low to carry to Caroline, but his rejection of Tina was obvious. Her cheeks stained with color, Caroline hurried into her bedroom.

She sought sleep in vain, disturbed by the encounter she had intercepted at Tina's door. Sitting opposite Eric while they played chess, she had been conscious of emotions that startled and alarmed her. When their hands had brushed accidentally, she had felt color flood her cheeks.

She was relieved that Eric had not gone into Tina's bedroom. It would be awful to lie here and know that Eric was in the next room making love to Tina.

No other man had ever made her feel this way. Ever since he had kissed her on the cheek, there at the Kimball House, she had been assaulted by wicked fantasies. Eric holding her in his arms, telling her he loved her. Eric kissing her until she was dizzy with delight.

She must stop this nonsense. Eric was a philanderer, a man who charmed every girl he met. She would not allow herself to be another of his conquests. She closed her eyes, ordering herself to sleep.

CAROLINE AWOKE early the following morning. As she lay in bed dreading the long day of idleness that lay ahead of her, she could hear her grandfather talking with mock ferociousness to Alexander. It was too early to go downstairs. She wished that she had brought a book up from the library so that she might read a while.

She left her bed, crossed to a window to gaze out on the golden splendor of the day. She loathed this self-enforced inactivity. Perhaps she would go for a walk today. She must discover where the streetcar could be boarded. Unwarily she remembered the small tableau at Tina's door the night before, and was again discomforted by its inference.

This morning Tina joined her on the verandah for breakfast, chattering about her plans for the day.

"Mama will take forever to decide what she wants to buy at Chamberlin's. And then we'll go to the house for lunch and to rest a bit until it's time to go to the reading club. It's so hot I don't know why they don't postpone the meeting." She brushed a lace-edged handkerchief across her forehead. "Why don't you have Zeke take you for a ride over through Piedmont Park this afternoon, Caroline? The park is beautiful."

"Miss Tina—" The tall, spare black woman whom Caroline knew was Tina's personal maid and had earlier been her nurse, hovered in the doorway.

"What is it, Lucinda?" Tina asked.

"Mist' Chad on your telephone," Lucinda explained.

"All right, Lucinda, I'll go right up." Tina rose to her feet with a sigh. "Chad's probably calling to make sure I'm not going to be late. He hates to be kept waiting. Wasn't it sweet of Grandpa to put in a private phone for me when I married Eric? He knew how close I am to my family. You do what I said, Caroline," she urged as she moved toward the door. "Have Zeke take you over to Piedmont Park. Folks say the grounds are even prettier than the Paris Exposition back in 1889."

TINA walked into her elegantly French pink-and-white bedroom. Lucinda was at the chest of drawers putting away freshly laundered chemises.

"Lucinda, go somewhere else," she ordered with an ingratiating smile, dropping to the edge of her bed.

"Yes, ma'am."

She knew Lucinda loved her, but sometimes she suspected her of tattling to Chad. Chad could be such an old maid sometimes.

She waited for Lucinda to close the door, then picked up the phone.

"I'm surprised you're up so early, Chad," she mocked. "What brought that on?"

"Orders from Mama," he said calmly. "She was waiting for me when I got home last night. Papa told her he sees no chance of getting that contract from the city that he's been after for the last four months, and he absolutely needs that business. She wants you to talk to the General. The old man can push the right people to get it through for Papa."

"Chad, he isn't going to listen to me," Tina protested.

"Sugar, you turn on your special brand of charm and Josiah Hampton will make it his business to see that Papa gets the contract," Chad said with cynical amusement. "He thinks you're the prettiest thing that ever came out of Atlanta."

"I'll try," she promised. "I'll talk to him tonight." He'd do that for Papa, she thought complacently. He'd do almost anything she asked, the way he felt about getting Eric into politics.

"Arrange it, Tina," Chad emphasized crisply. "And how's the 'prodigal granddaughter'?" he asked with veiled sarcasm.

"Grandpa's awfully upset, Chad," she said seriously. "He doesn't want her in Atlanta. She brings back bad memories."

"Is he upset enough to send her packing?" Chad asked bluntly.

"He's not even sure she's his granddaughter, though Sophie and Eric seem to think so. I heard him talking to Cyrus Madison over at the mill. He told Madison to send a man to London to find out if Caroline really is Francis' daughter."

"If the General decides she is his granddaughter, it could cost Eric and you your inheritance," Chad warned.

"Chad, don't be ridiculous," Tina laughed. "The General adores Eric and me. Eric will inherit everything."

"I hear it's fairly certain your friend the Councilman is going to run for the Legislature next year," Chad said archly.

"Marshall?" she asked coolly. "You know I don't see him since he married that awful woman."

"Dolly Shepard is very rich, and a lot of men see her as a fine figure of a woman," Chad needled.

"She's forty-two years old and Marshall's twenty-six!" Tina's voice rose stridently. "He only married her because she was a rich widow!" Six weeks after he married Dolly, she married Eric. That showed Marshall how much she cared.

"Dolly's down in Florida now selling some property to that man Flagler, who built the Royal Poinciana down in West Palm Beach and then the Royal Palm in Miami last year, so she can put the cash into Marshall's campaign," Chad continued complacently. "I hear there was a high-level secret meeting at their house a couple of nights ago to map out their strategy. She means to make herself the Governor's lady one of these days."

"She'll be the laughingstock of Atlanta," Tina said distastefully.

"Nobody's turning down invitations to those fine parties she's been giving," Chad taunted. "Not that we've had the opportunity," he chuckled.

"Dolly's not inviting anybody young enough to be competition," Tina shot back sharply. Marshall always was ambitious. The Shepards were a fine family, but they had no money after the War. Now, with Dolly behind him, he was sure he was going to be somebody important. He was going to have competition, she thought triumphantly. Grandpa and she were pushing their own candidate, and the Hampton fortune made Dolly Shepard's money look like pin money. Marshall was in for a surprise.

"What are you doing today?" Chad asked lazily.

"I'm just staying home and washing my hair and resting. Don't call me back. I'll probably nap all afternoon. I wish this heat would let up."

"How's Eric?"

"Still being awful," she sighed. "Everybody in the house notices how he neglects me. Sometimes I think I'll pack up and go back home."

"No you won't," Chad said with silken confidence. "Not with all that money that's going to be yours. That beautiful house and the mill and Hampton Court."

"Chad—" She hesitated, debating about telling Chad. But she always told Chad everything. Of all the five children Chad and she were the closest, despite the difference in their ages. The youngest and the oldest. "I had a long, serious talk with Grandpa. He wants me to have a baby. He thinks it's important for Eric's image as a candidate for office." Chad knew how Grandpa was constantly at Eric's neck to run for office.

"You'd hate that. Walking around with a fat, ugly stomach for all those months," he derided. "You used to scream when Lucinda took a splinter out for you. How could you stand giving birth?"

"The General promised to build me a house in Inman Park," she said softly, knowing how much this would impress her brother. "The day I give birth he calls in the architect. I approve the designs. My house, Chad. In my name."

"What are you going to do?" he asked after a moment.

"Chad, I can't get pregnant by myself," she said impatiently. "Eric doesn't come near me."

"Arrange it, Tina." His voice was edged with excitement. "You got him hot enough to marry you. You can get him into your bed again."

"I asked him to come in and have a glass of champagne with me last night," Tina reported. "He just brushed the invitation aside."

"You work on him, Tina. I don't care how you manage it, but you get yourself pregnant. By Eric," he cautioned. "The General realizes you won't necessarily get pregnant right away," he soothed. "So it'll take six months. A house in your own name at Inman Park is fancy payment."

"Chad, I have to go. Lucinda's here to wash my hair for me. I'll talk to you tonight."

She put down the phone, a secretive little smile about her face. So Dolly was down in Florida. She had not seen Marshall alone since she married Eric. At parties Marshall avoided her. Now she understood why. The Councilman had higher ambitions. He was taking no chances on losing out with Dolly.

She reached for the phone again, gave the operator Marshall's office number. With her free hand she tapped nervously on the table beside the bed. When he married Dolly, Tina recalled, he had discharged the girl who had worked in his office. That was insurance, because the girl knew how many times she came into

Marshall's office while he was courting Dolly. She never truly believed he would marry Dolly, knowing the way he felt about *her*.

"Councilman Shepard's office," a brisk, mature feminine voice greeted her.

"Is the Councilman there, please?" Tina asked politely. "Mrs. Hampton calling."

Tina's eyes lit as she visualized his surprise that she was calling him. The last time she saw Marshall alone was the night before his wedding. He took her to the fine new house Dolly had furnished to begin her married life. Marshall and she initiated the connubial bed.

"Tina?" There was suppressed excitement in his voice.

"How many Mrs. Hamptons do you know?" she challenged.

"How are you?"

"Miss you," she said softly.

"Dolly's in Florida," he said tentatively.

"I heard," she drawled.

"Come to the house at two," he invited. "Tell Arnold you have a business appointment with me. You remember where it is?"

"I remember, darling. See you at two." She put the phone down and threw herself joyously back across the bed. *Marshall was still mad about her. Nothing had changed.*

She dressed with infinite care, determined to dazzle Marshall, then want to her bedroom door and called for Lucinda.

"Lucinda, have a carriage brought to the front of the house. But I don't want Zeke to drive me. Miss Caroline will probably want him to take her to Piedmont Park later. I want Jason to drive me." Jason was stupid and amiable. He wouldn't run to Eric and tell him where she had spent the afternoon. She never trusted Zeke, the way he trailed around after Eric, like Alex.

In the carriage Tina directed Jason to take her to Peachtree Street, one block beyond the Shepard house. She would retrace her steps. Jason was too lazy to turn around to see where she was going. Wouldn't Marshall be amazed when he discovered that Grandpa was priming Eric for a seat on the Council! Eric would have to give in eventually. Nobody stood up against Josiah Hampton for too long.

She could bring Grandpa useful bits of information about the

Council, now that she was seeing Marshall again. She could tell him what Marshall and Dolly were doing to prepare for Marshall's race for a seat in the Legislature. She could be useful, she told herself triumphantly. The General would be pleased. She would say that Chad was picking up gossip for her. Chad was right; the old man wasn't going to push her about getting pregnant. Sometimes a new bride didn't get pregnant for a year or two. She would carry Eric's baby to own a house in Inman Park. It wouldn't belong to Eric; it would be her house.

Jason deposited her as she directed and Tina walked back almost a block, aware that he had returned to the perch and sat there with his back to her, satisfied to be idle in the warm sunlight.

The Shepards' rambling Victorian house was set in the midst of picturesque landscaping. It was by far the largest house in its vicinity. The ballroom, Tina remembered, was said to be enormous. That was so Dolly Shepard could try to build herself a salon in the French manner while she groomed Marshall for the Legislature. Chad could be so catty. He said Dolly Shepard might have the wealth and the girth to become another Mme. de Staël, but Atlanta would never forget that her late husband earned his fortune in junk dealing.

Tina walked up to the door, knocked, and was immediately admitted to the dark, spacious main hall.

"I have a business appointment with Mr. Shepard," she parroted Marshall. "He's expecting me."

"Yes, ma'am." The impassive Arnold pulled the door wide so that she could enter and led her to the mahogany-paneled library to the right of the hall.

"Arnold, we have business to discuss," Marshall said. "I don't wish to be disturbed."

Marshall was as handsome as ever, though it seemed to her that he was more fleshy. All those dinner parties Dolly had been giving since their marriage. She watched with a tiny, anticipatory smile while he crossed to lock the door behind Arnold, then swung about to face her.

"I've missed you like the very devil," he murmured, moving to her.

"You've avoided me like the plague," she accused. "At the Cargills' dinner you wouldn't even meet my gaze."

"I was afraid I'd betray myself." He pulled her close to him. "And you're a married lady," he reminded with sardonic humor, while his thighs pressed against hers.

"Are you happy with Dolly?" she questioned.

"Tina, be realistic," he rebuked, one hand moving to her breasts. "I didn't marry Dolly to be happy. Only rich. Why else did you marry Eric?"

"He's terribly handsome; every girl in Atlanta was after him. And I was furious at you." She lifted her parted mouth to his and he needed no further invitation. She could feel her heart pounding against his chest as their mouths clung. It was so many months since Marshall had made love to her. "We won't be interrupted?" she asked when he released her.

"The door's locked."

Marshall scooped her up in his arms in the masterful fashion she adored and carried her to the comfortably upholstered sofa and dropped her along its length.

"Take off your clothes," he said, already removing his jacket.

"Marshall," she pouted. "Persuade me."

He tossed aside his jacket and sat at the edge of the sofa, amused by her demand.

"Tina, you are the most fascinating bitch I have ever known. When I'm with you I forget everything that's real." His hands lifted her so that he could reach behind to release the hooks of her dress. "But why must I also be a ladies' maid?"

"Because it pleases me," she said imperiously, and reached a hand to touch him. She smiled with satisfaction at the sound of passion that escaped him. There would be no more talk of ladies' maids.

He drew the bodice of her dress to her waist and burrowed his mouth in the hollow between her breasts, his hands moving to pull her silken skirts above her slender thighs. Her hands tightened at his shoulders.

"Marshall, I mustn't get pregnant," she warned him, her breathing uneven. She mustn't get pregnant by Marshall.

"Have you ever?" he countered. But he arose from the sofa and crossed to the desk. Frowning with impatience he fumbled in a drawer, found what he sought. She watched with obsessive excitement as he protected himself against the mistake both knew they could not afford to make.

"Marshall," she scolded because he was strolling so slowly to the sofa. She wished they were away from this house, where Marshall would strip to skin and urge her to kiss every inch of him. But he was uneasy with the servants just beyond the locked door.

"Marshall, I'm going to dress again," she warned.

"No, you won't," he defied, a glint in his eyes as her hand reached out to fondle him.

"*You* are." She pretended to sulk.

With one swift gesture he reached to enclose her face between his hands, brought her slightly parted mouth to him. Passion charged through her. In a few moments she would arouse him to the impatient roughness she relished.

"Tina, don't bite!" His voice was guttural with desire.

She released him, leaned back against the sofa, her eyes half closed, one foot trailing to the floor, the other arched provocatively.

"You fascinating bitch!"

He lowered himself above her, thrust himself between the slender thighs. It was going to be marvelous, she exulted. She reached to draw his head to her breasts while he probed with mounting urgency. His mouth enclosed one erect, dark nipple.

"Faster, Marshall!" she ordered. "Faster!"

His teeth tightened on the nipple. She ignored the pain, but when his passion burst within her she cried out.

"Sssh," he exhorted, lest the servants hear. "Quiet, Tina!" He lifted his mouth to hers to silence her.

At last they lay quiescent, his weight heavy but pleasant above her. She knew that in a few minutes they would make love again. In the next house a couple was singing, to piano accompaniment. Tina recognized the lovers' duet in which Faust seduces Marguerite.

Marshall smiled. He was remembering the time he had taken her to the Opera to see *Faust*. She had been so aroused they had left in the midst of the duet. They had made love in the carriage

79

en route to his house. No aria in opera, Chad always said, was so erotic.

"Marshall," she whispered, her hands reaching out to him. Her eyes ordered him to make love again. Marshall and she were alike; insatiable.

His mouth grazed hers for an instant, then slid to her throat, her breasts. With a faint sound of reproach at this dalliance she prodded him toward his ultimate destination. She clenched her teeth to keep back the sounds that welled in her throat. Damn the servants for being here!

"Does Eric make you this happy?" he challenged, pulling himself into a sitting position so that he could reach to the table behind her for a cigarette.

"Eric neglects me, Marshall," she sighed. "Even Grandpa's upset at the way he's never home. I meant to be the perfect wife to Eric." She ignored his skeptical grin. "I convinced myself I was so happy when we were first married."

"As happy as with me?" Marshall pushed.

"Darling, nobody makes me as happy as you. But Dolly had you," she pouted, "and I had to make do."

Marshall dropped his free hand to stroke her hip.

"Tina, we'll have to be awfully careful," Marshall warned. "For both our sakes."

"Nobody will ever guess," she promised, her eyes complacent. "We'll be so clever about arranging our meetings. Not that Eric would even care," she said with unexpected bitterness. "I know he's seeing other women. He makes no effort to hide it. But he was a catch," she added with a touch of pride. "All that Hampton money will come to us."

"Shut up and turn over, Tina," Marshall drawled, disposing of the cigarette. He slapped her on the rump before he lifted himself above her again. "Damn it, why don't they stop that singing?"

"Darling, that's the Love Duet from *Tristan and Isolde,*" she rebuked. "Doesn't it excite you?"

"You excite me," he gasped, and triumph blended with passion in her. *She had won Marshall away from Dolly.*

Chapter Seven

C AROLINE awoke early, aware almost immediately of a comfortable abatement in the heat of the past two days. Her instinct was to arise and go directly downstairs and round up Tina for a long walk. But Tina slept late in the morning. Nor would she be available for socializing. At dinner last night she had talked about meeting her brother Chad so that they might go together to shop for a birthday present for her father.

"Go get it, Alex!" Eric's voice was a welcome sound in the morning stillness. Caroline instinctively brightened. "Go on, boy!"

She tossed aside the coverlet and crossed to the window, slipping into her dressing gown en route. Eric was just below, romping with the Irish setter. How handsome Eric was. How charming.

"Good morning," she called down.

Eric gazed up with a brilliant smile.

"Get dressed and have breakfast with me," he commanded. "I'll tell Annie Mae you'll be right down."

"All right," she agreed, eager for his companionship. She felt herself encased in a brittle shell of loneliness. She had not taken Tina's advice and gone for a drive in Piedmont Park yesterday. That would only have enhanced her feeling of being alone in a barren desert. But in Eric's company she became alive.

She dressed with breathless speed, hurried down to the side verandah. Eric watched with amusement while Alex darted forward to greet her.

81

"He's always been such a woman-hater," Eric chuckled. "What did you do to fascinate him this way?"

"We were friends on sight." She dropped into a chair with a sense of well-being, just as Annie Mae, obviously pleased that she was not having breakfast alone this morning, arrived with a laden tray. "There's always been an Alexander the Great at the General's house, hasn't there?" she asked, fondling Alex's silken head.

"As far back as I can remember. How did you know?" He smiled, but his eyes were serious as they rested on her.

"My father talked about the Irish setter named Alex that had been at Hampton Court before he went to England."

"Do you have any plans for today?" he asked abruptly.

"No." The question startled her.

"Tell Seth to have Zeke or Jason bring you down to Jim Russell's office about two this afternoon," he decided briskly. "Seth will tell you where it is. It's time you did some sight-seeing about Atlanta."

"I'd love that," she said simply.

"I love this city," Eric said with sudden intensity. "It's unlike any other city in the county. With each new year it changes. You can't imagine what it was like after the War. I wasn't around myself," he acknowledged humorously, "but I've heard the General talk with great eloquence. In thirty years the city rose from the ashes, Caro." Again, she reacted to the diminutive. Oh, she must watch her emotions when she was with Eric! "When Sherman left, Atlanta was one enormous funeral pyre. Packs of wild dogs ran through the streets. Hardly a tree remained standing. But Atlantans came back as fast as the roads would allow. They struggled to put together houses from scraps of lumber, brick, rusty iron—or they lived in tents." Eric smiled. "Folks like to say that anybody who has lived in Atlanta is never satisfied anywhere else."

"My father was never truly satisfied in England," Caroline said nostalgically. "His heart was always with Hampton Court and Atlanta."

"No city has made such progress," Eric declared, then paused. "Physical and material progress," he compelled himself to be honest. His face suddenly somber, he reached to pour himself another cup of coffee. "We are wanting in other ways."

"In what ways?" Caroline inquired, sensing this was of importance to Eric.

"I'll show you the new State Capitol." Eric redirected his thoughts, disappointing her. "It was finished in 1889. And the site of our newest skyscraper," Eric planned. "It's going to be ten stories high. Our tallest office building. And the Aragon Hotel, which most tourists seem to favor. And, of course you'll see the Cyclorama."

"I read about it in the *Atlanta Constitution*," Caroline began enthusiastically, then stopped herself in dismay. She must not reveal her familiarity with the city, her awareness that Louisa Hampton had died only a few months ago. "Please don't tell anyone, Eric," she pleaded. "It seems so sentimental. My father ordered the newspapers sent twice a year to London, and when he died my mother did the same. Please, I'll feel happier if you say nothing of this to anyone."

"I'll say nothing," Eric promised, but his eyes were probing hers. "Caro, don't feel so harshly toward Grandpa."

"What have I said to make you believe I do?" she hedged.

"It's not what you say. It's what you feel." His eyes compelled her to listen to him. "It was a painful separation for your father, but for the General there was no other way."

"I understand him." She struggled to keep her voice even. "Pride in name comes before love of son. I understand how he feels, Eric. I can't understand why." She could have loved her grandmother without reservations, Caroline thought, because she knew that women of her grandmother's generation would never dare go against a husband's wishes. Her grandmother must have cried inside for her oldest son, her firstborn. How many nights, for how many years did she lie in her bed and cry for him?

"I'm a disappointment to Grandpa," Eric acknowledged unhappily. "I wish it wasn't that way, but I can't allow anybody to dictate my life. I won't allow it," he said sternly, "no matter how much I love that stubborn old man."

"He won't let me love him." Suddenly she was perilously close to tears. "He can't wait for me to pack up and run back to England."

"But you won't," Eric predicted.

"No." She lifted her head determinedly. "I've come home."

Eric rose to his feet. "Two o'clock at Jim Russell's office," he reminded Caroline. "I'll show you some of Atlanta, and then I'll bring you home."

Caroline watched him walk briskly toward the streetcar line. The hours till two o'clock seemed depressingly dull. She could go into Atlanta early, her mind pointed out. Let today have a dual purpose. Before meeting Eric she could visit the Fulton County Courthouse. *Why delay?* Exhilarated by this decision she went up to her room for her handbag and hat. She would *not* ask for a carriage to take her into town. No one need know her first destination.

Seth was startled but gently informative when she inquired about the locale of the streetcar stop and directions to Jim Russell's office. "Miss Caroline, one of them boys would be jes' happy to take you anywhere it pleases you to go," he protested indulgently.

"Thank you, Seth, but I'd like to ride the streetcar. I never have, you see," she improvised charmingly. "I'll be meeting Mr. Eric this afternoon, and he'll bring me home."

"Yes, ma'am." His obvious affection for her was heartwarming.

Caroline walked in the fragrant morning air to where Seth had told her the streetcar began its trip into the city. Her mind revolved about her morning objective. Mr. Lonsdale said that the clerk who wrote him could have made a mistake, she remembered optimistically. He might have been careless. *Pray that he had.*

Caroline inspected the electric streetcar as it arrived with lively interest. It was open on all sides but equipped with curtains. These would be let down in the event of rain, Caroline guessed. The streetcar stopped and Caroline climbed aboard. She consulted the conductor about her stop. He promised to alert her when they were approaching the corner of Pryor and Hunter.

Soon the streetcar moved onto an avenue where the houses sat

84

more closely together, their grounds resplendent with flowers and shrubs. Tiled sidewalks appeared, and the streets were paved with asphalt.

The streetcar moved with impressive speed away from the residential area into the bustling business section of Atlanta. Here carriages and drays rumbled over the streets paved with Belgian block. Streetcar tracks seemed omnipresent. The railroad tracks were laid through the heart of the city, providing an atmosphere of daring to pedestrians.

At last Caroline alighted from the streetcar. Her heart pounded as she stood before the august Fulton County Courthouse. What a picturesque structure! Her eyes moved admiringly over the multiple gables, the Italianate moldings and arches, the mansard roof which accommodated a tall clock tower at the corner.

Caroline roamed from one office to another with growing frustration. At last she arrived in an office served by a spare, middle-aged, spectacled man with a broad north country English accent. For a moment she was chilled by homesickness.

The English clerk, in Atlanta for two years, was delighted to help her. While he searched, he talked of home in Northumberland.

"I'm sorry, Miss," he said at last. "I find only the Josiah Hampton house at the edge of town. There's no record here of any Hampton Court."

"But it was one of the showplaces of the South before the War."

"You would need further information," he apologized.

"I have nothing. Could the records have been destroyed during the War?"

"The original Fulton County Courthouse remained intact. In fact, the building was used during the Yankee occupation, I'm told, as the Provost Marshal's headquarters. Not this building, of course. This wasn't finished until 1883. I'm sorry I couldn't be of more help."

"I do appreciate your efforts." She forced a smile. "And perhaps you could direct me to a friend's house. I have the address right here—" She fumbled in her bag. "On Peters Street."

With directions to Mr. Woodridge's house in her mind, Caroline set out to call on him. She fought against the depression

85

that sought to swamp her. Had she expected to walk into the Fulton County Courthouse and walk out with proof that she owned Hampton Court? Undoubtably the General had taken astute measures to conceal the truth. So she must spend weeks, perhaps months in search, but she would hold that proof in her hands one day.

A streetcar took her to the comfortable block where Mr. Woodridge lived. She stood on the sidewalk before the white, two-story frame structure with rambling verandah, high triangular roof and gables, and geared herself for this encounter. All at once she spied a small, slight, aged man bent lovingly over a rosebush at the side of the verandah. She walked toward him.

"Mr. Woodridge?" she asked, more loudly than normal because she recalled his hearing difficulty. "Oh, I didn't mean to startle you," she apologized as he tensed in shock at a sudden presence.

"That's quite all right," he said, squinting at her with a friendly smile. "Oh, but you have to be Louisa Carter's granddaughter!" He glowed with pleasure at this deduction. "She was Louisa Carter before she married Josiah Hampton," he reminded.

"I'm Caroline, Francis' daughter," she introduced herself.

"Come into the house," Mr. Woodridge invited with courtly charm that reminded her of Mr. Lonsdale. "Lula Mae will bring us iced tea and cookies."

He led her into a high-ceilinged, densely furnished parlor, talking pleasurably about his years as a young attorney in Columbus, when Louisa was barely in her teens.

"My wife and I moved to Atlanta just two years after Louisa married. Atlanta was called Marthasville then, after first having been called Terminus. Did you know that, Caroline?"

"No, I didn't." She would not spoil the old gentleman's pleasure by telling him how Papa had told her the history of Atlanta.

"It was re-named Marthasville in 1843 after Governor Lumpkin's daughter, but when the new Macon and Western line came into town, folks felt the town could do with a more high-sounding name. No more than four hundred living there at that time, Louisa—" He smiled, not realizing his slip. "Mr.—

Mr.—" He frowned. "Sometimes names don't come to me too clearly, but he was the engineer—he chose Atlanta because this was the terminus of the Western and Atlantic Railroad. That was in 1845."

"And now it's a great city." How could she lead Mr. Woodridge into talk about Hampton Court? "Papa always said it would be."

"How is Francis?" Mr. Woodridge asked, as Lula Mae brought them glasses of minted iced tea and a hand-painted plate laden with dainty cookies.

"Papa died some years ago," Caroline told him softly.

Mr. Woodridge stared uncertainly.

"I thought it had been a while since he had come calling on me." Lula Mae hovered anxiously in the doorway.

"Mist' Woodridge, you ain't to tire yo'self out, remembuh." She turned to Caroline with gentle apology. "He don't often has company, and when he does it's jes' for a lil' while. Even when his nieces, Miss Emma and Miss Mary, come over, they don't stay ver' long."

"I won't," Caroline promised.

"Lula Mae, now stop that," Mr. Woodridge said fretfully. "I'm enjoying having Louisa Hampton's little girl here. Now you just go away and leave us alone. I haven't enjoyed myself so much since last year when Mama had the fine party for Mr. Henry Grady."

But Mr. Woodridge's mother had been dead many years, and Henry Grady since 1889. All at once Caroline understood. Though he was right enough about Atlanta history, Mr. Woodridge jumbled facts and dates. His memory was failing. He wouldn't be able to help her. Even if he offered to testify in court in support of her claim to Hampton Court, he would not be accepted as a responsible witness.

Masking her second disappointment of the morning, Caroline remained a few minutes longer, until Lula Mae indicated with her eyes that it was time to leave Mr. Woodridge to himself. Despite the noonday heat she walked back toward the center of town. She felt a need for physical activity in the face of this fresh defeat. But her time would come, she reminded herself once again. Meanwhile she would live in her grandfather's house and appear the dutiful granddaughter, grateful to be taken in off the streets. She loathed this subterfuge, when she *knew* Hampton Court belongd to her.

All at once aware of hunger, she glanced about for some tea shoppe where she might have a light luncheon. Did young ladies eat alone in Atlanta? she wondered nervously. Then she spied a group of girls of her own age, no doubt employed in the nearby offices, and followed them into a modest tea shoppe where she was relieved to be able to settle in a comfortable corner and rest her hot, aching feet. She ordered, self-conscious at being alone, and mindful of the low state of her finances.

She lingered over her light, inexpensive meal, watching for the time when she was to meet Eric. Tina would not be angry that Eric was showing her about Atlanta, would she? Caroline wondered belatedly. She was family; Tina would realize that. Eric treated her as he might a young sister. But *sometimes* he looked at her, she recalled in unease, and there was nothing brotherly in his eyes. She left the restaurant and went to the offices of Jim Russell's newspaper. Opening the door, she could hear Eric's voice in conversation with another man.

Caroline walked into a large, square, utilitarian office with a desk close to the door and several others scattered about the room, though currently unoccupied. She saw Eric, his back to her, talking to a small, compact man in his mid-forties with ruddy, unruly hair and a flaming mustache.

"I was to meet Eric Hampton here," Caroline told the slight young man at the front desk who pounded a typewriter with such speed its position seemed imperiled.

The typing stopped.

"Eric, young lady to see you," he yelled.

Eric swung about to greet her with a warm smile.

"Come over here and meet Jim Russell," he ordered.

With quick, small steps Caroline approached the two men. On sight she liked Jim Russell.

"Jim calls himself a newspaperman," Eric said with obvious respect and affection. "Jim, this is the General's granddaughter, Caroline, born and raised in London."

"My father left Atlanta just before the War Between the States," she said, and saw Eric start at her candor.

"If I had been old enough to fight, I would have done the same," Jim Russell said, his blue-gray eyes scrutinizing Caroline.

"Jim's a great follower of the London *Times*," Eric jeered good-naturedly. "Can you imagine the publisher of a Populist newspaper stooping to that?"

"All Eric knows about London," Jim shot back with a smile, "is that he saw Buckingham Palace and the Tower of London. I like to read what's happening in their textile industries." Quickly he became serious. "Long ago the English passed the Factory Acts for the protection of child workers, something we haven't gotten around to doing. Of course," he conceded, "they're still having trouble ninety-five years later."

"With all the wonderful new inventions in the clothing factories they still have terrible workshops with their sweated labor," Caroline remembered with a shiver of distaste. "Not even the Factory and Workshop Act passed two years ago has helped. It's just ignored."

"And if the factory workers threaten to strike for higher wages, off goes the work to the sweatshops." Jim nodded, his voice compassionate. "Our Southern workers don't fare too well in their efforts to improve their conditions, either."

What kind of employer was her grandfather? Caroline wondered. Demanding, no doubt. He was in the mill himself at least twelve hours a day.

"Are there troubles in the mills in Georgia?" she asked, and Eric grimaced.

"Just last month the Fulton Bag and Cotton Mills had a strike," he reported. "Fourteen hundred men and women walked out."

"For higher wages?" Caroline asked.

"Because twenty Negro women were brought to work in the folding department," Eric explained dryly. "While the textile workers are considered the lowest on the Southern social ladder, even they consider themselves superior to the Negroes."

"The strike was led by white women," Jim emphasized, and Eric laughed at Caroline's glare of indignation.

"What happened at the mill?" Caroline asked.

"The president fired the Negroes," Jim told her. "The strikers were re-hired. This was on the condition that they would work overtime to fill some rush orders, which was why the twenty Negro women were originally hired," he said. "But I worry about what's going to happen at the Fulton Mills. I don't entirely trust the situation there."

"I don't understand." Caroline was bewildered. "They don't strike for higher wages, but they strike because twenty Negro women were brought into the mill. *Why?*"

"Caroline, don't try to understand their minds," Jim said seriously. "They value their so-called white supremacy above everything else. They're afraid of the Negroes more than the mill barons who have almost absolute power over them. In time this will change, but I suspect it'll be a long and anguished process."

Eric pulled out his watch, inspected the face. "I'm showing Caroline a few sights in the city," he said to Jim, and reached for her arm. "See you in the morning."

They walked from the office and down the stairs in companionable silence. Caroline was pleasantly conscious of Eric's hand at her elbow.

"Have you had lunch?" he asked when they were on the bustling street.

"Yes."

"We'll go to a drugstore for a drink," he decided. "You're not an Atlantan until you've had a glass of Coca-Cola. I know folks who have a glass of Coca-Cola in the morning instead of coffee. But *you're* a British tea drinker," he teased.

"I'm an American. My father never let me forget that."

They went into a small drugstore with a marble soda fountain at one side. Parallel to the fountain sat a cluster of tiny marble-topped tables flanked by wrought-iron chairs. Eric waved a hand to a tall, rather attractive girl who was serving someone at the counter. When a boy behind the counter made a move to go to Eric and Caroline's table, the girl put out a detaining arm and came herself.

"What's your orders, please?" Her eyes were amorous as they rested on Eric. She ignored Caroline.

"Two of my usual, Kitty." He turned to Caroline. "We'll go to the Cyclorama from here."

The waitress was annoyed that he had come into the drugstore with her, Caroline realized. This was probably one of Eric's romantic conquests. Caroline's smile lost some of its spontaneity.

The waitress returned to set tall glasses of a dark, ice-islanded liquid before them. Caroline sipped tentatively.

"Coca-Cola was concocted by a pharmacist named Dr. Pemberton—the title was a courtesy one. When he died back in 1888, every drugstore in Atlanta was closed during the hour of his funeral. He was buried in Columbus," Eric explained, "where he had lived for many years." Her grandmother had lived in Columbus, Caroline remembered with sudden alertness. Must she go there, to Louisa Carter Hampton's roots, to find the proof she needed? "How do you like it?" Eric probed.

"It's delicious!" Caroline said.

"How do you like Jim Russell?" Eric was more serious now.

"On sight I liked him," she said. "I can understand why you're so pleased to be working with him."

"He's lived just about everywhere in the country. He gave up law to work for all kinds of newspapers and magazines. He's the most clear-thinking, compassionate, rational man I've ever encountered. His wife and he broke up years ago because he was invariably involved in some reform that made him forget about ever leaving his current office. But he's in love with Atlanta, with the future he sees for it." He pushed his chair back. "Let's go find ourselves a carriage."

A carriage acquired, Eric minutely directed the driver on a circuitous route to the Cyclorama, helped Caroline inside, and climbed in beside her with a raffish grin. His earlier mood obliterated, he devoted himself to the role of tourist guide. He pointed out the site of the proposed new skyscraper, the *Atlanta Constitution* building, and the Grand Opera Theatre. Then he leaned forward, propelling Caroline toward the window on her side of the carriage.

"We're approaching the State Capitol. It's just ahead on the sunny slope there."

"What a grand building!" Caroline gazed admiringly at the

elegant, high-domed structure that appeared to encompass several acres of land.

"It was designed in the fashion of the National Capitol," Eric pointed out. "From the dome you can see not only all of Atlanta but towns for miles around. But don't miss the lady on top of the dome," he ordered with amusement. "That's Miss Liberty."

"It's a copy of the Statue of Liberty!" Caroline exclaimed. "We saw it from the ship coming into New York Harbor."

"There are several stories about this Miss Liberty, but I like the one that claims it was given to Georgia by Ohio back in 1884 as a good-will offering, because of the devastation that Sherman brought to the state. You see, Sherman was a native of Ohio."

Caroline was aware of the air of conviviality that Eric sought to bring to this outing, yet she sensed that behind the facade of banter Eric was evaluating her, and advantageously. The knowledge was simultaneously disconcerting and exhilarating.

How would Eric feel toward her if he knew she was here to claim her inheritance? No doubt the General expected Hampton Court to be passed on to Eric and Tina when he was no longer alive. The mill, Hamptonville, all the rest—yes. *But not Hampton Court.* What was legally hers by virtue of her great-grandfather's actions, she would fight for until it was hers.

Eric pointed out the Aragon Hotel, several churches and private schools.

"There're a lot of private schools in Atlanta," Caroline said curiously. "Are the public schools inadequate?"

"The middle and upper classes," Eric explained with cynical amusement, "like to send their children to private schools, to keep them away from the immigrant children. We're coming to Grant Park now," he added. "The Cyclorama is housed in a building right near the Augusta Avenue entrance."

The carriage deposited them before a massive, circular, wooden-shingled structure. Eric helped Caroline from the carriage and ordered the driver to wait for them.

"It's ironic that the Cyclorama was bought by George Gress, a former drummer boy in the Union Army," Eric said, propelling Caroline to the entrance. "After the War he made Atlanta his home. Recently he offered the Cyclorama to the city, provided the Council arranges for a new roof and repairs to the painting. I'm sure they'll accept, once the conditions are agreed upon."

Eric paid the ten cents' admission for each and escorted Caroline inside, explaining that Gress used the admission fees for relief of poor children in the city.

"Eric, I never imagined it would be so enormous!" Caroline's eyes tried to take in the magnificent yet menacing five-segmented panorama that seemed to engulf them.

"It's the largest painting in the world. Fifty feet high and four hundred in circumference," Eric reported. "It was done by a crew of foreign artists who spent several months here in Atlanta. Confederate veterans stayed by, describing the action for them. All this had to be interpreted because the artists didn't speak English. But the authenticity is amazing," Eric said with infinite respect. "This was July twenty-second, 1864, at approximately four-thirty in the afternoon. The Battle of Atlanta."

"It's so real," Caroline whispered. "I feel as though we're part of it."

"There's Manigault's brigade," Eric pointed to the first segment. "Confederates. They've broken and seized the Federal lines and are defending it behind those bales of cotton. Up center are the guns of the Federal battery."

"The dirt is so red." Caroline shivered. "Like the blood of the wounded."

"The red clay of Georgia," Eric reminded gently. "There's a story about that. A stranger asked, 'Why is the clay so red?' and the reply was, 'The Confederate soldiers killed so many Yankees the dirt just never turned back to its natural color.' "

They moved slowly along the circumference of the Cyclorama, Eric interpreting each segment for her. Caroline could almost smell the smoke of battle. Horses charged forward; foot soldiers waited for word to advance. Everywhere lay the dead and the dying. Eroded gullies, ammunition trains, ambulances, abandoned wagons, against a background of Georgia pines and the dome of Stone Mountain—eighteen miles east. So overwhelming were her emotions Caroline was relieved that they were alone here.

"The General came here once when it was first opened.

Sophie told me," Eric remembered. "He returned to the house and didn't emerge from his room for three days. Let's go back." Eric guided her to the segment that portrayed the torn-up track of the Georgia railroad. "That's the rear of the Federal lines," Eric indicated with one hand. "Manigault's brigade is at the left of the Troup Hurt House. The General's youngest son was with Manigault. He died right there. And over there," Eric pointed, "the General's second son, who was a courier, had his horse run free suddenly. He was bayoneted by Union soldiers. He was nineteen."

"Eric, stop!" Caroline closed her eyes against the carnage before them.

"For years," Eric said softly, "the General cursed himself for being alive when his two sons lay dead."

"But why punish my father?" Caroline demanded, her anguish fresh. "His letters were returned unopened! Even when I was born, all those years after, his letter was returned. When he died and my mother wrote, my grandfather must have known when he saw Elizabeth Hampton as the sender, that Papa was dead."

"He didn't want to know!" Eric said. "He kept praying that one day he would walk into the house and see his son Francis sitting there. He wanted Francis to come to him and ask for forgiveness."

"He wanted Papa to grovel!" Caroline blazed. "He couldn't have known his son very well."

"That pride runs in the family," Eric taunted gently.

All at once Caroline realized why Eric had brought her here. He wanted to make her feel compassion for her grandfather. There was no room in her heart for that unfeeling old man.

"Do you want me to leave Atlanta?" she challenged. "Leave the General in peace? Because I won't!"

"No, I want you to stay." Unexpectedly he clutched her by the shoulders. She was trembling at the touch of his hands, the mixed emotions she read in his eyes. He was pleading for Josiah Hampton, but he was startled to realize that *he* wanted her to stay for a reason beyond this. Dear God, what was happening between them? "Caro, you must stay," he insisted. "The best thing that can happen to Grandpa is to take his son's child into his heart.

94

That's the only way he'll ever make peace with himself."

"Eric, I'd like to leave now," she said.

They did not speak again until they were in the carriage and bound for the house.

"The War Between the States should never have been fought," Caroline said accusingly. "There should have been men on both sides to put a stop to it! Why couldn't slavery have been handled in a civilized manner? Look at what happened in England. Way back in 1833 liberation of the slaves was guaranteed by compensation to the planters. The House of Commons voted twenty million sterling for this purpose, and set up transitional stops to freedom."

"Caro, by 1860 there were four million slaves in the South. Prime hands were selling for twelve hundred to eighteen hundred dollars. Boys and girls from ten to fourteen were selling for five hundred fifty. If the Federal government had been so inclined, how could they have paid off planters with that staggering investment?"

"The statesmen in the nation should have avoided a fratricidal war," Caroline insisted. "I loathe any war, but what happened in this country was a sin against God."

"Now we have this mess in Cuba." Eric sighed. "Instinct tells me I should go down there to fight with the rebels." Caroline stared at him in alarm. "They're in the same position as we were at the time of our American Revolution," Eric said defensively. "And you've heard the constant stories of Spanish atrocities. They attack hospitals, beat prisoners to death. They poison wells, murder women and children."

"But something holds you back," Caroline said with intuition.

"I don't know how much of what we read is true," Eric admitted. "Jim claims we won't know the truth until American correspondents who work for somebody besides Hearst or Pulitzer can travel beyond Havana and see what's going on in the country."

"Is that possible?"

"If I'm down there with the rebels, there's a chance I might be able to smuggle out stories. A slim chance."

Caroline listened while Eric confided his inner conflict. How like Eric to want to go to Cuba to help the rebels gain their independence! But the mental image of Eric fighting side by side with the hot-headed rebels was terrifying. Eric dying in the jungle. How had she allowed herself to grow so close to Eric? So quickly!

Dear God, don't let Eric go to join the rebels. Don't let him go to Cuba, perhaps to die.

Chapter Eight

WHEN Caroline and Eric arrived, the house was still
except for the voices of the servants somewhere in
the rear. All at once Caroline was relieved not to
encounter Tina. Now she felt uncomfortable at having spent the
past three hours alone with Eric.

"Dinner won't be for quite a while," Eric said as they walked
up the stairs together. "Take a nap. You've had a hectic afternoon."

"I think I will." She still felt shaken from the confrontation
with Eric at the Cyclorama. How did he expect her to react to the
General? she asked herself defiantly. To throw herself abjectly at
his feet because he allowed her to stay at his house? Despite the
long-festering anger in her, she could have learned to love her
grandfather if he had received her as a granddaughter.

As she opened the door to her bedroom, she could hear Tina
talking gaily to Lucinda in her room next door. Tina must have
enjoyed the afternoon with her brother. Again, Caroline felt a
surge of guilt because *she* had spent the afternoon with Eric,
when Tina was so wistful about Eric's frequent absences from
the house.

In her room, Caroline ordered herself to sit at her slant-top
desk and write a letter to Mr. Lonsdale. She chose her words carefully, striving to sound confident that she would not be long in
uncovering the evidence she required. In truth, she was unsure of
where to turn next.

How long before she would see Hampton Court? She dared
not question anyone in the household. It would be unwise to

probe Seth, she warned herself, lest he inadvertently say something of this to her grandfather. Surely the family would go to Hampton Court for Thanksgiving.

She left the desk to stretch along the length of her bed, only now aware of her weariness. She lay back against the plump goosedown pillows, remembering her father's vivid description of Thanksgiving at Hampton Court.

From exhaustion, she fell asleep. She awoke with a start to hear the General speaking with a man in the downstairs foyer. Were they having a guest for dinner? The prospect was unnerving. How would the General introduce her? she wondered.

Caroline left the bed and hurried into her bathroom. Decades ago this must have been a huge closet, she conjectured while she refreshed herself. She debated about what to wear. She could not hope to appear as spectacularly gowned as Tina, but her meager wardrobe was neat and tasteful, thanks to her mother's skills as a seamstress.

She started at the light knock on the door.

"Come in."

The door opened and Patience, with dancer's grace, came into the room.

"Dinner be on the table in a few minutes, Miss Caroline," Patience said. "You lookin' mighty pretty." Her eyes moved admiringly over Caroline's dainty white-dotted Swiss frock.

"Thank you, Patience." Caroline smiled. "I'll be right downstairs."

When she entered the dining room Caroline saw the General in absorbed discussion with a tall, slight, sandy-haired young man, who appeared about five years older than Eric. His features were finely chiseled, almost aesthetic, his eyes gentle. No one else had arrived yet.

Caroline's instinct was to leave, but the young man had become aware of her presence and was smiling shyly in her direction. The General turned around and Caroline waited for him to introduce her. While he hesitated, Sophie walked into the dining room from the side verandah.

"Caroline, here is another Hampton for you to meet," Sophie said crisply. "One of the Savannah cousins. Andrew is the mill superintendent. He lives in that white cottage near the mill. Andrew, this is Caroline, from England." Caroline suspected that Andrew had been briefed on her presence here.

"I hope you're enjoying Atlanta." Andrew radiated a genuine warmth that was reassuring.

"It's an exciting city." All at once Caroline was insecure. Should she say that she had spent the afternoon sight-seeing with Eric? No, she decided. "I'm looking forward to seeing more of it," she finished diplomatically.

The General crossed to the table, seated himself. This was the signal for the others to sit. Within moments of each other Tina and Eric joined them.

"Grandpa, you're looking tired," Tina chided, her tone affectionate. "Andrew, you must make him stop working so hard."

"Andrew's no better," Eric said, and Caroline sensed that he respected his cousin. "Always bent over a piece of machinery. I remember the summer I spent in the mill. I was scared to death of you, Andrew."

"You're never scared of anyone," Tina contradicted. To Caroline it seemed a rebuke.

"Andrew's been with me in the mill since he was sixteen," Josiah said. "There's not a piece of equipment that he doesn't know as well as the man who designed it."

"Tina, when are you going to start showing Caroline around Atlanta?" Eric asked. She *was* to remain silent about their afternoon, Caroline understood. "She'll think our famous Southern hospitality is a colossal joke."

"Eric, I hesitate to go into the city with all this talk of yellow fever. And there's almost no social activity until the end of the month." Tina smiled at Caroline. The General scowled. "Though we could go for a ride in Piedmont Park tomorrow," she decided after a moment of reflection.

"Tina's right. It's too hot to go chasing around Atlanta, Eric," Sophie reproved. "But a ride in the park would be pleasant."

"Oh, yes!" Caroline forced herself to smile in gratitude.

"Did you go often to the theater in London, Caroline?" Andrew asked eagerly.

"After my father died, we couldn't afford to go more than two

99

or three times a year." Caroline was candid. "This season my mother and I saw *The Princess and the Butterfly* at the St. James, with George Alexander and H. B. Irving."

"Pinero," Andrew said reverently.

"And once a year we went to the D'Oyly Carte for Gilbert and Sullivan." Caroline was aware that the General was irritated by what he probably considered frivolous conversation. Suddenly her whole position here was unreal. She wished with fierce intensity that she was back in London.

"Andrew, are we going to have trouble with that man Coleman?" the General asked, and Andrew turned to give his evaluation of the situation at the mill.

Josiah monopolized Andrew through dinner, yet Caroline was conscious of Andrew's frequent glances in her direction. He was shy and lonely, Caroline guessed sympathetically while she listened to Tina's lively report on theater and opera in Atlanta, which Tina attended frequently with Chad. Tina's implication was that Eric was rarely available as an escort. Neither Eric nor Sophie contributed much to the table conversation.

After dinner Josiah swept Andrew off to the library to discuss mill business. In the parlor, Tina played the piano, Sophie did her needlepoint, and Eric and Caroline played chess. Tonight his mind was not on the game. Caroline beat him shockingly.

CAROLINE FORCED herself to settle in to the tenuous existence of living at Josiah Hampton's house without being actually accepted as a member of the family. Tina spent a brief period with her late each morning when she came downstairs to breakfast, then Tina disappeared on some vague activity involving her mother or her brother or one of the myriad friends who were returning to town.

Tina had filled in her curiosity about Andrew. Like so many planters, his parents had been financially ruined by the War. His father had struggled in the rough Reconstruction period to utilize what land he had been able to retain for raising peanuts rather than cotton, but his health had been broken by his years in a Confederate uniform, and he died when Andrew was eleven. Five years later his mother died of pneumonia, and Andrew came to live with Josiah Hampton and to work in the mill. He had lived in the house until six years ago when he became the mill superintendent and asked that he be allowed to move into the superintendent's cottage. A strange, sweet man, Caroline decided. It was unusual, she thought, for a man so involved in the mechanics of machinery to love theater.

ERIC WALKED from the streetcar line, perspiring in the late afternoon sun. At the house he lowered himself into one of the comfortable rockers that lined the west verandah. In moments, Seth came out with a glass of iced tea and the afternoon's Atlanta *Journal*.

A few minutes later he looked up from the *Journal* at the sound of Caroline's voice. She was walking toward the house with Alex at her heels.

"Oh, it's so hot," Caroline said when she spied him, "I didn't realize how hot until Alex and I turned around to walk back to the house."

"Come sit down and talk to me," he commanded.

"It's good to see that you're going to be home for dinner," she said with a smile. He had not been home one evening since he had taken her to see the Cyclorama, he realized. Tina must have been crying to her about his neglect. If he were married to Caroline, he would be home every night. Damn, what was the matter with him, thinking of Caroline that way? But why not, his mind retaliated. She was young and beautiful and desirable.

"Seth!" He called without stirring from his chair, confident his voice would carry. "Bring Miss Caroline a glass of iced tea, please."

With Alex collapsed into a russet heap at their feet, they sat on the verandah, switching companionably from one subject to another until Jason pulled up before the house with the carriage, and the General and Sophie emerged.

"When is this heat going to break?" Josiah complained. "Sophie, I hope we're having something not too heavy for dinner?"

"Bluepoints, fresh lobster, asparagus, and celery salad. And tutti-frutti ice cream with cake for dessert," she added, indulgent over his taste for sweets.

"I'm going to sit out here for a while," Josiah decided while Sophie went into the house. He glanced at the newspaper that lay across Eric's knees. "Anything in this afternoon's paper about the Penitentiary Committee's action on convict labor?"

"Not yet," Eric reported. "But they'll have to take some action soon."

"For twenty years they've allowed that damned bartering in bodies. It's contemptible."

At dinner Josiah pointedly ignored Caroline, as always. Eric was uncomfortable in the tense atmosphere at the table. Now the others were waiting for Josiah to finish a second portion of ice cream and cake.

Seth came into the dining room to announce that a telegram had arrived for Eric.

"I figured you'd want it right away, Mr. Eric," he said with a faint apology, approaching Eric with the envelope.

"Thank you, Seth. Yes." He ripped open the envelope. Who the devil was sending him a telegram? He read the message with astonishment.

"It's from that magazine I worked for in New York four years ago. They want me to go to Cuba to do an article on Evangelina Cisneros. Not much money," he conceded, "which is probably why they're offering it to me. But they'll pay all my expenses."

"That can run up high," Josiah said with an air of respect.

"I'll have to make them understand one thing," Eric stipulated, fighting against the excitement that swelled in him. Cuba! "I want the story to run as I see it, no matter whom it favors. The truth," he said doggedly. If he could ferret out the truth.

"Work it out with them before you leave for Cuba," Caroline suggested, her eyes luminescent. She was as pleased about this as he, Eric realized.

"I wish I could phone them. You can phone from New York to Chicago, but you still can't phone New York to Atlanta," he said in exasperation.

"Chad says the phone lines to New York will probably be in by spring," Tina remembered.

"Tina, that doesn't help me now," he shot back at her.

"Send them a telegram," Caroline urged. "That'll be fast."

"Right." He pushed back his chair. "I'll drive straight to the Western Union Office. A wire to New York takes no time at all."

"Eric, don't forget, they've moved to Jersey City," Sophie cautioned, and stopped dead as Eric stared at her in sudden comprehension.

He turned to Josiah, his face black.

"Damn it, Grandpa, you arranged this!"

"Because Sophie reminded you that the magazine moved from New York to New Jersey?" Josiah refused to be irked. "You know she's the most efficient woman in the state."

"How could Sophie *know* that the magazine had moved to New Jersey?" Eric demanded. "*I* didn't know it!" Distraught, Sophie looked at Josiah in apology. "Sophie knew," Eric continued ominously, "because you told her to contact the magazine and set up this deal. Her letter was forwarded to the New Jersey offices. *That's how she knew.*"

"Josiah, I don't know how I could have been so careless." Sophie was pale.

"That's all right, Sophie," Josiah dismissed this. "So he knows."

"When are you going to stop trying to run my life?" A pulse hammered in his forehead. "I am a man, Grandpa. I know what I want to do, and how to do it."

"You want to go to Cuba," Josiah shot back. "You've talked enough about it!"

"I've thought long and seriously about going to fight with the rebels," Eric acknowledged. "You must have guessed; that's why you arranged this deal. To keep me from that."

"Why should you fight for the Cubans? It's not as though this country is at war," Josiah objected. "You call yourself a journalist. Here's your chance to cover a big story."

"You figure this magazine up North will blue-pencil my article to please you," Eric accused.

"No," Josiah denied, "I'll have nothing to say in the matter." His eyes held Eric's for a long moment.

"I'm not going," Eric said. "You're manipulating again."

"What the devil's the matter with you?" Josiah's voice was loud with irascibility. "You've been dying to go to Cuba! You've got an assignment!"

"You've bought me an assignment."

"What damn difference does it make?" Josiah demanded. "You want to know what's happening in Cuba." He was deceptively soft-spoken now. "Here's a way for you to find out."

"Jim Russell is willing to send me down to Cuba if he can raise the funds for the first issue of a new magazine. He knows I'll bring back the truth, and that I can handle it. Will you finance that first issue, Grandpa?"

"No." Josiah was truculent again. "I won't support that damned Populist."

"And I won't go to Cuba for a magazine that knows me as little more than an errand boy. I worked for them fresh out of Princeton. They don't know what kind of a story I'll bring back. They're letting you buy them, Grandpa, and I want no part of that."

"Eric, stop being childish!" Tina chided.

"No, Grandpa. Thank you, but no." Eric rose to his feet. "Excuse me, please."

He strode from the dining room and down the hall to the door. All at once he felt a compulsion to talk with Jim. Jim would probably still be at the office. He'd have Zeke drive him; he was in no mood for streetcars at this moment.

Leaning back in the carriage a few minutes later, his fury at the General's manipulations subsiding, he visualized Caroline's face at his tirade. She approved of his rejection of a bought assignment, though she had been as excited as he about his going to Cuba. He was going to have to watch himself around Caroline. She was a fascinating combination of wide-eyed innocence, quickness of mind, and an unexpectedly sensuous loveliness.

How the hell had he allowed himself to fall into Tina's trap? He was bored and restless, and she was beautiful and charming as only Southern girls could be. The most beautiful and desirable girl in Atlanta, he had thought. He was overheated every time he was around her, and he had figured the only way into her bed was to marry her. He had done exactly what the General wanted; he had taken himself a beautiful bride with impeccable background, who would do fine in the receiving line at the White House.

"Don't wait for me, Zeke," he said, jumping down from the carriage. He glanced up to the second floor of the building and saw the light in Jim's office.

"I've been trying to get you on the phone," Jim greeted him with an air of quiet satisfaction. "We're going to sit down tonight with an old buddy who's just back from Cuba. Roger Ludlow. He's in town for a couple of days, en route to Detroit. We're meeting him at Cleo Hastings' place."

"Cleo Hastings?" Eric lifted an eyebrow in amusement. "I hope he can afford to lose a bundle."

"Roger's a fiend at blackjack, and unconscionably lucky," Jim chuckled. "We'll be able to talk in one of Cleo's private rooms."

They left the office and took a carriage to Cleo's gambling casino, remodeled a year ago at a cost of half a million dollars. Not a mansion in the state could surpass the establishment in decoration and furnishings. Cleo had acquired, somewhere in her career, one of the finest private art collections in the country, all of which was on display. Supper, along with champagne and cigars, was served without cost from ten o'clock in the evening until dawn in the magnificent basement supper room. The public gambling rooms were on the lower floor. Private rooms for special patrons occupied the second floor. Cleo utilized the third floor as her personal apartment.

Eric occasionally visited the casino with Jim, who only gambled in moods of deep depression, and then with commendable restraint. Eric seldom allowed himself to be more than an on-looker, though on occasion he amused himself with one of the pretty waitresses who served in the supper room.

They arrived at the casino, its windows draped with heavy damask, appearing to the public as another of Atlanta's magnificent mansions. They were speedily admitted, and Jim led Eric upstairs to the private blackjack room. Five players and a dealer sat around a table. A husky, dark-haired man looked up with a debonair smile at their entrance. One hand holding the card just dealt to him, he indicated with the other that he would shortly be with Jim and Eric.

"Blackjack," Roger said a moment later, exposing his hand.

When they were out in the hall, Jim introduced them.

"Where can we talk?" he asked Roger.

"Cleo's holding a room for us down here." He stalked over the carpeted corridor toward the rear of the floor. "We're old friends," he said with a deprecatory spread of his hands. "I once bailed her out of a rough spot in Frisco."

The room was small, furnished with a table for playing, a circle of comfortable armchairs, and a sofa for relaxing. A bottle of choice bourbon and three glasses waited for them on the table.

Jim inspected the label on the bourbon and whistled in approval.

"Cleo must have been in a rough spot in Frisco."

Over Cleo's fine bourbon they talked about Cuba.

"Don't let the newspapers fool you," Roger said brusquely. "Cisneros is guilty of sedition. She's admitted it. She's living in two clean rooms of her own. She's well fed. She would have been pardoned already if those damned New York newspapers weren't pissing up such a storm."

"Don't you think the Cubans deserve independence?" Eric challenged.

"Give the Spanish time," Roger pleaded. "They've just organized a new Cabinet. They'll give the Cubans self-government. The rebels are too damned impatient to wait. They know they don't have a chance in the world at beating Spain militarily. They want to steam up this country so we'll do the fighting for them."

For hours they discussed the Cuban situation. Eric was convinced that much of what Roger Ludlow told them was true. He would not go down to Cuba to join the rebels, despite his sympathy for their demands for independence. Like Roger said, give the Spanish a chance to offer self-government.

"I tell you, if the *Journal* and the *World* will stop distorting the truth, we won't be dragged into war." Roger's pronouncement brought Eric back to the stream of conversation. "If we fight Spain, it'll be a war of imperialism. Men like Roosevelt and Lodge are looking for an empire."

Jim pushed back his chair.

"I didn't have dinner. Let's go downstairs to see what Cleo's supper room offers tonight. We'll come back up here later."

In the supper room Eric discovered a provocative waitress who made it clear his attentions would be most welcome. Eric hesitated fleetingly. Jim and Roger would talk till dawn. There would be another bottle of bourbon in the room upstairs, and the political dialogue would give way to personal reminiscences. He was being offered something more substantial.

"I can leave in half an hour," Lola whispered at an opportune moment, and pulled a key from the titillating cleavage of her frock. "I'll have a terrible headache." The key changed hands as she whispered her address. "Wait for me."

Eric let himself into Lola's shabby flat, found a lamp by the bed and lit it. He lay back against the pillows, his mind racing. He knew that the impulse to go to Cuba to join the rebels was dead. But he was increasingly intrigued by the thought of a Cuban assignment. He believed what Roger had told them, yet there was this drive within him to see for himself. If he had accepted the assignment the General bought for him, he could be leaving for Cuba in twenty-four hours.

He'd miss Caroline, he thought. He frowned. Caroline had such a damnable way of intruding on his thoughts. How was he ever going to bring the General and her together? One was as stubborn as the other.

Why hadn't Caroline come to Atlanta a year ago? A year ago he was not involved with Tina. Caroline and he were such distant cousins as to make the relationship nonexistent. He could have married Caroline and been happy with her.

He rose to his feet at the faint knock at the door and strode to admit Lola. At this moment he felt little arousal; but Lola, he promised himself, would take care of that.

"What took you so long?" he reproached as Lola came into the room.

"I didn't want to lose my job," she pouted, sliding her arms about his neck and leaning backward to provide an advantageous view of her curvaceous bosom. "I had to make it look good."

"You are a devastating woman," he told her glibly. "More devastating without your clothes."

"Would you like some wine?" she asked, swinging about so

that he could help with the hooks of her dress.

"Let's not waste time on niceties." He finished the final hook, pulled the dress down to her waist, and along with it the lace-trimmed low-cut chemise. His hands swept about her to encase the voluptuous spill of her breasts, and she nestled her rump against him with a small sigh of pleasure.

This one was passionate. Immediately his body was responding. With swift gestures he thrust her attire to the floor, spun her about to face him.

"You, too," she ordered, her eyes bright. "Take off your clothes."

She stood before him, arms on her hips, watching him strip. Her mouth was moistly parted when he stood before her, lean, trim, hard.

"Satisfied?" he mocked.

"I'll let you know later," she parried.

He reached to pull her to him, his mouth opening as it came down to meet hers. He heard the small sounds of excitement in her throat as his tongue moved about hers and his hands fondled her Rubenesque buttocks.

He released her mouth to drop his own to her breasts. Her hands closed in about his head in encouragement when his tongue swept about one taut nipple, then the other.

"Don't be wasteful," she rebuked, a hand reaching to caress his hardness.

"Honey, I can keep this up all night," he laughed. But he prodded her toward the bed.

She lay with thighs parted in welcome, waiting for him to lift himself above her. He drove within her with a frenzy that she returned. The room echoed with the muffled sounds of their passion. For a few exhausted moments they lay limp together, sweated from their efforts, gloriously relaxed.

"Honey," she urged, pushing at his shoulders.

His mouth moved with erotic, punishing slowness down her torso, and then he found her. Her hips writhed beneath the ministrations of his mouth, her nails tearing at his shoulders.

Then he pulled himself above her again, to pour his mouth

into hers, and felt the shuddering sigh that surged through her.

"Stay all night," she whispered when he lifted his mouth from hers.

"I can't," he hedged, swinging over onto his back. He made a point of coming home, no matter how late. "But you don't see me running away."

She laughed and pulled herself to her knees. Her hand reached between his thighs. She lowered her face to him.

"Show me how good you are, Lola," he dared.

He lay motionless, knowing she would bring him to desire again. No rush, he told himself. Savor every minute of this bitch's talents. But then his body demanded and he pulled her above him, thrusting toward her with towering desire. They moved together again with the knowledge that they would arrive together at orgiastic climax.

But when Lola and he lay still again, exhausted and exhilarated by their coupling, Eric found his thoughts focusing where they had no right to focus. He would lay odds that Caroline was passionate. But he could never truly know.

Chapter Nine

CAROLINE sat in the blue velvet upholstered chair before the fireplace and poked at the smoldering logs in the grate. These past five days of unceasing rain had brought a welcome release from the heat, an autumnal chill that she relished; but the enforced confinement to the house made her tense.

When he was at the house, Eric seemed moody. He had been home for dinner every night since his confrontation with the General, Caroline considered, as though in expiation for his refusal to accept the Cuban assignment; but he went immediately to his room when they left the dining table. He had been *right* in rejecting the assignment. She wished that she could arrange a private moment to tell Eric that she supported him in this.

Why didn't this rain let up so she could leave the house for a while? Even if only to walk about for an hour. She was alone, except for the servants, for most of the day. Bless Seth for showing her in so many small ways that he was happy for her presence in the house. His way of bringing her tea in the library when she was reading, or lemonade on the verandah on a hot afternoon. Sometimes he would talk to her about Papa, and she would feel less alien in this house.

Tina slept late each morning. They spent some time together at the midday meal, where Tina talked vivaciously about the newest fashions from Paris and local gossip that Chad passed on to her about people who were faceless strangers to Caroline. Then Tina returned to her room to talk incessantly on the telephone.

Poor Tina. She was being particularly charming to Eric at dinner each night, yet he gave no indication that he was aware of her efforts. The General was irritated by Eric's indifference; he made a point of being attentive to Tina.

When was her grandfather going to abandon his suspicions of *her*? She gave him so many little proofs of her identity. At night she lay awake, thinking of some small fact to mention next evening that could only be known by Francis Hampton's child. She was grateful for the silent sympathy she sensed in Sophie. Dinner conversation was always strained because of the General's veiled hostility toward her.

In a burst of restlessness she left the fireplace and crossed to gaze out a window. The drizzle had stopped. The sun was pushing wanly through a cluster of clouds. The ground was wet, but with sturdy shoes she could go for a walk. She changed into oxfords, brought out a cape. She felt immeasurably brighter at the prospect of putting the house behind her for a while.

Alex lifted up his head in welcome as she emerged onto the verandah, and she bent to caress him, viewing the lush greenness about her with pleasure. Droplets of rain on the leaves shone like small diamonds in the emerging sunlight. The air was fragrant with the scent of flowers coaxed into bloom by the badly needed rain. She tensed as her eyes rested on the mill and, beyond, on Hamptonville, eerily veiled by a rising mist now. Hamptonville, her grandfather's kingdom, she thought with distaste.

"Alex, let's go for a walk," she invited, and leaving the verandah, deliberately strolled in the opposite direction from the mill.

She walked swiftly, impatient to put distance between the house and herself. Alex trotted beside her, darting off at odd moments in fleeting pursuit of some small animal. Not until she saw the streetcar pulling to a stop just beyond Alex and her did she realize she had traveled in that direction.

Eric stepped down from the streetcar, the sole passenger to ride to the final stop. He spied her and waved. Smiling, she waved in return and waited for his approach. She realized how delighted she was for this encounter.

"Going somewhere?" he teased, gazing down at her with a tenderness that accelerated her heartbeat.

"To meet you," she said flippantly, though of course she had no way of knowing he'd be coming home so early. She felt color rushing to her face because Eric was inspecting her with an ardor that was unseemly. How could she allow herself to feel this way? She would *not* become another of Eric Hampton's camp followers. "I haven't had a chance to tell you," she stammered, while Eric fell into step beside her. "I think you were so right in not allowing the General to buy you that assignment."

"I stormed out of the house that night and went to Jim's office." His eyes lit up with ironic amusement. "Jim had been trying to reach me by phone. An old newspaper buddy of his had just arrived in the city, just back from Cuba. The three of us talked till all hours."

"How fascinating! What did he tell you about Cuba? Did he talk about Evangelina Cisneros? Does he think she'll be freed?" Her words tumbled over one another in her excitement.

Caroline listened as though mesmerized by all that Eric had to relate as they walked back to the house; their pace slowed to a dead stop as they became emotionally involved in the Cuban situation.

"Eric, do you believe the newspapers are lying about Evangelina's treatment in jail?"

"I believe," he said, "these are the kind of stories that sell newspapers."

"But the conditions in Cuba are horrible for the people! Your friend admits this."

"The Spanish are ready to capitulate," Eric insisted, "if the warmongers will give them a chance."

Alex chased off, barking furiously.

"Alex, get back here!" Eric commanded. "Alex!"

After one final show of ferocity Alex rejoined them.

"We have people living under terrible conditions in this country, too," Eric said. "In the five months I spent in New York I saw situations that appalled me. The sweatshops, much like they have in England, only you call them 'sweated shops,' " he recalled with a touch of humor. "The squalid tenements in the slum areas. Jacob Riis wrote about it in a book called *How the Other Half Lives*. We have depressing poverty right here at home that's dressed in the sanctimonious garb of paternalism." Caroline lifted her face to his with a frown of incomprehension. "The mill village, Caro. It's today's version of the prewar plantation system." His voice was sharp with sarcasm. His eyes smoldered with contempt. "The summer before my sixteenth birthday, Grandpa insisted I work in the mill. He had visions then of my taking over in the distant future. I hated it. After that summer I refused to set foot in the mill again."

"Maybe things have changed, Eric."

"They haven't changed. Ask the General to show you through the mill. Go to the mill village. See for yourself."

"I will," she whispered, unnerved by the intensity of his scrutiny. He looked at her, at this moment, as though she were the most desirable woman in the world.

"And don't let me hear about you signing any more petitions for Evangelina Cisneros," he said with mock sternness, shattering the deeply personal moment between them. "She's the over-romanticized pawn of the Cuban revolutionaries."

FOR THE next few days Caroline thought often about Eric's condemnation of the mill village system, which she knew was engrained in the South. Her curiosity expanded to obsessive proportions. She could go to the mill and ask to see it, she told herself, yet she hedged from this invasion of her grandfather's personal domain without his invitation. How could she ask him, she taunted herself, when she hardly addressed a word directly to him?

At Sophie's urging, Tina took her for a drive about Inman Park, Atlanta's picturesque suburban community of fine Victorian houses on curving landscaped streets, styled in the fashion of Frederick Law Olmsted who had designed Central Park in New York City. Caroline recalled the harshness in Eric's voice that first night when he had talked about Tina's expectation of a house in Inman Park as part of marriage to him.

"You must meet Chad soon," Tina said when Jason turned the carriage around and headed back for the house. "I'll make him take us to lunch at the café in the Kimball House!" But Caroline doubted that she would.

Did the General believe that her appearance in Atlanta would revive what happened thirty-six years ago? She had told the Congressman and Mrs. Bolton that Francis Hampton was her father; they had not been disturbed.

WHEN CAROLINE arrived at the dinner table, the others were already seated. She pantomined her apology, as Tina chattered, and Sophie dismissed this with a smile.

"Chad told me he read in the *Constitution* that the Parthenon in Greece is absolutely doomed," Tina said wistfully and turned to Caroline. "Eric and I were in Greece on our—" All at once she faltered, aware of Eric's cold stare. Her eyes fell to her plate.

"I'd like to visit the mill some day soon," Caroline filled in the uncomfortable silence that fell about the table. Her eyes moved from Sophie to the General. "May I?"

Josiah stared at her in astonishment.

"Whatever for?"

"Because my father was so interested in the cotton mills." How dare he look skeptical! "Papa read everything he could find about the progress of the cotton mills in the South. He felt they were crucial in the South's recovery." Her eyes softened. "He told me about going through the cotton mills in Columbus when he visited his grandparents." The General was staring at her now with fierce intensity. "He wrote several articles for a small periodical in London about the mills in the South. I have them." She was trembling at this first real verbal exchange with her grandfather since her first night in Atlanta. "Would you like to read them?"

"Yes." His voice was harsh, but Caroline knew it was from the effort to control his emotions. He was overwhelmed to realize that his oldest son had known enough about the mills to write about them.

"I'll bring them to you right after dinner," Caroline promised.

As soon as they left the table, Caroline went up to her room and removed her father's articles from the tea caddy. For a moment she held the clippings against her cheek, feeling a poignant closeness to him. Tonight she was making a breakthrough in her relationship with her grandfather. She had something to give him.

Caroline went downstairs to the parlor. The General was watching for her appearance. She went to him and silently offered the sheaf of yellowing pages.

"Thank you," Josiah said brusquely, clearing his throat. His hand trembled as he accepted the clippings. Without a word he left the parlor and disappeared behind the closed door of the library.

Tina sat down at the piano to play, as she did each evening. Sophie settled herself with her needlepoint.

"Let's play some chess," Eric invited Caroline.

"Not tonight," Caroline declined politely. She was furious at the way he had humiliated Tina at the dining table. "I have not yet read today's *Journal*," she fabricated.

Caroline focused on reading the newspaper. After a few moments of fidgeting, Eric excused himself and went upstairs. At last Josiah returned to the parlor.

"Thank you, Caroline." His eyes were pained as he extended the clippings.

"Would you like to keep them?" she asked, knowing his pain.

"Yes, I would." His voice was low. "Thank you, Caroline." He hesitated a moment. "Come to the mill tomorrow. Andrew will be pleased to show off the new equipment we've just received. He'll talk you to death about it."

IMMEDIATELY AFTER breakfast Caroline left the house to go to the mill. She walked with eager swiftness in the refreshing morning sunlight. Approaching Hamptonville, she was startled by the horrendous noise that emerged from the rectangular, red brick structure. None of this was audible at the house. The mill's multi-faceted windows were opaque, like so many unseeing eyes. None of the sunlight that bathed the grounds about the mill in golden glory could penetrate those windows. Caroline visualized the dreariness within.

She walked up the small flight of wooden stairs to the landing that adjoined the entrance door. She opened the door and walked inside, flinching at the noise, the heat, the sweet, damp scent that assailed her. At rows of machinery, workers labored as though mesmerized, not bothering to look up at her approach. She fought an impulse to flee.

"Caroline!" Andrew approached her with a glow of delight.

"Sophie said I might come for a tour," she said, warmed by his pleasure at her appearance. "Have I come at a bad time?"

"No," he said quickly, pulling a handkerchief from a pocket to wipe the perspiration from his face. "I hope you don't mind the heat." His eyes were apologetic.

"Of course not," she denied. But the noise and the heat were overwhelming. Lint was flying everywhere. How could these people work in such dreadful ventilation, by such poor lighting? She fought to conceal her revulsion.

"We have to keep the mill windows closed against drafts. Even the slightest draft breaks the yarn," Andrew explained.

He guided her along the aisles through the varied sections of the mill, his face close to hers in an effort to be heard above the clamor. Here and there he paused to indicate recently acquired machinery. He explained the work of each operator in minute detail. The carders and spinners, the dressers and finishers, the dyers and weavers.

"Most of the work requires little skill," Andrew pointed out. "The women easily handle the looms and the children the spinning frames. Only the loom fixers and the weavers require real ability. The machines are like animate objects. As long as we care for them properly, they work for us. They never tire. They're a magnificent labor force."

Caroline listened attentively, conscious of the dead-white skins, the stooped shoulders, the listlessness of the workers bent over their machines. At last, to her relief, Andrew led her into his small private office at the far end of the floor, meagerly isolated from the heat and the noise of the machinery. He showed her to an armchair that flanked his cluttered desk, and sat down facing her.

"You're shocked," he said, sensitive to her reactions despite her efforts to conceal them.

"Andrew, those children!" Her voice was unsteady. "How many hours a day are they at those machines?"

"They work a full day, like their parents," he acknowledged. "From sunrise to sunset, when we're on full schedule. The General works the same hours," Andrew said defensively. "So do Sophie and I."

"But those children," Caroline protested. "They belong in school."

Andrew's face was somber as he sought for words to explain the mill system to Caroline.

"It's not an easy life, Caroline, but the farmers work harder and with less security. Their children right beside them. These people know they have a roof over their heads, food to eat. They're grateful. They come to us from the farms looking for work."

"Andrew, it makes me sick," she whispered. "Do those people ever see the sunlight?"

Andrew forced a wry smile.

"On Sundays and when the mill is shut down. But it's their way of life, Caroline. They feel safe here. Even when the mill is shut down, the company store is open to them. Nobody has ever gone hungry in Hamptonville," he said with uneasy pride, yet Caroline sensed that Andrew was troubled by the ugliness of working conditions in the mill.

"Thank you for showing me everything, Andrew." She rose to her feet with a feeling of suffocation. "I wanted very much to see the mill."

On the landing outside the entrance, Caroline stood immobile for a few moments, grateful to feel herself in the fresh air, out of the monstrous oversized steambath that seemed to be her grandfather's whole life. Her eyes moved to the cluster of houses along the river. The mill village. Josiah Hampton's fief. He ruled the mill and the mill village, she guessed, the way he tried to rule the family.

On impulse she walked toward the village, obsessed by a need to see how the millworkers lived. Even at a distance there was a barren, sterile look about the village. She had seen the slums of London, but this was a new style of deprivation. Already she was repelled by what met her gaze, filled with hostility that her grandfather could allow this drab village, wrapped in an aura of hopelessness, to bear his name.

She slowed her footsteps as she approached the rows of houses. They were squalid, monotonously identical frame boxes, supported by stilts that dug into the red clay earth. Not a tree stood here to provide comfort from the hot summer sun or to ease the winter winds. Caroline's eyes swept about in search of relieving greenery. Not a flower met her eyes, only straggly patches of parched grass here and there.

She walked along the strip of dirt that separated two rows of houses, conscious that no one here bothered to cultivate a vegetable garden or to raise a few chickens for the table. When would the millworkers have time for this?

Fresh rage welled in her while she considered the situation of the women, who must come home from twelve hours or more bent over those infernal machines in the mill to cook for their families, wash clothes, clean houses. What about the young children? she wondered curiously. Who cared for them? Where did they go to school?

Then she spied a small, white building, surprisingly neat, with a fresh coat of white paint. The church, she realized. She heard the voices of young children inside. The church, then, was also the classroom.

She moved past the church. On a sagging porch on her left a pair of men sat staring idly into space. At sight of her they stiffened suspiciously.

"Good morning," she called out politely.

" 'Morning," one of the men grunted. The other scowled in silence.

Refusing to be intimidated, Caroline pursued her tour. Ahead of her on the right was a building that might have been a small barn. Several tobacco-chewing men sat in front on rickety chairs. Not a barn, she comprehended when she saw a man emerge, clutching a bag of potatoes. This was the company store. The men here viewed her with the same suspicion she had encountered earlier.

"Good morning," Caroline called to them, as she walked past the store.

Not one of the men replied to her greeting. Plainly they considered her an intruder.

THAT EVENING the family retired to the parlor after dinner without the diversion of Tina's piano playing awaiting them. Tina had left late in the afternoon to have dinner at her parents' house, since this was her father's birthday. Eric had made an effort at dinner to coax Josiah into a less reproachful attitude toward him. For all the hostility between them, Caroline thought, he dearly loved the General.

"Andrew tells me you were at the mill this morning," Sophie said to her with a quizzical smile.

"Impressed by what you saw?" Josiah demanded, a glint of pride in his eyes. He was looking at her as though she were a human being, Caroline thought. Was he at last admitting to himself that she was his granddaughter? "We have one of the best-equipped plants in the South."

"I was shocked," Caroline said, and saw him bristle. "I couldn't believe the archaic conditions in Southern mills. In England, a law was passed fifty years ago prohibiting more than ten hours of work a day. Even before Victoria came to the throne Parliament passed the first Factory Acts to protect children."

"The Ten Hour Law was not enforced!" Josiah shot back. "There were legal difficulties."

"Which were removed by additional acts," Eric reminded. "The law became a reality with the Factory Act of 1874."

"I've kept my workers from starvation!" He glared for an instant at Eric, then focused on Caroline. "Even during the Depression my workers ate. They have roofs over their heads, houses that are snug against the rain, which is more than they had on the farms. They have money in their pockets. A family man has more wages in his hands in two weeks than he would see in a year on the land!"

"With himself and his wife and half a dozen children working," Eric supplemented.

"And didn't the whole family work on the farm?" Josiah asked pugnaciously. "I have a fine relationship with my people. I know most of them by name. I know what's happening with their families. I allow them to take all the wood they need from company land. Those that own a cow pasture them on my fields. I pay for the school and church. Every Fourth of July I take them on a big barbecue. They even vote with me."

"Do they dare do otherwise?" Caroline challenged. Sophie looked unhappy.

"I don't threaten them," Josiah said tautly. "I have never once threatened a worker with repercussions if he voted differently. I talk to them. I explain what's for their own good. The South needs cotton mills. It's our salvation, our way to compete with the North. The mills make their lives more tolerable. There's something you don't understand, Caroline." Her heart pounded at the unfamiliar sound of her name on his lips. "The millworkers are the lowest white class in the South. They come from farms with absolutely no training. They have to be taught to work in the mills. They have to be taught habits of punctuality and regularity. Damn it, I'm educating them," he blustered. "They ought to go to church every Sunday and thank God I'm alive to take care of them!"

"Have you ever truly looked at them?" Caroline refused to be intimidated. "They're colorless from lack of sun, scrawny. I doubt that they even have enough to eat."

"They have more than they had on the farm," Josiah said tersely. "Why do you think they stay here?"

"You don't know what it means to be poor," Caroline began zealously, but Josiah interrupted.

"I know," he corrected her. "I was the son of a poor Presbyterian minister, who never knew for sure that there'd be food on the table next week. But he fought to better himself. He skimped every way possible to send me to Princeton. My great-grandmother was an indentured servant, who slaved for seven years to earn her freedom. She educated herself and married a Georgia farmer. But most poor whites—and blacks—are not capable of raising themselves, or they would." He rose from his chair with a slowness that betrayed his age. "I'm tired. I'm going up to my room."

"I'll send Seth up with some hot milk," Sophie said solicitously.

Josiah turned to Caroline.

"I read those articles you gave me. Damn good. I didn't know Francis knew that much about the mills."

He mentioned Papa by name. For the first time since her arrival he said Papa's name aloud. Tonight she felt the wall between them begin to crumble.

Chapter Ten

CAROLINE watched with fresh hope for signs that her grandfather was relinquishing his doubts about her relationship to him. He had been furious at her condemnation of the mill system, yet it had opened up a communication between them. When he talked about Papa's articles, it was, she suspected, his first reluctant admission that she was his grandchild. And in accepting her, Caroline told herself, he would be taking Papa back into the family. She wanted that, she thought recklessly, even more thán she wanted Hampton Court.

The others in the household were aware of the shifting in the General's attitude toward her. Eric was pleased. Sophie, too, she analyzed. But last night, after inveigling her into a game of chess, Eric warned her not to rush him.

"Give him time, Caro," he had urged, their conversation covered by Tina's inept rendition of a Tchaikovsky concerto. "There's a thirty-six-year wound to heal."

This morning she sat alone in the small octagonal dining room where breakfast was served on chilly or rainy mornings. She particularly liked this cheerful room with its delightful Chinese wallpaper, its detailed ceiling. But as she lingered over a second cup of coffee, she recoiled from the prospect of yet another day of idling about the house.

Would Mrs. Bolton be back in Atlanta yet? With sudden decision she left the table and sought out the telephone in the library. She had never used a telephone before, but she understood the mechanics of making a phonecall.

In the Atlanta phone directory she searched for the Congressman's number, went to the phone and called the Bolton house.

"I'm sorry, ma'am," the elderly maid who answered told her. "Miz Bolton's up in Washington with the Congressman. Nobody here 'cept Miss Laurette." Caroline knew that "Miss Laurette" was the Congressman's elderly mother. "You wanna talk to her?"

"Thank you, no."

She left the library and went down the hall to the stairs. She would go into Atlanta by herself. It would be good just to roam about the streets of the city. Everywhere in Atlanta there was a feeling of excitement, of things happening.

"Good morning, Caroline." Tina's sweet, soft voice drifted down the stairs to her. "Isn't this a glorious day? You can just smell autumn coming, though we'll swelter for sure again before it's here to stay."

"It's lovely," Caroline agreed. "I was out walking for an hour with Alex earlier." She observed Tina was dressed for leaving the house. "Are you going into the city?"

"Why, yes I am, honey."

"May I drive into Atlanta with you? I'd like to go to one of the bookstores," Caroline improvised.

"Of course. Go on upstairs and get your things while I send for a carriage."

Caroline hurried up to her room for her bag and a cape, eager for this excursion into the city. When she came downstairs, she found Tina on the verandah, annoyed that Jason was taking so long to bring out the carriage.

"Caroline, I'm having lunch with Chad before I go to my UDC meeting. Why don't you have lunch with us? Then Jason can take you over to the bookstores," she said vivaciously. "He won't have to pick me up until four-thirty."

"If Chad won't mind." *Tina wasn't afraid to ask her out now.*

"He'll be delighted," Tina reassured her. "I've told him how smart and pretty you are. He's been dying to meet you."

They met Chad at a prearranged point in the spectacular lobby of the Kimball House. The only physical resemblance between Tina and Chad, Caroline thought as Tina introduced them, was in the emerald of their eyes, though Chad's eyes seemed to view the world with an amused detachment. He was at least four inches shorter than Tina, with hair that was corn-silk yellow and fine. Not handsome, Caroline assessed charitably, but arresting in appearance.

Chad guided them into the dining room, intent on charming Caroline.

"Aren't these stained-glass windows exquisite? This hotel would do honor to Paris. Did Tina tell you that I lived in Paris for over a year?"

"Yes, she did." Caroline was discomforted by the intensity of Chad's scrutiny. It was as though he were trying to see within her soul.

"Tina should have lived in Paris a hundred and fifty years ago," he mused between narrowed eyes. "She should have been another Madame de Pompadour, mistress to a king."

"Chad, don't let Mama hear you talk like that!" Tina laughed, but her eyes lighted. "She'd kill you."

The waiter arrived and Chad concentrated on ordering for them. He reminded her of the London gentlemen in their opera cloaks and opera hats and white gloves who frequented the Café Royal and Kettner's and Romano's, who were in and out of hansom cabs, never arriving home until dawn.

Their luncheon arrived. Green turtle soup, broiled pompano, Duchesse potatoes and green peas. With this Chad ordered a bottle of sauterne, and promised a chocolate mousse for dessert. Caroline enjoyed Chad's manner of dashing from one subject to another, talking eloquently on theater, art, the newest novels, yet she wondered why he was making such an obvious effort to entertain her. Or was it simply that Chad entertained for each new audience? "Tina never reads a book, you know," he teased. "I think the last novel she read was *Trilly*, and that came out four years ago!"

"Caroline, you won't be upset if I leave you here with Chad, will you?" Tina asked with appealing wistfulness before their dessert was brought to the table.

"Where are you going?" Chad demanded, his voice testy.

"I want to do some quick shopping before I go to the UDC

meeting. Take Caroline to the bookstores, honey. You know the best ones in town. She'd like to buy some books."

For a moment her eyes clashed with Chad's, and then he was smiling inscrutably.

"Go along, darling," he drawled. "Do your shopping. Then come back and collect Caroline. We'll be an hour over our mousse and crème de menthe and coffee. Take Caroline with you to the UDC meeting."

"Chad, she wants to shop for some books." Tina's smile was sweet, but Caroline saw the fire in her eyes.

"She can shop for books any time," Chad dismissed this. "Take her with you." It sounded like an ultimatum. *What was this strange bargaining between Chad and Tina?*

Tina turned to Caroline with an engaging smile.

"Would you like to go to that terribly stuffy old meeting?"

"It's an experience no Southern young lady should miss," Chad insisted. "And Caroline is Southern," he pointed out, "by virtue of her Georgia grandmother."

"I'd like to go," Caroline said.

"Then it's arranged," Chad smiled and turned to Tina. "What are you waiting for, darling? Go do your shopping."

Tina swept off and Chad focused on entertaining Caroline. He must never miss a theater or opera engagement, she was thinking, while he casually mentioned having seen James O'Neill twice in *The Count of Monte Cristo.*

"Oh, that man is a magnificent performer," Chad said with nostalgia. "I can still remember him on the stage of the Springer in Columbus two years ago."

"You were in Columbus?" She was listening attentively. *Her grandmother had been raised in Columbus.*

"It's only a little over four hours from here by train. Our Uncle Harry lives there. Mama's brother and his family."

Her father used to go to Columbus regularly as a young boy to visit his grandparents, his aunts and uncles and cousins, Caroline remembered. But his grandparents had died within months of each other during his fourteenth year, and the cousin to whom he wrote from England made it clear he wished no further communications with him. Were aunts and uncles, cousins, still living in Columbus? Would they feel the bitterness now that they had shown all those years ago?

Somehow, through Tina, she must contrive to visit Columbus. She would have to wait for the proper moment, but it would come, she promised herself. There was a quotation in the Bible that her mother had particularly liked. *To everything there is a season.*

For a little while Hampton Court had receded in her mind, in the excitement of hoping that her grandfather was coming to accept her. But Hampton Court still belonged to her, and she meant to have it.

In exactly one hour Tina returned to the restaurant. She carried no parcels. She was cold to Chad when she turned down his suggestion that she have coffee before Caroline and she left for the UDC meeting.

"Let's go." Tina was sulky. "Jason's waiting."

Caroline walked with Tina into the large, airy clubroom, adorned this afternoon with masses of chrysanthemums, where the UDC was meeting. Small clusters of ladies of varying ages gathered about the room. Caroline was suddenly self-conscious. Had some of these ladies known her father? Would they remember that the oldest of the Hampton sons had not fought for the Confederacy?

"Tina, how lovely you look!" A small, dark-haired, middle-aged woman came forward effusively. "I'm so glad you came to our first meeting of the season! That means you'll be here every meeting."

"Mrs. Swift, I'd like you to meet my cousin Caroline from London," Tina said with the deferential sweetness she used toward the General. "She's just arrived in Atlanta." But the day she arrived, Caroline recalled, Tina was supposed to have been at a UDC meeting.

"Caroline Kendrick?" Mrs. Swift asked.

"Caroline Hampton," Caroline herself supplied, inwardly gearing herself for an icy glare.

"The General's grandniece?" Mrs. Swift inquired with a smile.

"His granddaughter," Caroline explained.

Mrs. Swift beamed.

"Welcome to Atlanta, Caroline."

"Thank you, Mrs. Swift."

Tina escorted her about the room, introducing her to the members. The older ladies obviously adored Tina. The ones her own age welcomed her with a show of warmth, yet Caroline sensed their envy. Tina's beauty dominated any gathering.

"Isn't your mother coming, Tina?" a voice asked sharply, and both Tina and Caroline swung about to face a tall matriarch in depressing black.

"She was so sorry she couldn't come, Mrs. Johnson." Tina apologized for her mother. "She wasn't feeling well today. But she'll be here at the next meeting. This is my cousin, Caroline, Mrs. Johnson. She's recently arrived from London."

"On your mother's side or your father's side?" Mrs. Johnson probed.

"She's a Hampton," Tina explained guardedly.

"Francis Hampton's daughter?" Mrs. Johnson's voice was faintly shrill. Her face forbidding. Caroline tensed. "At a UDC meeting?" Clearly she considered Caroline's presence an affront.

"Excuse me, Mrs. Johnson," Tina said in confusion. "My mother asked me to speak with Miss Emily about her Garden Club committee." She smiled abjectly at Mrs. Johnson as she tugged at Caroline's arm.

Struggling to conceal her rage, Caroline allowed Tina to propel her across the room. Tina had not wanted to bring her, she recalled. She had been thoughtless in accepting the invitation. But how dare that smug old woman stand there in judgment of Papa!

In a few minutes the meeting was called to order. Caroline sat erect in a small gilt chair beside Tina and tried to dismiss Mrs. Johnson's hostility from her mind. Everyone else had been cordial. But she had been wrong in coming, Caroline chastised herself, while she listened to the lively discussion of the coming Reunion.

"We mustn't wait until the last minute to start setting up our committees," Mrs. Johnson acidly interrupted an earnest young member describing the Reunion held in Richmond, where thousands of veterans—many of them penniless—slept in parks, on rooftops, on sidewalks.

"This is going to be a mammoth affair. Far larger than the one in Richmond." Tina had said that committees for the Reunion had already been set up. Caroline recalled the discussion at the dinner table, her first night at the house. Why had Tina lied? "There'll be at least forty thousand visitors to the city," Mrs. Johnson forged ahead. "We'll all have to make sacrifices and take these people into our homes." A distasteful prospect, her face said, but as a Daughter of the Confederacy she would make this sacrifice. "Our hotels can't accommodate everyone."

At last the business of the meeting was over. Refreshments were brought in and served by genial white-jacketed Negroes.

"I was thinking that before the Reunion we ought to arrange for a monument on the road coming into town from Decatur," a pretty young matron said enthusiastically. "Something simple that shows we remember. A Confederate soldier with a gun in his hand."

"But we have dozens of those statues," somebody reminded. "A soldier with a gun in his hand, pointing North."

"Isn't it doing the South an injustice to perpetuate the breach between the North and the South?" Caroline protested.

For an instant the room was deadly silent. Eyes ablaze with fury focused on Caroline. Then a half dozen voices were simultaneously attacking her. It was as though they were at the eve of defeat, their wounds still raw.

"I'm sorry," Caroline whispered with constraint, and stumbled to her feet. "I'm sorry." Head high, she left the room, with Tina at her heels.

"Caroline, I'm so sorry," Tina said. "I was afraid something like this would happen."

"You know about my father?" Caroline struggled to keep her voice even.

"Sophie told me," Tina said sympathetically. "This was all my fault," she sighed. "I shouldn't have allowed Chad to persuade you to go with me."

"It's over," Caroline said. "The UDC will have to realize soon that we're living in the New South. Eric was right when he said they were making a religious cult of the Confederacy."

"It's not just the UDC," Tina said softly when they were inside the carriage and Jason was driving them home. "The whole South still remembers what it was like before the War. Papa said that during the Reunion in Richmond, the Richmond *Times* gave nineteen of its twenty-four pages to articles about the Confederacy and the South the way it used to be. No matter how much Eric and other people talk about the New South, nobody's forgetting the old."

"I guess I won't become a Daughter of the Confederacy," Caroline said with an effort at lightness. "Though by virtue of my grandmother I'm entitled."

"Did you have a pleasant time with Chad?" Tina asked, determined to put the ugliness in the clubroom behind them. "Don't you think he's charming?"

After dinner, Tina begged off from her usual musical interlude in the parlor.

"I'm just exhausted from the UDC meeting this afternoon," she explained, prettily apologetic. "It was awful the way they attacked Caroline."

The General froze at attention.

"You took Caroline to a UDC meeting?" he demanded in amazement.

"Chad thought she would enjoy it," Tina said wistfully. "I didn't expect them to hound her that way."

"Tell me exactly what happened," Josiah demanded tersely.

Eric leaned forward grimly in his chair while Tina, after a glance at Caroline that begged her forgiveness, haltingly reported the events of the afternoon. Caroline sat motionless, her face hot, conscious of Eric's compassion for her ordeal.

"Damn it, Caroline, how could you make a statement like that?" Josiah exploded.

"Grandpa, she was right," Eric said gently. "After decades of sweating to make the South solid, now in the last few years we're trying to exhume the old plantation aristocracy!"

"Eric, have some respect for your traditions." Josiah's face was florid. "Nobody can steal that away from us." He stared at

Caroline with such fury that she was suddenly cold. Again she was the enemy. She had hoped, for a pitifully few days, that her grandfather and she could become close. He swung his gaze from her. "Tina, this Reunion will be the most spectacular the South has ever seen. Naturally I plan to contribute heavily. We'll hold a reception. I want you to make all the arrangements," he said with a flourish. "Your mother will help you. You're to spare no expense to make this a brilliant social event that Atlanta will remember for years to come."

Caroline lowered her eyes to the floor. This was a rebuke for her behavior at the UDC meeting. Eric was moving about in his chair, irritated by this whole discussion. She felt his eyes on her, knowing he was sympathetic.

"I expect to ride in the Reunion parade with the men who remain from my division," Josiah said with towering pride. "I'll ride and remember my two sons who gave their lives for the Confederacy."

"And while you're riding," Caroline said with unleashed anger, "remember your son Francis who died after saving two of his students from drowning and then, exhausted, attempting to save a third. He was as much a hero as his brothers!" Tears fell unheeded upon her cheeks.

For an anguished moment Josiah recoiled. Suddenly he seemed a very old man. But Caroline saw the pride that shone from his eyes as he digested what she had told him.

"Tina, did you tell me you were going to Columbus to visit your uncle and aunt?" Eric said with a studied nonchalance.

Tina gazed warily at him.

"I've been thinking about it," she conceded. "I don't recall mentioning it to you."

"You did," he said calmly, and Caroline sensed that it was a lie. "Why don't you take Caroline with you? She'd enjoy seeing Columbus."

"I'd love to go to Columbus." All at once her heart was pounding. The moment for which she had been waiting! She brushed aside the realization that Eric was seeking an excuse to put distance between her grandfather and her for a few days.

"Why not plan to leave at the end of the week?" Eric suggested.

"I'll have to write Aunt Agatha and make sure it'll be all right then," Tina stipulated. "Though I imagine it will be."

"Write tonight," Eric pushed. "I'll mail the letter for you in the morning."

"I'll go up and write it now," Tina said demurely. "I'll bring it to your room later."

Caroline lowered her eyes before the limpid invitation Tina was offering her husband. Guiltily she sought to brush away the disturbing image that floated across her mind. *How had she allowed herself to fall in love with Eric?*

Tina rose to her feet, walked over and kissed the General good-night. Caroline intercepted the exchange between Josiah and Tina. He was thanking Tina for removing *her* from the house for a few days. He would be less smug if he realized why she was so eager to go to Columbus.

Chapter Eleven

IN the garnet dressing gown that was the twin to the one he had bought for the General in Paris, Eric stood before the comfortable warmth of the fire Zeke had started earlier in the grate because the night temperatures were dropping sharply. He stared at the flames curling about the small birch logs without seeing them; his mind re-played Tina's report of what had happened at the UDC meeting. That fiendish Chad had urged Tina to take Caroline to that meeting. He enjoyed making trouble. Caroline had been right, of course. They had too many statues already of Confederate soldiers with guns.

What was he going to do about himself and Caroline? Sometimes she looked at him, and he would swear she felt the same way about him as he did about her. But what future could they possibly have together? The best thing for both of them was for him to stay away from her as much as he could. He smiled; he was spending more evenings at the house since she arrived than at any time since Tina and he had come back from Europe. He came home because Caro was here.

If Sophie had not bumbled that way, if he had not found out about the old man's manipulating that assignment, he would be in Cuba now. Maybe it would have been better if he had not found out.

He started at the knock at his door. That would be Tina with the letter to her aunt in Columbus. He strode to the door, opened it slightly. Tina stood there, her hair down in a dark cloud about her shoulders, her silk dressing gown not quite concealing the bodice of her transparent nightdress. His gaze involuntarily focused on the high rise of her breasts. For a moment he felt the first stirring of desire. Only for a moment.

"I'll mail the letter for you in the morning," he said, extending a hand.

"Eric, can I come in for a little while?" Tina gazed at him with the potent blend of wistfulness and passion that eight months ago had convinced him he could not live without her in his bed.

"I'm tired, Tina," he said brusquely. "I'm going to sleep." The envelope in hand, he closed the door on her. Tina knew it was over between them. It was over in Paris.

He put the envelope on his writing table, untied his dressing gown, and settled himself in bed. It would be a long time before he fell asleep tonight. He was haunted by visions of Caroline at that UDC meeting. If ever there had been a girl especially designed to fit into his life, that girl was Caro. But nothing was possible for them. She was unapproachable.

RIDING ON the streetcar to downtown Atlanta, Eric was conscious of the seemingly endless growth of the city. Everywhere there were new buildings rising. For decades people had been saying that Atlantans were a different breed from the rest of the South because of the way they had fought to rebuild. No Atlanta merchant considered himself putting in a full day unless he was at his place of business by 7:00 A.M., there till nightfall. None of the leisurely ten-to-four working hours of the Savannah merchant or professional man here in Atlanta. But increasingly Eric was aware of the shadows of the old Confederacy moving over them. Jim made him aware.

Eric walked into the office and Mike, who never failed to greet him with a broad grin, didn't even look up from his typewriter.

"Mike, that's going to land in your lap," he warned as he headed for Jim's desk.

"Eric, the son-of-a-bitch did it!" Jim pounded on his desk with one fist.

"What son-of-a-bitch?" Eric demanded.

"Hearst! That Cisneros girl was rescued by some of his people!"

Jim reached for a cigar. He smoked only in moments of deep stress.

"That should make a lot of people happy," Eric conceded with an uneasy frown.

"This was an illegal act, Eric. To the government of Spain it's a blatantly unfriendly act. That could push us even closer to war." He sighed. "I don't know why the hell I'm blowing off this way about a newspaper headline. We've got problems of our own."

"You still haven't heard from your money people," Eric guessed.

"I've heard," Jim acknowledged. "I was called into a meeting last night. They're not coming across. We don't seem a financially solid investment," he said. "We talk out against racism. We backed the legislation to control convict-leasing. We warn against disenfranchisement. I've got enough bankroll to cover salaries for the next five weeks. After that issue, we're finished."

"No, we're not!" Eric contradicted. It was inconceivable that a man of Jim Russell's capabilities should fail. "As of today, I'm off salary. If we have to, we can put out the paper between us."

"Take me off salary, too," Mike ordered. They had not been aware that he had abandoned his typewriter to approach them. "That'll keep us moving a little longer. You'll find somebody, Mr. Russell. I know you will."

"The typesetters have to be paid, but without other salaries I can handle that for a couple of months. I can stall on the rent, even on the paper. I've got a contact in New York," Jim said thoughtfully. "He's a weak possibility."

"Go to New York," Eric prodded. "Mike and I will keep the paper rolling till you get back." He grinned. "I've got my quarterly check due in this week. I'll throw that into the pot." Tina could stay out of the stores for a while.

"I could make it to New York and back within a week," Jim gauged. "Of course, it may be a wasted trip."

"Take it," Eric insisted.

Jim squinted at Eric.

"It's pointless to tackle the General for financing?"

"Useless," Eric confirmed.

"We want the same thing. A vital city that can compete with

any in the Northeast. We just arrive at it by different routes." He gazed from Eric to Mike. "I'll go to New York next week."

SEVERAL EVENINGS later Tina announced that Caroline and she were leaving for Columbus the following day. Eric was startled by his instant sense of loss at the prospect of Caroline's absence. He had fostered this trip, he taunted himself, to give the General a few days' breathing space.

"You're taking the morning train?" he asked.

"Honey, at 5:20 in the morning?" Tina reproached. "We'll take the 4:40 P.M. train. It arrives in Columbus at 9:10 P.M. Aunt Agatha said she would have a carriage waiting for us at the depot."

"I'll see the two of you to the Union Depot," Eric offered, and saw the General brighten at his offer.

Why the devil had he said that? He would have to hurry home, take Tina and Caroline to the station, then rush back to the office. He was playing the gracious Southern gentleman, he mocked himself, because he wanted to see Caroline tomorrow before she left for Columbus.

CAROLINE WAITED impatiently for the day to move past. It was unseasonably cool, and she had spent most of the afternoon in the library before the fire. Twice Seth brought her tea.

"Seth," she asked impulsively as he placed the second cup of tea on the table beside her, "when will the family be going up to Hampton Court?"

Seth smiled affectionately.

"Oh, you'll be goin' up for the Thanksgivin' week, Miss Caroline. And won't you be lookin' forward to that!" His eyes were bright with sympathy.

"Yes, Seth." He understood how eager she was to see the house where Papa grew up. The house that belonged to her, though Seth could hardly know that.

By the time Eric appeared with the carriage, she was already sitting on the verandah with her modest canvas suitcase at her

135

feet. Patience was hanging out an upstairs window, waiting to see her off. And to wave to Zeke, Caroline thought.

Eric bolted up the steps two at a time.

"Isn't Tina ready yet?" His eyes rested on Caroline with an intensity that brought color to her cheeks.

"I'll call her," she said, rising from the rocker.

"Sit down." It was a brusque command, contradicted by the tenderness in his eyes. "Patience!" he yelled up to the second floor, "go tell Miss Tina to come right downstairs. She has a train to catch."

Tina came downstairs immediately. She was followed by Jason carrying her handsome stateroom trunk, which he hoisted up to the carriage perch, along with Caroline's suitcase. Tina was in a convivial mood this morning. Eric helped Caroline and Tina into the carriage, arranging to sit beside Caroline.

Tina chattered about Columbus all the way to the depot. Her Uncle Harry, her mother's brother, had lived there for thirty-five years, since his marriage to a Columbus girl. Caroline gathered there were three unmarried daughters, well past the age favored by matrimonial-minded young men.

"I guess it's too late in the year to go out to Wildwood Park. Just everybody goes there for swimming and picnicking. I love to go boating in the moonlight or dancing in the pavilion." Tina smiled sentimentally, her gaze focused on Eric, but he was staring out the carriage window.

At the depot Eric escorted them onto their train, kissed Tina on one cheek, and then bestowed a cousinly kiss on Caroline's cheek. She felt a fleeting pleasure at the touch of his hands at her shoulder.

"Have a good trip," he said perfunctorily, but his eyes were warm when they rested on her for a moment. Then he sauntered down the aisle to the exit.

"You were smart to bring along something to read," Tina said. "Four hours is an awful long time just to sit on the train." Her eyes swept with odd expectancy toward the exit. The train began to move. Tina frowned.

At that same moment a last-minute passenger appeared at the

136

head of the aisle. He walked toward a vacant seat just opposite theirs.

"Marshall!" Tina exclaimed. "Whatever are you doing on this train?"

"I have business in Columbus," he explained. "And you?"

"Caroline and I are going to visit my uncle and aunt," Tina said effervescently. With a sudden unease, Caroline intercepted the secret exchange between them. "Oh, Caroline, this is Councilman Marshall Shepard. My cousin, Caroline Hampton," Tina introduced her.

Tina knew Marshall Shepard was going to be on this train. Caroline sat with a strained smile while Marshall and Tina exchanged small talk across the aisle. She must not think harshly of Tina, she exhorted herself. Eric was responsible for Tina's turning to someone else for affection. Yet it was a disturbing realization.

"Caroline, you're going to be reading. Would you mind if I moved across the aisle and talked with Marshall a while?" Tina asked with an ingratiating smile.

"No, of course not." Suppose Tina enjoyed sitting with Marshall Shepard on the train, what was so wrong about that? If Eric did not neglect her, she would not be looking for affection from another man.

Caroline tried to read, but her mind was too occupied with the visit to Columbus. Papa had talked with such affection about his mother's hometown. The family had moved to Columbus from Savannah when she was barely eight. She had been married in Columbus. The town was older than Atlanta, with streets planned to be broad and tree-lined, running parellel with the Chattahoochee River. Papa said it had a storybook air of elegance.

She would walk the streets that Papa had walked, see the church where her grandmother was married. For a moment her pleasurable anticipation was tainted by recall of her grandfather's antagonism toward her. *Don't think about him now.*

She must not forget her real mission in Columbus. To find someone—aunt, uncle or cousin—who would know about the entailment in the deed to Hampton Court. But would those who remained of her grandmother's family wish to talk to Francis Hampton's child?

When the train pulled into the depot, Tina immediately spied her aunt's coachman waiting for them.

"Marshall, we can drop you off at your hotel," Tina said gaily. "Where are you staying?"

"At the Rankin," Marshall said. "Is that convenient?" Caroline felt uncomfortable in the secretive exchanges between them.

"It's right on our way. Uncle Harry lives on lower Broad."

They deposited Marshall at the Rankin Hotel, where Caroline admired the inviting two-story cast-iron verandah. They rode along wide, gaslit streets, with Tina promising a daylight tour of beautiful Columbus.

"Marshall's doing very well for himself," Tina said with a show of admiration. "Of course, Dolly's been a big help to him politically. I know she's so much older than he is, but she was a rich widow when he married her, and a politician needs money to get ahead. Folks say Dolly already has her eyes on the Governor's mansion."

In a few minutes they were drawing to a stop before a sprawling white frame house with a verandah that extended on three sides. It was a large, comfortable house, though hardly as fine as the Hampton mansion.

The front door opened and a short, heavy, bespectacled woman pushed open the door to greet them. Caroline, too, was engulfed in Aunt Agatha's welcome.

"Girls, Tina and Caroline are here!" Agatha called exuberantly. "Come on downstairs this instant."

"We're arriving awfully late," Caroline apologized.

"Honey, you're family," Agatha chided. "Family's welcome any time. Uncle Harry will be home soon," she told Tina. "He's at a Bar Association meeting tonight. He's so delighted you'll be with us for a while."

"Did you have a good summer?" Tina asked. "Mama said you were at Warm Springs for a month."

"It was pleasant. Mike Rose brought his orchestra out to the hotel and played at luncheon every day and for the Saturday night balls. Your uncle stayed with us for one week, but after that he took the train into Columbus every morning to be at his office during the day, and took that long, hot trip back out to Warm Springs every night."

Tina's three cousins, Edith, Eleanor, and Elaine, appeared, though Caroline suspected their graciousness was forced, considering the lateness of the hour. Agatha talked brightly about plans for their entertainment.

"Aunt Agatha, you are not to put yourself out," Tina ordered. "I just want to see you-all and wander around town the way I always do. No parties," she ordered. "I've been telling Caroline how beautiful Columbus is, and she's a great one for walking. Let her wander about town seeing everything at her leisure."

"We're going to the Springer tomorrow night," Agatha said enthusiastically. "I have the tickets already. Eugenie Blair and her own company are presenting *Carmen*. It's the first time the opera has been here. And then our church is having a fair the day after—" She paused breathlessly.

"We're all going to the oyster roast at the end of the week," Eleanor, the youngest of the sisters, said. "At Papa's club. You'll like that," she told Caroline. Her eyes were bright with curiosity. "You're English, aren't you?"

"Ellie, with that way of talking, she sure isn't from Georgia," Tina laughed. "Caroline grew up in London, but she's a Hampton. That makes her one of us."

They must know that Louisa Hampton had been a Columbus girl, Caroline thought, her heart pounding all at once. But she would not ask questions tonight.

Caroline was relieved when they were at last shown to their own rooms. Only now did she realize how tired she was—from the train trip, from the need to face a houseful of strangers, from her constant awareness of her real purpose in being in Columbus.

SHE AWOKE early from custom, to a bright, sunny morning. She dressed quickly, eager to be downstairs and asking questions of her hostess. She liked Tina's Aunt Agatha; her aunt was a warm, unpretentious woman.

Agatha looked up with a smile as Caroline hesitated at the entrance to the dining room.

"Come on in to breakfast," she invited cordially. Elaine and her father smiled warmly. "Edith and Ellie are off to school already." Now Caroline remembered that they were teachers. "Elaine and her father will be leaving in a few minutes." Elaine worked in her father's law office. "But you and I can sit and visit," she said fondly.

Caroline's shyness evaporated before their genuine friendliness. The family maid brought her a plate laden with scrambled eggs and grits. A platter of ham sat in the center of the table, beside a basket of hot-from-the-oven biscuits, tall and golden. In a few moments Elaine and her father excused themselves, and Caroline and Agatha were alone at the table.

"My father used to come to Columbus often as a little boy," Caroline volunteered, battling against self-consciousness. "To visit his grandparents."

Agatha gazed with polite incomprehension for a moment.

"Oh, yes, Tina told me. You're General Hampton's granddaughter. He married one of the Carter girls. Louisa," she pinpointed. "They lived in a lovely house out on Wynnton Road."

"Perhaps you knew my father." Caroline's voice was uneven from excitement. "Francis Hampton."

"My memory's not too good," Agatha apologized. "I probably knew him when I was a child." Her face clouded in recall. "Those were good days before the War. I was a child, but I remember our beautiful house out in the country, in the hills, with just about everything we wanted. After the War we were left with almost nothing."

"Mrs. Williams," Caroline asked earnestly, "do you know if any of my grandmother's family remain in Columbus?"

"If I recollect correctly, two of her brothers died in the War. The third just a few years later. Her two sisters moved out to Texas, oh, twenty-five years ago. I heard they both died. But there's a cousin over on Second Avenue. She lives there with her husband and a son and his family."

"Do you suppose it would be all right if I went calling on her?" Caroline fought to mask her excitement.

"I think that would be very nice, Caroline," Agatha agreed. "She's Mrs. Madden now. Bertha Madden."

"I'll go over this morning," Caroline decided. "Tina will sleep late."

Agatha turned away at the sound of a knock somewhere toward the rear of the house.

"Miss Agatha," a voice called leisurely from the kitchen. "Vegetable man."

"Excuse me, Caroline, I've got to pick out the vegetables, then give Lily a list of groceries for the day."

After breakfast Caroline left the house to call on Bertha Madden.

"Miz Madden ain't home," the smiling Negro maid told her good-humoredly. "She's over to the dressmaker's. She be there all mornin'."

"I'll call again," Caroline said, and left before the maid could inquire further.

Disappointed, Caroline walked toward the center of town. Broad Street was divided by a mall of grass and trees. She dallied at the shop windows of the fine J. A. Kirven store, and Blanchard and Booth. She listened with amusement to a bevy of ladies inspecting hats in the window of Lee's Millinery.

"Would you believe it," one was saying, "when Lee's opened for the season on the sixth, ladies were crowded out on the sidewalks waiting to get in!"

Caroline walked uptown, enjoying the crisp morning air, admiring the fine houses beyond the business area. She saw the cotton mill far uptown, beside the muddy river, so like the mill at Hamptonville, and a somberness settled about her. All over the South were workers like those she saw in her grandfather's mill.

Now she returned to the downtown area. She realized with surprise that she was hungry. Her eyes roamed about the street. Oh, there was a tea room. She crossed to the Cricket Tea Room, opened the door and walked inside with an inquisitive smile. She stopped dead, her eyes fastened to a couple at a corner table, oblivious of her arrival. *Tina and Marshall Shepard.* Caroline spun about and left the tea room.

She spent most of the afternoon sitting on the verandah and

talking with Tina's aunt. They watched barefoot children play in an adjacent yard. Down the street a firm-voiced nurse called loudly, "Susie, you get yo'self home this minute. It's time for yo' bath!"

It was growing late. When was Tina coming home? Caroline wondered nervously. Moments later, Tina sauntered up the walk and onto the verandah.

"Oh, I have been visiting all day," Tina announced. "What a lovely time I had! I know I promised you a tour of the city, Caroline," she remembered with engaging apology. "Tomorrow for sure."

"Uncle Harry's coming home early from the office," Agatha told her, "so we can have supper and get over to the Springer. I'm so looking forward to the play."

Caroline struggled to mask her distress over Tina's behavior. She had no right to censure Tina, she told herself. Eric was responsible for this. But she wished that Tina would be more discreet. To be seen with Marshall in a tea shoppe, when each of them was married!

After supper, with the ladies dressed in their finest and Mr. Williams in his silk top hat, they crowded in the carriage for the short trip to the Springer Opera House.

"The Springer's the finest Opera House between New York and New Orleans," Mr. Williams boasted as they approached the elegant Victorian structure, brilliantly alight for tonight's performance. "It's presented some of the finest talent in the country—Madame Modjeska, Edwin Booth, Fanny Davenport, Lillie Langtry."

"Harry, remember the night Oscar Wilde lectured at the Springer?" Agatha smiled sentimentally. "Oh, it was way back in 1882, but I can remember so clearly. All the ladies tossed flowers in his path."

"Agatha, we don't talk about Oscar Wilde," Harry rebuked her, and Caroline remembered the painful trial in London two years ago.

The carriage took its place in line to discharge its passengers. They left the carriage and walked beneath the pillared balcony into the handsome lobby, its floor a lovely gray-and-white marble. Patrons were moving inside to their seats, and Caroline's party followed. Her immediate impression was of a charming baroque elegance, red plush and gilt everywhere, frescoed walls. Her eyes swept the scene with admiration. Three tiers of boxes on either side, a total of eighteen boxes, a delicate chandelier above each. There were gilt chairs in the boxes, and red velvet portieres.

"We're sitting in the orchestra." Mr. Williams led them to a group of center seats only a few rows from the stage, which was concealed now by a painted curtain.

"How many people can attend a performance?" Caroline's gaze swept the two balconies, each adorned with gold tulip lights.

"Twelve hundred fifty," Mr. Williams reported with pride. "And the stage is enormous."

Then a quietness fell on the Opera House. The curtain was about to rise. Caroline, long a theater-lover, was completely absorbed by the drama of the opera. As the curtain fell on the first act, she turned spontaneously to Tina. But Tina was gazing at the occupants of a box to their right, where a middle-aged couple sat in lively discussion with Marshall Shepard. Caroline saw him acknowledge Tina's presence with his eyes.

At the conclusion of the performance the audience demanded repeated curtain calls from Eugenie Blair and her company. At last the house lights came up, and the audience, convivial after a delightful performance, moved slowly from their seats.

"Shall we go over to Spano's for supper?" Agatha asked her husband. "Tina and Caroline would enjoy that."

"We'll go," he decreed in high good humor. "But let's hurry before all the tables are taken."

In a few minutes they were walking into the dark-paneled restaurant, some tables already occupied by those who had attended the Springer performance.

"Nothing plush about Spano's," Mr. Williams said expansively. "Not like some of the fancy restaurants you find in Atlanta and New Orleans, but the food is the best."

A white-jacketed Negro waiter, beaming his pleasure at serving this festive gathering, hovered over their table while they debated about what to order.

"I always have the same thing when we come to Spano's,"

Elaine said with anticipation. "The oyster pan roast."

Caroline had lost interest in this late supper. Her eyes followed Tina's gaze to a table across the room. Marshall sat there with the couple who had been with him at the Springer. He was rising to his feet, walking toward them in response to the silent summons from Tina.

"Tina and Caroline! How nice to see you again."

Tina and Marshall were using her to cover their covert relationship, Caroline realized. This was why she had been invited to come to Columbus. Did Eric suspect? Did he care? The General would care. He would be furious.

Chapter Twelve

CAROLINE slept later than normal the following morning. Again she awoke to a gloriously sunny day. Guilty at having slept so late, she dressed with calculated swiftness and went downstairs. Right after breakfast she would go over to Bertha Madden's house. Hopefully her cousin would be home this morning.

Agatha sat alone at the dining table, drinking coffee and consulting Lily about the day's grocery list.

"I'm glad you had a good sleep," Agatha greeted her fondly. "Lily will bring your breakfast now. But don't eat too heavily because we're going to the church fair and we'll have lunch there."

"What time will we go?" Caroline tried to conceal her disappointment. *She wanted to call on Bertha Madden.*

"Oh, we'll leave in about an hour," Agatha said, glancing at the grandfather clock that stood in a corner of the dining room. "Lily, the biscuits and the corn muffins must come out of the oven just as we're ready to leave," she cautioned with an air of anticipation. "A lot of the gentlemen will be coming there from their businesses for the noonday meal," she explained to Caroline. "It's to raise funds for the church."

"Do you suppose Mrs. Madden will be there?" Caroline asked.

"I shouldn't think so," she guessed. "The Maddens don't belong to our church."

Shortly before noon the carriage took Caroline, Tina and Mrs. Williams to the church, where the ladies had set up a varied assortment of tables and chairs to accommodate the already arriving patrons. Mrs. Williams took a plate piled high with Lily's hot biscuits and corn muffins to the small tent where family cooks of several church members supervised the improvised kitchen.

"Uncle Harry, over here!" Tina called, sweetly enthusiastic, as he surveyed the growing assemblage in search of his family.

They sat down to be served by some of the prettiest young ladies of the church, all who greeted Tina with warmth. Obviously Tina's visiting, Caroline noted, had not extended to them. She doubted that it had extended beyond Marshall Shepard.

Caroline enjoyed the crisp fried chicken, the ice cream and the chocolate layer cake served with fragrant hot coffee. After lunch the gentlemen returned to their businesses. The ladies began to circulate among the attractive booths that offered take-home delicacies and dainty handiwork. Caroline walked toward a booth in charge of an elderly, white-haired lady who appeared to be about Louisa Hampton's age.

She picked up an elaborately beaded pincushion in a floral design, inspected the tiny tag indicating the price. "I'll take this one, please." A present for Sophie. "This is my first visit to Columbus," Caroline confided as her pincushion was being wrapped in tissue. "It's a beautiful town." She hesitated. "My grandmother was born here. Perhaps you knew her?" The woman at the booth smiled in inquiry. "Louisa Hampton. She used to be Louisa Carter."

"Oh, my, you're Louisa Carter's granddaughter!" The woman beamed at her. "Our families moved to Columbus the same year." She squinted in recall. "Once she went away, we didn't see much of Louisa."

"Did you know her parents?" Caroline pursued with dwindling hope. Well enough, she meant, to be aware of the conditions of their will.

"Oh, our families met at balls and plantation barbecues," she said vaguely. "Fine folks." She turned with a smile to greet fresh comers to her booth.

Tina corralled Caroline for a walk to town when her aunt declared herself too tired to stand on her feet another minute. They escorted Agatha to the waiting carriage, then headed toward Broad Street.

"I'm absolutely dying for something to drink," Tina said in high good humor. "Let's go to a soda fountain."

At the soda fountain Tina was greeted effusively. The owners had heard that she was married and were eager to know about her husband.

"The next time I come to Columbus, Eric must come with me," Tina vowed.

Caroline was relieved when they were alone at the small table at the window. How could Tina carry on that way about Eric when he treated her so coldly?

"Wait till our Coca-Colas come," Tina said. "I'm sure you've never tasted anything so delicious." Caroline stopped herself from confessing that she had drunk Coca-Cola with Eric in Atlanta. "There's a kind of feud going on between Columbus and Atlanta about where Coca-Cola was first made," Tina confided.

"Don't let anybody tell you Doc Pemberton first made Coca-Cola in Atlanta." A spry, elderly man with a gleam in his eye eavesdropped. "It was made at the soda fount at his Eagle Drug Company right here in town. Then he called it 'French Wine of Cocoa.' Miz Etta Blanchard Worsley says the City Drug Store here in Columbus bought the first can of Coca-Cola syrup for two dollars."

A teenager brought two glasses and set them down before Tina and Caroline. The old gentleman continued to reminisce.

"Poor Doc Pemberton didn't see much money from his formula. He was having bad times financially and health-wise. Before it was even called Coca-Cola, Doc sold out for a total of $1,750. And I hear that the Candler folks expect to sell over half a million gallons this year, and that's only the beginning," he predicted.

"I believe you folks here in Columbus are right," Tina answered. "Anyhow, it's awfully good."

Caroline and Tina returned to the house, where Tina declared she would perish if she did not take a nap. But no more than an hour later Caroline, standing at a window in her bedroom, saw Tina being driven away in the carriage. Her aunt supposed she was calling on girlfriends, Caroline surmised.

At dinner, Tina announced that Caroline and she would be leaving on Sunday morning.

"I feel guilty being away from Eric so long," she said wistfully, "though I adore visiting you-all."

"At least you'll be here for the oyster roast on Saturday," Agatha reminded.

THE FOLLOWING morning Caroline left the house as soon as she felt a respectable visiting time had arrived. She was not making a formal call, she coddled her unease while she walked toward the Madden house on Second Avenue. She was just dropping by on a morning's walk to see if her grandmother's cousin was at home.

The maid who had come to the door on Caroline's earlier visit greeted her with a smile.

"Miz Madden's home this mornin'," she said brightly. "Come on into the parlor. Who shall I tell her is callin'?"

"Tell her it's Caroline Hampton. Louisa Hampton's granddaughter."

Caroline sat on the horsehair sofa in the parlor, inspecting a group of family photographs that were grouped on the wall above a console table. She rose to her feet as a tall, spare, older woman dressed severely in black appeared in the doorway.

"I'm Caroline Hampton," she said with a quick smile. "I'm visiting the Williamses with Tina Hampton. She's Mr. Williams' niece." Why was she talking so rapidly? "Mrs. Williams told me that you were my grandmother's cousin."

"I'm Bertha Madden." Her voice was cold. "Please sit down."

"Thank you." Caroline was suddenly uncomfortable.

"I was unaware that Louisa had a grandchild." Mrs. Madden's eyes scrutinized her. "Though there is a strong resemblance."

"That's what Papa always told me," Caroline's voice was soft.

"I don't understand. Her two boys died at the Battle of Atlanta."

"There was a third son." All at once Caroline was trembling. "Her oldest child. Francis."

Bertha Madden's face tightened. "The family prefers to forget about Francis Hampton. He was a disgrace to all of us. Because of him, poor Louisa lost her reason."

"My father was not responsible for that!" Color stained her cheekbones. "My grandmother lost two sons, as you yourself just said. She lost two brothers."

"She couldn't bear the disgrace of a son who refused to fight for the Confederacy!" Bertha Madden said contemptuously. "We all gave of our loved ones, but your father ran."

It all might have happened yesterday, Caroline thought, as she felt the rage in her grandmother's cousin. She knew they would never understand the anguish that sent her father to London, away from a war that never should have been fought. *But would they never forget?*

"Excuse me." Caroline rose to her feet. "I'm sorry I bothered you by coming to call."

She hurried from the house, tears of humiliation and anger spilling over. Someday people would think differently about her father. Someday Georgians would fight for her favors, she swore. She would make them respect Papa's memory.

SHORTLY BEFORE noon the family left the house for the pleasingly cool drive to Mr. Williams' club, where the oyster roast was to be held.

"We don't get to see the club often," Agatha explained to Caroline. "That's a strictly male preserve. But three or four times a year members are allowed to bring their family and friends. For a cotillion or an oyster roast like today."

At the handsome red-brick clubhouse they were escorted into the basement. Convivial voices of early-comers greeted them as they walked down the stairs. At one side of the enormous room a group of young Negro boys were tending hickory coals in the brick grills. Several barrels of oysters stood ready for roasting. Tables were set up on the other side of the room in readiness for dining.

"These oysters came up by boat from Apalachicola this morning," Mr. Williams said with satisfaction. His eyes settled on the fires, already beginning to glow darkly red and sending pungent hickory aromas across the basement. "They'll go on the grills within an hour."

Immediately they were engulfed in small talk. Tina was welcomed affectionately by those who knew her and her mother. Caroline was introduced simply as a cousin from Atlanta.

The ladies separated from the gentlemen to discuss fashions and children and social news, the men talking about business and politics. Caroline was conscious of the admiring masculine glances that settled at intervals on both Tina and her. She tried to appear to be enjoying herself, listened attentively to what the other ladies said, but it was the conversation of a group of men with Tina's uncle that captured her interest.

"I tell you, last year's strike at the Columbus mill bodes no good for the future," a pompous older man warned. "Can you imagine what would happen if the unions got their demands? Higher wages, lower hours, send the children to school instead of to the looms . . ."

"They ought to bar that man Debs from Columbus," another contributed. "Why can't he stick with his railway union and stay out of the mills?"

"The workers went back," Mr. Williams reminded. "And they took the ten percent cut that sent them out. I suspect the Southern organizers won't make much headway. Without a strong treasury a union has no power, and the millworkers can't afford union dues. They're doomed," he said with confidence.

Shortly before one o'clock the oysters were pronounced ready to be served. The guests ate endlessly as fresh trays of delicately roasted oysters appeared on the tables. At last two exquisite cut-glass punch bowls were brought in by the waiters, with a brandy punch for the gentlemen and a rum-laced eggnog for the ladies. Everyone agreed that this had been a most successful oyster roast.

The hours until bedtime dragged for Caroline. She was impatient to be on the train and bound for Atlanta. And Eric. In bed she found it difficult to fall asleep, though Tina and she must be awake and dressing shortly after five.

She awoke minutes before her alarm clock was to ring its warning message, turned it off, and went to the next bedroom to awaken Tina. When she was sure that Tina would not drift off again to sleep, she returned to her room to dress, shivering in the chill of the morning.

Despite the early hour, Tina's aunt was at the dining table. Lily brought in a lavish breakfast, which Caroline and Tina forced themselves to eat. Tina insisted that neither her aunt, nor her uncle, who put in a tardy appearance at the breakfast table, should accompany them to the depot.

"It's cold and drizzling," Tina pointed out solicitously. "And the train will be at the depot waiting for boarding."

Tina's aunt and uncle stood on the verandah while Caroline and she hurried under a protective umbrella to the carriage. Nobody stirred on the still dark streets. En route to the depot they encountered no more than half a dozen carriages.

At the depot a porter came forward to take charge of their luggage. Stifling yawns, they followed him to the waiting train. Approaching the train, Caroline understood why Tina was so firm about her aunt and uncle's not accompanying them to the depot. Marshall Shepard stood talking with the conductor, waiting to board the early morning train to Atlanta.

Chapter Thirteen

ARRIVING at the Atlanta house, Caroline hoped that her grandfather had relaxed his anger toward her for speaking out at the UDC meeting. He was at the mill, despite its being Sunday; but at dinner he made it blatantly clear that he still harbored his rage. Sophie was touched that Caroline had thought to buy her a gift at the Columbus fair. Again, Eric treated her as though she were an adored younger sister. Only Tina seemed unaware of tensions at the table as she chattered about their activities in Columbus.

"We're playing chess tonight," Eric told Caroline when they left the dining room to go into the parlor. "As I recall, I owe you a good trouncing."

"Grandpa's still furious at me," she said when they were seated at the chess table, too far from the others to be overheard.

"Give him time," Eric urged. "He's old and stubborn."

"Eric, you keep telling me that," she said with whispered intensity. "Is that supposed to make everything all right?"

"Caro, you don't know what battles are going on inside him," Eric said soberly. "You gave him back something he thought he had lost. His hold on immortality. His blood."

"Which he shuns!" Why did she allow herself to be so hurt? For a little while the wall between them seemed to be crumbling, and she had rejoiced. "If I had any pride at all, I'd leave this house."

"No," Eric said sharply. "It's enough that *he's* allowing pride to stand between you."

Caroline was disconcerted by the warmth with which Eric was

inspecting her. His eyes told her how much he had missed her.

"What's happening with the newspaper?"

"We're holding our breath," Eric said. "Jim should be back from New York any day." He chuckled. "He'll be sure to be here for Election Day—you can count on that."

But Election Day arrived and Jim Russell was still in New York, fighting to raise funds for the newspaper, Eric reported at the breakfast table.

"You've voted already?" Caroline asked.

"As soon as the polls opened," he confirmed.

"It's dreadful that women are not allowed to vote in the United States. In New Zealand they've been voting since '93."

"Zeke will vote this afternoon," Eric said. "I was able to arrange that." He looked up as Seth came into the room with a pot of fresh coffee. "Seth, you're going to vote in the next election."

"No, sir," Seth said uneasily. "I'll jes' let the General take care of that."

"Feel like going for a ride in the country?" Eric asked Caroline when they were alone again. She looked up from her breakfast plate in surprise. "It's a glorious day. I'm not going back to the office. We'll have Jason drive us," he said humorously, "if you're concerned about the proprieties. We'll be properly chaperoned."

"I wasn't concerned about that," she said swiftly. "We're cousins."

"Distant cousins." His eyes were challenging.

"I have to write some letters," she fabricated.

"You'll write them later," Eric brushed this aside. "There's something I want to show you about our great Southern states."

"What?" Caroline's eyes searched his.

"You'll see," he said gravely. "Finish your coffee and go up for a coat. It'll be cool in the country."

When she came downstairs again, she saw the open landau in front of the house, Jason on the perch. Eric helped her into the carriage and joined her there. They rode first along the river, then cut away from this charming view at Eric's instructions.

Caroline enjoyed the crisp morning breeze against her face, Eric's presence beside her, though ever conscious that nothing could come of her feelings toward him. He was talking about the violence and corruption in so many Southern elections with a vividness that made her cold.

"Jason, cut left here." Something in his voice alerted Caroline to the fact that they were about to arrive at his chosen destination.

They rode in silence now. They were approaching a huge pine forest, the air fragrant with the aroma of the trees.

"Stop here, Jason," Eric commanded. "We'll walk through the woods here." His face was taut.

Caroline and Eric left Jason with the landau, followed a foot-path through the pine forest. Then Eric put a staying hand on her arm, pointed to a cluster of laborers fifty yards or so beyond them.

"Those men sawing trees there," he said tersely. "Look hard, Caroline."

She stared, trying to assimilate the lineup of men—all ages, all sizes, most of them black—bare to the waist, each wearing leg shackles connected by a short chain. Longer chains connected each man to the next.

"Eric?" She looked at him, cold with horror yet uncomprehending.

"Chain gangs," Eric explained. "In 1879 convict labor was leased for twenty years to three companies owned by Georgia political leaders and businessmen. Not only does this relieve the state of the costs of providing for convicts, but it brings in a handsome revenue. It gives the companies like Senator Brown's Dade Coal Mines three hundred able-bodied men to work at about eight cents a day per hand." Caroline's eyes swung to Eric in shock. "The convicts work the mines, the forests, farm, make bricks, build railroads. Occasionally there's an investigation into the abuse the convicts receive. Ten years ago Governor Gordon ordered an investigation, then fined two of the companies $2,500 for cruelty. Last year Governor Atkinson fined the Dade Coal Mining Company. But what's a fine to them when they're building fortunes on convict labor?" His voice was harsh with frustration.

"I don't understand." Her soul recoiled from understanding. "How can they do that?" Caroline's eyes were riveted again to the lineup of men, unaware that they were being observed. Beyond caring, she suspected.

"It's the system in all the Southern states, Caro. Barbaric. Detested by all decent-minded folks."

Now Caroline remembered the General's contempt for convict labor when they talked about the Penitentiary Committee at dinner one night, but she had not truly understood what Eric and he had meant. She had not envisioned this animalistic treatment of human beings that was worse than slavery. Those men, shackled, chained together, working how many hours a day like that?

"When their day's work is done," Eric pursued grimly, "they go to over-crowded camps, filthy and infested with vermin. No bedding to speak of, inadequate food."

"Why doesn't someone do something about it?" she challenged. "Where are those decent-minded people you talk about?"

"The penitentiary ring is a power, Caro. Corrupt power. The money interests are strong."

"Strong men could fight this," Caroline refuted.

"Only a Don Quixote would try. A change in the system was part of the Populist platform. You know what happened to the Populists. But after fifteen years of struggle—and the General contributed heavy financial support," Eric pointed out, "reformers seem about to push through the first legislation against this. It's meager," he acknowledged. "If the legislation goes through, it will amend the leasing system when the contracts expire in '99. There'll be a prison farm for the young and the old and the sick, where they'll work to help earn their keep, and they'll be separated from the hardened criminals. Those sentenced for five years or less will go to the counties, to build roads—"

"On chain gangs?" Caroline demanded, stumbling over the unfamiliar words.

"On chain gangs," Eric conceded. "Those whose sentences are longer than five years will be leased at one hundred dollars a year each."

"What will be the benefit?" Caroline's eyes flashed. "That the young and the old and the ailing will be separated from the others?"

"It's a beginning," Eric said stubbornly. "And those sentenced for less than five years will work for the county, not for private companies."

"Will that be any better for them?" Caroline asked.

Eric sighed.

"I doubt that it will be better."

She forced herself to turn away from the chained humanity in the work area beyond.

"Eric, why are you showing me this?"

"Because I need to share this with you," he said with an urgency that seemed fraught with anger, yet Caroline understood. "Since the first night I walked into the house and saw you stand up that way to the General, I knew we could share so much."

"Eric, we'd better go back to the carriage." All at once she was trembling. If he reached a hand out to touch her now, she would be drained of all restraint. *Don't touch me, Eric. Please, don't touch me.*

For a poignant moment his eyes held hers, loving her. Her heart pounded absurdly. She had never thought it was possible to love any man the way she loved Eric. And for them there could be nothing. Why? Why did it have to be this way?

"We'll go back to the carriage," Eric agreed with unexpected gentleness.

JOSIAH SAT forward in his chair, elbows on the desk, his eyes never leaving Cyrus Madison's face as the attorney read the full report delivered by the man sent to London. Had he expected anything different? Josiah rebuked himself. How many times did his blood turn to ice when his eyes dwelt on Caroline and he saw a tilt of the head, a smile, an inquiring gaze that might have been Louisa's?

"That's about it, Josiah." Cyrus laid his report on the desk. "The girl is who she says she is. Francis married Elizabeth Heath, an Englishwoman, in 1871. Their only child was born eight years later. Caroline."

"So she's Francis' child. I'll see that she has a home." His voice was devoid of acceptance.

"Josiah, she's your only grandchild," Cyrus chided. "Find room in your heart to love her. Don't be a stubborn old man."

"You're a sentimental fool," Josiah shot back. "I have a moral obligation to see that she's fed and clothed. I'll accept that." Cyrus knew nothing about the insane entailment in the deed to Hampton Court. No one alive knew. The truth lay buried in the Courthouse records. "But don't expect more from me," he warned.

"Caroline could bring you such happiness, Josiah, if you'd let her," Cyrus tried again. "She's a lovely, fine young lady—"

"And she's here because she discovered her grandfather is a rich old man," Josiah interrupted, his color high. "She has no feeling for me. I'll see that she never starves. That's all I'm obliged to do. Eric—not Caroline—will inherit when I die."

Francis robbed him of his grandchild. His flesh and blood. How much that child could mean to him, could have meant to Louisa, if Francis' shame didn't stand between them! "Thank you, Cyrus." He forced himself to be gracious. "I knew you'd handle this well."

"Wait till you get the bill," Cyrus chuckled. "You'll be swearing for a week."

"Any election news around town?" Josiah asked, but he hardly heard the speculations about the election returns that Cyrus was reporting to him. Francis had given him a grandchild. He had always pictured Francis living alone in London, doing penance for his shame. But he had married and had a child. He had died a hero. Pain surged through him as he considered the long, wasted years. Francis, his firstborn, destined—he had thought—to fulfill his own thwarted ambitions.

"I have to get back to the office." Cyrus rose to his feet. "But I wanted to bring this report to you as soon as it arrived."

"Any fresh word on the convict bill in the Legislature?" Josiah forced himself back into the present.

"No more than you already know," Cyrus said philosophically.

"If there's a question of more funds to help fight it through," Josiah said, "I'm available."

Cyrus left and Josiah tried to focus on the figures before him. His mind refused to cooperate. Too many times he looked at

Caroline and saw Francis in her. Not the physical resemblance—she was a small, young replica of Louisa—but little mannerisms he remembered so well in Francis he saw in Caroline, and each time he saw this he felt a fresh sense of loss.

"I saw Cyrus leave." Sophie stood in the doorway. Her voice was calm, but he sensed the undercurrent of concern in her.

"You were right," he conceded. "She's Francis' child."

"Now will you stop this hostile attitude?" Sophie came into the room and sat down. "Josiah, enjoy her, for God's sake! She's beautiful and bright—and very like you," she added with a faint smile.

"Me?" he recoiled.

"Caroline is every inch your granddaughter, Josiah, and don't you think otherwise," Sophie said flatly.

"She's stubborn and hot-headed and devious," he shot back.

"And you're not?" Sophie laughed.

"What's Eric up to these days?" He leaned back in his chair, aborting the talk about Caroline.

"You know as much as I do." Sophie's face softened. She loved that boy as much as if he were her own, Josiah thought. As he did. When the devil was Tina going to get herself pregnant? She wanted that house in Inman Park.

"Cyrus says Leonard Baker is quite impressed with Eric," Josiah said. "He thinks Eric would have no trouble at all making it into the Town Council next year if we handled it right."

"Baker's aware of Grandpa's financial backing." Sophie's smile was cynical. "Also, Baker has an eye for the ladies."

"Tina?" Josiah's eyes narrowed.

"I'd say Leonard Baker was more impressed with Mrs. Eric Hampton than with Eric Hampton. He couldn't take his eyes off her when you had him and his wife to dinner early in September."

"Tina could be a big help all the way," Josiah sighed. "If only Eric would cooperate."

"Josiah, stop trying to run Eric's life for him," Sophie ordered. "You'll only drive him away from you. And remember you have a granddaughter."

Josiah's face tightened.

"As I told Cyrus. I have a moral obligation to provide for Francis' child. Nothing more."

CAROLINE CAME down to dinner determined to avoid a game of chess with Eric this evening. For endless times today her mind had replayed those moments when Eric spoke with unseeming candor to her. *He loved her.*

While part of her rejoiced in this, another part rebuked her. Eric was married. Eric was accustomed to winning over every girl he met, she taunted herself. Was she so weak as to succumb, also, to that highly charged charm?

Dinner conversation revolved about the day's election. A tradesman had reported near violence at the polls, which Josiah found exacerbating. Tonight, Caroline thought, he seemed to be especially ignoring her presence.

"Dammit, what's the matter with McKinley?" he demanded of the table at large. "I hear they just missed outbreaks at the polls because of that rumor he was considering a Negro postmaster in this area."

"It was a false rumor," Sophie said dryly.

"I don't understand how a man with McKinley's awareness of the country's needs can go about making Negro appointments that he knows will exasperate the whites, at a time when race relations are so improved."

"Are they improved, Grandpa?" Eric challenged.

"You know they are." Josiah bristled. "Ever since Booker T. Washington's speech at the Cotton Exposition two years ago."

"It was the first important occasion in the South on which a Negro made a speech before an audience composed of both whites and blacks," Eric told Caroline. "Of course," he added with a flicker of humor, "the invitation came through only after much pressure from Clark Howell of the *Constitution.*"

"I've read about his speech." Caroline suppressed a smile at the General's start of surprise. At least he was aware of her presence at the table. "Mr. Washington pleaded for economic opportunity for the Negroes, but three months ago that was denied at the Fulton Bag and Cotton Mills."

Josiah turned accusingly to Eric.

"You've been filling her head with that business of the strike!"

Eric ignored the General's anger.

"I realize Mr. Washington is a skilled diplomat, but I don't understand how he could bring himself to tell his people to avoid politics and ideas of social equality."

"I liked what he said." Josiah was belligerent. "No race can prosper until it learns that there is as much dignity in tilling a field as in writing a poem. Nor can every man among us be a lawyer or doctor or industrialist."

All at once a terrified outcry was heard from the rear of the house, jarring everyone at the table.

"Seth!" Josiah yelled, while Eric jumped to his feet. "What's happening in the kitchen?"

"That was Mattie!" Sophie pushed back her chair. Eric was already at the door.

"Seth, what's happening?" Eric asked with reassuring calm as Seth approached.

"Mattie saw Zeke and she got frightened." Seth appeared in the doorway. "But he'll be all right, General. Annie Mae, she's lookin' after him. Don't you fret, suh," he reassured Josiah.

"Seth, what happened to Zeke?" Josiah demanded.

"He got beat up at the polls. He got beat up somethin' awful."

"I'll take him over to Dr. Ashley!" Eric charged past Seth and down the hall toward the kitchen.

"How did it happen?" Caroline asked solicitously.

"He'd been waitin' for three hours to vote, but it was necessary to oblige the white gentlemen first," Seth explained. "When he wanted to go to vote, they tole him the polls was closed. When he said they had to let him vote because he was on the votin' list, they beat up on him."

"I'm sure he'll be all right, Seth," Caroline comforted, struggling to mask her shock.

"Damn fool thing to happen," Josiah growled when Seth left the room.

"I'm glad that Eric isn't here for a few minutes," Tina said with an air of girlish conspiracy. "His birthday is Thursday. I thought it might be nice if we had a small dinner party as a surprise."

"That's day after tomorrow, Tina," Sophie cautioned.

"You go ahead and arrange it with Annie Mae," Josiah ordered. "Nobody has been over to the house for months except Andrew and the Bakers."

"We'll have Mr. Madison and his wife," Tina planned. "My mother and father and Chad. Perhaps Marshall and Dolly Shepard," she said ingenuously. "You'll enjoy talking politics with him."

"And ask the Bakers," Josiah instructed. "And Andrew, of course."

Tina's smile lost some of its brightness.

"Do you think Andrew will enjoy all that political talk?"

"He stays too much in the mill and his cottage. Tell Andrew we'll expect him," Josiah told her.

"Of course, Grandpa," Tina agreed sweetly, yet Caroline sensed her covert annoyance. In Tina's eyes Andrew was a mill employee, hardly the family's social equal even though he was a Hampton.

"Put Mr. Baker next to you, Tina," Josiah said. "I'd like you to be especially nice to him." Caroline saw the secretive glance between them. Mr. Baker must be influential, Caroline surmised. When would the General stop trying to manipulate Eric's life?

"You'd better tell Eric about the party," Sophie warned. "He might just decide not to show up for dinner that night."

CAROLINE STOOD in the center of her bedroom while Patience manipulated the hooks at the back of her dress. She fought incipient panic as she visualized herself walking into the dining room. There would be seven among tonight's guests whom she had never met. But Andrew would be there; she clutched at this knowledge.

"Miss Caroline, you look jes' beautiful," Patience said with proprietary admiration when she had finished hooking Caroline into her frock. "That yellow goes so nice with your hair."

"Thank you, Patience." She strived for a convivial air. Tonight the General would have to present her as his granddaughter. Had he realized that when he approved of Tina's giving this party? "I suppose I'd better go downstairs now."

161

"Yes'um." Patience nodded. "Folks arrivin' already."

The dining room wore a festive air, with masses of yellow chrysanthemums in cut-glass vases on display. The table had been set with Louisa Hampton's fine Spode china and Sheffield silver. At the far side of the room the General and Sophie were in lively conversation with two men and a lady whom Caroline had never met. Neither Eric nor Tina was down yet; but Andrew, appearing ill-at-ease, darted eagerly toward her as she walked into the room.

"You're looking beautiful, Caroline," he said with quiet appreciation.

"Thank you, Andrew."

"We're sitting next to each other. I checked the place cards," he confessed.

Sophie called to her to come and meet Cyrus Madison and his wife and distinguishedly graying Mr. Baker, who explained that his wife was down in Florida with their daughters. Sophie was deliberately taking on the task of introducing her to spare the General, Caroline understood. Obviously they had all been briefed on her presence in the house; but, nonetheless, her grandfather seemed uncomfortable.

In the foyer Seth was opening the door to Mr. and Mrs. Kendrick and Chad. Simultaneously Tina was coming down the stairs. The hall echoed with their animated conversation as they walked toward the dining room. Caroline steeled herself for the introduction to Tina's parents.

"Caroline, you look like a Dresden shepherdess." Chad came toward her with an air of having known her forever. "I've told Mama how beautiful you are." He glanced slyly at Tina, exquisite tonight in white taffeta trimmed in white chiffon; but Tina was busily greeting the Madisons and Mr. Baker. "Mama, this is Caroline Hampton, the General's granddaughter."

Mrs. Kendrick was a small, slender, graying woman, with a petulant mouth and bitter eyes. Her husband, short and paunchy, blond like Chad, wore a constant, specious smile. He left them as soon as he could politely do so to approach the General, almost fawning on him, Caroline thought with distaste.

A few minutes later Marshall and Dolly Shepard arrived. For

an unguarded instant, Caroline saw Tina's dislike for Marshall's tall, imposing wife, still handsome at forty; but then Tina was welcoming her with an over-abundance of graciousness. Caroline respected the strength, the confidence that Dolly exuded. Marshall might dally with Tina behind his wife's back, but Dolly knew her hold on him was potent. Again, the General waited for Sophie to introduce her as his granddaughter from England.

Eric arrived and was engulfed in birthday greetings. Tina ostentatiously clung to his arm. In moments they were seated at the table, according to the place cards arranged by Tina. Tonight Tina sat at the foot of the table, Josiah at the head as customary. Caroline was pleased to be sitting between Andrew and Chad.

Mattie had prepared a sumptuous meal. Green turtle soup, Georgia quail on toast, roast duck with mushroom sauce, a sweetbread glacé with French peas, and salad. Seth served an array of fine wines in the fragilely beautiful stemmed glasses. Caroline had seen earlier, at Annie Mae's invitation, the magnificent two-tiered birthday cake.

Conversation, as Caroline had expected, was largely political. Both Tina and her mother were annoyed that Tina's efforts to lighten the table conversation were ignored. The men, as well as Dolly and Caroline, were immersed in serious discussion of local problems. Tina's smile was bright but artificial. She had envisioned herself as the sparkling, beautiful young hostess.

"Look at all the office buildings going up in the city," Cyrus Madison said with vigor. "That's positive proof that Atlanta's economic state is strong. Best thing we ever did was to invest in the Cotton States and International Exposition. That brought close to a million people into the city."

"The Confederate Reunion will bring a lot of folks here," Tina said vivaciously. "It'll be a big help to business."

"I think these Confederate Reunions are terrible for the whole South," Eric contradicted. "What is this one? The eighth?"

"Eric, you shock me." Mrs. Kendrick was coy in her reproach. "As the wife and daughter of Confederate officers I feel these Reunions are important to us."

"Mrs. Kendrick, it's time we considered the welfare of the nation at large," Eric said with pained politeness. "We can't live forever in a storybook world."

"Eric's right," Caroline supported him. "My father, too, was anxious to see the South reunited with the rest of the country."

Josiah's fork clattered to the floor. Seth moved forward to replace it with another.

"How did your father like living in England?" Dolly asked.

"He always felt he was living in exile." Caroline's voice was soft. "Though he had many English friends. People seemed to gravitate toward him. I remember one friend saying to me, 'Caroline, if your father had been English-born, he would be in the House of Commons with me now.' " Caroline was aware of her grandfather's sudden anguish. Did he, at last, realize what he had done to his oldest son?

"I see you got that city contract you were angling for, Mr. Kendrick," Leonard Baker commented. "That's a nice piece of work."

"It's always good to have an important friend at court," Andrew said with rare irony, his voice lowered to reach only Caroline.

By mutual agreement the party ended early, since Friday was a business day and most of the men kept early hours. Caroline was relieved to escape to her room. The encounter with so many strangers had been tortuous at moments.

She had told Patience not to wait up for her, but her bed was turned down and a robust fire crackled in the grate. She settled herself tiredly in the chair before the fireplace. In a few moments she would undress and prepare for bed.

"What the hell do you mean by using Grandpa to get contracts for your father?" Eric's voice startled her as it bounded from the next room. Tina's bedroom.

"Honey, all I did was to mention that Papa was anxious for that city contract. I didn't ask him to do anything," Tina said plaintively.

"You turned on your girlish charm, and he pulled strings."

"Eric, darling, do you have to be mean to me on your birthday?" Tina's voice was strident.

"Stop using Grandpa!" Eric ordered. "And stop charging to his accounts all over town!"

"Who told you I was?" Tina countered.

"I went into the library to pick up a book just now. I saw some bills on the desk. Grandpa isn't buying a pale blue pompadour satin evening gown or a raccoon cape for himself. Among a dozen other stylish items," he said derisively.

"Grandpa told me to go shopping," Tina defended herself. "He said he enjoyed seeing me look pretty."

"Stop it, Tina. Stop it!"

Caroline flinched as Eric slammed the door behind him. She rose from the chair and began to undress before the warmth of the fire, which would soon begin to wane. Almost since her arrival she had suspected there was no marriage between Eric and Tina. Why did she allow herself to feel so distraught at hearing them fight this way?

There was no future for Eric and her, though he had blatantly conveyed the depth of his affection for her. For now he loved her, she taunted herself. The way he must have once loved Tina. When would he turn to somebody else? Next week? Next month?

How had she allowed herself to fall into this trap? No matter how sternly she denied it, she knew that Eric was the only man she would ever love.

Chapter Fourteen

TINA lay in bed, sulky and unresponsive to Lucinda's efforts to raise her spirits. She had already sent a note to Sara Ballard saying she was not feeling well and could not attend the whist party that afternoon. She was so bored with these endless silly parties and club meetings. How had Mama endured them all these years?

"Lucinda, go away and leave me alone!" she shrieked at last. "You're a stupid, meddling old woman. It was a dreadful birthday party last night. I wish I had never given it!"

"You call Mist' Chad," Lucinda coaxed, refusing to be upset by Tina's diatribe. "He'll make you feel better. He always do." Lucinda left Tina's bedroom, closing the door softly behind her.

Marshall had been deliberately nasty to her last night. She never should have invited them. Dolly never once invited Eric and her to their parties. But, of course, Dolly was pleased to attend a dinner at General Hampton's house. She had no idea that the General would never lift a finger to help Marshall's political career; it was his grandson's career that concerned him.

With sudden decision she pulled herself into a sitting position and reached for the telephone. Marshall had ordered her never to call him at his office, but to the devil with that.

"Mr. Shepard, please," she said to the homely young woman who graced his office. Dolly would never have tolerated a beauty. "Mrs. Hampton calling." She leaned back against the pillows, an anticipatory smile on her mouth.

"Tina, I told you never to call me here." Marshall was furious. "We can't see each other for a while."

"Why can't we, Marshall?" she demanded. "We're always so discreet."

"I can't afford any problems now. I expect to be running for the Legislature next fall, Tina. Things will change in a few months." He changed to a conciliatory tone. "We can wait this out."

"No, we can't!" Tina slammed the receiver down.

All Marshall cared about was becoming Governor of Georgia. Maybe Eric would push him right out of the running. Not now, but in ten years. The General would do anything to put Eric in the Governor's mansion. He didn't care what it would cost. How much longer could Eric go on fighting him?

The General was waiting impatiently for her to come and tell him she was pregnant. She'd been so sweet to Eric. She had invited him to come to her room half a dozen times. What would she have to do to bring him to her bed? *She was willing to give him a child.*

She hated the prospect of walking around for all those months, looking misshapen and ugly. She wouldn't allow herself to think what it would be like to give birth. It would be awful. But once she had the baby she would own her house in Inman Park, and the General would spend a fortune to push Eric ahead in politics. Eric was in a stronger position than Marshall. He had the Hampton name behind him.

In a burst of frustration she leaned across the bed to pick up her telephone, called her family's house. Her mother was out. Chad was home, but irritated at being awakened.

"Tina, you know I sleep till noon unless I have a specific appointment," he complained querulously.

"Chad, it was an awful party," she wailed. "And all you did was sit there and sulk or make nasty remarks to Caroline."

"How do you know they were nasty remarks?" he asked.

"Because I know you. And Caroline looked uncomfortable."

"The party was a success, Tina, though it was painfully political," Chad conceded. "Even Madame Pompadour and Madame de Staël found their salons dominated by politics. You looked exquisite. Leonard Baker had you naked on your back all evening."

"What are you talking about?" she demanded.

"In his mind, darling. I understand he's quite the Don Juan around town. He's in fairly good condition for a man pushing fifty. Handsome in a distinguished fashion. And he could be helpful to Eric," Chad pointed out, "if Eric ever stopped playing the moralist and settled down to politics."

"The General told me to invite Leonard Baker," Tina admitted.

"Josiah wants to be the power behind the throne," Chad drawled. "He wants to rule the White House."

"Chad, do you think Eric could someday be President?" Excitement spiraled in her. She thought about the Governor's mansion, but Chad—like the General—thought big. "It would be fascinating to be the youngest, most beautiful First Lady ever to live in the White House."

"I don't think you'll ever make it as the youngest," Chad rejected. "Unless the old man pushed Eric into the Presidency within the next two years, which is hardly possible. But the most beautiful, yes."

"Who was the youngest First Lady?" Tina demanded.

"Frances Folsom Cleveland. She was twenty-two. But don't let that disturb you, Tina. Make it by thirty-five and you'll be doing fine."

"I'll be old!"

"You'll be beautiful at fifty," Chad corrected. "Darling, I want to go back to sleep. I have a dreadful headache. It's all that champagne last night."

"We didn't serve champagne."

"I didn't go directly home," Chad explained. "Tina, I'll talk to you tonight."

Chad always annoyed her when he was secretive about his social life. Usually he would tell her later where he had been, but these little games he played were so stupid. She knew his friends. Supercilious, ineffectual dilettantes with illusions of talent.

Tina stared at the phone, thinking about Leonard Baker. He *had* been entranced with her last night. The General had been delighted. A faint smile lifted the corners of her mouth. Chad was right; Leonard Baker was handsome in a distinguished fashion. All at once she was decisive. She reached for the telephone directory, sought Baker's office telephone number. In moments she was talking with him.

"I know it's an imposition to bother such a busy man with my minor problems, but somehow I thought you would understand," she purred.

"Tina, I'll be happy to do whatever I can to help," he said instantly, and she heard the anticipation in his voice.

"Eric and I had a silly misunderstanding, and I want to buy him a present. I thought, perhaps, some unusual cufflinks or some especially fine luggage, but I know absolutely nothing about these things."

"I'll be delighted," Baker said. "Let me just look at my appointment schedule." Tina waited, knowing the effect she had on Leonard Baker. In a moment he was back. "I'll be free from two o'clock on this afternoon. Perhaps you'd like to see my personal collection of cufflinks. I collect them the way some men collect fine paintings. If you see something you like in my collection, I can have my jeweler make up a matching pair."

"Mr. Baker, that would be so gracious of you." His wife was in Florida with their daughters last night; it was hardly likely they were back today. She waited for his next move.

"The most practical way would be for you to drop by the house. I'll ask Raymond to assemble the cufflinks and bring them down to the library. Would about two-thirty be convenient for you?"

"Perfect," she assured him. "I'll be there."

She had Jason take her to the house, then sent him away. Leonard Baker would put her into a cab later. She walked up the path to the fine Victorian house on Edgewood Avenue, which spoke eloquently of Leonard Baker's financial success, and she rang the bell. As though waiting for her arrival, the Bakers' houseman admitted her and led her down the wide corridor to the library.

"Tina, how nice to see you so soon again," Baker murmured, crossing the room to relieve her of her raccoon cape. His eyes lingered on the high thrust of her breasts that edged provocatively above the neckline of her green taffeta frock. "I'm truly flattered that you turned to me for advice."

"I knew your taste would be superb." She heard a door open and close somewhere on the lower floor. She knew that Raymond had been sent on some manufactured errand.

"I couldn't sleep last night," he said playfully. "All I could think of was you."

"It was a dull dinner party," she apologized, her smile silken. Raymond off on an errand and the other servants away.

"Not when I could feast my eyes on you," he contradicted.

"You said Raymond would bring the cufflinks to the library," she reminded.

"I'm afraid Raymond's rather remiss." His eyes were making passionate love to her. "And now he's gone off for the afternoon. But I'll bring them down to show you. First, let's have a glass of wine. I'm especially proud of this Chablis." He was crossing to the breakfront to bring forth a bottle and two wineglasses.

"I'm not a connoisseur of wine," she warned. Chad prided himself on being that. "Wine takes on the flavor of my company." Chad had taught her to say that. Her eyes were telling Baker that his advances would not be rejected.

Baker poured the pale, faintly green liquid into the pair of glasses, handed one to her.

"To us," he said with candor.

"To us," she accepted, her eyes bright.

"How do you like the Chablis?" he asked, when she had sipped experimentally.

"Marvelous," she murmured. "Like my company."

"You should always wear green," he said, mentally divesting her of the taffeta dress.

"To match my cat's eyes?" she mocked. He was dying to take her to bed.

"You are the most desirable woman I've ever encountered." His gaze held hers. "Dinner last night was agony for me because I couldn't make love to you right then and there."

"I'm here now."

Her smile dazzling, she walked to the crimson medallion-back sofa and sat down. With a look of heated anticipation, he joined her. She sipped at the Chablis, relishing the way his eyes devoured her.

170

"You don't want the rest of that wine, do you?" he asked after a moment, reaching to take the glass from her.

"Not really," she acknowledged.

He deposited the two glasses on the marble-top table behind the sofa, and reached to pull her to him. He kissed her experimentally, then with greater ardor. She felt nothing; but she would, she promised herself. Marshall was not the only man who could make her passionate.

"Raymond won't be coming back?" she asked when he released her.

"Not for hours," he promised.

He reached behind to undo her frock, pulled the bodice to her waist.

"You're exquisite," he whispered, fondling the milk-white, perfect breasts. "As I knew you would be."

He drew her to her feet and began methodically to strip away each garment that concealed her from him, whispering paeans of praise for her tiny waist, the slender hips and long, narrow thighs. Slowly he was arousing her, though her closed eyes and parted mouth gave an indication of instant heat.

"You, too," she ordered when she stood nude before him, and she saw his start of surprise. "I'll help." She reached to unbutton his shirt, then allowed a hand to slide inside his trousers. Was he afraid he would show up less than perfect? "Leonard—" she reproached because he was slow in removing his clothes.

"You won't be disappointed," he promised.

He was self-conscious about his middle-aged paunch, but except for that he was remarkably well-preserved for a man of his age. Almost as good as Marshall. Would he be as passionate as Marshall? *She* could make him that passionate.

"Are you surprised that I came here this way?"

"I'm delighted." His eyes glowed with anticipation.

"Show me," she commanded, feeling in superb control of this situation. She was a famous courtesan, extending her favors, she dreamed fancifully. He was an envoy from the court of France, her absolute slave. "Leonard, show me how much you want me," she coaxed.

He lowered his mouth to the hollow between her breasts while his hands moved about her hips. She closed her eyes, envisioning herself in an extravagantly luxurious bedroom at Versailles, such as the one in which the Marquise de Pompadour received Louis XV.

"Leonard, make me passionate," she ordered, though already he was arousing her.

His mouth traveled down the length of her flat, firm belly with an artistry she had not expected. Her hands closed in about his head. Her heart was pounding. His mouth found her. She whimpered, holding him to her, and—at last—cried out with abandon.

She lay back against the crimson sofa, waiting while he lifted himself above her. With devious gentleness his hands parted her thighs. She tightened her arms about him, lifted her hips to meet him as he thrust himself within her. It was like being with Marshall. *She didn't need Marshall.* She had Leonard now.

"Leonard," she warned at the height of his passion. "I mustn't get pregnant!"

"One more moment," he pleaded, and then he was withdrawing. Perversely she wished he had ignored her.

"Leonard—" She reached to hold him to her. Too often her desire was simulated. Today it was real.

"Wait." He smiled, understanding her. Exhilarated that she wanted him yet again. "Wait."

She lay back, naked and beautiful, watching the small, masculine ceremony. Now Leonard was returning to her. His face was flushed, his eyes brilliant. She extended one hand to him, rested the other against the back of the sofa. Again, he crouched above her. She closed her eyes, giving herself up to passion.

All at once Leonard was pulling away from her. She opened her eyes in reproach. He tried to rise, stumbled to the floor. His breathing was terrifyingly labored. His face was etched with pain.

"Leonard?" Terror turned her cold. She dropped to her knees, beside him. His face was ashen. He was unconscious. He was *dead*, she told herself hysterically. She was alone in the house with a dead man!

She struggled to her feet, swaying in shock. Call Chad! No,

she rejected. Chad would take forever to get here. Call Caroline. *Caroline would know what to do.*

Where was the telephone? Her eyes swept frenziedly about the library. There. She darted to the phone, deliberately turning her back on Leonard as she asked for her private phone at the Hampton house. She waited, fighting not to give way to hysteria. *Why was it taking Lucinda so long to answer?*

At last Lucinda was on the phone.

"Lucinda, find Caroline!" Her voice was shrill. "Quickly, Lucinda!" *Let Caroline be home.*

"Miss Tina, is you all right?" Lucinda asked worriedly.

"Just go get Caroline!" Tina shrieked. "Fast."

In a few moments Caroline was on the phone. Obviously Lucinda had imparted some of her alarm.

"Caroline, don't say anything," she ordered. "Something awful has happened. You've got to come to me immediately."

"Where are you?" Caroline asked, and with meager relief Tina gave her Leonard Baker's address.

"Hurry, Caroline! And don't tell anyone where you're going!"

"I'll be right there," Caroline promised.

Tina collapsed into a chair, her eyes fastened on the rug at her feet. She was not conscious of her nudity, fearful of moving her eyes and seeing Baker's body prone on the floor. She was numb, waiting in a trance-like state, blotting out reality. Not thinking; just being.

CAROLINE ORDERED Jason to take her within a block of her destination and to wait there. Instinct told her she must not allow him to see exactly where she was going. What had happened to Tina? She had sounded on the brink of hysteria.

Jason pulled up at the corner she had indicated, leapt down to help her from the carriage.

"Wait right here, Jason," she said gently. Jason was good-natured and willing; she had early discovered he had the mind of a child.

"Yes'um." Docilely Jason climbed up on the perch again, facing away from the direction she intended to take.

She walked swiftly, fearful of what she would find. Why had Tina called *her*? Why not Chad? Why not the General? At the door she rang sharply, waited to be admitted. Anxiously she checked the number of the house. This was the address Tina had given her. Had Tina given her the *wrong* address? Tina's frantic words repeated in her mind. *Something awful has happened.*

After a moment of inner debate she tried the door. It was unlocked. She walked into the ornate foyer, called out cautiously.

"Tina? Tina, are you here?" Only silence greeted her. *But Tina had given her this address.* "Tina?" Where were the servants?

The double doors to the parlor were shut. Her heart pounding, she forced herself to open them. No one was in the parlor. She closed the doors again and hurried down the hall to a door that was ajar.

"Tina?"

She peered into the library and turned cold with shock. Who was the unclothed man lying face down on the floor? *Leonard Baker.* Her eyes swept the room. Tina sat in a chair by the window, naked, staring unseeingly at the floor.

"Tina!" Caroline ran to her. "Tina!" She shook Tina by the shoulders. When that elicited no response, she slapped her across one cheek.

Tina looked up, trembling uncontrollably.

"Caroline," she whimpered. "What am I going to do?"

"Tina, put your clothes on," Caroline said with calculated calmness. "Right away." She darted across the room and dropped to the floor beside Baker. She reached for his wrist. There was an erratic pulse. He was alive. "Tina, what's the name of the hospital?" Her eyes sought the phone. "Tina!" she repeated because Tina seemed unaware that she had spoken. "The name of the hospital?"

Tina was on her feet, reaching for her clothes.

"Grady," she whispered shakily. "Why?"

"He's alive." Caroline reached for the phone. "But he won't be for long if we don't get help for him."

"Don't call!" Tina's voice rose to a hysterical pitch. "I have to get out of here!"

"You have to dress and get control of yourself, Tina," Caroline said sharply. "We can't leave him like—" She abandoned conversation with Tina. A hospital clerk had picked up the phone. "An ambulance immediately," Caroline ordered. "The Leonard Baker residence. Mr. Baker appears to have suffered a heart attack or a stroke." Tina was staring in terror at Baker. "Please hurry." She gave the address.

"We have to leave, Caroline!" Tina's hands were too unsteady to cope with the hooks of her frock. Caroline went to help her.

"We can't leave him like that," Caroline rejected, color flooding her face. "We have to get him into his clothes."

"I can't," Tina shivered.

"Tina, I can't manage alone." Caroline braced herself for what must be done. "Come help me. I'll get him into his shirt. You pull on his trousers." Her mind was racing. "We'll say we came here together to talk to Mr. Baker about a contribution to a charity. Nobody responded to the door, but we heard outcries inside," she improvised. "We came in and found Mr. Baker on the floor. Tina, listen to what I'm saying!"

"Raymond knows I was here," Tina whispered. "Leonard sent him off on an errand."

"Raymond will say nothing," Caroline assured. "Fix your hair, Tina."

She knelt to put a pillow beneath Baker's head. He was still breathing, lightly and irregularly; but he was alive. She tried to brush aside her distaste for the situation. How many other men had consoled Tina, besides Marshall Shepard and Mr. Baker, her mind queried unwarily. Eric's fault, she told herself. Tina was beautiful and spoiled, accustomed to much attention. How dare he treat her so shabbily!

"Caroline, you won't tell Eric and the General?" Tina implored. "You won't tell anybody?"

"Nobody, Tina," Caroline reassured. "Just remember what I told you. We came here to talk to Mr. Baker about a contribution to a charity."

"I thought he was dead," Tina whispered. "It was awful."

"There's the ambulance!" Caroline hurried into the hall. She pulled the door wide to admit the doctor and attendants. "He's in the library," she said without preliminaries, and the ambulance crew rushed to the door where Tina stood, pale but composed now.

Raymond returned as Baker was being lifted into the ambulance. Quickly Caroline explained the situation. Her eyes held his; she knew he would be silent about Tina's interlude with Baker.

"You'd better notify Mr. Baker's wife down in Florida," she suggested, then expanded on this as she saw his bewilderment. "Telephone his office. They can send a telegram."

"Yes, ma'am," he promised gravely.

Caroline led Tina to where Jason waited with the carriage. All the way home she coached Tina in what they must say at the house. She loathed having to lie to Eric, but how could she go to him and tell him to what lengths he was pushing Tina?

"I was so lonely," Tina said contritely as Jason pulled up the carriage before the house. "Eric neglects me so, and Mr. Baker was terribly sweet to me."

"You're going to be all right, Tina," Caroline said with determined confidence. "If you like, when we come downstairs to dinner, I'll explain to the family about Mr. Baker's illness."

"You tell them," Tina whispered. "I'll have dinner in my room."

Caroline accompanied Tina upstairs and went to her own room. Only now, when no demands were made of her, did she realize how shaken she was by this afternoon's experience. It would be a long time before the image of Leonard Baker, unconscious on the library floor, and Tina, naked in the chair by the window, would be erased from her mind.

She had been woven into the ugly tapestry of the marriage between Tina and Eric. She was being pushed into deception, which she loathed. She was not in love with Eric, she told herself strongly. She was obsessed by him—and she *would* free herself from this obsession.

Caroline remained in her room until she heard the sounds

downstairs that told her dinner was about to be served. She had wished to call the hospital to ask about Leonard Baker's condition, but discretion warned against this. She went down to the dining room, framing a speech in her mind that would convey what she must report to the family.

The General and Eric were discussing the situation in Cuba. It was odd how the General and Eric seemed to be switching sides. Now it was Eric who hedged on the necessity for American intervention in Cuba, and the General who anticipated war and felt it necessary.

When they were seated at the table, Caroline told the others that Tina would not be down to dinner.

"She's upset about what happened when we went to Mr. Baker's house this afternoon."

Avoiding Eric's eyes, Caroline related the fabricated story about Leonard Baker.

"Why didn't Tina talk to him about funds when he was here last night?" Eric asked.

"At a dinner party in her own home?" Sophie chided. "That would hardly have been hospitable."

"I'll call Grady to ask about his condition." Eric rose to his feet, obviously dismissing any suspicions that had been hovering in his mind. How could he be suspicious? She had presumably been with Tina.

Seth almost collided with Eric at the door. His eyes followed Eric questioningly.

"Go on and serve dinner," Josiah ordered. "Mr. Eric will be back directly."

In a few moments Eric returned to the table.

"Baker's in serious condition but they expect him to recover," he reported. "I gather he's alive only because the hospital was alerted so promptly." His eyes turned to Caroline. "I assume *you* phoned for the ambulance."

"I called," Caroline confirmed coolly. Why did he take every occasion to slight Tina? "He was still breathing. I knew he needed immediate help." She was conscious of her grandfather's intense scrutiny.

"Thank God, he'll be all right." The General withdrew his

gaze from her and focused on Eric. "We won't be going to Hampton Court for Thanksgiving week this year," he pursued. "I can't be away from the plant just at this time."

Caroline clenched her teeth to hide her dismay. She had been counting the days until they would go to Hampton Court. The family always went to the plantation for the Thanksgiving week. But she was here—and her grandfather refused to go.

She was lagging in her campaign to win Hampton Court. She was allowing herself to be lulled into the hypnotic Southern leisureliness. She had not come to Atlanta for this.

Stop sentimentalizing about the General. He'll fight me into the courts before he'll relinquish the plantation. But I'll have it. I don't need the General. I don't need Eric. All I want is Hampton Court. Hampton Court and Atlanta will be my life.

Chapter Fifteen

C AROLINE was plagued by restlessness. Thanksgiving arrived and passed with little joy in her heart for the traditional American holiday, which she had anticipated since her arrival. Tina was touchingly subdued, poignantly sweet to Eric. Often Caroline saw her grandfather gaze with pained bewilderment from Tina to Eric. He could not fathom what had gone wrong in their marriage. Nor could he guess, Caroline thought with fresh, young bitterness, how far Tina wandered in search of the love denied her by Eric.

Caroline awoke this brisk December morning with the instant recall of her grandfather's elaborately casual statement as they all left the parlor last evening to go to their rooms.

"We'll leave two days before Christmas for Hampton Court. We'll return for New Year's Eve."

At last she would see the plantation. Papa's home. She leaned back against the pillows with a surge of exhilaration. Eric had told her on Thanksgiving night that the General had not been able to bring himself to go to Hampton Court in the knowledge that this year Louisa would not be with him. She had not expected sentiment from Eric.

The General had not gone to Hampton Court because he knew the plantation no longer belonged to him. *It was hers.* He was forcing himself to go for the Christmas holidays because it was unnatural for the family to remain away. But he was not averse to collecting rentals from his tenants, she thought with resentment. That, too, belonged to her.

When Hampton Court was hers, she dreamed extravagantly,

she would give fabulous parties that would bring out all of the important people of Atlanta. Not just the rich, she emphasized, but people like Jim Russell, who fought so hard to make Atlanta a finer city, not merely for the powerful but for the poor and downtrodden. Her parties would bring together people who could make things happen. Atlanta could lead the way to a greater South. That was what Papa wanted to see, above all else.

She thrust aside the plump, warm comforter, crossed to the fireplace. Earlier Patience had moved silently into the room and laid fresh logs on the grate, coaxed them into a blaze that would lend warmth to the room when she awoke. The temperature had dropped these past few days. She dressed before the fireplace, thinking about Hampton Court.

She waited until Eric had left the house before going downstairs to breakfast. She made a point now of never being alone with him. Jim Russell had raised funds in New York, though far less than was genuinely required to launch the magazine. Again, he was struggling to operate. The newspaper had run its final edition last week. The first edition of the magazine was due out in three weeks. Eric, who loathed selling, canvassed Atlanta businesses daily, striving to sell advertising.

"Eric, the man's a failure," the General had argued last night at dinner. "He failed at running a newspaper in Chicago," he added with contempt. "Let him go back to being a lawyer."

"Grandpa, Henry Grady failed at running four newspapers before he bought a piece of the *Constitution*," Eric pointed out with the calm that exasperated Josiah.

Eric talked so mesmerizingly about the reforms that were needed in Atlanta. She read every issue of *The Mirror*, Jim Russell's newspaper, which Eric brought to her. Eric wrote the way he talked, but it irritated her that he avoided issues that would show the General in a bad light. Jim and Eric wrote against disenfranchisement, against the convict-leasing system, about the inadequacies of the public school system. But there was never a line in *The Mirror* about child labor in the mills, or about the conditions in the mill villages. *The Mirror* avoided those issues.

On impulse, after breakfast, Caroline walked to the mill village. This morning she would not run away at the first sign that she was unwelcome. She walked swiftly, her eyes fastened to the rows of shabby, weather-stained frame houses that speedily came into view. Little difference, she surmised, from the rows of cheaply constructed cabins that had been the antebellum slave quarters.

This morning she ignored the suspicious eyes of the men who slouched before the company store. She walked to the church, which she knew was also used as the schoolroom. She tensed as she paused at the door, hearing voices of the children in recitation. Did she dare intrude? She lifted her head with determination. She dared.

A tall, spare, graying man of about fifty, with gentle brown eyes, smiled as she walked into the church. Small, colorless faces swung about to inspect her with curiosity.

"I didn't mean to intrude," Caroline said, intimidated by the sudden silence. "I'm Caroline Hampton—"

"Children, that's all for today," their teacher said briskly, and strode up the aisle, a hand outstretched. "How nice of you to call on us, Miss Hampton."

"I didn't mean to disrupt the class," she stammered.

"I was letting them go in a few minutes anyway," he reassured her, while the children scrambled from the pews and out of the church. "They're up at dawn with their parents. By this time of day, they're ready to go home and eat. I'm Henry Roberts. Minister and teacher. But come to the house and meet my wife. Grace will be so pleased that you've come to see us."

He led her through a side exit to a cottage she had not noticed on her first visit. Like the church, it had been freshly painted. A low white fence enclosed a small, carefully tended garden area where late roses still bloomed in startling contrast to the barren area around the other cottages.

"Grace doesn't garden as much as she used to," he explained, "because she helps me with the teaching and organizes the children in play activities in the afternoons."

He pulled open the door to the cottage. The sitting room was tiny, modestly furnished and immaculate. A small, well-worn sofa and a Boston rocker flanked the fireplace. A pine table and four chairs sat on one side. The windows were curtained in much-washed white muslin, the drabness of the walls relieved by colorful, framed needlepoint.

"Grace," her husband called with lilting warmth, "I've brought you company."

A small, rounded, dark-haired woman, who appeared to be in her late forties, came into the sitting room with an air of delighted astonishment. Obviously guests were a rarity. When Henry Roberts had introduced them, he showed Caroline to the sofa, while his wife went off to make tea.

"We've been here in Hamptonville for close to nine years," he said, his smile telling Caroline how much he enjoyed her presence. "There're just the two of us—we were never blessed with children."

"I'm the General's granddaughter. I was born and raised in England." He probably knew nothing about her father. She sensed he would be sympathetic.

"Your first winter in Georgia?"

"Yes." She laughed. "I hadn't expected it to be so cold in the Deep South."

"Wait till the temperature drops to six or eight degrees," he cautioned whimsically. "When Grace started complaining about the cold winters up in North Carolina, we moved down here, thinking it would be much warmer. But we stay. As mill villages go," he qualified, "Hamptonville is one of the best."

"Now, Henry," Grace chided, coming into the room with a tea tray, "don't you go running down the General. He's good to his workers."

"I think the whole system is horrible!" Caroline burst out, startling the Robertses. "I went into the mill and I saw these children working there. They ought to be in school!"

"The time will come, Miss Hampton," Grace said, emboldened by Caroline's sympathy, "when no child under fourteen will be denied an education."

"Caroline," she said impulsively.

"Caroline," Grace agreed, pleased with her guest.

"The families couldn't survive without those children working." Henry Roberts was unhappy in this admission. "Often the fathers come to the mills with hands too callused from farmwork to work with machinery. Too old at forty to learn a new trade. With his wife and half a dozen children drawing wages, they manage to eat, keep themselves clothed. By skimping on food there's occasional tobacco and snuff, candy or soda pop for the children."

"The workers seem so spiritless, so tired." Caroline was troubled.

"How else would they look when they work from sunrise to sunset?" Henry ignored his wife's reproving gaze.

"Wouldn't they live better on the farms?" Caroline asked. She knew that vast acreage at Hampton Court was leased to tenant farmers. At least, the farmers must eat well.

"They come to the mill villages for company," Grace's voice was compassionate. "Country roads are bad. For weeks on end they don't leave their farms, don't see another living soul other than their own family. When the weather is good, they get to the county church maybe once a month or go to the country store on some Saturday afternoons. They don't feel so isolated in the mill villages."

"The farmers are always owing to the country stores," Henry explained. "They get little for what they sell and pay high for what they buy because they need the credit the country stores extend. And when crops are bad, they're near starvation. To the farmers the mills offer a certain security. A roof over their heads and food, of a sort, on the tables."

A brisk knock at the door brought Henry to his feet. He crossed to the door, pulled it wide. A young man and a boy, with packs on their backs and tanned from the Southern sun, stood on the porch.

"Noah and David Kahn!" he said with rich welcome. "Come in!"

Grace rose to her feet to greet them.

"How good to see you both!" She extended her hand to the older of the two arrivals, then embraced the younger. "You haven't been in these parts in weeks," she reproached affectionately.

Henry marshaled the Kahn brothers into the sitting room and introduced them to Caroline, while Grace hurried off for more cups and saucers. Noah, the older, could hardly be more than a year older than she. David, the younger, was thirteen. They had lean, almost aesthetic faces, with dark hair and intelligent brown eyes. Noah spoke with an accent that Caroline recognized as German. David's speech bore no trace of his origins, though only slightly touched by the Southern pattern.

"Noah and David have been in Georgia for almost a year now," Henry told Caroline. "They peddle between here and Columbus and Augusta."

"We came here after two years in New York," Noah said shyly. "Before that we lived in England for a year."

"I came from London in September," Caroline confided, feeling an instant tie to Noah and David. "You lived in Germany before you went to England?" she said with lively curiosity.

Noah's face darkened.

"We speak German, yes. But we lived in a small town near Riga. David and I were away from our town when the Cossacks came. When the pogrom was over, David and I had no family. Our father and mother, three brothers and two sisters had all been murdered." Caroline paled with shock. "Friends helped David and me to make our way to England. We worked hard, saved what we could, and came to America, to live in a democracy."

"I've been studying the mathematics book you gave me," David told Henry. "I believe I understand it all. Would you have a harder book for me?"

"You understand the geometry?" Henry asked in amazement.

"If you have time later, I will show you," David offered.

"I'll have time," Henry promised.

Grace returned with cups and saucers and a plate piled high with cookies. With an indulgent smile she put the plate of cookies directly in front of David.

"I hear there's trouble in Atlanta again at the Fulton Mills," Noah said, his face serious.

"What's happening?" Henry leaned forward intently.

"The union says Mr. Elsas is firing the leaders of the August strike, though he had agreed that wouldn't happen. It appears that a thousand workers are preparing to walk out."

"I hope not." Henry's eyes looked troubled. "Strikes are hard on the workers. And little is ever accomplished."

"I do not understand the cotton millworkers!" Noah said, frowning in impatience. "Their salvation lies with the unions, yet they regard them as the enemy."

"Noah, how can these millworkers afford to pay union dues?" Grace countered. "They earn barely enough to survive."

"They have no spirit!" Noah shot back. "They listen to the fancy speeches of the orators at picnics and rallies. They believe what the *Constitution* constantly tells them, what they hear on every side. That the mill owner is their benefactor, providing charity beyond anything in history." Contempt deepened his voice. "Begging your pardon, Mr. Roberts, but they accept everything as the will of God. Their women spit blood from the lint that fills their lungs. They have back pains and ringing in their ears from too long hours at the machinery. They die too young and too often from pellagra, but nobody tries to find out why. And they think that education is a fine thing, until their children arrive at nine or ten and can become doffers at the mills!"

"Things will change," Grace reiterated with stubborn optimism. "You must be patient, Noah."

Caroline sat on the edge of the sofa, absorbing the lively conversation. Eric would enjoy talking with these two immigrant boys, she thought. Perhaps Noah Kahn could push Eric into writing about these children in the mills in Jim Russell's new magazine. Their wretched situation nagged at her more than anything she had encountered in her young lifetime. Perhaps, she thought, because Papa had been so involved in the betterment of child labor in the English textile mills.

Feeling that David was eager to work with Mr. Roberts on his mathematics study, Caroline rose to leave when she would have preferred to remain with these people and talk a while longer. She thanked the Robertses for their hospitality, promised to return soon, and inquired about when Noah and David might be again in the mill village.

"When we're near Hamptonville, we come often," David said

with quiet pleasure. "We'll be selling to the farms around here until after Christmas."

"Then I'll be sure to see you," Caroline said. "We'll have to talk about London next time," she added, all at once homesick, though she knew this would be short-lived. *Atlanta was her home.*

Approaching the mill en route to the house, Caroline paused, her mind racing. She was so restless in her idleness. Tina seemed to be avoiding her. She was a reminder of the awful experience at Leonard Baker's house. With sudden resolution she directed her footsteps to the mill entrance, frowning as the clamor reached her ears. All at once she was obsessed by the idea that had taken hold of her. She would help Sophie in the mill office. Her grandfather would see her as something besides an intruder, a parasite. *Let him learn to respect her as a person. His granddaughter.*

She sought out Sophie and told her what she wished to do. Sophie was skeptical.

"Caroline, you would never survive the noise here," Sophie remonstrated.

"You do," Caroline countered. "I'm very good with figures. I could help."

"Two afternoons a week," Sophie stipulated. "You can begin tomorrow, if you like."

ERIC WAS intrigued when Sophie mentioned during the evening that Caroline was coming in to help at the mill office two afternoons a week. Josiah, whom Sophie had obviously briefed, was simultaneously irritated and amused. At irregular intervals Caroline felt the weight of his covert, curious glances in her direction. Tina was horrified that Caroline would expose herself to the mill environment.

Caroline watched the clock the next day, counting the time when she could go to the mill and put herself at Sophie's command. She was excellent in mathematics, which Sophie loathed. She would make herself useful. Sophie was very close to her grandfather. In some fashion, Caroline reasoned, this might bring *her* closer to her grandfather.

Andrew was delighted with Caroline's presence at the mill. He made excuses to come to Sophie's office several times in the course of her first afternoon there. Sophie was pleased with her unexpected efficiency. As she and Sophie prepared to leave for the day, Josiah stalked into Sophie's office.

"You still here?" he said to Caroline. She knew his gruffness was manufactured.

"Why not?" she demanded. How rare it was to be in direct communication with her grandfather. "Sophie says I handle figures satisfactorily."

"She's fine," Sophie said flatly. "She'll be here two afternoons a week."

"I've been curious about something," Caroline said on impulse, emboldened by Sophie's approval. "The lighting here in the mill is—" She paused, searching for a diplomatic description.

"What about the lighting?" Josiah interrupted with an air of defensiveness.

"It's so dim." Caroline abandoned diplomacy. "You complain often about there being too much breakage in the machinery. Andrew says that, too. If the lighting were stronger, there might be less breakage."

"They can see the equipment!" Josiah derided.

"Not every worker in the mill has perfect eyesight," Caroline shot back. "With better lighting there would be less waste at the machines, too."

Their eyes clashed for a heated moment. Then Josiah turned to Sophie.

"Sophie, experiment for a month with higher wattage on two rows of spindles," he said gruffly. "See if we come out ahead."

"Josiah, that's going to run our electric bills way up," Sophie protested.

"Try it for a month," he insisted. "Figure the results."

CAROLINE FELL into a more relaxed pattern of existence. Twice a week she worked in the mill office. On the other afternoons she was with the Robertses. She was involved with Grace in arranging a Christmas party for the millworkers. On three occasions Noah and David, working close by, stopped at the Roberts house when she was there.

Noah and David were touchingly pleased to see Caroline. Henry Roberts said that their access to intelligent conversation was meager. The farmers, their sole social contact except for the Robertses, were ill-read, semi-illiterate. Both Noah and David were intelligent and voracious readers.

The week before they were to leave for Hampton Court for the Christmas holidays, Mrs. Bolton, home from Washington until the next session of Congress, invited her to dinner at their fine Atlanta house.

The Boltons lived in a lovely red-brick Queen-Anne residence on Ponce de Leon Avenue, with multiple half-timbered gables, molded chimneys, scalloped wooden shingles, and with the terra-cotta ornamentation that, Caroline observed, adorned much of the Victorian houses in Atlanta. It reminded Caroline of houses she had known in London.

The Boltons greeted her affectionately and introduced her to the elderly Mrs. Bolton—"Miss Laurette"—whom Caroline found charming. The huge double parlor and the spacious dining room were furnished with Belter rosewood furniture that had been presented to Miss Laurette by her parents when she was a bride in Augusta, and had been saved from the carnage of the Union soldiers by shipping it by wagons to south Georgia, only hours before the arrival of Sherman's men.

Caroline enjoyed the evening of socializing. Much of the talk was about Washington, which she found fascinating. The invitation to the Congressman's house had impressed the General, she remembered. He approved of her having friends in high places. Perhaps he thought that one day the Boltons might be useful to Eric, she told herself realistically.

The night after she had gone to dinner at the Boltons' house, Caroline left the mill alone with Sophie. Josiah was remaining late for a conference with Andrew on the purchase of new machinery.

"You're doing well in the office," Sophie confided in the privacy of the carriage. "And you may be right about increasing the wattage in the mill. Josiah is already convinced you are."

"But he's not convinced that I'm his granddaughter," Caroline said with a rare display of bitterness.

Sophie seemed to hesitate. "Don't ask how I know, Caroline, but Josiah is aware that you're his granddaughter. Don't try to rush him. He'll come around to accepting you," she promised.

"Eric says that, too," Caroline conceded. "But I still feel like an intruder."

"He's changing, Caroline," Sophie insisted. "Surely you can feel that already."

"Sometimes I think so," Caroline said slowly. But he said nothing about her ownership of Hampton Court.

At dinner that evening Josiah brought up their imminent departure for Hampton Court. If he felt any guilt about keeping her inheritance from her, Caroline thought, he made no show of it. Tina brightened at the prospect of going to the plantation for close to two weeks. Tonight she was more like the Tina of old, Caroline decided. No longer wistful and subdued. Caroline knew that Mr. Baker had left Grady Hospital a week ago and was well on his way to full recovery. Only Raymond, the Baker houseman, and she knew the circumstances under which he had suffered his heart attack.

"Will we be back in Atlanta for the New Year's Eve *Bal Poudre*?" Tina asked eagerly, then smiled disarmingly at Eric. "You *will* take me, Eric?"

"Of course he'll take you," Josiah said with ominous firmness. "We'll return in time," he promised.

"I hate those affairs," Eric complained.

"You'll take Tina," Josiah commanded, as Patience appeared with their desserts. He pushed back his chair and rose to his feet. "Go ahead with dessert. I'll only be a few minutes."

Eric dug stubbornly into the almond mousse, his face set with annoyance. Sophie was talking about the coming performances in the city of James O'Neill and of Mme. Modjeska, who had not appeared in Atlanta for four years.

"Andrew is counting the days," Sophie said with gentle amusement. "He rarely misses a performance of any truly fine artist."

Caroline had been touched when Andrew shyly asked if he

might escort her to the performance of *Macbeth*, starring Mme. Modjeska, late in January. She had accepted with delight, only later realizing that Andrew might conceive this as an encouragement to courtship. She was deeply fond of Andrew. She would never love any man but Eric.

Josiah returned to the dining room. In his hands was a square velvet box. He walked to Tina's side, placed the box before her.

"Let me see this on you, Tina," he said with the ingratiating charm he displayed on rare occasions. "I think it will suit you perfectly."

Tina's eyes glowed. Quickly she lifted the lid of the box and brought forth the emerald-and-diamond necklace. "Oh, Grandpa! It's exquisite!" She brought the necklace about her throat, fastened the catch.

"My Christmas gift to you," Josiah said with a gallant bow. Eric stared in disbelief. The necklace was worth a small fortune. "You'll wear it to the ball. It was Louisa's necklace." His eyes were nostalgic. "I gave it to her on our tenth wedding anniversary."

Caroline gazed anguishedly at the splendor of emeralds and diamonds about Tina's throat. She could hear her father's voice lovingly describing each detail of this necklace.

Mama adored it. She wore it to every important social event in Atlanta. If I had a daughter, she used to say, it would be hers, either on the day of her wedding or on her twenty-first birthday, whichever arrived first.

But now the necklace was Tina's. It could never be hers.

"It's magnificent," Caroline stammered when Tina turned to her for the expected admiring comment. "The most beautiful necklace I've ever seen."

Caroline fought back tears of rage and hurt. The General must know that necklace was meant to be hers. How dare he give it to Tina! How dare he disregard Louisa's wishes!

Chapter Sixteen

C AROLINE was astonished when Sophie conveyed a message from Josiah that she was to charge to his accounts in the stores whatever Christmas presents she wished to buy for the family and servants and any clothes she might like. Tina would take her shopping.

Together Caroline and Tina spent several afternoons in Rich's Department Store. Tina protested Caroline's self-conscious scrutiny of price tags before she made any purchase.

"Honey, you don't have to do that," Tina laughed. "Grandpa is as rich as Croesus. He won't mind what we spend. He won't even notice!"

Emboldened by Tina's urging, Caroline bought a selection of fine English teas, which she knew Henry and Grace Roberts would enjoy but could never afford. She bought a book on calculus for David Kahn, and for Noah *The Will to Believe*, the new book by William James. While Noah and David did not celebrate Christmas, she knew about their own joyous holiday of Hanukkah, which arrived about Christmastime. At Tina's insistence, she chose for herself an emerald green velvet evening gown that Tina declared was just right for her.

The Christmas party was to be held the evening before the family was to leave for Hampton Court, in the church. Josiah, as was his custom, had ordered quantities of candies supplied by the company store. For three days prior, Annie Mae and Mattie baked in preparation for the party. An enormous turkey, hams, roast beef, endless loaves of bread. Caroline and the Robertses pushed the pews to two sides of the church, set up cypress tables on which to place the food and a keg of sarsaparilla. Henry Roberts had gone out with two of the millworkers on the previous Sunday and chopped down a tall pine, which the children decorated with stringed popcorn and cranberries.

The Christmas party brought out even Josiah. He seemed to enjoy the occasion. Tears sprang to Caroline's eyes when she saw the way the children viewed the feast prepared for the mill villagers. A banquet such as this was a miracle to them, to be savored twice a year; at the Christmas party and the July Fourth barbecue. She looked at their pale, thin faces and was angry with a world that denied them the food that should be their birthright.

Eric came to the table to help Caroline and Grace in the preparation of sandwiches for the avidly waiting children. Josiah was drinking sarsaparilla with a group of the older men across the room.

"Caro, you're not supposed to look sad at a Christmas party," Eric chided, but his eyes told her he read her mind.

"The children are enjoying it," she said unsteadily. Those who had been given sandwiches piled high with their choice of meat or poultry were standing about the church room eating ravenously, their eyes bright with appreciation.

"And the older workers," Eric added, his gaze on his grandfather and the men about him, "they're grateful to have a roof over their heads and something on their tables. But the younger workers are growing resentful. They want a larger share of the industrial kingdom. I keep telling the General that times are changing in the South," Eric reiterated, "but he refuses to face change."

"Write about this in Jim's new magazine," Caroline urged. "Make people see."

"I can't. Jim's hands are tied," Eric confided ironically. "His financing comes from a New England textile manufacturer. We can fight against convict labor, racism, the poverty of the farmers who feed the South; but we can't lift our voices against child labor or cry for higher wages in the mills."

"Jim Russell?" Caroline stared at him in disbelief. "He would compromise himself in that way? Jim Russell?"

"Caro, I would have felt that way once, too," he soothed, "but you have to weigh the benefits. Without that money Jim can't fight at all." Eric frowned, his gaze again on the General. "How can I write what I feel about the employment of children in the mills? How can I vilify a mill system that is Grandpa's way of life? I can't be the one to hold him up to public contempt."

"The unions will come into Georgia and they will change things," Caroline insisted. "They're beginning. You've told me this, Eric."

"In some instances," he conceded. "But they're making pitifully small headway. The millworkers are skeptical. They're afraid of losing what security they have. Look what's happening now at the Fulton Mills. Elsas is still resisting since a thousand of his workers walked out on December eighth. He's operating with some non-strikers, some strike-breakers from towns around here, and strikers who're returning because they're hungry. I hear that Prince Green, who's worked so hard in Columbus, is coming here to help the strikers."

All at once Caroline wished that she had power in the Hampton Mill. She would bring about reforms for their workers! The mill earned high profits. Why couldn't some of those profits be used to raise wages, improve working conditions? Why wasn't there a law to protect those children who should be in school?

"Eric, has there ever been a strike in our mill?"

"There were some slight rumblings," Eric admitted. "A bright young worker named Tom Coleman tried to take out the workers. The General talked to the men, and they turned their backs on Coleman."

"What was the matter with them?" she asked with contempt. "Why didn't they listen to him?"

"Caro, this is one of the best operations in the South, no matter how you and I look upon it. Even during the Depression years, Grandpa kept the mill open. The company store was never closed to the workers."

"All right, everybody," Henry Roberts called out. "Some of the children have prepared carols for us. Let's gather 'round and listen."

The following morning Caroline, Tina, Sophie and the General settled themselves in the wagonette, which could comfortably seat six, for the ride to Hampton Court. Eric would arrive in the evening. Was he being detained by Jim Russell, as he claimed, or by some smitten young lady who had taken his fancy? Caroline asked herself.

Caroline fought to mask her excitement as they drove out on field-flanked country roads, south of Atlanta. At last she was going to see Hampton Court. *Her plantation.* She could hear her father's voice:

"We'll ride up that quarter-mile curving driveway lined with pecan trees and flowering dogwoods, and we'll pause at the great circle in front of the house. I can almost smell the camellias and jasmine."

Neither Caroline nor Josiah spoke much during the hour-and-a-quarter drive in the bleak cold. Tina talked vivaciously about the *Bal Poudre,* to be held at the Capital City Club on New Year's Eve. Yesterday the gown she had ordered designed for the ball had been delivered, and she was entranced with it.

"I'll wear my emerald and diamond necklace, of course," Tina said with a soft glance at the General. Caroline clenched her teeth in secret rage that her grandfather had dared to give the necklace to Tina.

At last the carriage turned into the private roadway that led up to the house. Pecans and dogwoods towered high above the road. Nuts still littered the ground beneath the trees, not yet fully gathered by the servants. Caroline leaned toward the carriage window, her heart pounding in the knowledge that in moments, she would see Hampton Court. Not in her parents' company, as Papa had plotted, but beside her grandfather, who callously ignored her ownership.

The huge white house rose tall and stately behind a circular driveway flanked by evergreens. Eight massive, round white columns on the verandah reached up beyond the second floor to support the roof. As she gazed at the filigreed balcony over the entrance, she visualized her grandmother standing there watching her three sons at play on the sprawling lawns below. This was the mansion that, despite its distance, had dominated her childhood.

The carriage came to a stop before the house. Here Papa had

spent the first nineteen years of his life. Years that remained forever etched in his memory. But because of her grandfather, Papa died in exile. Fresh anger welled in her, to be masked by a tense little smile.

"Look at those clouds," Sophie said when they had alighted from the carriage. "We'll have snow this Christmas."

They walked up the wide steps to the verandah. Several smiling house servants swarmed through the elegantly lovely Georgian doorway to greet them in rich welcome. Caroline gazed in admiration at the hand-carved woodwork of the entrance, was awed—despite her awareness of its presence—by the graceful, free-standing spiral stairway that rose unsupported to the second floor. The ceilings seemed even higher than the seventeen feet about which her father had boasted.

When the servants had been properly greeted, the family retired to the handsome parlor, whose walls still wore the beautiful hand-blocked French Auber wallpaper chosen by Louisa Hampton as a bride. A cut-glass gaslit chandelier illuminated the room in deference to the outdoor grayness. Electricity did not yet reach this far out into the country. The furniture was the Hepplewhite favored by Louisa; the rug was a seventeenth-century Persian which had once lain in a sultan's palace.

Coffee was served in delicately decorated Haviland china cups, which Caroline guessed had belonged to Louisa's wedding china, first imported from Limoges, France, at that period. When they had finished their coffee, Sophie suggested that they rest in their rooms until the midday meal was ready to be served.

Hallie, one of the maids, escorted Caroline to a corner bedroom that looked out upon the Chattahoochee. The large, square room, daintily papered in blue and white, was furnished with lightly graceful Hepplewhite pieces. The four-poster bed was canopied in a cloud of sheer whiteness. Whose room had this been when her father was a boy? Caroline wondered. Had it been her father's? Her grandmother's?

Delighted to have company at the house, Hallie chattered about various tenant farmers on the plantation, as though Caroline was familiar with each. When Caroline questioned her, Hallie said that she had been born at Hampton Court a few years before "the bad times." She had never lived any place else. Hallie told her how Miss Louisa had saved Hampton Court from the Yankee soldiers.

"Miss Louisa, she was somethin' in them days," Hallie said emphatically. "The soldiers come trompin' into this heah house and she meets them, proud as you please, right downstairs in the foyer, and she tells them her husband comes from Saratoga Springs, New York, and he's a spy for the Union Army. Nobody is to tech this house, she tells that fine Yankee officer, less'n they git their heads knocked off. And then," Hallie said with dramatic emphasis, pausing in her ironing, "Miss Louisa takes that Yankee officer into the parlor and she shows him how she's nussin' six Yankee soldiers who wuz wounded in the fightin' nearby and brought to Hampton Co't." Hallie chuckled. "He never once guessed they wuz Confederate soldiers under them sheets. All he seen wuz the Yankee caps lyin' on the flo' beside them."

"She was a very brave lady," Caroline said softly.

A servant knocked at the door. Hallie want to answer with a proprietary air. Caroline was her lady for the Christmas holidays.

"What do you want?" she asked.

"Miss Sophie say to tell ever'body to come down to the family dinin' room."

"Miss Caroline be right down," Hallie said loftily.

Caroline saw the first flakes of snow falling outside as she smoothed her hair before the mirror. It would be a storybook Christmas. She hurried down the stairs and to the dining room, where a pair of logs blazed in the grate, extending pleasing warmth to the table. She was the first to arrive.

Her eyes moved slowly about the room, admiring the sideboard with its graceful front and delicate fruitwood inlay. Ten chairs flanked the dining table, set now with a blue-and-white Canton table service. Caroline knew about the magnificent formal dining room, never opened since the War, where Louisa and Josiah Hampton had entertained as many as a hundred guests at banquets.

In a few moments the others appeared in the dining room. The General seemed somber, preoccupied, though Tina strived to brighten his mood. It was his first Christmas at Hampton Court without her grandmother, Caroline remembered. Though her mind had broken all those years ago, Eric said, the General had loved her to the end, treated her with the utmost devotion. It was difficult to envision Josiah Hampton showing tenderness.

After the meal, Caroline went to her room for a coat and more substantial shoes. Despite the snow that was falling steadily, she was eager to explore the outdoors. A bright shawl protecting her hair, she walked away from the house, seeking the path along the river that her father had talked about through the years. In a few minutes she jubilantly discovered the well-beaten trail. Feeling poignantly close to her father, she followed the path, unmindful of the snow that clustered about her shoulders and clung wetly white to her head shawl. *She was home. She was at Hampton Court.*

About a hundred yards beyond the house she stopped short. To her left was a wrought-iron fenced enclosure that she swiftly identified as the family cemetery. Her throat tightening, she opened the gate and moved inside. Granite benches flanked the fence. Evergreens stood tall and friendly at each corner. A feathery blanket of white covered three graves, each with a simple headstone.

She paused before the headstone that bore Louisa Hampton's name. Tears welled in her eyes, spilled over unnoticed as she read the inscription. Her grandmother lay here, with a son on either side. She remembered the afternoon at the Cyclorama, when Eric had so visually described the death of her two young uncles, and she shivered with a cold unrelated to the weather.

One day, Caroline silently vowed, she would bring her father and mother to lie here at Hampton Court.

ERIC ARRIVED at the plantation that evening. He was astonishingly tender with the General, striving to lift the old man from the depressed mood that had imprisoned him since they had left the Atlanta house. His first Christmas at Hampton Court without Louisa, and the realization seemed to weigh unbearably upon him.

Sophie had said the General knew she was his granddaughter,

Francis' child. Why was it so difficult for him to accept her? The two of them were all that remained of their line. Eric and Andrew were distant cousins. Why did he persist in shutting her out of his heart? There were a precious few moments when their eyes met, and she felt something stirring in him and hope spiraled in her. But those moments were rare and evanescent.

The following morning Eric and two of the servants went out to choose a Christmas tree. That evening they made a festive display of decorating the tall pine. Presents were deposited under the tree to be opened in the morning. Afterwards they gathered in the music room, where Tina played Christmas carols for them while they sipped the hot chocolate Seth brought in delicate Haviland cups.

Later Caroline moved restlessly about beneath the pile of comforters on her bed, unable to sleep. She was here in her grandmother's house, and she ought to be discovering facts to support her claim to Hampton Court. Instead, she was abandoning herself to sentiment.

Had she been foolhardy in choosing her grandfather's Christmas present? Would he comprehend what she was giving him? Not a fine, expensive gift, but what she most cherished among her possessions.

At last she fell asleep, to awake in instant realization of being in a strange bed. Moments later there was a tentative knock at her door.

"Come in."

The door opened. Hallie came in with her morning coffee and kindling wood for the fireplace.

"Merry Christmas, Miss Caroline. I thank you fo' your Christmas present."

"Merry Christmas, Hallie." Caroline smiled in return. Sophie had bought presents for each of the plantation servants, ascribing them to various members of the family.

"We is havin' a lotta snow this mornin'," Hallie said cheerfully. "Looks like it ain't gonna stop till night."

"I adore the snow." Caroline sipped the strong black coffee while she watched Hallie coax the embers in the grate into a flame with kindling. Now Hallie reached for small logs piled high in the box beside the fireplace.

When Caroline arrived downstairs, she discovered the others, except for Tina, already at the table in the family dining room. Platters of eggs, ham, steak, grits and biscuits sat on the table.

"The servants are anxious to be done with breakfast," Eric chuckled. "As soon as the table is cleared, they are free until tomorrow morning. They go visiting their folks."

"It's been a tradition at Hampton Court for twenty years," Sophie told her. "We always go for a mid-afternoon Christmas dinner at the McElveys'. They're at the next plantation."

"I don't know why we have to go this year," Josiah complained, digging into a slab of steak. "I'm in no mood for it."

"Josiah, they would be hurt," Sophie insisted. "And the servants expect the day off."

A daring thought took root in Caroline's mind. The servants would be away from the house. The family would go to the McElveys' in the afternoon. If she contrived not to go to the Christmas dinner, she would be alone at Hampton Court. She could go into the room that had been her father's without the fear of being discovered. She could go into her grandmother's room. Her heart pounded at the prospect.

After breakfast, the family went to the parlor for the ceremony of opening presents. Caroline was sure that Sophie had shopped for the bottles of French perfume that her grandfather gave to both Tina and her. From Sophie there was a volume of poetry by Walt Whitman, and from Eric the book by Jacob Riis, which she had expressed a wish to read. Tina gave her a beautiful pendant on a gold chain, which she was sure had been charged to the General.

While Caroline admired her gifts, she covertly watched her grandfather. Slowly, his face inscrutable, he was turning the pages of the leatherbound scrapbook she had bought and filled with the carefully treasured mementos of her father's life in England, dating from his first appointment as a county schoolmaster to letters of gratitude received by her mother from the parents of the two students whose lives he had saved. Josiah Hampton knew only of his first nineteen years. Now he was learning about Francis Hampton, the man.

At last he lifted his head from the scrapbook, appearing tired and old. He gazed with piercing intensity into her eyes, as though trying to see within her soul. *He loves Papa, she thought with dizzying exultation. He'll come to love me.*

"Thank you, Caroline," Josiah said gently. It was not necessary for him to say more.

CAROLINE STOOD at her bedroom window, watching the others climb into the carriage for the trip to the McElvey plantation. Sophie herself had prepared a pot of tea and brought it up to her room when she had begged off going to the Christmas dinner, feigning a sore throat. Eric promised to bring her hot milk and rum at bedtime. His solicitude elicited guilty pleasure from her.

She watched until the carriage disappeared from view. Now she left her bedroom and went to the room she knew had once been her father's. Her pulse quickened as she reached for the doorknob, turned it, pushed the door wide. The bedroom was exactly as her father had described it. But someone—his mother, Caroline suspected—had directed that a child's bed be set up in a corner of the pleasantly furnished room. On the bed had been placed a cluster of toys. Her father's toys, she realized, gathered together by his mother.

One wall was hung with small framed certificates indicating school honors awarded to Francis Hampton, several papers her father had written at various stages in school, a daguerre of her father and a classmate—smiling, arms about each other—taken at the college at Princeton. She could hear his voice explaining to her why he had fled to England. *"How could I take up arms against my classmates at Princeton, my cousins in the North? My soul rebelled."*

At one side of the room sat a bookcase holding her father's books. On a table was a cabinet that he had made, she recalled, under Seth's tutelage, for his father's birthday. The yellowed birthday note had been painstakingly pasted across the front. How often, before her anguished mind cracked, had her grandmother come into this room and cried for her son in England?

Caroline left and went into her grandmother's room. She was conscious of an eerie sense of having been here before, until she realized her father had described the charming colonial furnishings in such minute detail that they were etched in her memory. How many precious hours he had spent in this room as a small boy! And in this room he had told his mother what he had already told his father, that he was leaving for England; and she had held him to her and cried.

Feeling deeply at peace with herself, comfortable at Hampton Court as she had never been in the Atlanta house, Caroline returned to her own room. She sat before a cozy blaze, not bothering to light a lamp, feeling close to the grandmother she had never seen.

She stiffened at a sound on the floor below. Had one of the servants returned to the house? She crossed to a window. There were no carriage tracks in the lush white blanket of snow that covered the road to the stables.

Was a carriage sitting in front of the house? This would not be visible from her room. Had one of the family returned? Was someone ill? Anxiously she left her room and hurried downstairs.

Now there was only silence on the lower floor. She pulled open the front door. No carriage sat outside. Again, there was a sound somewhere in the house. She whirled about with sudden trepidation. *Someone was in the kitchen.*

Wary now, she moved on silent feet into the library, reached into the breakfront drawer, where she knew her grandfather kept a pistol. Pushing aside her revulsion, she picked up the pistol. Bullets lay in a box before her. Determined not to give way to panic, she took a bullet from the box, slid it into position. Refusing to acknowledge the terror that gripped her, she moved stealthily toward the kitchen.

At the kitchen door she paused, pistol outstretched before her. The intruder sat with his back toward her. A tall, burly black man in the striped attire of a chain-gang convict.

"What are you doing here?" she demanded coldly, masking her fear.

The man spun about in shock.

"Missy, don't shoot!" he pleaded, stumbling to his feet, a chunk of bread and a slab of ham clutched in his hands. "I thought nobody was home. I didn't see no lights, I didn't mean no harm, Missy." His dark eyes, bright with terror, were riveted to the pistol in her hand.

"How did you get here?" Caroline asked quietly.

"When the guards got drunk from Christmas likker, the fella that was chained to me broke loose and took off. Then I figured I'd go, too. I got whupped somethin' awful yesterday—" He shifted a shoulder so she could see the raw welts where his shirt was torn. "I got whupped for sayin' it was too cold to work without shoes."

Caroline shivered at the sight of his bare, ripped feet, the leg shackles. But even as she responded emotionally, her mind was racing.

"Why were you arrested?" She must know this, she told herself.

"I stole a sack of potatoes 'bout three years ago when things wuz so bad. We didn't have nuthin' to eat at home, and I got five kids. My wife, she couldn't get no work, either."

"Sit down and eat," Caroline said calmly, but her mind was active. "I'm going to the barn to search for a file. You can travel faster if your legs are free." Christmas dinner would be lengthy, she estimated. It would be a while before the family returned from the McElveys'. "There's a pot of coffee on the stove. Heat it up." She smiled faintly at his stare of disbelief. "It's all right," she said with infinite gentleness. "I'll help you get away."

The man dropped into the chair with a look of abject gratitude that brought a tightness to Caroline's throat. She hurried to the library to put away the pistol, carefully removing the bullet. She hesitated a moment, a hand on the box of bullets. No. The terrified convict in the kitchen would do her no harm. She hurried upstairs for a coat and sturdy shoes, then, equipped for the weather, raced to the barn and searched frenziedly for a file.

When she was about to despair of finding it, she located the file and returned to the house. The man at the table started as she came into the kitchen with the file.

"Will this do?" she asked.

"Yes'um," he said eagerly.

While he worked to free his legs, Caroline went upstairs again, shed her coat, slipped again into the slippers she had worn earlier. She went to Eric's room, ignoring her sensation of guilt at this intrusion. He would hardly miss a pair of trousers, shirt and a sturdy coat from his closet, she told herself with shaky confidence. Never mind if he did, the man downstairs needed them. On the point of leaving Eric's room she remembered to take a pair of boots.

In the kitchen her unexpected guest was cleaning up evidence of his having eaten. His shackles were removed. Still, he jumped at her reappearance.

"Change into these," she ordered matter-of-factly, while her mind plotted the course of action ahead of them. "You'll leave those in the stable." She pointed to the shackles on the floor. "I'll burn your clothes in the fireplace. Take a horse and head across the state line." He could be far away before the guards sobered up and discovered his escape.

"Missy, you so good to me." He hesitated. "Iffen you can find the time, would you write a little letter to my missus? She can read," he said with a touch of pride. "I'd like her to know I'm all right."

"Tell me where she lives," Caroline agreed. "I'll see that she receives word."

"God bless you, Missy." His eyes were tender with gratitude as he waited for her to leave the room so that he could change.

"I'll bring you some money," she resolved. Her funds were low, but this man needed railway fare to guarantee his freedom. "You'll have enough to take a train up North. You'll be safe," she reassured.

"I'll find a job and save money, and I'll send for my family. They won't bring me back from up North," he said with growing courage.

"Hurry," she ordered, fearful of an unexpected early return of the family. "I'll bring you the money."

Within ten minutes Caroline stood at the kitchen door and watched the man charge toward the stables. She waited while the snow fell heavily, blanketing his footsteps from the house to the stables, watching until she saw him emerge on horseback and disappear into the woods. Now she went back into the kitchen, picked up his tattered convict clothes and took them into the library where logs had been piled high to keep the fire going until the others returned.

She watched while the garments disintegrated in the flames. The family would return and discover a horse had been stolen, she calculated. Eric would notice his clothes were missing. She must say that she had been sleeping in her room, had heard nothing. She had complained of a sore throat; it would be reasonable to assume that she had slept.

She remained in her room, waiting self-consciously for the family's return. As the early winter night settled about the house, she heard the approach of a carriage. A few minutes later the family was coming into the house. Shortly after, a servant came from the stable to report a horse was missing.

"There must have been an escape from the convict camp!" Josiah yelled angrily.

"Caro?" Eric was coming up the stairs two at a time. "Caro?"

Trembling, aware of the solicitude for her in his voice, she opened the door of her room and moved into the hall.

"Are you all right?" His eyes searched hers.

"My throat's much better," she reported.

"There were no intruders?" he asked impatiently while the others gazed up at them from the foyer.

"I was sleeping," she apologized. "Has there been a robbery?" she asked with a show of alarm.

"A horse was taken from the stable, that's all," Eric soothed. "Thank God, you're all right."

"I'm fine," she reassured him. *He must not show such concern for her.* "I was just preparing to come downstairs."

"It was a cold drive home," Sophie shivered faintly. "I'll go out to the kitchen and make us coffee." Caroline tensed. Had they cleaned up evidence of the convict's meal?

"The horse must have been stolen by an escaped convict. We ought to notify the convict camp," the General said reluctantly.

"He's probably taking this route across the state line."

"Grandpa, on Christmas Day?" Eric reproached. "Poor devil, 1 hope he gets away."

"Damn sentimental fool," Josiah rebuked. "The man could be a murderer."

"I'll ride over first thing in the morning," Eric promised. "They're not going to find him in this weather, anyway. The snow will cover his tracks."

They gathered in the library, Caroline excusing herself to go help Sophie with the coffee. When she returned, a tray in hand, she saw Eric stooping by the fireplace. He picked up a button from the floor. *A button had fallen away from the jacket she had burnt.* She saw him toss the button into the fire while Tina and the General talked about the new loco-steamers that were appearing in the country, one recently having been seen in Atlanta. Did he know the button belonged to a convict jacket?

Her eyes cast down, Caroline brought the tray and set it down on the pedestal supper table that sat between two windows. Coffee would be served buffet fashion tonight. Gratefully she allowed Tina to draw her into conversation about the *Bal Poudre,* which dominated Tina's thoughts this week.

Throughout the evening Caroline was conscious of appraising glances from Eric. Was he suspicious of her part in the convict's escape? She doubted that he would be censorious if he were. In truth he seemed in rare high spirits tonight. When Sophie rose to go out to the kitchen to bring in the cold supper prepared this morning by the cook, he insisted on serving them himself. Still, Caroline was relieved when the time arrived for them to retire to their respective rooms.

In nightdress and dressing gown, she settled herself in her favorite chair to read for a while before going to bed. She started guiltily at the light knock on her door. Even before she pulled the door wide, she knew her caller was Eric.

He stalked into the room and closed the door behind him.

"What the devil happened here this afternoon?" he demanded quietly.

"What do you mean?" she hedged.

"Who was eating out in the kitchen?" he said with a flicker of humor. "Whose clothes were burnt in the fireplace with a button carelessly left behind?"

Haltingly, she told him what happened, omitting nothing.

"Eric, I'm sorry I took your clothes," she apologized, "but I had to help him escape. Three years ago he stole a sack of potatoes, and still he was serving time on a chain gang. He was beaten for complaining about working in the dead of winter without shoes. What kind of justice do we have in Georgia?" Her indignation spilled over, a catalyst that evoked an emotional response from Eric for which she was unprepared.

"Caro—" He moved toward her. The atmosphere in the room was electric as their eyes clung. She knew he was on the brink of pulling her into his arms, but she could muster no resistance.

"Eric, I had to help that man—"

But instead of taking her into his arms Eric reached for her hand and brought it to his lips.

"Caroline Hampton, you are a very special young lady."

Far into the night she lay sleepless beneath the mound of comforters on her bed. The logs in the grate were gray-laced smoldering embers, spreading a fanlight of pale color about the hearth, sending meager heat into the night-cold room. She could not erase from her mind those moments when she had stood so close to Eric, knowing how desperately he wished to make love to her. *She had wanted him to make love to her.*

Why was she behaving in this absurd fashion? How could she love Eric, knowing what she knew about him? How many women before her had fallen prey to that charm? How many women had Eric thought he loved?

He was several men in one. The philandering husband who drove Tina into an ugly search for love. The devoted grandson, despite his refusal to be manipulated by the General. A man with such rich compassion she felt a frightening compulsion to join her life with his. If he had taken her into his arms tonight, she would not have repulsed him.

She might tell herself she would not allow herself to love Eric—but she would love him all the days of her life.

Chapter Seventeen

CAROLINE awoke to discover that yesterday's snowladen sky had been replaced by a display of azure and gold. Immediately she remembered her promise to the escaped convict. She must write a letter and, somehow, see that it was mailed without the family's knowledge.

She dressed before the fire that Hallie had lit early in the morning while she still slept, and went downstairs. In the library she found paper and pen and envelope. She wrote a brief but reassuring note, cautioning herself not to sign it. The woman would understand.

With the letter folded over and concealed in the bodice of her dress, Caroline walked to the dining room. Eric sat alone at the table. Her heart pounded as she remembered those few charged moments last night when she had thought he would surely take her in his arms.

"Have breakfast with me," he ordered in high spirits. "Then ride over with me to the country store. I want a newspaper. It's a beautiful day for a drive."

"All right." She ought to refuse, her mind chastised. She had no will in Eric's presence.

A smiling house servant came into the dining room to inquire what she would like for breakfast.

"Just biscuits and coffee," Caroline told her.

"Peggy, you bring her bacon and eggs," Eric instructed.

"Yessuh." Peggy grinned. "They be ready directly."

"You'll be starving by the time we reach the country store if you don't eat," Eric scolded when Peggy left them. His eyes were quizzical. Was he going to ask more questions about that man last night? But he *approved* of what she did.

"Eric, I—I have to deliver a message to someone. A letter." She took a deep breath. "That man last night. I promised to get word to his wife that he was safe. She lives a few miles from here—"

"I'll have it hand-delivered from the country store," he promised.

After breakfast Caroline went upstairs for her coat. She tucked the envelope in a pocket and returned to the lower floor. Eric was outside on the verandah. The buggy was waiting. In moments they were on their way. Just the two of them, Caroline thought with a blend of pleasure and unease.

While they traveled over the near-deserted roads, Eric drew her out about her life in England. They were so engrossed in conversation that she was surprised when they drew up before the small country store. They left the buggy and went inside. Several customers hovered before a pot-bellied stove, talking about a lynching in a neighboring state.

Eric corralled a bystander and arranged for Caroline's letter to be delivered.

"I want it delivered today," he emphasized. "I have to know if she's available for a housemaid's job." He was covering lest anyone connect the woman with the escaped convict, Caroline comprehended.

"Yes, sir," the delegated messenger assured him. "I'll take it over this mornin'. I gotta go that way, anyhow."

Eric bought a copy of a two-day-old Atlanta *Journal*, then escorted Caroline from the store. In the buggy, he paused to scan the front page and swore under his breath.

"Excuse me, Caro. But every time I read of another lynching I want to go out and bash in heads."

"I thought there was a Georgia law against lynching."

"A law that's ignored," Eric said grimly. "For the past eight or nine years there've been almost two hundred lynchings each year in this country, most of them in the South. It's mob murder."

"Doesn't anyone try to stop it?" Caroline asked indignantly.

"Caro, nobody in the South is ever going to vote to convict a white man for killing a Negro. Not in our time."

"You mean they don't even go to trial?" She stared incredulously.

"They go to trial," Eric conceded, "though there are those who scream about the waste of money for this. But with all the anti-lynching talk up North, they know they must put up some show if they're to get Northern investments down here."

"Suppose the man is innocent?" Caroline pursued.

"Honey, they don't ask questions," Eric said bluntly. "I remember a lynching when I was twelve. I had nightmares for years afterward. It happened right near here. We were at the plantation for the summer, and I had wandered up along the river to fish." His face became taut. "I saw a mob of about three hundred people gathered around a young Negro man, chained to a log. There were women in that crowd," he said with painful recall.

"Oh, Eric!" Caroline was sick with shock.

"They had piled leaves all around his feet, and then they poured on gasoline. When the flames shot up, I went berserk. I pushed through the mob, yelling for them to stop. One of the men picked me up and held me over his shoulder, forcing me to watch. Inch by inch they cooked that man to death. Every few minutes they would add fresh leaves, more gasoline. And he didn't utter a word. Not once did he beg for mercy." Eric stared ahead, visualizing the horror of those minutes. "They brought his wife and his little boy to watch."

"Eric, don't tell me any more." Caroline's face was drained of color.

"Caro, I'm sorry!" he apologized.

"Didn't anybody try to stop it?" She struggled to keep her voice even. "Besides you?" She was touched by the vision of the small boy charging to the rescue.

"The sheriff knew," Eric said. "But I heard him tell the General, who was furious about it, that nearly every man, woman and child in the county wanted to see the man lynched. The sheriff said he didn't have a chance."

"Why, Eric?" Caroline asked.

"I've asked myself that a hundred times," Eric admitted. "Jim says it's the dullness of their lives, both at work and in their homes. They lynch from an uncontrolled love of excitement. And too often their lives are dominated by a ministry that preaches hell-fire and brimstone," Eric reminded contemptuously. "Men like Henry Roberts are rare in these parts." He removed one hand from the reins to brush hers comfortingly. "But enough of this for today. I'm driving you up along the river. It's a beautiful view on a day like this."

AFTER TWO more days of idleness at the plantation, Josiah insisted on making the tedious drive to the mill, despite Sophie's protestations that Andrew could manage without him until they returned. Philosophically Sophie accompanied him to Hamptonville and back each day.

Tina slept late, remained much of the day in her room, reading the fashion magazines that were her delight. Eric, too, remained much of the time in his room. He was struggling to finish an article for Jim's new magazine. It was a relief not to be alone with Eric, yet perversely she longed to roam about the massive acreage of Hampton Court in his company.

Two mornings before they were to return to Atlanta Eric came into the library, where she was reading.

"The article's finished," he told her, his eyes appraising. "Would you like to read it?"

"Yes," she said eagerly and lowered her eyes, lest she give away her pleasure at this invitation.

"I'll bring it down for you later," he promised. "Do you have a riding dress?"

"No," Caroline acknowledged, "but I have a bicycle skirt."

"Do you ride?" he questioned.

Her eyes glowed with recall.

"When I was five, my father put me in trousers and lifted me on the back of a horse. I rode constantly until I was nine, when he died. After that, I rode two or three times a year with my mother's pupils, in Battersea Park."

"Astride?" he challenged.

"Sidesaddle in Battersea Park," she conceded.

"We'll ride this morning," he decided, and her eyes widened in faint rebellion. He might ask if she cared to ride. "Or are you still suffering from a sore throat?" he teased.

"I'll go upstairs and change, if you'll excuse me," she added politely.

"You're excused. Go change." His eyes held hers for a heated moment. Disconcerted she hurried from the library.

Within half an hour they were astride a pair of fine riding horses as eager for a canter as Caroline. Eric talked about the General's vow not to sell an acre of their land in the awful days following the War; his realization that the South could not afford to depend upon agriculture to restore its economy.

"Other planters were selling their land for pittances, just to survive. The General divided most of the land here at Hampton Court into tracts and rented them to both whites and Negroes. He borrowed money from cousins up in Saratoga Springs, sold shares to hundreds of small investors, and struggled to build the mill. Most of the mills were built with the help of people who had meager funds to invest but knew, like the General, that the South's salvation lay in industry."

"The farmers are painfully poor," Caroline surmised compassionately, viewing houses that were no improvement over those in the mill village.

"Many of them leave the farms for the mills," Eric reminded. "They spend their lives in peonage to the country store." Caroline lifted her head inquiringly. "The farmers buy from the country store on credit during the months before they pick their crops. Their food, their clothes, whatever they need to exist. They pay exorbitant prices because they're at the mercy of the country merchants. Higher prices than at the mill village stores," he said strongly. "If the crops are bad and they can't pay, the country store carries over what they owe and no other store will give them credit."

"Then it's the country stores with their high prices that keep the farmers poor," Caroline said with fresh indignation.

"That's part of the trouble," Eric agreed, "though there are country merchants who accumulate so many bad debts they fall into bankruptcy."

"What can be done about it?" Caroline demanded.

"Tom Watson and the Populist Party had ideas," Eric said. "They wanted to set up a system of warehouses on a nationwide basis, where farm produce could be stored until market conditions were favorable. They wanted the government to provide loans against the crops deposited by each farmer."

"Mist' Eric!" a deep young voice called jubilantly. "We ain't seen you since last summer!"

"How are you, Cassius?" Eric asked warmly, and Caroline and he reined in their horses.

"We gettin' along, Mist' Eric. Cotton came in good, but the price is so low and ever'thing costs so much." He shook his head. "But we're gettin' along." The tall, amiable young black man smiled at Caroline.

"How's the family?" Eric dismounted, reached a hand to Caroline to help her down.

"Papa's got some stiffness in his legs, but he do all right. Ever'-body else jes' fine."

"Cassius was born and raised here at Hampton Court," Eric told Caroline. "His father was born here. Cassius, this is the General's granddaughter." Caroline saw his start of surprise. He thought she was Tina, she realized. "Mr. Francis' daughter."

"My Papa knowed Mr. Francis," Cassius said respectfully. "He knowed the whole family. He worked in the big house." His eyes shone with unexpected tenderness. "I growed up hearin' about how the General took care his slaves after the War. Most nobody wanted to leave, and them that did wished they hadn't."

Caroline's smile was strained because she knew Eric watched for her reaction to Cassius' story. She concealed her astonishment at hearing her brusque, bitter grandfather discussed with such love by the son of a man who was once his slave.

"You still do watercolors?" Eric asked.

"Yessuh." Cassius smiled shyly. "If you-all wait here a minute, I'll bring you the one I jes' finished."

Cassius hurried toward a tiny drab cottage a hundred feet away. How could Cassius feel so kindly toward the General? His father had been her grandfather's *slave*.

Cassius returned with a watercolor of a colorful tanager.

"It's beautiful!" Caroline admired with obvious sincerity. "Cassius, you've a real talent."

"I'd be happy if you'd accept it as a gift, Miss Caroline." His eyes shone.

"Thank you. I'll have it framed and hang it in my room," Caroline promised.

They left Cassius and rode in silence for a few moments.

"Caro, you have to understand that to men like the General, the slaves were a responsibility that could not be shirked," Eric said slowly. "Not possessions but a responsibility," he emphasized. "The typical Southern planter had the strongest contempt for any master who misused his authority. Bad masters existed, Caro, but they were a minority. I suppose you've read that book by Harriet Beecher Stowe," he said, "but that was a rare situation."

"Eric, you're not defending slavery?" she accused, pulling her horse to a stop to confront him. "Not you!"

"You know better!" he admonished. "But I want you to understand the General. It was the only way of life he knew, and he carried on honorably."

"Eric, please, not that word!" Caroline tensed in distaste. "Because of the General's obsession with honor my father was in exile. Because of that obsession I never knew my grandmother!"

"Grandpa loved your father, Caro. You saw his face when you gave him that scrapbook for Christmas." Eric's eyes held hers. "But you look at him and I still feel rage in you."

"Yes, I feel anger," Caroline acknowledged, "and hurt and disappointment. I've tried every way I know to make him feel that I belong to him, but he shuts me out!"

"He's easing up, Caro," Eric said strongly. "You must feel that."

"It's not enough," she resisted. He still denied her inheritance. Perhaps because of that he withheld his love. "I don't want to talk

213

about him, Eric." She tugged at the reins, swerved her horse about and galloped away. She was relieved to discover that Eric made no effort to follow her.

THE FAMILY was in residence at the Atlanta house again by dinner-time of the evening before the *Bal Poudre*. Tina had confided her wish to rest up the day of the New Year's Eve ball, and the General had approved this early return. Caroline would spend New Year's Eve with Josiah, Sophie, and Andrew, who was traditionally invited for a New Year's Eve supper.

On the drive into Atlanta, Caroline had promised herself that the new year, 1898, would be a more active one for her. She would persuade Sophie to allow her to spend more time at the mill. She would involve herself with the Robertses in their efforts to help the mill families.

Clearly she was not to be included in the rounds of parties to which Tina took off with amazing frequency. Her outspoken behavior at the UDC meeting had made her a social pariah. Nor did she genuinely regret this social ostracism. She had no patience for the endless small talk, the petty quarrels that evolved among the club groups.

The day of the ball, Tina remained in her room until minutes before Eric and she were scheduled to leave. She arrived in the parlor to wait for him, resplendent in a frosty-white dance gown adorned with winter flowers, her hair powdered, a black patch provocatively placed on one cheekbone. Louisa's emerald and diamond necklace was a perfect foil for her green eyes.

"Tina, you look like one of the famous beauties we read about in the grand French salons of the eighteenth century," Caroline exclaimed, compensating for the guilt she felt for coveting her grandmother's necklace.

"Thank you, Caroline." Tina smiled and went to kiss Josiah. "I won't see you, Grandpa, until 1898," she laughed.

Eric arrived, cool and detached, and Tina and he left for the ball. A few minutes later Andrew arrived. Despite his painful shyness he was transparent in his delight at spending New Year's Eve in Caroline's company. Sophie was aware of his growing fondness for her, Caroline realized in dismay. Sophie was pleased. But she must not allow Andrew—so sensitive and vulnerable—to expose himself to a courtship of her. She admired Andrew; she could never love him.

Mattie had prepared a sumptuous supper for them, served by Seth. Tonight Josiah was in a reminiscent mood. He talked about the painful Reconstruction years with a vividness that mesmerized Caroline.

"Atlanta was a city unto itself. From all over the South men came here with hope in their hearts. With anything over a hundred dollars in their hands they opened up a grocery or dry goods store. And we welcomed them, so long as they came with a will to better themselves and Atlanta."

"There were no fine houses built in the city in those first years." Sophie was misty-eyed in reminiscence. "Houses were plain and inexpensive, meant only to provide shelter. The concentration was on rebuilding stores."

"Most of the merchants had shipped their goods to safe places days before Sherman marched into Atlanta," Josiah explained. "The stores were destroyed, but the merchants went to work with their own hands to rebuild. I laid bricks out there," Josiah pointed toward Hampton Mill. "I worked side by side with the laborers until there were walls and a roof. And when the funds were raised to buy equipment, I went to New England myself. I wanted none of the out-dated machinery Northern mills tried to pawn off on the South. I bought the best equipment."

How she would have relished living in those days, Caroline thought, her love for Atlanta entrenched with a strength that astonished her. She could understand how Jim Russell, new to Atlanta like her, was enslaved by his visions of its future.

Andrew remained until a few minutes past midnight, then wished them a happy 1898 and left for his cottage. Josiah seemed reluctant to go up to his room tonight. By silent consent Caroline and Sophie remained with him. Far earlier than Caroline expected, Tina and Eric arrived home.

"It was a magnificent ball!" Tina told them.

"Tell us about it," Caroline encouraged.

"There were several hundred guests, all in fascinating costumes," Tina's voice was effervescent. "Mistletoe and holly and garlands of smilax everywhere. And you should have seen the Christmas tree! Hung with lights and souvenirs for the ladies."

"And you were the most beautiful young lady there," Josiah said with a sly smile, covertly inspecting Eric.

"The two most popular ladies were undoubtably Tina and Dolly Shepard," Eric said with ironic amusement. "Mrs. Shepard has a very keen mind."

They had left early, Caroline interpreted, because Tina was piqued at Dolly Shepard's success.

"It's late," Josiah decided. "Let's call it a night."

While Caroline reached for the door to her bedroom, she saw Tina lean toward Eric, a detaining hand on his arm. She went into her own room and closed the door, her face hot with color.

ON A crisp, cold, early January morning, Caroline sat with Grace Roberts in the tiny mill cottage sitting room and listened to David Kahn explain how he was teaching himself calculus from the book she had given him at Christmas.

"David, you ought to be in school!" David was a mathematical genius. "Suppose we arranged for you to be admitted to a school in Atlanta?" The prospect was exciting.

"I have to work with Noah," he reminded.

"Where is Noah?" Caroline asked.

David looked uncomfortable.

"It's not right, I think, but he's selling to customers he's made among the villagers. Only three or four," he explained. "Most of them still buy at the company store."

"Here's Noah now." Grace smiled as Noah came into the room and shifted the pack from his back to the floor.

"Noah," Caroline demanded without preliminaries, "if I were to find some way for David to go to school, would you let him?"

"But how would he live?" Noah stared in bewilderment. "We make little money—" He spread his hands in an eloquent gesture of futility.

"I'll try to find a place for him to board in return for chores,"

Caroline plotted. "I'm not sure that I can," she admitted, "but I could try it."

Noah looked intently at David, whose eyes glowed with the possibilities that lay ahead; but before Noah could respond, David brushed this aside.

"It's good of you to make this offer, Caroline," David said with rare formality, "but Noah needs me. We're brothers—we must stay together."

"If you can arrange this, Caroline," Noah said sternly, "David and I would be forever grateful." He turned to his brother. "When we came to America, we heard everywhere that America is a land of opportunity. But of what use is opportunity if you do not take it when it is offered?"

"I'll know in a few days," Caroline promised.

She would talk to Eric about how they could get David into a proper school. He had gone to school in New York for only two years; but he was capable, she was confident, of advanced high school studies despite his tender years. Her mind sought for a possible place for him to live and earn his keep. No point in approaching the General, who was sarcastic now about "those damn immigrants pouring into the country," though he had boasted on New Year's Eve about how Atlantans had appealed to earlier immigrants to come and help rebuild their city.

Caroline's face lighted. She would talk to Mrs. Bolton. She would call her as soon as she returned to the house. Hopefully Mrs. Bolton was not in Washington.

The Boltons were in Atlanta. Marian Bolton immediately invited Caroline to come over for tea that afternoon. It was one of her afternoons to work in Sophie's office, but she was sure Sophie would not be angry if she asked to change the day.

Promptly at three, Caroline arrived at the Bolton house and was ushered into the parlor, where the two Mrs. Boltons greeted her with gratifying warmth. Earnestly, Caroline explained David's situation.

"I don't know of anybody," the younger Mrs. Bolton said, frowning in thought, "but I'll talk to the Congressman tonight."

"I know somebody," the elder Mrs. Bolton—Miss Laurette—

said firmly. "We've got all those empty rooms in this house. He can live here and help with the yards. That no'count Sam is always lagging behind," she said with an affectionate glint in her eyes that belied her words. "You set him up in a school, and then you bring him here," she commanded. "I can do with some company with all that gallivanting to Washington that goes on with this family."

"But we don't know much about the boy," Marian objected.

"We in the South know what it means to need help." Her eyes kindling, she turned to Caroline. "I was here during the siege of Atlanta. The most horrible twenty days this city ever knew. I hid with my sister and two of my daughters-in-law and their children in a cellar. We heard the constant bombardments all about us. Red hot cannonballs were setting fire on all sides. We had little food, no milk for the children. We brewed chicory with dried beans."

"That's over," Marian said gently.

"We'll never forget those days," Miss Laurette shot back. "For more than a month after the siege we had a hundred thousand Federal soldiers billeted in Atlanta. When the order came through for us to leave, we were given ten days to evacuate the city."

"Out of four thousand five hundred buildings in the city only four hundred were left standing. And while Atlanta burned," Marian said with fresh bitterness, "General Sherman, in the Federal camp on the Capitol grounds, was serenaded by the strains of 'Miserere' from Il Trovatore."

"We came back," Miss Laurette said triumphantly. "That spring there was not one bird to be seen or heard anywhere, but sunshine kissed the earth that had been red with blood and brought forth daisies and brown-eyed Susans in a carpet of white and gold. Atlanta became a frontier boomtown."

"Remember how dangerous the streets were after dark?" Marian's voice was electric with recall. "The lawlessness was awful. And rents were so high. A shack cost fifteen to twenty dollars a month. Some folks lived in old army tents. The city always seemed ankle-deep in red mud, with sand and bricks and scaffolding all around as folks built stores and houses."

"But we overcame it all," her mother-in-law reminded with pride. "We led the way for the rest of the South. There's a glorious spirit of hope and courage in Atlanta. A bright, buoyant mood that'll be forever with us."

Leaving the Bolton house, Caroline headed for Jim Russell's office. Since the day at Hampton Court when Eric had introduced her to Cassius, she had made a point of not being with him; but there was no one but Eric to whom she could turn in this situation.

Mike, typing as furiously as he had on her first visit to Jim's office, looked up with a grin of recognition.

"Eric's in the little room at the back," he pointed good-naturedly.

"Thank you."

"Eric, young lady for you!" he yelled, as Caroline started toward the rear of the large office.

Eric emerged from a door to the left, greeted her with an expansive smile.

"Welcome," he drawled, strolling toward her.

"Eric, I need some help," she said quickly in answer to the curiosity in his eyes.

"Honey, anything you want," he promised, pulling out a chair for her beside one of the desks. He dropped onto the corner of the desk, waiting for her to explain her mission.

Talking so swiftly that her words tumbled over one another, as was her habit in moments of stress, she explained about Noah and David Kahn, about what she hoped to do for David.

"I don't know anything about the public schools here in Atlanta," she said breathlessly. "He's only had two years of formal schooling, but Eric, he's a genius at mathematics. He taught himself calculus from a book I gave him at Christmas. I thought he would go to Mr. Roberts for help—or even to me." She paused, too conscious of what his eyes were saying to her. *He had no right.*

"I know a few people. We ought to be able to get him into a private school, where he can move along fast." He squinted in thought. "They'll want to test him," Eric warned.

'That'll be no obstacle," she said confidently.

'I'll make some calls. Stay right here," he commanded. "I want to get hold of Jim's phonebook. Did you come in a carriage?"

"No, I took the streetcar," she said, and he chuckled.

"Then we'll go home together. As soon as I have your protégé scheduled to meet some people who can do him some good," he told her and sauntered off, whistling.

She was doing what she had sworn not to do, she chastised herself. She was allowing Eric to come close to her again.

JOSIAH FINISHED the lunch tray that Seth had brought him from the house, as usual, and reached for the newspaper still folded on his desk. He scowled as he scanned the front page. Strikes again in the New England textile mills. They were a hotbed of labor agitation.

He put down the newspaper and frowned. Was Sophie right in holding him back from firing Tom Coleman? Don't make a martyr of the man, she kept insisting. Not many of their people bothered to read the newspapers, but Coleman would use these new strikes to try to stir up trouble.

"Josiah, you're supposed to leave at three for that directors' meeting," Sophie's brisk voice intruded.

"It's just past one," he snapped. "Zeke knows to come by and pick me up." He picked up the paper and handed it to her. "A strike in New Bedford."

"We don't have to worry. Elsas just broke the strike at his mill. His workers lost a lot of wages, and still had to go back without winning any of their demands. That's what the Georgia workers will be talking about."

"Elsas made no effort to force his men out of the union," Josiah said narrowly.

"That would have been stupid and you know it," Sophie shot back. "The unions have too much internal trouble to cause us headaches, Josiah."

"Sophie, what the devil's going on with Caroline?"

"What do you mean?"

"I see her going over to the village all the time. Why is she seeing so much of the Robertses?"

"She's lonely and they're friendly to her," Sophie said bluntly. "She wants to come in more often to the office."

"Let her," Josiah said. "It'll keep her out of trouble." Why did Caroline have to create a rumpus at the UDC meeting? Half of Atlanta probably had heard about it within twenty-four hours. He chuckled, envisioning her stubbornly announcing her feelings. Spunky little beauty; he had to give her credit for that.

Sophie returned to her office. He rose to his feet and crossed to a window that faced the village. In sudden decision he left the office and strode down the long corridor to the front door. He could use a little exercise after that heavy lunch Mattie sent over today. He'd walk to the village and stop in to see Roberts for a few minutes.

He stopped in at the church. Grace Roberts was there, organizing the children in some activity. He quietly closed the door and went to the Roberts cottage. Henry welcomed him with warmth.

"Am I keeping you from your sermon?" Josiah asked perfunctorily, noting the sheaf of papers on a worktable by the window.

"No problem, General," Henry assured him. "It's always a pleasure to see you, sir."

Josiah wasted little time in bringing the conversation around to Caroline.

"She's quite taken with Grace and you."

"You can be proud of Caroline," Henry said. Josiah stared hard at the minister. "The way she's campaigned for the young Kahn boy."

"Caroline doesn't talk too much about such things at the house. What exactly has been happening?" he probed. He had seen the pair of young peddlers moving about the village. Little happened there that he missed. He wasn't concerned about losing business at the company store. A peddler could hardly afford to extend much credit.

With lively pleasure Henry Roberts explained how Caroline had arranged for David to study at a private school on a scholarship, while he lived at the Bolton house.

"The boy is a genius. He'll do us all credit," Henry said with pride.

"You say there are two brothers?"

Josiah listened intently while Henry briefed him on the two Kahn brothers and their backgrounds.

"When the older boy shows up, send him over to me," Josiah ordered, rising to his feet. Henry stared in alarm. "Don't worry about that one," he soothed. "I just want to discuss a business proposition with him. Just between the three of us," Josiah warned. "If you say a word to Caroline or anybody else, he'll get no help from me."

"It'll be confidential, General Hampton," Henry assured him.

Two days later Noah Kahn showed up at his office, diffident and uneasy but striving for an air of confidence. Josiah liked that.

"Noah, I hear you've been doing a little business in the village."

"Yes, sir," Noah acknowledged warily. "Just a little."

"How do you manage to sell to these people, when they can charge at the company store?"

"I sell only to four families, sir. That's all I can afford to carry. I choose them carefully. And I sell for less," he said with a faint spurt of defiance.

"Noah, I'm going to see that you're set up in a store in Atlanta," he said matter-of-factly, ignoring Noah's stare of incredulity. "Not a fancy place," he warned. "You'll start small, with credit from the bank. I'll endorse your notes. I expect you to work your backside off to meet the payments when they're due. Is that clear?"

"Yes, General Hampton." Noah's accent, usually slight, was guttural in his excitement.

"Don't expect to get rich quick," the General warned caustically. "You'll have to put every cent of profit into building up your inventory. You'll live worse than you do now maybe for years—but you're building for a future in one of the great cities of this country. And nobody is to know about my part in this, Noah. Do you understand? If anybody learns about it, the bank will call in your notes immediately."

"General Hampton, I have heard about opportunities in America," Noah said, "but I had not expected this."

"You stick to your side of the bargain and I'll stick to mine. I consider you a fairly good investment. Now get out of here," he said with mock gruffness.

He leaned back in satisfaction. Wasn't that going to set Caroline on her ear? She was taking care of the young boy's education, but he was setting up the older in business. And she'd never know, he told himself complacently, that he had any part in it. Let her go on thinking he was a hard-headed, hard-hearted son-of-a-bitch.

Chapter Eighteen

CAROLINE was pleased to be spending four afternoons a week at the mill. Sophie gave her increasing responsibility, and Andrew was never too busy to answer her endless questions, though at times he was disconcerted by her zeal for reforms. She was jubilant about Noah's good fortune. As soon as she became aware of his going into business in Atlanta, she had gone to Miss Laurette. It was arranged that Noah would share David's room at the Bolton house.

Caroline avidly followed the news of Cuba. Eric was convinced that the new Liberal government in Madrid would yield now to President McKinley's demands.

Three days earlier, the battleship *Maine* was ordered to Havana. It was officially a peaceful courtesy call, but Eric admitted he was uneasy.

Tonight Caroline was going with Andrew to the Grand Opera House to see Mme. Modjeska in *Macbeth*. Andrew was coming to dinner at the house prior to the performance.

Everyone was in the parlor when she went downstairs. Andrew's eyes softened as she walked into the room.

"Caroline, you look exquisite."

"Thank you, Andrew." She was conscious that both her grandfather and Eric were staring inscrutably at her. "I hope I haven't held up dinner."

"Mattie's not ready yet," Sophie told her. "But we'll sit down to the table in a few minutes. You won't be late for the theater."

Caroline was uncomfortable in Sophie's pleasure at her going to the theater with Andrew. Sophie was developing romantic ideas.

"Caroline, I know what would be perfect with that gown," Tina said vivaciously. "My emerald necklace. Grandpa, you won't be angry with me if I loan it to Caroline, will you?"

"That would be very generous of you, Tina," Josiah said with unfamiliar formality.

"I'll go right upstairs and get it. If Seth's ready to serve, go in without me," she coaxed.

Eric launched into a volatile discussion with the General and Andrew about the Cuban situation.

"I know I've done an about-face," Josiah admitted, "but with all the news that's coming out of Cuba, how could I do otherwise?"

"All the biased news," Eric emphasized. "McKinley's right to try to keep us out of war."

"Even if we accept the premise that Spain is oppressing Cuba—" Andrew began and Eric interrupted.

"We know it's happening, but why can't we give Spain and Cuba a chance to work out their differences?"

"I agree," Andrew nodded. Josiah snorted. "Oppression goes on all over the world. England is oppressing Ireland, India and Egypt; Turkey is oppressing Armenia; France is oppressing Madagascar and Siam. We can't step in and be a referee for the entire world."

Seth arrived to say that dinner was ready to be served. Walking with Sophie into the dining room while the three men followed, Caroline was conscious that Eric was irritated that she was going to the theater with Andrew. What right did he have to feel that way?

Tina arrived as they were seating themselves. She went directly to Caroline and with dramatic flair fastened the necklace about Caroline's throat. The necklace that was supposed to be hers.

"Honey, the necklace is perfect with your dress," she said with satisfaction.

Josiah was pale, his eyes over-bright as they clung to Caroline. He was seeing her grandmother wearing this necklace. Their hair, their features were identical. He looked at her and saw Louisa Hampton.

Caroline was relieved when dinner was over, and Andrew and she were in the carriage bound for the Grand Opera House on Peachtree Street.

"The DeGive Grand Opera House is the third largest theater in the country," Andrew told her. "Mr. DeGive spared no expense to make it a masterpiece. And I'm particularly partial to *Macbeth*."

Jason left them at the theater. Andrew escorted her through the arriving hordes into the elegant marble-tiled lobby of beveled glass and quarter oak with ornate friezes. The auditorium elicited an instant exclamation of admiration from Caroline.

"The murals are by Paolo Payesich, who decorated the Sultan's palace in Constantinople and the palace of the Czar in St. Petersburg," Andrew told her. "Just look at those allegorical figures across the proscenium."

"Andrew, it's magnificent," she murmured in awe, gazing from proscenium to the display of electric chandeliers, from orchestra to mezzanine to gallery and then to the fine boxes on each side.

Andrew led her to their orchestra seats, close to the stage. The house curtain depicted a scene of Shakespeare reading a play before Queen Elizabeth. Caroline was eager for the curtain to part and the performance to begin. How her mother would have adored this theater with its terra-cotta, blue and gold colors, its lush abundance of old rose plush.

Caroline was entranced by the performance, preferring to remain seated with Andrew between acts to discuss the splendid performance of Mme. Modjeska, who was playing *Mary Stuart* at matinées.

"She's marvelous in any play," Andrew said with elation, "but *Macbeth* is her greatest triumph."

To Caroline's astonishment, Eric and the General still sat in the parlor when she returned from the theater. Tina and Sophie had gone to their rooms.

"I assume the evening was a success," Eric drawled as she hovered at the parlor entrance.

"I enjoyed the play tremendously." Her heart was pounding. *Eric was jealous because she had spent the evening with Andrew.* "I'll go up to Tina's room and return the necklace. I adored wearing it tonight," she said, her eyes faintly defiant as they clashed with her grandfather's. "I saw several ladies look at it with much admiration."

She returned the necklace to Tina, not lingering because Tina was talking with Chad on the telephone, and went to her room. It was disturbing to recognize that Eric was jealous of Andrew. Had the others noticed? she asked herself with alarm. No, she decided after a moment of recall. But she knew Eric so well now, and she sensed his reaction.

He would not be jealous if he did not love her, she thought, and she sighed in frustration. What did it matter if Eric loved her and she loved him? Tina would be forever between them. And if there were not Tina, she forced herself to face reality, with how many others would Eric fancy himself in love?

EARLY IN February Josiah was much involved with the Manufacturers Convention in Atlanta. Two hundred delegates from seventy Georgia towns were present. Josiah attended the morning session called to order by Governor Atkinson and, grumbling, went to an evening session at the Kimball House that took the form of a bohemian smoker.

"We have to bring more industry into the state," Josiah proclaimed at home. "Governor Atkinson is right. We must give whole, or at least partial, exemptions to manufacturing enterprises coming into Georgia. I told him I agree wholeheartedly. Most other Southern states are already doing this."

Caroline listened and remembered how many New England mills had moved to the South for cheaper labor. The mills that remained in New England were paying a sixteen percent dividend, but were cutting wages by ten percent.

With the deepest of sympathy and admiration she had read in the *Constitution* about Mrs. Harriet Pickering, a striker in the Massachusetts mills, who rallied the women workers when the men were ready to give up their fight.

"In God's name," Mrs. Pickering said to the men, "let the women be heard! The Massachusetts mill owners denounced slavery in the South, but now they're trying to fasten white slavery on us!"

Why couldn't the General understand the needs of his own millworkers? Caroline asked herself with recurrent frustration.

On February 17, the New York newspapers ran extras announcing the sinking of the *Maine* two nights earlier. Hearst's *Journal* blazoned a headline that read: THE WARSHIP MAINE WAS SPLIT IN TWO BY AN ENEMY'S SECRET INFERNAL MACHINE. Quickly the Associated Press spread the news across the nation. Atlantans, like all Americans, were stunned by the news that two hundred fifty-two officers and men were dead or missing; more lay in Havana hospitals.

Eric brought the news to the Hampton house. Josiah's face was florid as he read the headline of the newspaper Eric gave him.

"This should be enough to show McKinley we have no alternative but war!" he sputtered. "How much does he expect the American people to take?"

"Do they know that the Spanish are responsible?" Caroline asked Eric. "Couldn't it have been an accident?"

"No accident!" Josiah brushed this aside. "The Spanish want war!"

"It's preposterous to believe that Spain blew up the *Maine*." Eric was losing his battle to remain cool. "Spain knows she hasn't a chance in a war with us. She's swallowed insults to stay out of war. It's quite conceivable that the ship blew up because of an explosion of her own magazines. She could have been sunk by Cuban rebels trying to throw us into war. It could have been a group of Spaniards, hating the new Spanish government and plotting trouble for it."

"It was a mine," Josiah insisted inflexibly. "Set to destroy the *Maine* and kill her crew."

"Our Minister in Madrid is convinced we can have peace." Eric leaned forward urgently. "He says the Spanish government will go the limit to avoid war. But if Hearst and Pulitzer have their way," Eric predicted, "we'll have war in sixty days."

"May I see the newspaper?" Caroline asked, and Josiah handed it to her.

"We know that a Spanish cruiser went out and picked up survivors," Eric said. "Even while the explosions continued. They saved American lives at the risk of their own skins."

"The American public won't accept this," Josiah thundered. "You'll see."

"Grandpa, do you think there will be a war?" Tina seemed fascinated by the prospect. Caroline shivered. Tina envisioned war as a romantic affair. Growing up in the shadows of the War Between the States, how could she feel that way?

"Like Eric said," Josiah agreed, "we'll be at war within sixty days."

Each day the disaster stories grew more horrifying, though sabotage had not been proved. The New York *Journal* printed Cuban news in blood-red letters. Clear-thinking minds exhorted against an impetuous leap into war, but the public at large was not thinking clearly.

Josiah returned from a joint meeting of the National Grand Army of the Republic and the United Confederate Veterans, held in Atlanta, and was outraged because they called for support of the President, who remained against intervention. Across the country thousands were giving themselves up to emotional excesses. Tent-meeting revivals were spreading the "war fever." McKinley was burned in effigy in Colorado. In New York people hissed at his photograph. Assistant Secretary of the Navy Theodore Roosevelt was said to have declared that "McKinley has no more backbone than a chocolate éclair."

Swayed by the public clamor for war, the President sent a bill to Congress asking for fifty million for national defense. It was passed without a "nay." With stolid determination, Jim Russell and Eric kept to a pacifist road in Russell's new magazine. But the voices of intelligent Americans were being drowned out by the "yellow press."

TINA CELEBRATED her twentieth birthday at a dinner party given by her parents at their house. Caroline was invited, though she sensed Mrs. Kendrick's inner hostility the moment she walked into the Kendrick house. Chad, however, was at his most charming in his efforts to amuse her.

To Mrs. Kendrick's vexation the conversation turned to politics. Her husband was expressing contempt for a small group calling for legislation against child labor. Eric shot a warning glance at Caroline, lest she speak her mind on this subject.

"I think it's absurd," Mrs. Kendrick said disdainfully. "If working children are not physically abused and prefer working, then the matter of their going to school is the business of their parents and nobody else."

"Caroline, Tina says you're forever reading," Chad twitted her, bored with the political talk. "How do you like Ouida?"

"I don't know her books," Caroline acknowledged. "Right now I'm reading *Kreutzer Sonata*. I think Tolstoy is fascinating."

"I never allowed Tina to read *Kreutzer Sonata*." Mrs. Kendrick grimaced in distaste. "The man wrote the book just to make vice seem inviting. For a young girl to read that kind of fiction is to deprive herself of her lovely young innocence."

Again Caroline caught Eric's warning glance. He knew she was on the point of making an explosive retort. Mrs. Kendrick's way of thinking was what kept women from gaining what was rightfully theirs.

Not until the end of the evening did Josiah announce his birthday gift to Tina. The members of the dinner party were invited to go out to the verandah to see the present that had just been delivered. Before the house sat one of the new loco-steamers, about which Tina had prattled with girlish enthusiasm on several occasions of late, but which none of the family had ever seen.

"Oh, Grandpa!" Tina threw her arms about him delightedly. "You couldn't have chosen anything I wanted more!"

"Is it safe?" Mrs. Kendrick viewed the loco-steamer with dismay.

"Mrs. Kendrick, in fifteen years there won't be a horse left on the streets," Josiah predicted and turned to Tina. "A man who has come down from New York to demonstrate the loco-steamers in

Atlanta will drive it out to the house for you tonight. He'll come to give you lessons every morning until you've got the hang of driving it."

"And tomorrow night," Chad announced, "I'm taking Tina and Caroline to see Mademoiselle Anna Held at the Grand. That's my birthday present," he said with an exaggerated bow.

Caroline accompanied Tina and Chad to the Grand on the following evening for the performance of *Gay Deceiver*. The audience was visibly disappointed that Mlle. Held did not appear until the third act. They seemed disappointed, too, that her songs were hardly naughty at all, though the play had been publicized as daring. Still, the atmosphere in the theater was festive.

AT THE end of March Marian Bolton returned from Washington. Caroline went to visit Marian and Miss Laurette.

"I was so tired of all the socializing in Washington," Marian confided. "I simply could not bear another ladies' luncheon. And now, of course, everybody is so upset about the Cuban business."

"Is everyone in Washington expecting war?" Caroline asked.

"Honey, it's unbelievable what's happening in the Capital," Marian declared. "All the Congressional wives are at the Capitol doors by eight A.M., hoping for a seat in the gallery. They're all for the war, Caroline," she said. "Proctor sobbed aloud when he reported to the Senate on what he had seen in Cuba. He told them that two hundred thousand people had died of malnutrition or starvation in the concentration centers during the last few months."

"I understand that Clara Barton has been very active in relief work in Havana," Caroline said, and Miss Laurette beamed.

"Now there's a great lady. Seventy-seven years old and she's still helping folks."

"It's rumored that Assistant Secretary of the Navy Roosevelt is going to resign to form a volunteer unit as soon as war is formally declared," Marian confided. "Though he's barely forty," she teased her mother-in-law.

Caroline was disturbed by what she had heard. War was breathing down their necks. Would Eric go? *He was against fighting*

231

Spain. The vision of Eric in uniform, a gun in his hand, was unsettling. Eric wounded. Dying on a field of battle. *No, don't think about that.*

ERIC emerged from the parlor as Caroline came into the house.

"What's the news from Washington?" he asked lightly, but his eyes were serious.

"Caroline!" the General's voice called from inside the parlor. "Come tell us what Mrs. Bolton has to say about things in Washington."

Josiah and Eric listened to what Caroline had to relate to them. One man intent on war, the other on peace.

"This whole war business has mushroomed into absurdity. War will cost American lives," Eric said exasperatedly. "We don't have to fight. The way talks are going with Spain we can eventually dictate our own terms."

"Mrs. Bolton says that there are rumors in Washington that the Assistant Secretary of the Navy plans to resign to form a volunteer regiment," Caroline said somberly.

"Theodore Roosevelt?" Eric said with surprise.

"Our regular Army won't be able to cope," Josiah pointed out. "We'll have to train a lot of volunteers."

"It's only a rumor about Roosevelt," Caroline reminded. The zealous glow about Eric's face disturbed her.

"It's only a rumor because he can't form a regiment until a Volunteer Army Act is passed," Eric explained realistically. Now he seemed to sense her inchoate concern for him. It unnerved her sometimes, the way they seemed to exchange thoughts without a word between them. "How's your young mathematic genius coming along?" He deliberately brushed aside further talk of war.

Caroline reported on David's progress. The General pretended to have returned to his newspaper, but she was aware that he was intrigued by the anecdotes she passed along about Noah's canny efforts at bringing customers into his small store on Decatur Street. He might be General Hampton today, Caroline realized, but he had not completely forgotten a boyhood where money was hard to come by and his family denied themselves to put him through college. He would have respect for Noah Kahn.

On April 5, President McKinley recalled U.S. Counsul Fitzhugh Lee from Cuba. The nation waited impatiently for a declaration of war. Jim Russell entrained to Washington, to return the afternoon of April 12. Eric waited for his arrival at the office.

"It's not good," Jim said to Eric without preliminaries. Mike arrived with coffee for them, lingered to hear the latest news from the Capital. "The inside word is that the Spanish minister advised the Pope that the Governor General in Cuba would call a halt to hostilities pending a settlement of the Cuban situation. The message came through to McKinley while he was meeting with the Cabinet. A few level heads urged that the Cuban message be postponed, but most of the Cabinet members voted to go ahead, just adding the offer of armistice at the end. Congress will declare war within the week," Jim predicted.

"It's insane!" Eric exploded. "Spain's accepted our three-point plan. They've agreed to an armistice. What more can we ask of them?"

"Don't ask for reason," Jim snorted, then turned to Mike. "Any more of this bilge you call coffee around?"

"I'll make another pot," Mike offered.

"Did McKinley recognize the independence of Cuba?" Eric asked.

"No," Jim reported. "We're intervening on humanitarian grounds in part, but mainly to protect 'our endangered American interests.' "

"I want to cover the war," Eric said.

"Why?"

"My damnable curiosity." Eric lifted one eyebrow in self-mockery.

"A magazine the size of ours won't be able to get credentials from Washington." Jim squinted in thought. "If we could come up with a strong angle, I might be able to sell my Detroit contact on sending you out."

"What kind of angle?"

"Something to increase his circulation."

"Suppose I could get permission to accompany Roosevelt's regiment?" Eric offered.

"Why Roosevelt?"

"He's the kind of man the public likes to read about. I like what he did as Police Commissioner in New York City. I like the way he fought for two years to stamp out graft in the city's police force. I loathe his views on Cuba," Eric acknowledged. "But I figure your friend will be impressed by a volunteer regiment led by the former Assistant Secretary of the Navy."

"Let's play this from both ends. You tell whatever Washington connections you can use that the Detroit *Weekly Advocate* wants you to do a series of articles, following Roosevelt's regiment from its inception until victory. I'll tell Charlie Freeman in Detroit that you've wangled permission to cover the regiment, but you're looking for a magazine that'll print your articles the way you send them in. Freeman owes me a favor. He'll come through."

"I'll leave for Washington tomorrow." Eric was stimulated by the need for action.

"Hold it for a day. Let me see if I can work this out with Freeman. Then you can go to Washington with an actual commitment. But you're not in business until you have credentials. And that's not going to be easy, Eric."

Jim sent a telegram to Freeman in Detroit. They would have a reply within twenty-four hours, he promised. Mike brought them more coffee, paused to listen to Eric's plans to go to Cuba.

"If they're going to take volunteers," Mike decided, "I'll go with a company from Atlanta!"

"Mike, you stay here," Jim said tersely. "We have a magazine to get out."

Riding home on the streetcar, with the first dogwood of spring blossoming along the avenues, Eric listened to the war talk that dominated commuter conversation. How could Americans consider the imminent war with such a sense of righteousness? This was a military aggression.

Late in the evening Eric announced his plans to leave for Washington within two or three days, explaining his mission.

"You're going to be a war correspondent?" Tina was disappointed. Tina wanted to be able to talk about a gallant husband fighting against the Spanish. In contrast, Caroline looked stricken.

"Then you admit we're going to have to fight," Josiah said with acerbic humor. Eric knew the General was burying visual images of his bringing military glory to the Hampton name.

"I deny that we have to fight," Eric contradicted. "But we will. I want to be there as a correspondent."

"How do you expect to acquire this status?" Josiah pushed. "Jim Russell's magazine won't help you. I might be able to use some influence with the *Constitution* or the *Journal*—"

"No," Eric rejected. "I can handle this myself."

Carefully Eric explained the strategy Jim and he were employing. Caroline laughed at their caginess, but her eyes were serious.

"You're going to need people to open doors for you in Washington," Josiah warned. "Those things can drag on forever without the right people behind you. This war won't wait for you."

"Maybe Congressman Bolton can help," Caroline said impulsively. "I can write him."

"We can't waste time on letter-writing," Josiah dismissed this. "Eric, you go to Washington the day after tomorrow. The New Orleans to New York *Limited* leaves Atlanta at noon. Take Tina with you. A pretty face goes a long way in Washington. Take Caroline, too," he ordered. "Make reservations for a Pullman drawing room for them. I'll give you letters to people who owe me favors. Sophie, you'll have to get them out tonight. We'll be too busy at the mill tomorrow."

"I'll phone Mrs. Bolton and ask her for their Washington address." Caroline leapt to her feet. "I'll call right now." Sophie had already left the room to go for her notebook.

The General was looking at Caroline with grandfatherly pride, Eric thought. Despite himself, he was coming to love her. Caroline and the old man were past the rough hurdles in their relationship.

"I'll need Lucinda with me." Tina's eyes shone. "There're so many parties in Washington."

"We'll only be there a few days," Eric reminded. "You won't need Lucinda."

Tina turned beseechingly to Josiah, but he was unaware. His eyes were fastened on the portrait of Louisa Hampton. His wife was gone, but his granddaughter was home with him at last.

Chapter Nineteen

C AROLINE, Tina and Eric arrived in Washington, D.C., shortly before 7:00 A.M. Already the streets were showing signs of activity, the number of cyclists amazing Caroline. She leaned toward the hack window, eager for her first sight of the Capital city, while Tina smothered a series of yawns and Eric stared from the other window. He was pleased that Charlie Freeman had wired acceptance of him as the correspondent of the Detroit *Weekly Advocate*.

"We're staying at the Oxford Hotel," Eric said. "It's at Fourteenth and H, just three blocks from the White House."

"Honey, you wired for reservations?" Tina asked.

"I wired," Eric assured her, his voice edged with irritation. Tina's constant chattering on the train yesterday, particularly in the dining car, had strained his patience, Caroline thought uneasily. "This is hardly the time to come to Washington without reservations."

"How exciting to be so close to the White House!" Tina placated him. "Do you suppose we'll be able to visit there?"

"I'll ask Congressman Bolton," Caroline said. She felt a peculiar guilt because so often she lifted her eyes to discover Eric's eyes resting on her with an intensity that brought color to her cheeks. But he barely tolerated his wife.

They were shown to a four-room suite at the Oxford, three large, airy bedrooms and a sitting room, all with large gilt mirrors and marble mantels. Eric immediately took off to call on people with letters the General had written about Eric's mission in Washington. He instructed Tina and Caroline to meet him at the hotel at three. Probably there would be a dinner invitation. Caroline and Tina unpacked and sought out the dining room, where breakfast was being served.

"Mama said we must go shopping at Saks," Tina said, happy in the admiring glances they were receiving from other tables. "It's a marvelous store, something like Wanamaker's in Philadelphia."

"I have to try to get through to Congressman Bolton," Caroline reminded. "Though he'll probably be at the House until all hours."

"You try to reach him, then we'll go shopping," Tina decided. "We can't just sit in our rooms all day."

A quartet of men, in volatile conversation, were coming into the dining room. Caroline recognized one of them as a leading Congressman.

"Tina, be still," she said, as the four men sat at a table behind them. Tina stared aggrievedly at her. "I want to hear what they're saying," Caroline appeased. "Those are Congressmen at the table behind us."

Caroline and Tina listened, ostensibly occupied with breakfast.

"When will the Foreign Affairs Committee come to terms about the question of recognizing Cuba?" one of the Congressmen demanded. "Smith of Michigan is opposing any resolution which doesn't include this! I hear the meeting was stormy."

"A second meeting's scheduled," another of the Congressmen said calmly. "They'll arrive at an acceptable intervention resolution. They have to do it fast," he emphasized. "The Army is already moving its regulars from the West to New Orleans, Mobile and Tampa." Then, as though aware that they were the cynosure of other guests, they fell silent.

Caroline and Tina finished breakfast and walked to Congressman Bolton's office. Bandannaed black women sold colorful bunches of daffodils and violets along their route. Between buildings, high-spirited black children played hopscotch or marbles, darting dexterously beneath clotheslines. As Caroline suspected, Congressman Bolton was attending the session at the House. She left word that she was at the Oxford Hotel and was most anxious to speak with him, after which Tina carried her off to Saks.

Tina was intrigued by the shop windows, which displayed pictures of Army and Navy heroes, of battles dating as far back as the Spanish Armada. Everyone seemed to be wearing tiny American flags, peddled on the streets for five cents. Clusters of youngsters whistled "The Star-Spangled Banner." And everywhere—at the large stores, churches, theaters—Caroline saw the rows of stalls where bicycles could be stabled.

Promptly at three, Caroline and Tina returned to the hotel, though Tina sulked at Caroline's insistence on their punctuality. A message was waiting from Congressman Bolton. The three of them were invited for dinner at the Boltons' Washington house the following evening.

Eric arrived, frustrated that two of the General's most powerful contacts were in New York on business, though due back shortly. The Congressman beholden to the General was in Garfield Hospital recovering from pneumonia. A fourth contact—a Southern Judge—had invited them to dinner that evening, and Caroline and Tina were to attend a luncheon with their hostess on the following day and a tea that afternoon.

Caroline was uneasy when she arrived with Tina and Eric at the Judge's elegant town house to discover there would be a dozen at dinner, but this unease was short-lived. Table conversation was largely about the war, and she listened, engrossed, to every word, contributing at intervals when she realized that among the guests were those who agreed with Eric and her that the imminent war was a grave mistake.

Caroline's eyes moved slowly about the table, contemplating who among the guests might be helpful to Eric. Their host, unfortunately, had no direct Army contacts, though he had promised Eric he would make inquiries on his behalf.

Caroline was restless at the luncheon they attended the following day with the Judge's wife, though no one would guess that she was any less delighted than Tina at this Washington socializing. The over-dressed women, the overly elaborate luncheon table, the inane conversation made her wish wistfully to be free to sight-see alone in the Capital. Through ten courses, concluding with a spectacular dessert of ice cream in the form of pink roses in a pink sugar basket, Caroline contrived to be polite. The afternoon tea was equally straining. She took a deep breath of relief when the "good mornings" had been said, amused that it appeared to be morning in Washington until dinnertime arrived.

Congressman Bolton lived on Capitol Hill. This was the most expensive part of Washington, Tina pointed out to Caroline and Eric, though she was candidly unimpressed by the obvious smallness of the houses. Three stories tall but little more than twenty-five feet wide.

They were admitted by a smiling black maid who led them across the foyer to the pleasantly furnished double parlor. In moments the Congressman joined them, delighted to see Caroline again, welcoming Tina and Eric.

"Marian won't be back for two or three weeks, but she leaves me well cared for here in Washington," the Congressman assured them.

Over dinner, Eric explained their mission in Washington. The Congressman listened attentively.

"I've heard the rumor about Roosevelt and Wood forming a volunteer regiment," he confirmed. "I've known Leonard Wood for a number of years," he confided. "He's McKinley's physician, you know, as well as being an Army surgeon. He won a Medal of Honor for leading troops against Geronimo, the Apache Chief. He'll be your best approach to Roosevelt. Give me a few days to reach Captain Wood," he stipulated. "Everything is in such an uproar in Washington right now that it's sometimes difficult to talk with people."

Tina was enchanted when the Congressman offered to arrange for them to call on Mrs. McKinley at the White House. He would have their cards sent to the hotel as soon as he could arrange this, he promised. Eric was pleased that, at last, he seemed to be making some progress in reaching the Assistant Secretary of the Navy.

The following morning Eric left early as usual, determined to follow through on the General's leads in the event Congressman Bolton should fail to make contact with Leonard Wood. Caroline persuaded Tina to join her in sight-seeing before they were to attend a reception in the afternoon.

They visited the five-hundred-foot Washington Monument and the red sandstone castle that housed the Smithsonian Institution. They dallied at the colorful public market, an institution patronized by every strata of Washington society. Expensively gowned society ladies, accompanied by a retainer with basket, moved from stall to stall beside boardinghouse keepers and budget-conscious housewives.

Caroline easily persuaded Tina to dawdle with her along the small area becoming known as Embassy Row, where the diplomatic missions were located. They sat on green iron benches in the warm sunlight at Lafayette Square, across from the White House, and watched the pigeons strut and squirrels dart about the grass. Nursemaids sat gossiping on nearby benches while their charges played Prisoners' Base. Here and there a man sat reading the *Washington Post* or *Times*.

Late in the afternoon Caroline and Tina presented themselves at the reception given by the wife of a Southern Senator, a longstanding friend of Josiah Hampton.

"Are there only women here?" Tina whispered in contempt, gazing into the large ballroom where pretty girls were dancing together to the beautiful music. "How awful."

"We don't have to stay," Caroline said tentatively.

"We'll leave," Tina decided with a shudder.

They arrived at the hotel to discover that Congressman Bolton had sent over their cards for visiting the White House. They would be received the following afternoon. Tina was jubilant.

"It was worth coming to Washington just for this," she declared dramatically.

Eric returned to the hotel to tell them that he was to call on Roosevelt's Army surgeon friend, Captain Wood, on the 20th.

"You'll get your credentials," Tina said, already envisioning herself talking to Atlanta friends about her husband, the war correspondent. Didn't they wonder, Caroline asked herself, why Chad was more often her escort than Eric?

"*Perhaps* I'll get them," Eric cautioned. "I'm still calling on the General's contacts when they return to the city. But your Congressman Bolton is my best hope," he told Caroline conscientiously, his eyes saying much more.

The next morning Tina insisted on remaining in their suite until time to leave for the White House. It was her fashion to stay abed as long as possible on days when she wished to appear her most beautiful. Caroline was covertly pleased to be able to roam about the Capital alone.

When Caroline returned, she found Tina with her entire wardrobe scattered about her bedroom.

"I have absolutely nothing that's right," she wailed. "And why isn't Lucinda here to iron for me?"

"Tina, you have three dresses that are perfect," Caroline said firmly, her eyes sweeping about the room. "Here, wear this. Dress immediately," she ordered. "We must not be late."

Sulky but beautiful, Tina at last conceded she was ready to leave for the White House. She was briefly affronted when Caroline rejected her wish to order a carriage.

"Tina, it's three blocks," she laughed.

"Nobody arrives at the White House on foot," Tina objected.

"We will. It's a beautiful day, Tina."

They walked leisurely in the early afternoon sunlight. Caroline marveled that she was here in Washington, about to meet the President's wife. Tina was talking without a pause about Mrs. McKinley, whose poor health had kept her husband from long campaign tours.

"Can you imagine, Caroline? He absolutely refused to leave her. Mr. Hanna arranged for thousands of visitors to go to Canton, Ohio, and he talked to them on his front porch."

"He won," Caroline laughed. "She didn't hold him back."

They stopped for a moment to admire the red tulips in a big round bed before the White House portico, and then they approached the door. They were asked for no identification other than their cards. An officer ushered them into the Red Parlor where Caroline inspected the portraits of Andrew Jackson and Mrs. Hayes. Tina's eyes were brilliant with anticipation as she posed on one of the blue velvet sofas.

After a short wait they were instructed to go upstairs. Another young officer met them at the elevator and escorted them to a room where Mrs. McKinley waited to receive, with two women in attendance. Caroline was filled with compassion for the frail First Lady. Most of Washington knew that Mrs. McKinley was subject to fainting spells and epileptic seizures, though she re-fused to allow this to prevent her from performing her official obligations.

Tina was the charming young Southern matron to the core, intent on making an impression; but Caroline sensed that the President's wife was feeling ill. The two ladies in attendance were exchanging anxious glances. Mrs. McKinely ought not be put through these receptions.

When Caroline saw other guests approaching, she thanked Mrs. McKinley for her graciousness and, despite Tina's annoyance, ushered Tina from the room.

"Caroline, why did you rush me out?" she whispered furiously.

"There were others arriving," Caroline said. "She's ill. She ought not to be receiving."

Tina sulked all the way home, went directly to her bedroom and shut the door. Caroline settled down to read the *Washington Post* in the sitting room. She was tired from the day of socializing. She hoped there was no dinner to attend this evening.

Eric arrived at the hotel later than usual.

"We must be at the Capitol tomorrow at ten," he announced grimly. "The resolutions from the Committee are to be heard."

"It'll mean a formal declaration of war?" Caroline's face was somber.

"Most likely." Eric dropped into a chair. "Some Senators will balk, but the House is heavily in favor of war."

"The Senate could reject it," Caroline said. "And McKinley's against war. Eric, there *is* a chance for peace," she insisted.

"Don't count on it," he warned.

Tina's door flew wide.

"Where are we having dinner tonight?" she asked, ignoring Caroline. "I had such a dull afternoon."

"We'll have dinner at the Ebbitt House," Eric said cajolingly. Caroline was astonished; Eric usually cared little about Tina's sensibilities.

Tina lifted an eyebrow in reproach.

"We're not invited anywhere?"

"We are on the brink of war," Eric reminded with strained

patience. "Tomorrow we learn if Congress votes for intervention in Cuba. There'll be little entertaining in Washington tonight."

"We're going to the Capitol tomorrow, Tina," Caroline placated. "Eric says the resolutions from the Committee will be heard."

"It'll be dull," Tina prophesied.

"You don't have to go, Tina," Eric said, and she stared at him warily.

"I'll go," she said with suspect sweetness. "What time must we be there?"

The morning was sunny and unseasonably warm as Caroline, Tina and Eric paused before the Capitol at shortly before 9:00 A.M. Caroline remembered that Eric had told her the Atlanta Capitol was modeled on this structure. She felt an unexpected surge of pride as she viewed the gleaming, white-domed building invaded and burned by British troops in 1812 and rebuilt seven years later.

"Let's get in line," Eric urged. "There's a mob waiting at the doors already."

They found seats in the gallery. Caroline leaned forward avidly, mesmerized by the activity. The House met and wished to adjourn till noon, but the Senate refused to agree. The vituperative debate that ensued astonished Caroline. How rude these gentlemen could be to one another! Speaker of the House Reed was a tyrant.

Little seemed to be happening, yet no one relinquished a seat when the lunch hour arrived, though the gallery was stifling.

"If I don't go out to lunch immediately," Tina whispered, "I'll faint right here. Eric rushed us so at breakfast I hardly ate at all." She rose tentatively from her seat.

"I'll come with you." Admittedly the proceedings were painfully dull, but Caroline would have preferred to remain. "We'll come back later."

Caroline and Tina went to a restaurant for lunch, after which Tina insisted they go shopping on F Street. The heat was far more intense than she had anticipated, Tina complained. She must find something more comfortable to wear.

By the time Caroline could get Tina back to the Capitol, the House had recessed till 8:00 P.M. She suspected it would be far into the night before the votes were taken.

Caroline and Tina dined alone when Eric did not show up at their hotel suite. Tina was annoyed that there were no scintillating receptions for them to attend this evening, though Eric hinted that they were to be guests at several foreign embassy affairs within the next few days.

"I'm going to bed," Tina decided upon their return to the hotel. "I look just awful if I don't get enough rest."

Caroline sat on the sitting room sofa to read the *Washington Post*. She wished that she had returned to the Capitol, but it would have been unseemly to do this alone. Exhausted from the tensions of the day, she leaned back and closed her eyes. The newspaper dropped to the floor as she fell asleep.

"Caro—" Eric's voice was a gentle intrusion. She opened her eyes with a start.

"Did they vote on the resolution?"

"At three A.M.," Eric reported, and she realized how long she had slept. "The Senate vote was forty-two to thirty-five. Four more Senators on our side," he said in frustration, "and the resolution would not have passed the Senate. But the House passed it three hundred ten to six. It went through with an amendment for Cuban independence. We can be grateful for that."

"The President will sign it immediately, won't he?" Caroline felt cold. The nation would be at war.

"I should think within hours." Eric's eyes seemed to be memorizing her face.

"You'll go to Cuba soon." How would she survive if anything happened to Eric?

"The General would be happier if I joined a volunteer unit."

"It's enough that you're covering the war!" Her eyes betrayed her fears for him.

"Caro, I'll miss you—" He reached for her hand.

"Don't be foolhardy, Eric," she urged.

"Honey, I can't cover a war without being with the men who're fighting it," he reminded.

"This war is so wrong." Eric was going to a war and he had never even held her in his arms. *She loved him*. He was going away, maybe never to return. These minutes now might be all the time they would ever have alone together.

"You'll be going back to Atlanta in a day or two." His eyes told her he wanted to make love to her. "Caro, I've been silent too long. Ever since I walked into the parlor and saw you there that first night—"

"Eric, it's late." She pulled her hand away and rose to her feet, with an air of not having heard him. There could be nothing for Eric and her.

"Caro, wait." He leapt to his feet and pulled her close. She felt his heart pounding against her. Her instinct was to forget everything except being in Eric's arms. "Caro—you must listen to me—"

"Eric, no." Reason returned. She marshalled all her strength to push him from her. How could she harbor such wicked thoughts? And Tina sleeping no more than twenty feet from them! "Good-night, Eric," she said firmly, and walked into her bedroom.

She leaned against the closed door, trembling, aware of the thumping of her heart. There had been one instant there when—if Eric had swept her from her feet and carried her into his room—she would have forgotten everything except that she loved him.

How many women before her had felt this way, with their men about to go off to war? But Eric was not hers to love; she must never forget that. Tonight never happened. She would wash it from her memory. But she found it impossible to fall asleep again. She was too conscious that Eric lay in the bedroom across the narrow corridor from her own. Shortly after daylight she became aware of the sound of marching feet somewhere in the streets. Troops!

Immediately after breakfast Eric went off on a series of appointments. Tina seemed revitalized by the war spirit that swamped Washington. Caroline was recurrently astonished by the feeling of those about them that they were embarking on a glorious adventure. The city seemed almost festive.

246

Later in the morning word circulated through the city that the President had signed the resolution as expected. Eric returned to announce that his credentials would come through, though Roosevelt and Wood could not publicly announce their volunteer regiment until Congress passed a Volunteer Army Act, which would permit this.

There was no reason for Caroline and Tina to remain in Washington, yet Caroline was glad that Tina pressed for a few more days in the city. On the 22nd the Volunteer Army Act was passed, and the First Volunteer Cavalry, under the command of Leonard Wood—now elevated to Colonel—and Theodore Roosevelt, was recognized. Eric would be among the war correspondents following their activities.

That same day all Cuban ports were blockaded, and the gunboat *Nashville* captured the Spanish ship *Buena Ventura*, the first prize of the war. The following day President McKinley issued a call for 125,000 volunteers to fight in Cuba.

On April 24, Eric took Caroline and Tina across the river to the train that would carry them back to Atlanta. He was to remain in Washington until Roosevelt would head for San Antonio, where a camp was to be prepared to train the First Volunteer Cavalry.

"Why is the training camp to be in San Antonio?" Caroline asked bewilderedly. "It's so far from Cuba."

"San Antonio's in fine horse country," Eric explained. "It's near the Gulf, and we'll probably head for Cuba from some Gulf port."

"When do you suppose you'll be leaving for San Antonio?" Caroline was grateful for these few moments alone with Eric. Tina had discovered among the waiting passengers an older woman from South Carolina whom she knew slightly, and the two were discussing the Confederate Reunion to be held in Atlanta in July.

"Not too long," Eric said quietly. His eyes told her he would miss her. "The Colonel is impatient for action."

"Caroline, here comes the train," Tina said, and turned to the acquaintance from South Carolina. "My husband will be going to Cuba soon as a war correspondent."

"Eric, be careful," Caroline whispered, her eyes clinging to his. He was going as a war correspondent, but once in Cuba he would be in as much danger as any soldier. "Please."

"It won't last long," he soothed. "It can't."

"Eric, we have to board the train," Tina said with honeyed tones. Her eyes were moving oddly from Eric to Caroline, and Caroline forced herself to smile impersonally at Eric.

"Write to the General," she reminded. "He'll be anxious."

"I'll write," he promised. He would write to the General, Caroline interpreted, because he could not write to her. He leaned forward to kiss Tina lightly on one cheek, turned to kiss Caroline in a like manner; but the pressure of his hands at her shoulders, the ardor in his eyes when they fleetingly met hers, told her he loved her. "Have a good trip."

In moments Caroline and Tina were seated in their drawing room and Eric was striding off into the distance. Tina's slight secretive smile distressed Caroline. Did Tina suspect how she felt about Eric? It was *wrong*, she told herself. *She had no right*. But surely Tina knew there could never be anything between Eric and her.

Eric had wired Josiah of their arrival in Atlanta the following afternoon. Jason was waiting at the station with a carriage to drive them home. Tina was irritable after the long, boring train ride from Washington, refusing to be coaxed into a more pleasant frame of mind.

"I'm going straight to sleep," she said sulkily to Caroline when they approached the house. "I don't know if I'll come down for dinner."

"The General will be so disappointed," Caroline rebuked Tina softly. "We've been away ten days." She realized now that she was eager to see her grandfather. *She had missed him.*

Tina's air of irritability vanished.

"Caroline, you're always so considerate of everybody," she said affectionately. "Of course I'll come down to dinner. Grandpa will be full of questions about our trip."

At the house Seth greeted them with genuine warmth, yet Caroline felt a slight sadness in him.

"Seth, you seem unhappy," she probed. "Is something wrong?"

"Not exactly wrong, Miss Caroline," Seth said. "But I ain't feelin' too happy with Zeke goin' off to the Army."

"Zeke volunteered?" Caroline asked, cold with alarm.

"He went out and enlisted." Seth sighed. "I know I oughta be proud he's fightin' for his country, like the General says, but I worry, Miss Caroline."

"Is he with a Georgia company?" Tina seemed fascinated that Zeke had been drawn into the war.

"No, ma'am," Seth reproved gently. "Miss Tina, we knowed the Governor wasn't asking for black men when he called fo' volunteers. Zeke, he went out to enlist in the Tenth Cavalry out in Fort Assiniboine, Montana. That be one of the four black regiments that wuz started out in New Orleans after the War Between the States. They takes only the strongest and biggest men. Can't nobody shoot better than Zeke, and he rides like he was born on a horse," Seth said with pride. "He's hopin' he gets to Cuba." Pride gave way to anxiety. "The General, he right pleased that Zeke went out there. He give him the money for the train and a letter to the officer of the Tenth Cavalry. We expectin' they's lettin' him enlist."

"The war can't last long, Seth," Caroline soothed. "Mister Eric says it'll be over in a few weeks. The Spanish don't have a chance."

"It won't be over before Eric gets out there?" Tina asked with concern.

"We should pray that it is," Caroline said, unfamiliarly brusque. "Every day that it continues will cost more lives."

"Caroline, we have a moral obligation to the women and children of Cuba," Tina reproved.

Lucinda appeared at the top of the stairs, as Jason lumbered upward, burdened with luggage.

"Jason, you don't drag them bags on the stairs," she reprimanded. "Miss Tina, you come right upstairs and rest until dinnertime. Mist' Chad called three times already to see if you got home."

Caroline went up to her own room. Moments later Patience arrived to unpack for her.

"Seth say Mist' Eric stayin' up there in Washington," Patience said with none of her normal exuberance. "He goin' to Cuba, too?"

"He expects to." Caroline was aware that Patience had been crying. She was upset that Zeke had gone off to enlist with the Tenth Cavalry. "But the war can't last long, Patience. Mister Eric and Zeke will both be home soon."

"I'm scared, Miss Caroline," Patience acknowledged. "When men take guns in their hands, it means some of them gonna be killed. Ever'body acts like the war was jes' a big picnic," she said defensively. "It ain't right."

"I know, Patience." Their eyes met in mutual concern. "Let's hope it's over before Mister Eric or Zeke gets to Cuba."

Caroline went down early to dinner, amazed at her impatience to see the General and Sophie. She sat in the parlor, where Seth had laid a fire against a slight evening chill, her eyes drawn to the portrait of her grandmother. Would Louisa Hampton have wished for Hampton Court to belong to her husband, Caroline asked herself with fresh comprehension.

She leaned back in the wing chair, her mind focused on this probability. She had never before considered this. The deed entailed the house to her. Legally it should be hers. Yet the prospect of fighting her grandfather for Hampton Court was becoming repugnant to her.

During the General's lifetime, she could conceive of Hampton Court belonging to him, Caroline rationalized. But someday it must come to her. It was disconcerting to realize that the General expected Eric to inherit the plantation someday. She loved Eric, she acknowledged; but she would fight for Hampton Court.

"So you're home." Josiah's booming voice swung her about to face the doorway of the parlor. "Have you heard that war was formally declared today?"

"We heard nothing on the train." Caroline restrained her initial inclination to go to her grandfather and embrace him. Yet despite his impassive inspection of her, she sensed he was pleased that she was back from Washington.

"Eric's telegram said only that he would be traveling with the First Volunteer Cavalry and that Tina and you were arriving this afternoon. Tell me what happened in Washington," he commanded, sitting in a chair close to hers.

Caroline gave him a detailed account of happenings in the Capital. Josiah listened, nodding at intervals.

"Welcome home, Caroline." Sophie smiled affectionately from the doorway.

Caroline darted forward to kiss her.

"Eric sent his love," Caroline told Sophie. "He promises to write regularly."

"He'll be too busy to write," Josiah contradicted. "He has a war to cover."

"Andrew talked about joining a volunteer unit," Sophie reported. "We managed to talk him out of that. He's needed here at the mill."

Andrew would hate war, Caroline thought tenderly. He made this gesture out of respect to the General.

"I understand two of the cracker factories here in Atlanta are already preparing to switch over to making hardtack for the troops," Josiah said with satisfaction. "In two weeks the first detachment of Georgia volunteers should be leaving for the camp that's being set up at Griffin, on the State campgrounds. There'll be a hospital at Fort McPherson to care for the wounded." Suddenly his face was taut with recall. "This generation of soldiers won't encounter what we of the Confederacy endured." His voice deepened with anguish. "I remember the surgeons cutting off arms and legs and throwing them in a pile behind the shack where they operated. I remember the screams of the men because we had no morphine."

"Grandpa, how lovely to see you!" Tina swept into the parlor and leaned forward to kiss Josiah. "Isn't this exciting? We're at war!"

Chapter Twenty

E RIC made himself as inconspicuous as possible about
Roosevelt's offices, colorful now with evidence of his
affiliation with the newly formed First Volunteer Cavalry.
Offered the Colonelcy of the regiment, Roosevelt had arranged to
serve, instead, as Lieutenant Colonel under his close friend,
Army Surgeon Leonard Wood, whose military experience was far
more extensive than his own. Eric chuckled when he was told
that Colonel Wood had organized Georgia Tech's first football
team. At the time he was a lieutenant at Fort McPherson and had
enrolled at the college to play football.

Roosevelt's office was swamped by telegrams from men who
had known him and were eager to join up with the First Volunteer Cavalry. Graduates of Harvard, Yale, Princeton and Colum-
bia; cowboys and plainsmen; men who had served under
Roosevelt when he was Police Commissioner of New York City.
The fathers of many of these volunteers had served one side or the
other in the War Between the States.

After a long day in Roosevelt's offices, Eric went back to the
small room he now occupied at the Oxford Hotel. He was restless
for action, which he suspected would come shortly. He stretched
on his bed, too stimulated to sleep, though it was well past midnight. He reached to the night table for the letter he had received
from Caroline, who had been delegated the family letter writer.
He was disturbed that Zeke had enlisted.

His mind had a traitorous way of closing in on the image of
Caroline as he said good-bye to her at the station. How the devil
was he going to go back and live under the same roof with her,
feeling the way he did about her?

Women had been chasing after him as long as he could remember. He had taken his pleasure where he liked, making no commitments until he allowed himself to grow hot enough over Tina to be trapped into marriage. He was never in love with Tina. He had wanted frantically to sleep with her.

Caroline was unlike any girl he had ever known. He felt tender and solicitous and passionate toward her. Damn! In a fit of restlessness he rose from the bed. Go out for a walk. Maybe then he could sleep. He dressed and left the hotel.

"Extra! Extra *Post!*" The night-quiet streets seemed to explode with newsboys. "Extra *Post!* Extra *Post!*"

"Here!" Eric reached into his pocket for a coin, extended a hand for a newspaper.

Windows were opening along the street. People were calling to newsboys. Eric scanned the front page. Admiral Dewey had attacked the small Spanish fleet at Manila in the Philippines, which few Americans even knew existed. The Spaniards had gone down with their ships. The American fleet, the newspaper stated, was almost untouched. But a final sentence brought the war into painful perspective. *"The American fleet withdrew to the west side of the bay to land their wounded."*

Eric hung about Roosevelt's offices, impatient to go on to San Antonio, where Colonel Wood was training the First Volunteer Cavalry, which had been just dubbed the Rough Riders by a member of the press. At last he received approval to go out to San Antonio. Not until he was aboard the train did he realize he would pass through Atlanta. When the train pulled into the Atlanta depot the next afternoon, he sought out the conductor.

"How long will we be here?"

"Oh, about twenty-five minutes," the conductor gauged. "If you want to get out and stretch your legs, you got time."

"I'll do that." Eric sped down the aisle to the door.

He located a phone. He ought to call the mill first and talk to the General and Sophie, his mind exhorted. He thrust aside reason and phoned the house. Seth answered.

"I'm only in the city for a few minutes, Seth," he said gently. "I'm on my way to San Antonio. Has Zeke written to you?"

"Yessuh," Seth said somberly. "Patience read me the letter.

He's got hisself in the Tenth Cavalry."

"Seth, is anybody home?" he asked.

"Miss Caroline jes' came in," Seth told him, and he sighed with relief that he would not have to talk to Tina. "I'll call her, Mist' Eric."

Moments later Caroline's voice came over the phone.

"Eric, why didn't you write you'd be in Atlanta?" she scolded.

"I have to get right back on the train," he explained. "I just wanted to hear your voice."

"Are you on your way to San Antonio?" He could hear her effort to be casual.

"Yes." He hesitated. "I suppose I ought to try to reach the General and Sophie."

"You should, Eric," she urged.

"Caroline, I love you," he said softly, and hung up.

AT THE railroad station in San Antonio hung a sign announcing: "This Way to the Roosevelt Rough Rider Camp." Colonel Wood might be the commanding officer, but this was obviously Roosevelt's outfit. A small band, apparently capable of only one tune, blared "There'll Be a Hot Time in the Old Town Tonight," a popular new song, particularly apropos at the time.

Within a few days Colonel Roosevelt arrived from Washington. Everyone was impatient for orders to move out to Tampa, where half the regular Army and a few volunteer regiments had been stationed since war was declared. The Rough Riders were issued khaki-colored canvas suits trimmed in yellow, and broad-brimmed hats. The Army had decided that soldiers fighting in the tropics would require clothing of lighter material, such as the British had worn in India for over forty years. But material was hard to come by. Most of the American forces went into the tropics wearing woolen shirts and trousers.

At last, on the 29th of May, the Rough Riders received orders to embark for Tampa. From there they would sail for Cuba. Eric was relieved to be on the move. Too often here in San Antonio, as in Washington, his mind turned homeward to Caroline.

The whole regiment—one thousand strong—piled their

horses into seven trains. Eric traveled with the enlisted men in dirty, decrepit day-coaches. For four hot, humid days and nights they rode the trains.

They arrived in Tampa famished, their unappetizing rations exhausted en route. No one met them to tell them what they were to do, to show them to their camp. Eric's quick mind already formed accusative paragraphs for his next article to the Detroit *Weekly Advocate*. How like the War Department, Eric thought cynically, to bring a crack volunteer unit to Tampa and leave them stranded.

Camp was set up on a huge flat of sandy soil, devoid of trees except for pines and palmettos, with tents arranged in long streets. A bale of straw was issued to each four-man tent, to be divided and spread on a rubber poncho and then covered with a blanket.

The following day Eric left the camp, deciding to billet himself at the five-hundred-room Tampa Bay Hotel, built in 1889 by railroad tycoon Henry P. Plant. He stood before the huge Moorish structure with endless balconies and mosque-like windows, topped by a huge silver dome and thirteen silver minarets with crescent moons, and laughed. This in the midst of endless sand!

"Eric Hampton, what the devil are you doing in this Godforsaken hole?"

Eric swung about in delighted astonishment.

"Chuck!" He had known Chuck Greyson, a free-lance artist, in New York. "I'm with a Detroit magazine. How long have you been down here?"

"Ten days. Not a bad place if you keep to the hotel."

"Let me register and get something cold to drink." He inspected Chuck quizzically. "What the hell brought you into this war?"

"Glory," Chuck drawled. "I'm sending back sketches of the great American troops rescuing the downtrodden Cubans."

They walked across the broad verandah of the hotel into the airy interior. The public rooms abounded in statuary, flowers, potted palms and obsequious waiters. Correspondents from every prestigious newspaper in the country were billeted here, along with John Jacob Astor, now the Assistant Inspector General,

British military attachés, and a representative of the Kaiser. The atmosphere was electric.

Eric and Chuck collapsed into comfortable wicker chairs and waited for tall glasses of iced tea to be brought to them. Two hours later they went out to inspect the town. The population of 10,000 had been swelled by nearly 30,000 troops, transforming the normally small, neat town into wild confusion. Miles of railroad tracks were loaded with cars containing government supplies, for which no invoices appeared to be available and, hence, could not be unloaded. Eric was conscious of how the Rough Riders in their khaki-colored uniforms would stand out among the blue worn by most of the other soldiers.

"People here make cigars, of course," Chuck explained leisurely. "Except for the Cuban-Americans out in Ybor City who've given up making cigars to plot against the Spanish. Tampa has three banks, several general stores, one theater, a trolley line, and a single-track rail to Fort Tampa, nine miles away," he continued in mock tourist-guide fashion, "from which we'll have to embark."

"With all the troops here, why haven't temporary rail lines been laid?" Eric asked curiously. "They can put down miles of them in twenty-four hours."

"Eric, whoever is running this son-of-a-bitching war isn't long on organization," Chuck said bluntly. "But you'll find out soon enough. Come on, let's go over to Pendleton's news store and read the back numbers of the *Police Gazette*."

Alerted to problems, Eric left Chuck to head back to the Rough Riders' camp. The men were drilling. With the temperature at ninety-eight in the shade, everybody in the Tampa area sweltered.

Eric sought out the plainly harassed Colonel Roosevelt.

"Nobody has any definite information to give us," the Colonel related with frustration. "And what we've unearthed on our own account seems to be wrong. General Miles is here and General Shafter. Washington orders Shafter to embark, strangely figuring this can be done in a day or two. Nobody here has any experience handling a force of this size."

"When do you expect we'll be leaving?" Eric asked.

"Nobody knows. This is the worst confusion yet. It's a break-down of both the railroad and the military system of the country. But let me tell you," he summed up grimly, "when the expedition finally takes off, we're not going to be left behind!"

WORD CAME through that the regiments were to sail on June 8th at daybreak. The correspondents and artists were instructed to board the headquarters ship *Seguranca* at 2:00 A.M. Cagily Eric ignored the order and infiltrated the eight troops of the Rough Riders who were to sail to Cuba. On the night of June 7th the Rough Riders went to the track to meet the train that was to take them to the embarkation point at Fort Tampa. The train did not appear. At dawn Roosevelt commandeered a coal train to take the Rough Riders to the quay.

The mile-long wharf was packed with troops. Wood and Roosevelt sought out the Quartermaster General, who allotted them a ship and told them to take her immediately if they expected to keep her. Without bothering to ask permission, Wood borrowed a motorboat and took over the *Yucatan* and brought her in.

When the Second Infantry and the Seventy-First New York Volunteers, who had been earlier assigned to the ship, tried to take over, they were met at the gangplank by Roosevelt and a cluster of burly Rough Riders. Eric grinned as he watched the Colonel rebuff the Captain from the Seventy-First, despite the official papers the Captain carried. It was squatters' rights.

At last men and supplies were boarded. Enlisted men were moving out without their horses; only those of the officers were being transported to Cuba.

Just as the *Yucatan* was loaded, word came through that they were not to sail.

"What the hell goes on?" a cowboy from Texas demanded.

Knowing he would not be taken off ship at this point, Eric pushed his way through the men, packed shoulder-to-shoulder on the deck, until he found a lieutenant who filled him in. Washington had wired that they were to remain in Tampa Bay until further word.

The officers remained in their cabins except when inspecting the ship, so as to leave the overcrowded deck to the enlisted men. Day after day they remained in Tampa Bay under the semitropical summer sun, sleeping, playing cards, cursing the delay. The first enlisted men on board had been assigned bunks, four tiers high; most of the men slept on the decks, as best they could.

Their travel rations were meager. The men refused to eat the stringy, salt-free, tasteless, foul-smelling beef. The ship offered no cooking facilities. There was no ice and the water was hardly drinkable, though in the intense heat and winter-weight uniforms the men were perpetually thirsty. The water had been sealed for six weeks before sailing in casks used earlier for fish and kerosene. Only the crew had fresh water.

Eric watched uneasily as he saw some of the men grow depressed, lethargic. A few surreptitiously bathed morning and evening despite the danger from sharks. A few cases of malaria broke out. They were lucky there was no typhus. What kind of stupidity was keeping them hemmed up on this ship in this unbearable heat?

In the long, dragging night hours the men talked about their wives and their women, and Eric thought nostalgically about Caroline. Almost from her arrival in Atlanta he had known Caroline was special, the kind of woman he needed to make his life complete. He knew she loved him. Without her saying a word, he knew this.

"You know that song folks have been singin' this year?" one ebullient soldier demanded. " 'My gal is a high-born lady; she's black but not too shady.' When we land over there in Havana, I'm gonna find myself the sweetest, prettiest lil' thing in that city!"

On June 14th the orders came through to sail to Cuba. The *Yucatan* echoed with shouts of jubilation. Every man on board ship was at the rail to watch as the thirteen silver minarets of the Tampa Bay Hotel disappeared from view.

He alone seemed devoid of joy, Eric thought ruefully. His eyes swept the lighted up faces of the Rough Riders. Cowboys and college athletes, plainsmen and policemen. Irishmen, Italians,

Jews, Indians and Mexicans. How many of them would return from Cuba? How many would die on foreign soil in a war that never should have happened?

Chapter Twenty-one

ATLANTA was imprisoned in the grip of a heat wave that brought lethargy to a citizenry notably active for residents of a Southern state. Some of the very rich were leaving precipitately for Saratoga Springs. This summer Newport was considered too exposed to Spanish guns. The slightly less affluent were seeking comfort at resorts in White Sulphur Springs.

Despite the weather, the young society ladies who remained in Atlanta—and the not-so-young—were engaged in relief work on behalf of American soldiers. Two weeks ago word came through that the men of the Second Georgia Volunteers were not on the Army payroll as yet and would spend still another week without funds. The Atlanta Relief Association was organized.

Tina had accompanied her mother to the meeting this afternoon, but she had contrived not to be appointed to any of the committees. Now she was driving her mother home.

"Tina, you shouldn't drive so fast," Mrs. Kendrick remonstrated.

"Mama, I'm not driving fast," Tina laughed. "Barely eleven miles an hour." With Marshall last week she had reached twenty.

"But everybody comes to stare! And the horses get so frightened."

Tina drew to a stop before the Kendrick house and waited for her mother to alight. For all her mother's complaints, she had talked endlessly at the meeting this afternoon about "my daughter's loco-steamer."

"Aren't you coming in for a glass of iced tea?" Mrs. Kendrick asked as Tina remained seated.

"I promised to take Caroline to Inman Park to cool off," she fabricated, impatient to be on her way.

"Are you writing to Eric?" Mrs. Kendrick persisted, always dallying at moments of departure.

"Mama, I told you. Caroline does all the letter-writing for the family. You know how I hate to write letters."

"Where is Eric?" Mrs. Kendrick frowned.

"We had a letter yesterday from San Antonio. He was leaving for Cuba."

"You ought to write him," her mother said worriedly. "I don't like to see Caroline getting so thick with him."

"Mama, I'm Eric's wife. He can't ever forget that."

"When he gets back from this war, you make sure he remembers it," Mrs. Kendrick's tone was acerbic. Tina looked sharply at her. Had Chad told Mama about the General's offer of the house at Inman Park?

"Mama, I have to go. Tell Chad I'll phone him tonight."

Tina drove with a swiftness that would have terrified her mother until she arrived at the isolated suburban house of Marshall's absent friend. She had been meeting Marshall there twice a week for a month.

She left the car in the barn, lest it be noticed by a passerby, and walked into the house.

"Marshall?" she called tentatively from the foyer.

He strode into view at the head of the stairs, and pleasure stirred in her. He was a damnable handsome man.

"Come on up, Tina. Be sure you lock the door," he cautioned.

"I will." This was a rite with them.

She locked the door, conscious of his eyes following her every movement. She knew he was naked beneath that fine blue silk dressing gown he kept here at the house for their meetings. Now she slowly climbed the stairs. *He couldn't wait.*

"You're late," he reproached when she reached the landing. "I ought to beat the hell out of you."

"You wouldn't dare," she defied him, her eyes bright.

"I would dare," he shot back. But he never did. Sometimes she wished he would.

He pulled her to him and reached for her mouth while his

261

hands fondled her breasts. She relished this sense of power over him. What kind of lovemaking did he share with Dolly? she wondered contemptuously.

"Let's go into the bedroom," he said, an arm about her waist while he led her down the wide, carpeted hall. "Where were you this afternoon?"

"At the Capital City Club with Mama. There was a meeting of the Atlanta Relief Association." She lifted her eyes to his. "I don't suppose you feel like another donation?"

"Dolly thinks I ought to join a volunteer regiment." Suddenly he was serious.

"Why?" She stopped dead at the bedroom door.

"It would look good on my record," Marshall pointed out. " 'Captain Marshall Shepard served his country in Cuba.' I could wangle at least a captaincy."

"Are you going?" she demanded while he drew her into the bedroom. Eric should have volunteered instead of playing at being a war correspondent.

"I'm giving it consideration." He unfastened the dressing gown, pulled it off, and dropped it to the floor. "Would you like to see me in uniform?"

"I like you better this way," she laughed, her eyes inspecting him. Now she spun about so that he could undo the hooks of her frock.

When would the General persuade Eric to run for the City Council? When she told him she was carrying a baby? A house of her own in Inman Park, and in a few years a house in Washington as the Congressman's wife!

"Turn around," Marshall ordered.

She stood still, a secretive smile on her face while he methodically stripped away her clothes. She would see her husband in Washington before Dolly could do as much for Marshall. The General would see to that.

"We can't come here after today," Marshall told her, pulling her to the bed.

"Why not?" She lay back against the pillows while he sat at the edge of the bed, deliberately making her wait before he took her.

What kind of pleasure did he get from that? All he had to do was look at her naked and he was ready.

"Dolly's getting suspicious," he said with a wistful smile, lifting himself above her. "I can't gamble anymore." *He must have told her a dozen times that they could not see each other again because Dolly was growing suspicious.*

"I'll miss you," she reproached, desire beginning to spiral in her as he ran his hands over her breasts, down her narrow torso to her thighs.

"I mean it this time," he insisted. "I can't afford to take any chances now. I'm running for the Legislature."

"You'll miss this," she jibed, lying immobile while he hovered above her. What a silly game he played! Waiting until her impatience drove her to take the initiative. "Does Dolly make you feel this way?" Her hand shot forward to bring him to her. He grunted in approval. "Marshall, make love to me," she commanded.

She closed her eyes, lifting her hips to meet his as he thrust himself within her. Her hands tightened at his shoulders while her body moved with his. Dolly couldn't do to Marshall what she could do to him, she thought with triumph when the sounds of his passion echoed about the borrowed bedroom.

"Tina, you're marvelous." At last he lay limp above her.

Tina was conscious of a faint unease. Usually Marshall was meticulous about their not taking chances of her getting pregnant. Today he had been careless. Perhaps because he believed they would not be together again. He wanted today to be special.

Nothing was going to happen, she reassured herself. Not because of one time this way. Playfully she made an attempt to lift him from her.

"Let's go take a bath together." Her eyes were a candid invitation. Afterward he would make love to her again. This time they would be careful. "I'll run the tub. You bring us champagne." Marshall kept a bottle stashed here for their meetings.

Whistling, Marshall rose from the bed and strode naked from the room and downstairs for the champagne and glasses. Tina ran tepid water into the massive porcelain tub, reached for the bottle of bath oil she had left here on an earlier occasion. In moments the heady scent of roses filled the room. She lowered herself into the tub to wait for Marshall's return with the champagne. Eyes closed, moist mouth slightly parted, she rested her head against the back of the tub. She might have been Pompadour or DuBarry awaiting Louis XV. If she were not buried here in Atlanta, she might be loved by "Diamond Jim" Brady or the Prince of Wales.

"We can't stay much longer," Marshall interrupted her reverie from the doorway, with two glasses of champagne in tow. "Dolly and I are going out to dinner."

CAROLINE GAZED in concern at Noah as they stood in serious conversation at the door of his small store on Decatur Street.

"Noah, you must not consider volunteering," she insisted. "You can't walk out on your business."

"I feel bad that I'm doing nothing," he sighed. "Already three volunteer companies have gone from Georgia. I'm young and strong. People look at me and think, why is he not going to fight the Spanish?"

"The war can't last long, Noah." But Eric was en route to Cuba, and she was terrified for him.

"It would be my way of proving to Atlanta that I'm part of the city. As a Jew I feel I should go. Though in the South," he said with an ironic smile, "Jews are foreigners even when their fathers fought in the Confederate Army. Did you know, Caroline," he said with a touch of pride, "that forty Jews arrived at Savannah on the second ship on July 11, 1773? The first white male child born in Georgia was a Jew."

"And he was a foreigner," Caroline joshed sympathetically. "Noah, promise you'll do nothing so foolish as volunteering."

"You're right, of course," he capitulated with a touch of humor. "I owe too much money at the bank."

Caroline left the store and took the streetcar home. The weather was hot and humid. She was glad to be out of the heart of the city and, at last, off the streetcar. What was it like in Cuba? Had Eric's ship reached there yet? The troops were arriving at the most dreadful time of year when the fever was apt to be at its worst.

She clung to the memory of Eric's voice that afternoon when he called her from Union Depot. *"I love you, Caroline."* She cherished the memory, yet simultaneously she was furious with him for bringing their feelings for each other into the open. *He didn't have the right.*

Tina was sitting on the verandah, fanning herself peevishly when Caroline arrived at the house, tired from walking in the heat.

"This weather is awful," Tina complained. "And the General says we won't be going to Hampton Court until after the Reunion."

"England was never like this," Caroline admitted, lowering herself into a rocker beside Tina. She had not expected that they would go to Hampton Court with the Reunion scheduled for late July. Much of the General's conversation these evenings was about the Confederate Veterans' Reunion. He was obsessed by it.

"Here comes the carriage with the General and Sophie," Tina said with surprise. "They've closed the mill early."

Jason stopped before the house. Josiah and Sophie, both appearing drained from the heat, stepped down from the carriage.

"We shut down early today," Josiah said tersely. "We'll wreck the machinery keeping it rolling in this heat." Caroline suppressed a smile. He would not admit to a feeling of compassion for the workers.

Josiah and Sophie walked up the steps and sat beside Caroline and Tina. Seth came out onto the verandah with glasses of iced tea.

"I heard the carriage come up," Seth explained, dispensing the iced tea.

Josiah's eyes followed Seth into the house.

"He doesn't say a word, but he's scared to death for Zeke."

"Grandpa, Seth ought to be bursting with pride that Zeke was accepted by the Tenth Cavalry," Tina protested gaily, and began to chatter about the reception to be held at the house during the Reunion.

Her mind wandering from the inanity of Tina's conversation, Caroline interrupted this endless flow.

"I've been thinking about all the operations in the mill." Caroline leaned toward Sophie and her grandfather. "I'd like to learn them all. Not that I mean to work the machinery, but I want to understand each operation from the time the cotton is ginned and brought into the mill until it's shipped out." The General seemed galvanized with astonishment. "May I?"

"Talk to Andrew about it," Josiah said, his eyes opaque.

For the next few days Caroline spent long hours at the mill despite the heat, the noise, her physical exhaustion. Andrew assigned various workers to instruct her in the operation of whatever machinery it was possible for her to handle. He himself explained the mechanics of the more difficult operations.

Caroline was fascinated by the transformation of raw cotton into cloth. She amused Sophie each evening with a barrage of questions, though the General pointedly ignored this interest. Still, she strongly suspected that he was pleased.

"I've been wondering about something," Caroline began, one evening when Andrew had come to the house for dinner, and Tina laughed.

"Honey, you're always wondering about something. I never heard so many questions."

"What is it, Caroline?" Sophie asked with a glance of annoyance at Tina.

"Why do we ship all our goods to the North to be finished?" Caroline demanded. "Wouldn't it be less expensive to do that right here? We'd save the cost of shipping, and labor is higher up North—"

"It's easier this way," Sophie explained. "We have enough to do to bring the cotton this far."

"But it's wasteful!" Caroline declared.

"It's practical," Sophie insisted. "We can't do everything."

"I've thought for a long time about setting up a finishing plant here," Josiah admitted. Sophie stared at him. "She's right. It *is* wasteful."

"But, Josiah—" Sophie began impatiently and he interrupted her.

266

"Sophie, we know the salvation of the South is in our cotton mills. We've been slipshod and shortsighted in sending our goods up North."

"Josiah, it would cost so much to set up a finishing plant." Sophie's face was flushed.

"Andrew, what do you think?" Josiah challenged.

"I've long felt it would be advantageous to do our own finishing," Andrew said matter-of-factly.

"Then why the devil didn't you say so?" Josiah sputtered. "We have to sit here until a slip of a girl wakes us up!"

"Remember the demonstration at the Cotton States Exposition three years ago?" Andrew turned to Caroline. "Cotton was picked at sunrise, ginned and taken to the mill at seven A.M. The machines were ready to make the raw cotton into cloth and to dye it black and dry it. Tailors cut the cloth and made suits—and those suits were worn that same evening by Governor O'Ferrall of Virginia and Governor Coffin of Connecticut."

Josiah's eyes were bright with anticipation. "By God, we're going to do it! By 1900," he promised, "we'll be finishing everything right here at our own mill."

Josiah gazed at Caroline with a fresh awareness. With pride that she had challenged him, she decided. She had never felt so close to her grandfather. Her heart pounded in this realization.

"Grandpa," Tina shattered the poignant moment for Caroline, "do you think we should serve champagne at our reception? I do think champagne gives elegance to any social affair."

Chapter Twenty-two

ERIC was conscious of the feeling of excitement aboard the troop ship this morning of June 22nd. The order had been given to land. Like the others, he had discarded much of his belongings, keeping only his rubber poncho, canteen, food which he stuffed in his pockets, a six-shooter, and notebook and pencils.

All day yesterday they had followed the Cuban coast in view of the tall, barren mountains that seemed to rise precipitously from the shore. General Shafter had left the *Seguranca* in a Navy gig, along with Admiral Sampson, to meet with General García, leader of the rebel forces in Santiago province.

Eric knew that they were to come ashore at the village of Daiquirí, eighteen miles east of Santiago. It was defended, according to García's intelligence, by only three hundred Spanish; but no one knew what they would find ashore.

Eric's eyes searched the shoreline as the ships came to a standstill in preparation for the landing. Would they be attacked from the mountains, or would they meet the enemy on the beach? He wished frustratedly that he had dared to write Caroline an intensely personal letter—not meant for the eyes of the family—before they had left Tampa.

They were within a hundred yards of land now. Small boats were being lowered to take the men ashore. The Navy warships opened fire to cover them. The shells hit, uprooting trees, tossing rocks and earth into the sky. Eric could see the squat blockhouses high above the beach.

The waves were rough, making the progress of the boats

268

hazardous. The officers' horses and the mules were being shoved overboard to swim as best they could. When the smoke had cleared away, they discovered there were no Spanish soldiers in sight.

Like the others, Eric stripped to the waist under the hot sun to help unload the supplies, amid jubilant singing and bugle calls. He heard that the Tenth Cavalry was landing, but realized that it was impossible to search for Zeke in this melee. By mid-afternoon of the next day, when the Rough Riders received orders to head for Siboney, he learned that the Tenth Cavalry was already marching.

The road ahead of them was a hilly jungle trail, so narrow it was often necessary to march single file.

It was late at night when, exhausted, reeking of sweat in their heavy uniforms, they arrived at the wretched little railroad town of Siboney. Eric gazed apprehensively at the sky. A storm appeared imminent. He quickly joined the others in making fires to cook their pork and boil coffee. They had barely finished eating when a tropical downpour lashed the earth.

When the rain was over, the men relighted the fires and tried to dry their wet clothing. Eric knew that at sunrise they must start for Santiago. A force of Spaniards had dug in at Las Guasimas, about four miles ahead.

With feet still aching from the long march of the previous day, the Rough Riders began their advance at 6:00 A.M. The uphill pace was rough, the heat intolerable, their packs heavy. Eric pushed sternly ahead, conscious that men were dropping their packs. Some were falling out of line.

At the top of the hill they found some relief. Here was an exotic tropical forest. Magnificent royal palms, mango trees with foot-long, slender pointed leaves and tiny pink flowers, trees with dazzlingly scarlet blossoms. Varied-colored birds—some of them spectacular cardinals and tanagers—darted about the trees.

They marched for about an hour before they arrived at an opening near a fork in the road. All at once the air was heavy with the humming sound of Mauser bullets.

"Fill the magazines!" The order was passed along the lines.

They were being fired upon from both flanks at almost point-blank range. The Spanish were using smokeless powder and firing under cover of foliage.

"Get down!" Eric heard Roosevelt yell. "Get down!"

Eric stiffened in shock as he saw Sergeant Hamilton Fish, the grandson of the former Secretary of State, fall to the ground. Involuntarily he reached for a carbine dropped by another wounded soldier.

Now bullets flailed the Rough Riders from the Spanish defenses atop the hill. Eric, like the others, hugged the earth while trees around them were ripped to shreds. A man on the ground beside him rolled over with a faint groan. Eric leaned above him. The soldier was dead.

The word came through that they would charge. Eric was aghast. *They would be wiped out.* But retreat was hazardous. They were ambushed. A barbed-wire fence on one side, a precipice on the other. Carbine in hand, Eric moved ahead. A Rough Rider now.

All at once they heard the yell of reinforcements. Troops of the Tenth Cavalry were coming up behind them.

"Mist' Eric!" He turned around incredulously at the sound of Zeke's voice. "Mist' Eric, get down!" Zeke yelled in alarm.

Eric dropped. A burst of Mauser bullets zipped furiously into their midst, tearing up ground, ripping trees. A soldier beside Eric uttered one wild animal outcry and was silent. Of those still on their feet, several fell into inert heaps. Then, with startling suddenness, there was absolute quiet.

Eric cautiously lifted his head. Some of the men were crawling forward on their bellies. He lifted himself to a crouch. His eyes sought Zeke. Already the Spanish had resumed firing. All about him Rough Riders and soldiers of the Tenth Cavalry were slowly pushing forward. *Where was Zeke?*

Then Eric saw him, a few yards to the left. He lay motionless, his face in the dust. Eric scrambled to his feet and rushed to where Zeke lay. He put down the carbine and turned Zeke over. Blood oozed from a wound in Zeke's chest.

"Zeke," he said urgently. "Zeke!"

"I ain't doin' so good, Mist' Eric." Zeke managed a weak smile.

"I'm getting you out of here!"

Eric dropped to his haunches, struggling to lift Zeke's tall frame into his arms. Bullets were cutting down men on every side of them, but Eric charged toward a clump of underbrush. *How the hell was he going to get Zeke out of this ambush?*

"Mist' Eric," Zeke gasped. "Put me down. Lemme just lie down." He clenched his teeth to refrain from crying out in pain.

"Zeke, I'll get you to the field hospital." Gently Eric deposited Zeke on the ground. His eyes searched the area. Where was medical help?

"Mist' Eric, I ain't gonna make it." Eric had to lean over Zeke to hear him.

"You'll make it!" Eric stripped off his jacket, folded it and put it beneath Zeke's head. He was going to have to do something to stop that bleeding.

"You tell Grandpa I did what I could—" The words emerged between aborted grunts of pain. "He'll be right proud, like the General's proud of you."

"Zeke, don't try to talk," he ordered. "Save your strength." He was pulling off his shirt to use as a bandage.

"Mist' Eric, you tell Patience I—" His voice trailed off. His eyes gazed sightless at the Cuban sun.

"Zeke! Zeke!"

Despite the hellish heat Eric was suddenly cold. Zeke was dead. Twenty-four years old and he was dead. All around him lay the dead. Young Ham Fish with a brilliant future ahead of him. Zeke, who was convinced a new kind of freedom lay ahead for his race.

What the devil were they doing in this rotten hole shooting at men who were here because some American newspapers pushed their country into war? *Four Senators in Washington could have prevented this.*

With painful gentleness he closed Zeke's eyes. He removed the jacket he had placed beneath Zeke's head and put it on again. It was stained with blood. With one hand he touched the darkening stain. This was all of Zeke that would go home again.

The Rough Riders and the Tenth Cavalry pushed ahead through the undergrowth, yelling as though they had the whole

American Army at their rear while they fired and reloaded and fired again. Two and a half hours after it began, the Battle of Las Guasimas was over. The Spanish had been driven from their position on the mountain. Now it was time to help the wounded.

The doctors did what they could without supplies. The wounded would have to wait until they could be taken to the landing place, where Spanish houses along the beach would offer shelter. In the morning they would bury their dead. Already vultures were circulating overhead.

FOR THE next six days the troops camped along both sides of the Santiago road in a three-mile stretch of wagons, mules and tents. Eric was numb with the realization of Zeke's death. For two hours, while they advanced toward the Spanish, he had allowed himself to be swept into the savagery of war. *He had shot at men he had no real cause to kill.* For that he could not forgive himself.

How was he going to tell Seth that his grandson was dead? How was he going to tell Patience? Because of him, Eric agonized, Zeke was dead. Zeke had stayed on his feet to warn *him* to hit the dirt, when he should have done this himself.

With a new awareness of war, because only a fragment of the troops had faced an enemy before, the men stoically spent part of each day roaming about the forests for coconuts, mangos and plantains, as they were on half-rations and without tobacco, all the while dodging the packs of wild dogs and fighting off mosquitos. They bathed in the Aguadores River to find relief from the stifling heat. The engineers were laboring at long stretches each day to build bridges. The troops struggled to make the roads suitable for transporting supplies. And every evening it rained.

On June 30th the order at last came through to advance on Santiago. Eric stolidly remained with the Rough Riders as they marched through the jungle all day. That night they made camp in the open at highly elevated El Poso. About a mile and a half beyond rose a cluster of high ridges, known collectively as the San Juan Hills. Opposite was a ridge with a huge kettle for sugar refining at its summit, which was quickly dubbed Kettle Hill.

Early the following morning fire from the Spanish reached Eric's camp while they breakfasted on hardtack and cold water. When the firing ceased, the troops—and Eric was no longer a correspondent but a soldier—moved downhill on a slippery, muddy road through the jungle.

The Spanish began to throw volleys at them again. Shrapnel nicked the top of Eric's hat, missing his head by half an inch. He would take it home as a memento for the General, he thought with bitter amusement.

The Rough Riders were ordered to cross a small river ahead, then march along the stream until they connected with General Lawton. Roosevelt rushed them across the stream toward the right for a mile. Kettle Hill loomed ahead.

Mauser bullets were whistling through the trees and the high jungle grass. Eric, with a cluster of Rough Riders, lay behind a clump of bush. Roosevelt had sent back word for orders to attack. Eric was aware that man after man around him was being cut down by the Spanish fire. Damn it, they were sitting ducks!

At last the order came through to move forward. The Rough Riders were to support the Regulars as they fought to take the hills. The bugler sounded the charge. Yelling forcefully, the Rough Riders followed. It was a matter now of killing to survive, Eric reminded himself.

Pushing ahead with the Rough Riders, Eric saw the Ninth and Tenth Cavalries, the Third and Sixth joining the charge. They reached the summit of Kettle Hill with an ease that astonished everyone, to discover the Spanish had fled.

Eric was conscious of excitement as he watched the attack on San Juan Hill to their left. Despite the hundreds of miles between them he felt strangely close to the General. How many times in the long years of the War Between the States had the General been in this same position?

The American Gatlings came into the battle, moving closer and closer to San Juan Hill. The fire of the Spanish increased in frenzied intensity.

"Fire on the Spanish in the blockhouse and the surrounding trenches!" Roosevelt's orders were passed along to the Rough

Riders. Simultaneously they became the object of attack from the Spanish in another line of trenches.

On each side of Eric, men silently crumpled to the ground. Not bothering to reload his carbine, Eric reached instead for one that lay on the ground beside a fallen soldier. Damn them! Damn them!

He felt a sudden agonizing pain in his left shoulder. His eyes moved with an odd detachment to the blood that oozed through his jacket. But he lifted the carbine and fired again. All at once he was lightheaded. His legs were weak. He fought against losing consciousness.

Falling to the ground, Eric heard someone shout: "The Infantry's at the top of San Juan Hill! Hold your fire!"

ERIC REGAINED consciousness in a hill dressing station. Countless wounded lay around him. Many were unconscious or stoically silent. A few cried out in agony.

Eric lifted himself on one elbow. A bandage had been roughly applied to his wound. He doubted that it was serious, though the loss of blood had left him weak.

"Lie flat," an army surgeon ordered tersely, all at once hovering over him. "We'll move you to the field hospital in a while." He checked Eric's bandage. "You'll do till then."

Eric grinned.

"I'm too tough to kill."

Dazed and weak, running a high fever, Eric was placed in a wagon with other wounded. Soon they were en route via the tortuous Santiago road to the field hospital behind El Poso. In an open area of a wooded valley, surrounded by mountains and thick jungle, three large tents had been set up to serve as operating rooms. Half a dozen smaller ones plus a sprinkling of low shelter tents completed the facilities of the hospital.

There were no blankets, no pillows. The wounded lay in the tall grass on sodden ground or beneath clumps of bushes, which offered some relief from the blazing sun. Sometime during the night Eric was shifted to one of the larger tents. The surgeon removed the bullet in his shoulder. He could hear them cursing because of the lack of medical supplies, and remembered the General's pained reminiscences about similar situations in the earlier war.

At dawn, Eric's temperature dropped. He shivered from the chill of the early dew. But his mind was clear. He listened anxiously to reports of the fighting that came to the field hospital.

"The guerrillas were bad. They shot the doctors. Even the wounded on litters and the burying parties," Eric heard a newcomer report.

Beside Eric lay a member of the Twenty-Fourth Infantry.

"No more than twenty-five of us left to fight," the tall black sergeant said numbly when Eric questioned him about the hills.

At sunrise the Spanish again began fire. More wounded were brought to the field hospital in the course of the day. The word was that the fighting was becoming a siege. There were rumors of malaria and yellow fever breaking out among the troops.

Clara Barton arrived at the field hospital, bringing with her food and medical supplies. Morale leapt upward. Eric borrowed pencil and paper from one of the staff that had accompanied Miss Barton. He was determined that Seth would hear about Zeke's death from someone in the family.

He wrote the General, saying nothing about having been wounded, and asked that his report of the final few minutes of Zeke's young life be read to Seth and Patience. The next morning he entrusted the letter to a young infantryman being loaded on the ambulance wagon destined for Siboney. The letter would be on the next transport bound for home, the infantryman swore.

Eric refused to remain on his back. Shaky but ambulatory, he made himself useful to the hospital corps; but when he again began to run a fever, he was shipped to the Red Cross hospital at Siboney.

For three days he was barely aware of his surroundings, knowing only that he was being enveloped in cold, wet sheets, that strange faces hovered anxiously above him. And then, quite suddenly, in the chill of a Cuban night his temperature dropped, as it had in the field hospital.

In the darkness someone moved to where he lay. A nurse.

"What's happening with the war?" he asked.

"You're better," she said briskly, and told him that the Spanish fleet had been destroyed or beached by American warships and that General Shafter had demanded the surrender of Santiago. "But it appears that's not enough for Washington," the nurse said sarcastically. "Washington wants unconditional surrender."

"Will General Toral agree?" Eric asked skeptically.

"It appears he will," the nurse began, then stopped short at an urgent call from across the room.

"Katie, give me a hand!"

As the gray dawn seeped into the Red Cross hospital, Eric became aware of hunger. He struggled into a semi-sitting position, wary of his wounded shoulder.

"Would you like something to eat?" A small, pretty, flaming-haired nurse walked toward him. Kate, his mind attached the name. He recognized her by her voice from their earlier encounter in the night.

"Coffee?" He lifted one eyebrow with an air of skepticism.

"Coffee," she promised. "I'll bring it to you in a few minutes."

His eyes followed her. In some undefinable fashion she reminded him of Caroline. Her small figure, despite its air of fragility, was sensually arousing. Not that he was in any condition to exert himself, he mocked with wry humor.

Katie returned with his coffee and lingered to talk with him.

"I'm from Chicago," she told him in response to his inquiry. "But I was with the Red Cross in New York at the outbreak of hostilities." His eyes settled on the wedding ring on her left hand. "I'm married to a man with a hunger for travel. He's been in the Klondike for months."

"That's rough on you," Eric said sympathetically.

Katie shrugged.

"One day Adam will send for me."

"What brought you to Cuba?" Eric pursued.

"It's the United States' first involvement with war in my lifetime. I wanted to be a witness. Not that I see any glory in war." He started; she even thought like Caro. "I grew up hearing my grandmother talk about how upset she had been by the levity with which people in Chicago had looked upon the Civil War."

"My dear," he teased, "you mean the War Between the States.

But that attitude was the national response," he conceded with distaste. "Except for the men who were dying on the battlefields."

Katie was summoned and he was left alone to think about Caroline. He had not seen her since Washington. He had talked with her for only a few moments on the phone en route to San Antonio. How had she responded to his last words: *Caroline, I love you?*

Eric convalesced with a speed that amazed the doctors. In two days he was on his feet again, though the doctors made it clear he would not return to the troops. He insisted on helping the over-burdened medical corps in the hospital.

Siboney was a plague-ridden city now. A yellow fever camp was hastily set up. The hard-fighting Twenty-Fourth Infantry volunteered for duty. After lengthy negotiations, General Toral surrendered Santiago. But yellow fever, along with an especially virulent form of malaria, was striking hard in the army camps.

On the day of surrender, Katie asked for immediate transfer to the yellow fever camp. Eric sought her out when he learned of this.

"Katie, what's the matter with you?"

"Eric, I'm needed there."

"I'll ask to be sent with you." He could not bear the prospect of being separated from Katie. In an odd fashion she made him feel close to Caro.

"Eric, that's absurd!" she rejected. "You haven't recovered from your wound yet. Just because you're on your feet," she taunted, "you're not back to normal strength."

"I'm asking. I'm an 'immune'. I survived yellow fever as a child." It was a compulsion with him to be at Katie's elbow.

"They won't let you," she warned.

He grinned.

"Don't take any bets on that."

Eric went with Katie and three medical corpsmen to the yellow fever camp. Along with the others on duty there, he worked each day until he could no longer stay on his feet. He was amazed at the tenderness of the men of the Twenty-Fourth Infantry as they nursed the hordes of fever-stricken soldiers. He was amazed at Katie's strength, her fearlessness of contracting the fever.

Each death was a personal grief to Katie. At the end of their fifth day at the camp, when a young cavalryman died in her arms, Eric forcibly pulled her away from the camp and down to the beach.

"You'll kill yourself," he reproached, while they walked along the deserted strip of sand beneath a silvered sky.

"They're so young," Katie whispered. "Why do they have to die? He thought I was his mother. He said, 'Mama, hold me. Mama, don't let me die.' " All at once she was shivering, despite the warmth of the night. "Why, Eric? Why?" Her voice broke.

Eric stopped and pulled her close in comfort, as though she were a child.

"You've got to stop torturing yourself this way, Katie."

"If there's a God, why does He let this happen?" she demanded, lifting her face to his.

"Katie, you can't mourn for every soldier who dies."

"You're talking like Adam." Eric saw the sudden loneliness that engulfed her. "He used to say, 'Katie, a nurse has to be tough.' "

"Tough and tender. You're special, Katie." He lifted her face to his, kissed her lightly on the forehead.

Her arms tightened about his neck. They clung together in a silence disturbed only by the sound of the waves lapping at the shore. It was as though he were holding Caro, he thought, conscious of a frenzied stirring within him.

"Eric, love me," she whispered passionately. "Please, love me."

Eric brought her down to the sand, conscious only of her nearness, of his need. His mouth filled hers and her arms tightened about his shoulders.

"Eric, make me forget," she urged when he lifted his mouth from hers at last. "For a little while let there just be us."

"Katie, yes."

The moon hid behind a clump of clouds shrouding them in blackness. Eric's hands moved about her curvaceous small frame, while his mouth explored one small ear. All at once her hands were between them, unbuttoning her shirtwaist. His hands moved inside her chemise, fondling the velvet warmth of her breasts. He heard the swift intake of her breath.

278

"Eric, it's been such a long time." Her voice was rich with desire. "Damn Adam for leaving me alone all these months."

She allowed one hand to ease its way inside the waist of his trousers. The other stroked his thigh. All at once further preliminaries were painful for both. Katie helped him hoist her skirts above her hips, as he brought his mouth to the hollow between her breasts. She whimpered faintly as he found her and probed.

They moved as one, utterly absorbed in arriving together at the moment of ultimate climax. A small, low cry of pleasure escaped her.

"Oh, Caro, Caro," he murmured, and Katie laughed.

"I'm jealous," she chastised tenderly. "Who the devil is Caro?"

Chapter Twenty-three

ALTHOUGH the Confederate Veterans' Reunion would not officially open for two days, Atlanta was already in festive garb. From Union Depot to Grant Park and from the Exposition grounds to Fort McPherson the streets were colorful with miles of bunting, with the Stars and Stripes and Confederate emblems. Early this morning the veterans began to arrive at the depot.

Hospital trains came regularly to Atlanta, laden with soldiers sick with malaria and typhoid. In lesser numbers the wounded arrived at the Fort McPherson hospital. Like other Atlanta young ladies, Caroline visited the veterans two or three times each week.

This afternoon Caroline sat beside a wounded young veteran who talked grimly of the heated jungle fighting at Las Guasimas. She fought against tears because six days ago a dirtied, crumpled envelope bearing Eric's letter with the news of Zeke's death at Las Guasimas had arrived at Hampton house.

"I wish I could have lasted long enough to have been there at San Juan Hill," the young veteran said, his eyes bright with frustration. "That was something to talk about!"

Caroline left the hospital and returned to the house. Masking his grief, Seth was polishing furniture in the expansive, high-ceilinged double parlor, not in use since the Cotton States and International Exposition.

"The parlor looks beautiful," Caroline complimented.

"Thank you, Miss Caroline." Seth smiled, but the sadness in his eyes touched her. "The General be in the lib'ary if you want to stop and talk to him."

"Is he all right?" Caroline asked in alarm. He was never home at this hour.

"He's too excited about the Reunion even to stay at the mill," Seth said fondly. "He's been there in the lib'ary, walking back and forth for 'most an hour."

"I'll go to him," Caroline promised. The General was excited about the prospect of the Reunion; but he was worried, as she was, about Eric. They had heard nothing since the letter that told them of Zeke's death.

The door to the library was open. Caroline walked into the room. Josiah was at the desk, inspecting blueprints spread out before him.

"Will they break ground soon for the finishing plant?" she asked with lively interest.

"As soon as the Reunion is over," he reassured. "Where were you this afternoon?"

"I went to the hospital again. More wounded are arriving from Cuba. But I'm sure Eric is all right." She forced a cheerful smile.

"Of course," Josiah said brusquely. "He's in this war behind the lines with pencil and paper."

"Somehow I doubt that!" Today this disparagement angered her. "Eric is right there where the fighting is, in as much danger as any soldier!"

"They don't know what war is all about." Scowling, Josiah dismissed this. "The fighting in Cuba will be over before the summer is past."

"That's small consolation to Seth and all the other families who've lost sons and brothers and husbands!" Caroline shot back. "Until the Spanish surrender, we're losing men."

"You don't know what is was like in the War Between the States. For four years we fought! With terrible losses!" He leaned back in his chair, reliving with painful eloquence the terrible years that would forever remain with him. Caroline stood before him, listening with compassion. The Reunion was bringing both joy and anguish to him.

"I gave my two sons and my wife to that war!" Josiah's face was flushed with recall. He seemed unaware of her presence now. "I

281

lived through the shame of my oldest son's disgrace. How could Francis have deserted that way? He was a *Hampton!*"

"My father did not desert!" Caroline was white with rage. "When are you going to bury the War Between the States? You put pride and vanity above your love for your son. You doomed Papa to a life in exile!" Josiah was jolted from his reverie. He listened as though mesmerized while Caroline poured forth all her rage and hurt. "More than anything else in the world he longed to come home, and you kept him from doing that. He loved you. He loved his mother. And you kept him away. He died without ever coming home again." Her voice broke.

"Caroline—" His eyes glistened with painful comprehension. His armor crumbled. "I loved Francis more than life itself. I'm a stubborn, blind old man. Caroline, can you ever forgive me? Can I make you understand how much you've come to mean to me?"

"Grandpa, I love you," she whispered. Her face was radiant.

"My granddaughter." Josiah reached with trembling hands to draw her into his arms. "When the Reunion is over, we'll have a ball in this house. General Josiah Hampton will introduce his granddaughter to Atlanta. Francis gave me the finest gift in all the world, Caroline. Louisa and I live, in you."

By the next day Atlanta swarmed with veterans. Gray uniforms were splashed about the city. Every street was jammed, the street-cars packed to capacity. Every train that came into Union Depot disgorged fresh hordes. Wagonloads came in from neighboring counties. By night it was estimated that close to 23,000 visitors had already arrived. For Caroline and Josiah Hampton this was a special, personal celebration.

At dinner Tina prattled vivaciously about the various events honoring the sponsors and maids of honor, among whom she was numbered.

"Caroline, you'll go with Mama and me tomorrow afternoon to the meeting at the Capitol of the United Sons of Confederate Veterans. We'll be allowed to sit in the gallery. It's a shame that you won't be able to attend the formal opening of the Reunion tomorrow morning," Tina said with pretty apology.

"She'll attend," Josiah said, his eyes resting with overt pleasure on Caroline.

"But Grandpa, it's impossible," Tina reminded. "The only ladies present will be the sponsors and their maids of honor. And some of the Generals' wives," she added.

"Also, a general's granddaughter," Josiah decreed. Sophie's face was a blend of astonishment and pleasure as she gazed from Josiah to Caroline. She had prayed for this moment. Tina was disconcerted. "I'll make the arrangements, Caroline. You'll sit with me on the platform."

"Business might as well close down for the rest of the week," Sophie said humorously, but there was a tenderness in her eyes for the days gone past. "The entire city is turned over to the veterans."

"There isn't a hotel room to be had in Atlanta," Tina reported. "Chad told me that a thousand mattresses have been set up in the transportation building at Piedmont Park, to accommodate two thousand veterans. And the commissary is prepared to feed thirteen hundred at a sitting."

"We'll have at least a dozen billeted here in the house." Josiah's eyes glowed. "Men who fought with me when I was Major Hampton. And if need be, we'll set up tents on the grounds. This will be the greatest week Atlanta has ever seen! The largest Confederate Reunion ever!"

An hour later three slightly abashed, white-haired Confederate veterans in full uniform were admitted by Seth. Josiah charged into the foyer to welcome them. Caroline impulsively followed behind him.

"Gentlemen, my granddaughter." He introduced the sergeant and two corporals who had served with him thirty-four years ago. He had not seen two of them for thirty years. The sergeant he had seen regularly once a year at the earlier Reunions.

The younger of the two corporals, who might have been the General's son in age, wore one sleeve pinned up. Caroline was sure he had lost the arm in the War. Three days ago at the Fort McPherson hospital she had written a letter for a young lieutenant who had lost his right arm at the San Juan Hills.

"Major, you ain't changed one bit!" the older of the corporals said. "Excuse me, sir," he corrected himself with a grin. "General Hampton!"

"You must be hungry after your traveling," Caroline said. "I'll ask Seth to bring in supper to the dining room."

Beaming with pleasure, Josiah led the men to the dining room. Caroline knew they would sit there far into the night, reliving the terrible days of the battle for Atlanta. Tomorrow was the thirty-fourth anniversary of the Battle of Peachtree Creek.

Several times in the course of the evening Caroline, Tina, and Sophie—gathered in the parlor—heard the fresh arrivals. Tina retired early. Tomorrow she would be sitting on the platform in the auditorium at the Exposition grounds; she was determined to appear her most beautiful.

"You've made your peace with your grandfather," Sophie said gently when they were alone. "I've waited for this."

"He's a stubborn old man," Caroline said with mock reproach, "but I do love him."

"Eric will be pleased." Sophie's eyes were clouded. She too worried about him.

"We'll be hearing from him soon," Caroline told her.

"Why doesn't he write?" Sophie shook her head in anxiety. "It's not like Eric."

"He's upset about Zeke," Caroline reminded. "He's blaming himself for Zeke's death." *Was Eric all right?* If he were hurt, he would try to spare them.

"Let's go up to our rooms," Sophie said. "Tomorrow will be a busy day for you. And I'll be alone at the plant much of the day. Andrew will attend the meeting of the United Sons of Confederate Veterans. He feels he owes that to his father's memory." Her eyes rested on Caroline. "Caroline, Andrew's growing very fond of you."

"I dearly love Andrew." Caroline forced herself to meet Sophie's eyes. "He's been like an older brother to me."

CAROLINE WAS propelled through the throngs at the Exposition grounds of Piedmont Park by Josiah in full Confederate uniform, his head high, his eyes agleam with pride. By ten o'clock the heat was torpid, but no one seemed to notice. Every few feet they were stopped for a swift, joyous private reunion.

"We're on historic ground, Caroline," Josiah told her, his face somber. "Thirty-four years ago this was a battlefield."

Though the opening exercise was scheduled for 10:30 A.M., veterans had been arriving for hours. Josiah pushed Caroline into the huge auditorium and up the aisles toward the platform.

The auditorium was magnificently decorated, the flags of the Union blending with the Confederate flags. Banners had been erected to indicate the various delegations to the Reunion. Above the platform hung a life-size portrait of Jefferson Davis. To the right was a painting of General Lee on horseback and to the left a painting of General Stonewall Jackson. Caroline spied portraits of other soldiers and statesmen of the Confederacy on display about the walls. A surge of pride arose in her as she spied the portrait of her grandfather.

Tina was already seated along with a group of sponsors and maids of honor at the extreme rear of the platform. Caroline waved and took her place beside the General.

The audience good-humoredly waited for the exercises to begin. General Joe Wheeler arrived, fresh from Cuba, and cheers filled the air. It meant nothing that today he wore a blue uniform rather than the Confederate gray. There were more cheers for Fitzhugh Lee.

The band, stationed in a small balcony across from the platform, struck up "Dixie," and the gathering let out a rebel yell that drowned out the music. General Gordon arrived, and the building reverberated with shouts of welcome.

Caroline sat beside the General, enthralled with the proceedings, impressed by the demonstrations accorded the Confederate heroes. Mayor Collier was here, and Governor Atkinson. Every seat was taken, every inch of standing room. Thousands more remained outside.

"There're at least ten thousand inside here," Josiah whispered. "Atlanta is having the best attendance of any Reunion!"

Caroline leaned forward to absorb all that the speakers had to say, feeling herself truly part of Atlanta today. When a speaker talked of the July 20th thirty-four years earlier "when beleaguered by an overwhelming force, the boys in gray fought like demigods in Atlanta's defense," Josiah sat stiffly erect, his head high.

Caroline's throat tightened when Congressman Felder, formerly a Colonel of the Confederacy, talked about the war in Cuba, where Northerners served beneath former Confederate officers Wheeler and Lee. Governor Atkinson welcomed the veterans, then talked about Atlanta and other thriving Southern cities, denying their growth was due to Northern capital.

"Not a Northern dollar ever came South," the Governor declared, "until Southern genius had displayed its profits." And Josiah nodded in agreement.

The applause was tumultuous when battle-scarred General Gordon, Commander of the Confederate Veterans, rose to speak. He talked with an eloquence that brought tears to the eyes of many, about the return of the disarmed and disbanded Confederates to the blackened ruins of the South, where every home was in mourning, and then he spoke of the formation of the Association of Confederate Veterans in New Orleans in 1889.

"In what age or country have the shattered remnants of defeated armies banded together in a brotherhood so unique, a purpose so unselfish?" General Gordon demanded.

As General Gordon spoke, Caroline comprehended her grandfather's anxiety that the Confederacy not be misjudged by history, that history would respect the brave and patriotic men who had yielded to overwhelming numbers and resources. She felt Josiah Hampton's love, not only for the South but for the nation.

When the proceedings were over, hundreds of veterans made their way to the platform for a feast of handshaking. Caroline stood beside her grandfather, fighting tears, as he—like the other Confederate officers on the platform—was embraced by men with whom he had faced death. She was conscious of the empty sleeves, the empty trouser legs, and the black eye-patches among the hordes in the vast auditorium.

In the afternoon Caroline accompanied Tina and her mother

to the Capitol for the meeting of the United Sons of Confederate Veterans in the big Hall of Representatives. They sat together in the gallery, which was reserved for ladies. Caroline realized that Mrs. Kendrick had been ordered to be cordial to her on this occasion. The big hall was colorfully adorned, the audience enthusiastic and quick to cheer. But Caroline's thoughts wandered away from the meeting.

Santiago had surrendered, but the war was not over. The newspapers talked about much malaria among the troops, even an epidemic of yellow fever. Jim was confident the war would be over within a few weeks, but disease could be as bad as enemy guns. *When would Eric come home?*

Seth had opened the formal dining room because there were twenty at dinner tonight. Their guests talked ebulliently of visiting the Cyclorama out at Grant Park, crowded all day with veterans, of the hordes of people everywhere, the mobs on the streetcars. Some of them had gone out to Fort McPherson to talk with the soldiers back from Cuba.

"We've got to be at the Exposition grounds at nine A.M. tomorrow boys," Josiah finally halted the heavy stream of reminiscences about the dining table. His eyes wore a faraway glow. "The thirty-fourth anniversary of Manassas." He rose to his feet before more reminiscences could flower. "Let's call it a night."

Caroline made a point of coming downstairs to have breakfast with the General and his guests before they left for the Reunion. This afternoon he was to be host at a reception for the men of his regiment and invited Atlanta citizens. In the evening they were to attend a reception in honor of the sponsors and their maids of honor at the Confederate Auditorium in the Exposition park.

Caroline took charge of arranging the flowers for the afternoon reception. Tina remained secluded in her room; she would not emerge, Caroline surmised, until it was time to appear as the General's hostess. At intervals Tina sent Lucinda downstairs to inquire about some detail of the reception.

From three to five the Hampton house was thronged with callers. Caroline was suffused with happiness as Josiah made a point of introducing her to each new arrival. "My granddaughter,

Caroline Hampton, who has come from England to live with me." If anyone harbored resentment toward her father, none indicated it. Who would dare, Caroline thought humorously, when the General was obviously so happy in her presence.

A magnificent buffet had been prepared. Champagne flowed copiously. Tina was radiant as she moved among their guests in a brilliant green silk gown with an overskirt of white chiffon, made for her by Atlanta's finest ladies' tailor. About her throat she wore Louisa Hampton's emerald necklace. Caroline, lovely in sunlight yellow chiffon designed for her by the same tailor who made Tina's dress, was uneasy when Marshall and Dolly Shepard appeared; but Tina's behavior was exemplary.

"Atlanta has never seen a sight like this Reunion," Dolly said to Josiah, and Caroline laughed because Dolly had lived in the city only four years. "Do you know that the churches are opening their doors to provide sleeping quarters for the veterans? And folks with small homes have set up tents on their lawns. The newspapers are saying we have sixty thousand visitors!"

In the evening, Josiah and Andrew escorted Sophie and Caroline to the auditorium in the Exposition park for the grand official entertainment and reception in honor of the sponsors and their maids of honor. Caroline gloried in her grandfather's pride in her. At intervals Sophie beamed upon them. She, too, was happy in their private peace.

"You're more beautiful than any of those girls on the platform," Andrew whispered to Caroline as they settled themselves in their seats.

"Andrew, I adore your flattery," she said lightly, yet she was uncomfortable beneath the ardor she read in his eyes. How simple her life would be if she could allow herself to love Andrew.

On the platform sat the official sponsors who represented the various commonwealths of the Confederacy. In front of them were the camp sponsors and the maids of honor. The auditorium was filled to capacity; Andrew estimated there were 12,000 people present. The audience, vocally appreciative of the bevy of loveliness before them, received the program of song and speech with enthusiasm.

When at last they emerged from the auditorium, Caroline was disturbed at the overcast sky. Tomorrow afternoon was the crowning event of the Reunion, the parade of the Confederate Veterans and the Sons of the Confederate Veterans. The General was to ride with his regiment. The weather all week had been fine. Let it continue that way.

Josiah and Andrew escorted Sophie and Caroline through the throngs to where Jason waited with the carriage. Tina would be going with the other maids of honor to the Piedmont Driving Club, where the young lady sponsors and their maids of honor were to be entertained at an alfresco reception.

"Andrew, you'll take Sophie and Caroline to the parade tomorrow," Josiah ordered, his eyes aglow with anticipation. "It'll be a day that everyone will remember forever."

BY 4:00 P.M. the entire population of Atlanta and thousands of visitors—many of them veterans—were jamming the sidewalks, lined up ten deep at the curb for what promised to be the greatest parade the city had ever seen. The street vendors were moving along the parade route doing last-minute business in souvenirs and flags. The slight drizzle was no deterrent.

The formation for the parade was all but completed on the west side of Peachtree, between Ponce de Leon Avenue and Ellis Street. The Governor, the President of the Senate and the Speaker of the House of the General Assembly of Georgia, the Mayor and Council, officers of the UDC and other distinguished guests were taking their places on the review stand at Marietta Street.

In a dainty white organdy dress, Caroline waited at the curbside, protected from the drizzle by the umbrella Sophie held above them. Andrew stood at her other side.

"I hope the parade starts on time." Andrew glanced apprehensively at the sky. Dark clouds clustered together like witches over a boiling cauldron.

At last they heard the 5th Regiment strike up "Dixie." The parade was beginning. Excitement engulfed the hordes of watchers. The old rebel yell reverberated all along the parade route.

First came the mounted police, then the United Sons of Confederate Veterans as the escort.

"There's Chad!" Caroline said with astonishment. She had not expected him to participate.

All at once the cheers welled to a thunderous volume. The crowds along the earlier segment of the parade route were growing hoarse with approval.

"General Gordon must be approaching," Andrew told Caroline, a protective arm about her waist.

The hordes of people about them pushed forward as the commander-in-chief of the United Confederate Veterans appeared. Though weak and ill, the battle-scarred General rode a fine black horse with a pride and dignity that brought tears to the eyes of many onlookers.

General Gordon and his staff were followed by carriages containing such distinguished guests as Mrs. Davis and Winnie Davis, widow and daughter of the President of the Confederacy, General Gordon's wife and General Stonewall Jackson's widow. Behind them came General Stephen Lee and his staff, then General Lombard and staff followed by the Louisiana veterans.

General Clement A. Evans, commander of the Georgia division, accompanied by his staff, appeared. The voices of the crowd swelled in an ovation. Those in the parade and onlookers alike ignored the heavy rain that was developing. Caroline lifted herself on tiptoes, straining for sight of her grandfather.

"Here comes Josiah!" Sophie's voice deepened with excitement.

At the head of the column of Georgia veterans rode Colonel Waddell. Close behind, in the uniform of Lieutenant Colonel, which had been his rank at the Battle of Atlanta, rode Josiah Hampton. His back was ramrod stiff, his head high. He gave no indication that he was being drenched by the relentless downpour.

"Sophie, he's wonderful!" Caroline glowed. He was surely soaked to the skin. Rain streamed down his face. And Caroline knew he rode down these streets that thirty-four years ago today were a battlefield red with blood, and he was remembering his two sons who had died here. But none of his private anguish showed through.

"Josiah shouldn't be riding in this awful rain," Sophie worried. "But he'd rather die than miss this parade."

Caroline's eyes clung to her grandfather's erect figure as he rode past them. Never had she felt so close to him. Oblivious of the other veterans, she followed his progress down the parade route.

"The Georgians are receiving the loudest ovation," Sophie's voice was complacent. Many of them were in uniform. One entire company carried guns. Tattered flags, eloquent reminders of stormy battles, were carried high, evoking continuous cheers.

"There must be two thousand Georgia veterans marching," Andrew said with respect.

"Here come the carriages with their sponsors and maids of honor. Oh, there's Tina!" Caroline waved enthusiastically.

"Would you like to go home now?" Andrew asked when the Georgia section had passed. He knew that the umbrella Sophie held over Caroline and herself provided little protection against the downpour that was causing small rivulets to form in the streets.

"I would," Sophie admitted.

"Andrew, take Sophie home," Caroline urged. "I want to cut through to try and see Grandpa again." Without waiting for approval, ignoring her sodden shoes, her wet frock, Caroline pushed her way through the crowd, diminished now as onlookers fled for shelter. Breathless with exertion she thrust her way to a vantage point at Peachtree and Marietta, to wait for the Georgia segment to appear.

All at once a United States mail wagon drove across the parade line.

"That's the only thing save God Almighty that can stop this parade!" a spectator cried out exuberantly, and Caroline joined in the laughter. Only the U.S. Mail has the right of way anywhere in the nation.

Only when Caroline saw her grandfather again did she capitulate to the weather and seek her way to a streetcar that would take her home. At this point many spectators had fled for shelter. Some of the marchers had fallen out. But she knew that General Josiah Hampton would be there to the last, refusing to bow before the elements.

IN THE evening the General held open house for all the members of his regiment. Tina had left shortly before six to attend a grand reception being given by the Atlanta Chapter of the UDC at the Kimball House. Following the reception there was to be a cotillion in honor of the sponsors. Sophie devoted herself to the management of refreshments, which arrived in steady procession. Tonight Caroline was her grandfather's hostess.

Smiling, listening with respectful attention to the endless wartime stories told for her benefit, Caroline felt the General's eyes following her as she moved among their guests. If Eric were safely home, her happiness would have been complete.

Late in the evening Josiah began to cough. Sophie was watching him anxiously. Caroline, too, found her eyes seeking him out each time she heard the hacking cough that he had developed. Sophie was right; he should not have ridden in that awful downpour this afternoon.

When the last of the guests, except for those who were staying in the house, departed, Sophie ordered Josiah up to his room and instructed Seth to prepare a hot toddy and take it up to him.

"I was so proud of you when I saw you riding in that parade, letting nothing stop you," Caroline said when he bent to kiss her good-night at her bedroom door. "I wanted to shout to everybody, 'General Hampton is my grandfather!' "

"I was proud of you tonight. My beautiful granddaughter. My clever granddaughter," he acknowledged with a courtly bow. "But for you I would not have gone forward on the finishing plant."

Waking at intervals during the night, Caroline heard the heavy coughing from her grandfather's room. Semi-awake, she was conscious that Sophie had gone to Josiah. She heard Sophie consulting with Seth. Her instinct was to rise and go to her grandfather's room; but before she could bring herself to do this, she was asleep again.

Awaking at what she considered a scandalously late hour, she dressed with compulsive swiftness, impatient to question Sophie about Josiah's cough. He had always seemed indestructible to her. Last night he had appeared exhausted, older than his years.

Leaving her room she encountered Seth going downstairs with a barely touched breakfast tray.

"Seth, how's my grandfather this morning?" she asked.

"Cantankerous because Miss Sophie say he ain't goin' to the mill this mornin'," Seth confided. "She say if he don't stop coughin', she's gonna call the doctor. He don't wanna admit it but I know he's havin' chills."

Caroline went directly to Josiah's room and knocked at the door.

"Come in," Sophie called, and Caroline complied.

"How are you feeling?" Caroline asked Josiah.

"I'd feel a hell of a lot better if Sophie would stop fussing over me," he growled. "No reason I can't go to the mill this morning. And I have to go to the depot to see off the men."

"Josiah, you're not stirring from that bed," Sophie insisted. "Now try to get some sleep. Seth will bring up some hot soup and tea and lemon later."

Grumbling, Josiah settled himself against the pillows. His eyes were over-bright, his face flushed. Sophie urged Caroline to the door.

"Do you think it's more than a cough?" Caroline asked, while Sophie and she walked down the stairs.

"I'm sure he's running a fever," Sophie admitted, her face lined with worry. "I'm calling the doctor. Once Dr. Ashley's here, Josiah has to see him."

Within an hour Dr. Ashley had arrived and was examining Josiah. Sophie and Caroline waited in the library. The skies were overcast again, threatening a repetition of the previous day's downpour. Sophie stood at the window, staring outdoors, silent with apprehension. Caroline tried to tell herself they were being melodramatic in their alarm.

At last they heard a door open and close upstairs. Caroline

darted from the library, down the hall to the foyer. Sophie followed close behind.

"How is he?" Sophie's voice sounded almost harsh in her anxiety.

"I suspect he has pneumonia," Dr. Ashley said matter-of-factly, but his eyes betrayed his concern. "I'll arrange to have a nurse come to the house."

"Can't I take care of him?" Caroline offered. "I'll do whatever you say." Her heart pounded in alarm.

"He needs professional attention," Dr. Ashley said gently. "I'll send an experienced nurse."

"He's going to be all right?" Caroline asked, her voice uneven.

"He's a tough old man," Ashley said after a moment, "but there's no way of knowing how he'll handle this. I'll be back in a few hours."

"Josiah's never been sick a day in his life," Sophie said stubbornly. "He'll live to be ninety."

But Sophie was shaken, Caroline thought, and her own alarm soared. *Why did he insist on staying in the parade until the final moment?* She could hear Sophie's voice as they watched the Georgia segment of the parade. *"He shouldn't be riding in this awful rain, but he'd rather die than miss the parade."*

Chapter Twenty-four

THE Hamptons' houseguests, disturbed by the General's illness, had expressed their good wishes, their gratitude, and left for the depot. Within an hour of Dr. Ashley's departure from the house a tall, angular nurse arrived to take charge of the sickroom. She banished Caroline and gave orders that no one was to see the General until after the doctor's afternoon visit.

Sophie had gone off to the mill. Caroline realized that Sophie refused to allow herself to believe that the General might be seriously ill.

Tina at last emerged from her room. Somberly, Caroline informed her of Josiah's illness.

"He'll be all right," Tina said with confidence. "Grandpa's tough."

"Pneumonia can be treacherous for the old," Caroline reminded nervously.

"Honey, you're practically ready to bury Grandpa," Tina twitted, and Caroline winced. "He's going to be fine."

Anxious about Josiah, Sophie returned early from the mill, leaving Andrew in charge.

"We have trouble brewing at the mill," she told Caroline while they sat in the library over tea. Outside, a repetition of yesterday's rain lashed the earth. "Andrew suspects that Tom Coleman has been agitating among the weavers. They're the best paid in the South!"

Both Caroline and Sophie started at the sound of the doorbell.

"That's Dr. Ashley." Caroline was on her feet. She hurried

into the foyer, preceding Seth, and admitted Dr. Ashley.

"I never saw weather like this in Atlanta," the physician said, relinquishing his umbrella to Seth. "The streets are flooded. A lot of sewers are washed out. Union Depot is a disgrace."

"Not much of a farewell to our veterans," Sophie said.

"The nurse won't let us see my grandfather." Caroline's eyes clung to Dr. Ashley's. "Does that mean he's worse?"

"It means she wanted him to rest." He smiled. "The General's a fighter. Let's put the odds as much in his favor as we can."

But when Ashley came downstairs from Josiah's room a half hour later, Caroline sensed he was concerned.

"You can see him," the doctor said. "But as soon as he shows a sign of tiring, the nurse will send you out of the room. Do what she says."

"We will," Caroline promised.

"We're doing everything we can to make him comfortable," Dr. Ashley assured. "Pneumonia is hard on the very young and the old."

He was making an effort not to frighten them, yet he knew they must accept that this was serious. Carefully, in layman's language, he explained that the General's fever was high, that he admitted to chest pains. He was suffering from pneumonia.

Tina had been standing at the head of the stairs as they talked with Dr. Ashley. Now that he was gone, she joined them in the foyer.

"Shouldn't Grandpa be in the hospital?" Tina questioned.

"Everything's being done here at home. Josiah prefers to be here," Sophie told her.

"We ought to try to reach Eric," Caroline said.

"Caroline, he's covering the war," Tina rebuked. "It isn't over yet."

"We can't try to reach Eric," Sophie agreed. "Josiah would be furious with us."

"Let's go up and see Grandpa," Caroline said. Her mind was active. She was the General's closest kin. It was her feeling that Eric should be here. He would want to be here.

The three of them went up to Josiah's bedroom. By silent agreement they all pretended that he was suffering from nothing

296

more serious than a bad cough. Between bouts of coughing he talked about yesterday's parade.

"Did you see how General Gordon sat there, with his hat off, reviewing the parade until the last man had passed?" he demanded with relish. "Only the young ran for shelter from the rain," he said.

"The young and the bright," Sophie said with a touch of her old bluntness.

Josiah was indignant when the nurse dismissed them, but Caroline realized he was tired. She worried about the fever, which showed no indication of going down. But like Tina said, he was tough.

Despite the hazardous conditions of the streets, Caroline summoned Jason and instructed him to take her to Jim Russell's office. Jim listened with sympathetic attention to Caroline's report of Josiah's pneumonia.

"Sophie and Tina think we shouldn't try to reach Eric, but I want him to know, Jim," she said with resolution. "If—if anything happens, he'll want to be here."

"Eric's in Siboney," Jim told her. "I'm forwarding his articles to Detroit for him—that's how I know." He hesitated. "Eric was wounded at Kettle Hill."

Caroline paled.

"How bad was it?" *Eric was wounded and she knew nothing of it.*

"It was a shoulder wound," Jim soothed. "He's recovered already."

"Then he's on his way home?" Her eyes searched his. Her heart was pounding.

"No," Jim said. "He's helping with the sick in Siboney."

"The wounded?" Caroline tried to pinpoint.

Jim sighed.

"At first he was helping with the wounded. Now he's at the yellow fever camp." Caroline gasped in alarm. "He's immune," Jim explained quickly. "He's had the fever; he's not going to contract it again."

"How do we reach him, Jim?"

"There's a cable office in Siboney. I'll take care of contacting

297

him, Caroline. But it'll take close to a week for him to get home, even if he leaves the minute he receives the cable."

Caroline returned to the house. She geared herself to remain silent about the visit to Jim. Was Eric being truthful? Had he recovered from his wound, as he claimed? She would not be able to relax until she saw for herself that he was all right.

She said nothing to Sophie or Tina at dinner about Jim's cable to Eric. She would face that when he walked into the house. After dinner Tina returned to her room. Exhausted, Sophie fell asleep over her needlepoint as she sat with Caroline in the parlor.

Caroline went upstairs, hoping to be allowed to see her grandfather. Passing Tina's room, she could hear Tina in telephone conversation with Chad.

She knocked timorously at the General's door. The nurse pulled it open.

"You can sit with him for a little while," she said with unexpected gentleness. "But don't let him talk much. It only makes him cough."

"Caroline, I want to tell you something," the General said when the nurse left them alone. His breathing was labored.

"You mustn't talk," she objected tenderly. "Just let me sit here with you."

"No. I have to tell you," he insisted. "Hampton Court. It's yours. It would have been your father's if he had lived. Now it goes to you. You'll find the deed in the County Courthouse." She gazed uncertainly at him. "The Coweta County Courthouse," he stipulated.

"Don't talk now, Grandpa," she pleaded. Mr. Lonsdale had assumed Hampton Court was in Fulton County. *They had searched in the wrong courthouse.* Thank God that they had. Thank God the General would never know that she came here determined to fight him for her inheritance. "Rest, Grandpa. I'll stay here with you if you promise not to talk." He smiled faintly and pressed her hand.

For over an hour she sat beside Josiah, holding his hand. He dozed intermittently but clung to her hand in his. Finally the nurse firmly disengaged their hands and sent Caroline away.

"He'll sleep through the night," she soothed. "He's had medication."

Andrew spent most of Sunday at the house. Dr. Ashley came twice during the day. After his evening visit he admitted Josiah's condition was grave. They could stand by and hope he could fight the infection. Everything medically possible was being done.

Monday morning Sophie was too upset to go to the mill.

"Andrew will have to manage alone today," she said distractedly to Caroline.

"You were up all night," Caroline said gently. "I heard you going back and forth to Grandpa's room."

"I just wanted to see him." Sophie's face was drawn and pale. "I've been with him for over thirty years—"

"Go up to your room and get some sleep. If there's any change, I'll call you."

"I don't need to sleep."

"For Grandpa's sake you need to sleep," Caroline insisted. "Don't let him see you looking so exhausted."

"I'll go up for an hour," Sophie stipulated. "But I doubt if I'll sleep."

Two hours later Bart Menlow, a foreman at the mill, arrived at the house with a message for Sophie. Seth received no response when he knocked at Sophie's door. He sought out Caroline, found her in the library.

"A man came from the mill with a message for Miss Sophie," Seth told her. "I think Miss Sophie's sleepin'."

"I'll talk to him, Seth." She knew Bart Menlow. She disliked his crudeness, his way of staring at the young girls in the mill.

Bart lounged self-consciously in the foyer. His face brightened as Caroline approached. She ignored his brazen inspection.

"What is it, Bart?" she asked. "Miss Sophie is sleeping. You can give me the message."

"I don't know," he hedged, his eyes arrogant. "Mr. Andrew said I was to tell Miss Sophie."

"Tell me," Caroline ordered.

Bart hesitated, his eyes clashing with hers.

"The workers are walking out at the mill," he said sullenly. "We got a strike on our hands."

"Go back to the mill," she instructed. "Tell Mr. Andrew I'm coming to talk to them."

Caroline called Seth and asked him to order a carriage brought out before the house immediately. It would be faster than trudging through the mud that remained from Saturday's excessive rainfall. She waited on the verandah until Jason arrived and darted down the stairs and to the carriage.

"To the mill. Hurry, Jason."

As they approached the mill, abnormally quiet this morning, Caroline could see the workers gathered out front in small clusters, talking among themselves. Their faces were grim. At one side of the crowd a group of women were listening with fear in their eyes to a tall young woman.

"We have to be strong," the young woman was exhorting. "Remember Mrs. Pickering up in Massachusetts. We have to fight with our men to stay out until we've won!"

Some of the children, playing in glee at this unexpected respite from work, paused as they became aware of the carriage. The adult workers were eyeing her with suspicion. Most of the mill hands were out, she realized. No more than a handful remained at their machines.

"Wait here, Jason," Caroline ordered.

Heart pounding but head high, she pushed her way through the crowd to the short flight of stairs that led to the mill entrance. Her shoes were muddied, her skirts stained. She mounted the stairs and turned to lean against the railing, facing the workers in the glaring morning sun.

"I want to talk to you," she said loudly. "Please be quiet and let me speak." For an anguished moment she feared they would ignore her efforts, but then silence fell over the workers and their faces turned toward her. She took a deep breath. "My grandfather is very ill. He has pneumonia. With God's help he'll survive—"

"What about us?" a woman interrupted with anger. "How are we goin' to survive?"

"We can't live on the wages we get!" a man yelled from the rear of the crowd.

"It don't buy nothin' at the company store!" another voice shouted menacingly.

"Listen to me!" Caroline ordered, emboldened by her vow to avert a strike. "When my grandfather is well, he'll sit down with your committee. I promise you that. You must not walk out on him at a time like this!" Her eyes searched the crowd. "Tom Coleman!" she called out. "I'm asking you to form a workers' committee. My grandfather will sit down with you as soon as he has recovered. I swear to that." Her voice rang with a new air of authority. "There will be changes made. The time has come. But you must not walk out when my grandfather lies ill up there on the hill." She paused, breathless, while the workers muttered among themselves. *She must stop the strike.* "The General never locked you out," she reminded. "Not even during the awful years of the Depression. He's always kept the company store open to you when there was no work. No family in Hamptonville has ever been denied credit. Now the General needs you." Her face was a challenge to everyone who stood before her. *"Are you going to let him down?"*

The silence was heavy. The workers exchanged looks, debating within themselves. Her throat tight, Caroline waited for their decision. All at once Tom Coleman strode toward the stairs and mounted them. Caroline's eyes held his with mute gratitude. Then slowly, silently, the workers followed him back into the mill.

CAROLINE RETURNED to the house, relieved that the General was unaware of what had happened. In a little while he would have noticed the unfamiliar weekday stillness at the mill. Seth told her that Sophie was with Josiah. Caroline went immediately to his room. She winced at the sound of his dry, hacking cough as she opened the door.

"Dr. Ashley just left." Sophie made a stern effort to conceal her anxiety. "He says we're to keep Josiah from talking." She shook her head at him in mock reproach.

"You're looking better, Grandpa," Caroline lied. His face was flushed with the fever that refused to be lowered. His breathing was labored. She went to stand beside the bed. "You behave yourself." How worn he looked. She reached to take one of his hands in hers, felt the feeble pressure of his. His eyes focused fiercely on her, telling her he loved her.

In a few moments the nurse indicated they were to leave. Caroline followed Sophie from the room.

"Sophie—" She fought to keep her voice even. "What did Dr. Ashley say when he was here?"

"The same as before. We have to stand by and watch."

When would Eric arrive? Caroline asked herself in rising alarm. *He ought to be here.*

"Sophie, maybe we should bring in another doctor." Caroline was assaulted by a sense of helplessness. "We ought to do something to help him."

"Dr. Ashley is doing everything that can be done. He couldn't receive better care at the hospital. And I know he wants to be home."

One day blended into another as the family stood by at Josiah's bedside. Caroline prayed each night that Eric would arrive on the following day, though Jim reiterated that it would be the end of the week before Eric could possibly arrive.

Caroline moved in and out of her grandfather's room like a wraith. He seemed to watch for each of her appearances. She stayed until the nurse indicated she was to leave. Sophie, too, haunted his room. The General was waging a fierce campaign, but Caroline knew he was losing. Every sound before the house sent her to the window, hoping that Eric was arriving.

Late in the afternoon—exactly one week after Josiah rode in the parade—Dr. Ashley warned that the end was near. The nurse pulled a chair close to the bed so that Caroline could sit beside her grandfather. He reached a trembling hand to her.

"I thank Francis for giving me my granddaughter." His voice was a painful whisper.

"Grandpa, don't talk." She fought back tears. "Let me just sit here with you."

"I want to remind you," he insisted weakly. "It was the mills that were the South's salvation after the War. The mills will make

302

us great in the years to come. You've got my feeling for the mill."
He managed a triumphant smile. "You're a true Hampton,
Caroline."

She felt his hand go slack in hers. She heard the faint outcry
from Sophie as the doctor moved forward. Unconsciously
Caroline's eyes moved to the clock beside his bed. It was two
minutes past 5:00 P.M. She had found her grandfather, only to
lose him.

PART II

The Heritage

Chapter Twenty-five

ON this hot Friday afternoon the train moved with exasperating slowness through the busy Atlanta streets en route to the Union Depot. Eric rose to his feet and walked toward the exit, his eyes fastened to the passing panorama. A strip of bunting not yet removed reminded him that the Confederate Reunion took place a week ago.

He had been away little more than three months; it seemed three years. He had gone away knowing this would not be "a splendid little war"; time had proved him agonizingly correct.

The train chugged into the shed. Eric was the first to disembark. He pulled out his watch as he scanned the area for a hack. The train had come in almost an hour behind schedule because of a washout south of Atlanta. It was 5:07 P.M.

He had been shaken to hear that the General was down with pneumonia. Grandpa seemed indomitable, but Caroline would not have sent word if she had not been fearful of the outcome of his illness. His taut, sun-bronzed face relaxed as he visualized seeing Caroline again. God, the nights he had lain awake and thought about her.

He climbed into the hack that stopped before him and gave the driver the address. He settled back with wry realization that his appearance was necessarily disheveled. Two hours after he received the cable he was aboard a transport bound for Florida.

Arriving in Tampa he had learned that while he was aboard ship the Spanish government had asked for peace terms through the French Ambassador. Two days later the town of Ponce, the second largest city in Puerto Rico, had surrendered to General

307

Miles. The worst battle the American troops faced now was against yellow fever.

Eric leaned toward the window when the hack approached the house. Let Grandpa be well by now. He always swore he would live to be ninety. Eric reached for his wallet, impatient to be at the door of the house. Tonight he would sleep in a decent bed. He would soak in a bath till his skin was waterlogged.

He rang the doorbell, his heart pounding. After the months of heat and endless rain, of battles and disease and death, he was home.

The door opened. Seth stood there, his eyes infinitely sad.

"Mist' Eric—" He held out both hands and Eric grasped them. Later they would talk about Zeke. "Seth, is he—"

"He's gone, Eric." Pale but composed, Caroline stood on the stairway. "Just thirty minutes ago."

"That damn train!" Eric swore. "We had a washout." *The General was dead.* The words reverberated in his brain. "I should have been here!"

"Eric, you couldn't help the washout."

"I was on the first transport out after the cable arrived." How beautiful she looked; it took all his willpower not to draw her into his arms.

"Jim said you were wounded." Her eyes sought his, seeking confirmation that he was recovered.

"It was just a shoulder wound," he dismissed it. He turned to Seth. "Grandpa read you my letter about Zeke?"

"He read it to me, Mist' Eric." Seth's eyes reflected his grief.

"He saved my life, Seth. I held him in my arms those last few minutes of his life. He wanted you to be proud of him."

Tears spilled over onto Seth's cheeks.

"I'm proud enough to bust, Mist' Eric."

"Seth, would you please bring us iced tea in the library?" Caroline asked. "But, Eric, first go to Sophie. She's terribly upset."

"Eric!" Tina called from the head of the stairs. "Why couldn't you have come home earlier? Grandpa's dead!" Her voice rose to a hysterical pitch. "It was awful, seeing him try to hang on that way!"

"Go to your room and lie down, Tina," Eric ordered, and turned to Caroline. "Is Sophie in her room?"

"She's sitting with the General." Only now did Caroline's composure crumple. "Go to her, Eric." Her voice broke. "Eric, he's gone."

A LIGHT drizzle fell this morning as the caisson bearing Josiah Hampton's body and the two carriages transporting those closest to him approached Hampton Court. It had drizzled this way as the Confederate Veterans' parade left Ponce de Leon Circle, Caroline remembered.

In the first carriage rode the members of the family; behind them followed Seth, Annie Mae, Mattie, and the other family servants. The day before there had been an impressive, heavily attended public memorial service; another special service at the mill village church, conducted by Henry Roberts. Noah Kahn had closed his store for the day to be at the service with David.

The burial at Hampton Court was to be private. The service was to be conducted by the minister of the nearby country church, the same minister who had conducted the services for Louisa Hampton, and all those years earlier for her two sons. Reverend Jewett's first post had been the plantation church at Hampton Court, where he had arrived three years before the War Between the States.

"I should have returned in time," Eric said somberly when the entourage turned into the private driveway to the plantation. "I should have been with him."

"I thank God you're here with us today," Sophie comforted him. "I thank God that Caroline was with him at the end." Her red-rimmed eyes rested lovingly on Caroline. "He wanted her with him every moment that the nurse would allow it."

"He was magnificent in the parade." Caroline's face shone with recall. "I'll carry the memory of him astride that fine, black horse, ignoring the rain, so proud and erect, till the day I die."

The carriages pulled up before the family cemetery, where the plantation servants stood waiting, weeping softly. Seth and Jason held umbrellas over Caroline, Sophie and Tina while they gathered before the freshly dug grave. With deep affection, the minister began the service. Caroline fought back tears. Eric held an arm consolingly about Sophie. Tina dabbed at her eyes.

She must be grateful for the time she had with her grandfather, Caroline told herself, while she watched the simple pine coffin being lowered into the grave. She would carry the memory of that time forever in her heart.

Sophie insisted that Caroline, Eric and Tina remain at Hampton Court to avoid the heat wave that engulfed the city. Andrew and she would return in the morning because the mill required their presence. In the afternoon, according to instructions left by Josiah, Cyrus Madison was coming to Hampton Court to read the will.

Shortly before three, Madison arrived and asked that the family join him in the library. Though every window in the large, airy library was open, the room seemed an elegantly furnished steam-bath, with the afternoon sun beaming on that side of the house.

Drenched in perspiration, those closest to Josiah Hampton settled themselves in chairs about the room, as Madison unfolded the will. For the first time since the General's death, Caroline remembered his disclosure that Hampton Court was legally hers. Were the others aware of this?

Seth wheeled in a tiered tea cart bearing glasses of iced tea and a plate laden with pecan cookies. At a grateful nod from Caroline, who sat forward in the velvet chair lest her frock cling to the fabric, Seth began to serve.

Cyrus Madison cleared his throat and moved his eyes about the room.

"This is a will that the General drew up the opening day of the Reunion," he explained slowly. "It's legal," he emphasized with conviction. Why would they think otherwise, Caroline wondered? "He was in full control of his faculties at the time."

Carefully Madison began to read. There were bequests for the servants in the town house and at Hampton Court. Money was set aside for David Kahn's education. Caroline's eyes widened. The General had been David's secret benefactor. And she was sure, too, that the General had signed the notes that permitted Noah to open his store.

Small bequests were provided for mill employees with long service. Sophie and Andrew were each willed six percent of the fifty-five percent of the Hampton Mill stock owned by Josiah.

"To my adopted grandson Eric I leave a trust fund, which is to revert to the estate at his death." Cyrus took a deep breath before reading the substantial, though hardly luxurious, amount in the trust fund. Tina's color was suddenly high, her eyes bright with incredulity. "The remainder of my estate is willed to my grand-daughter Caroline, who already is the legal owner of Hampton Court, according to the deed filed in the Coweta County Court-house."

Caroline stared at Cyrus Madison, trying to assimilate what he had just divulged. Except for the bequests, the stock to Sophie and Andrew, and Eric's trust fund, the Hampton fortune was hers. A major portion of the mill stock was hers.

"I knew about this new will," Eric said quietly, and Tina swung her gaze to him, her mouth drawn tight in rage. "Mr. Madison explained to me that the General had drawn this up just before he took ill. He wished the bulk of his estate to go to his nearest kin. As always," Eric said with tenderness, "he was gener-ous to me."

"Nothing will change in our way of living," Caroline said quickly. "We're the General's family. Everything will be the same."

IN HER bedroom Tina screamed at Lucinda for not having ironed the dress she wished to wear to dinner.

"You're impossible, Lucinda!" She left her room and slammed the door behind her, strode to Eric's room.

Without bothering to knock, she opened the door and charged inside. Eric swung away from the window with a frown.

"Oh, you put on quite a show this afternoon," she said scath-ingly. "Do you know what you've done to us? You've lost us a fortune!"

"The General was generous to me," Eric said coldly.

"You should have inherited everything!" Her voice shook with fury. "You did this yourself, thwarting the old man at every turn!

We're going to be poor because of your stupidity!"

"Shut up, Tina. We'll have plenty to live on comfortably. Particularly with Caroline's insistence that things continue as they were," he reminded with ironic humor. "Excuse me. I want to go downstairs to talk to Seth."

Tina returned to her room and changed from the severe black she had worn all day. She sent Lucinda to order Jason to bring around the carriage. She was going to Atlanta.

"Miss Tina, we's gonna stay here till the heat lets up," Lucinda protested. "Whatcha goin' into the hot city for?"

"I'll be back. I have to go in to talk to Chad."

Tina instructed Jason to drive her to the Atlanta house and to stand by for the return trip. In the house, curiously silent today, she telephoned Chad.

"What the devil are you doing in the city?" Chad demanded.

"I have to talk to you, Chad." She was close to hysteria. "Right away."

"You're at the house?" Chad asked.

"Of course I'm at the house," she said impatiently.

"I'll be right there."

Tina paced about the library, waiting for Chad. At the sound of the doorbell she darted down the hall and across the foyer to admit him. The servants had not yet returned from Hampton Court.

"Let's go sit down in the library before you say a word," Chad stipulated.

"Chad, you're awful!" But she walked with him to the library and sat down. Chad settled himself opposite her. "Chad, the old man left almost everything to Caroline!" Her eyes blazed in recall.

"What did he leave to Eric?" Chad carefully refused to relinquish his calm.

"A trust fund," she said disdainfully, and named the figure.

"You won't be living in grand style," Chad conceded. "Unless you stay on at the house—"

"Caroline says everything is to go on as before," Tina conceded. "But how could the old man do that to Eric and me? He adored both of us."

"You didn't handle Caroline properly," Chad told her. "The prodigal granddaughter should have been shipped back to England months ago."

"It's too late now." Tina's voice was shrill. "And just now he has to die, when I'm so terribly upset."

"What are you upset about, Tina?" Chad asked with deceptive quietness. His eyes were watching her.

"Chad, I'm pregnant."

"You Goddam fool!"

"Is that all you can say?" she flared. "Chad, what'll I do?"

"Is it Marshall's baby?" he demanded. "It sure as hell can't be Eric's."

"Marshall's," she confirmed bitterly.

"Does he know?"

"I told him. He had the insolence to suggest that it wasn't his."

"Darling, he knows you," Chad chided.

"I haven't been near anybody except Marshall for four months!" she shrieked. "Chad, what am I going to do?"

"Shut up and let me try to figure this out." He squinted in thought. Tina's eyes clung to his face. "There's just one way," he said finally. "You've got to get Eric into your bed—"

"Chad, he hasn't touched me since we returned from Europe," she interrupted. "I've told you. He just ignores me."

"Darling, you'll manage it now," Chad promised, his smile cynical. "Eric's been down in Cuba without a woman for weeks. He's a passionate man. Seduce him."

"What good will that do? I'm two months gone already!"

"Nobody knows. They'll figure the baby is premature." He grinned. "It's amazing how many premature babies are born every year. Starve yourself to make sure the baby is small. Or," he paused significantly, "you can arrange not to have the baby. I can find someone."

Tina flinched.

"No. I'd be scared to death." In some vindictive fashion she wanted Marshall's baby. He would never have a child with Dolly.

"Then make sure Eric's in your bed tonight," Chad said smoothly. "He's upset about the old man's death. He's been without a woman all those weeks in Cuba. Don't fail, Tina.

You're running out of time."

"I screamed at him this afternoon. I'll apologize. Very sweetly." She was imagining herself in one of the filmy dressing gowns she had bought in Paris. Chad was right; Eric would find her impossible to resist after those weeks in the Cuban jungle. *He must believe this was his baby.*

Tina went directly back to Hampton Court and up to her room. Lucinda had laid out a black dress. She had bought it because black was so fashionable. Now it seemed she was in mourning for the General.

"Miss Tina, you gotta be down at the dinner table in a little bit," Lucinda scolded.

Lucinda was relieved that she was back. Did Lucinda guess she was pregnant? It was uncanny sometimes, how much Lucinda knew. Already—so quickly—she was aware of a faint swell in her belly. It was going to be awful, walking around looking like *that.* She wouldn't think about giving birth; she had heard too many terrible things. Why hadn't Marshall been careful that last time at his friend's house?

THE HEAT of the day had broken. A relieving breeze wafted into the parlor as they sat there after dinner. Sophie was talking about the Reconstruction years, when she first came to the mill to work for Josiah. Sophie was stupid, Tina thought arrogantly. She should have made sure the old man gave her all his stock in the mill.

Feigning tiredness from the exhausting day, Tina rose and excused herself. She ordered Lucinda to draw her a tepid bath, perfumed the water with exotic oil bought in Paris on her honeymoon.

"Lucinda, go downstairs and tell Seth I'd like a bottle of champagne chilled. Bring it up with two glasses when it's ready." Eric would not come up early, she surmised. He was so solicitous about Sophie's feelings.

Stepping into the bath, Tina touched her breasts with narcissistic pleasure. They were slightly fuller than normal. Was that because she was pregnant? Unexpectedly she felt a surge of passion as her long, slender fingers moved from her breasts to trace the faint swell of her belly. She was remembering that last afternoon with Marshall. Damn him, he had not touched her since. He had meant it about not seeing her again, except on social occasions where they met by accident.

She lowered herself into the tub and leaned back luxuriantly. Of all the men she had ever known, not one had truly excited her except for Marshall. They made her feel important and powerful, but they rarely brought her to passion. Marshall was like her. Ruthless. Demanding. Occasionally he was rough. Maybe that lent something special to their relationship.

She felt her body lose its tension. She enjoyed the pungent perfume that clung to her when she emerged from the water. Chad was right. She had little time. Eric must make love to her tonight. *He would.*

She pulled the white chiffon nightdress over her head, slid it into place about her lissome slenderness, and reached for the matching dressing gown. Her hair a dark cloud about her shoulders, her eyes brilliant, she inspected her reflection in the mirror above the exquisitely japanned commode. Early pregnancy had lent a slight, becoming voluptuousness to her.

Lucinda came into the room with a tray. Tina touched the bottle of champagne. Chilled sufficiently if Eric came up to his room shortly. The two stemmed glasses were from the fine glassware that was brought out on formal occasions.

"Get out, Lucinda." She reached for the tray and carried it to a table.

"Mist' Eric comin' up now," Lucinda whispered, then closed the door softly behind her.

Tina waited while Eric let himself into his bedroom and Sophie and Caroline retired to their rooms. Then, with a glass in each hand, the champagne bottle tucked precariously beneath one arm, she walked down the night-dark hall to Eric's room and tapped lightly with the toe of her slippered foot.

Eric opened the door. She moved lithely into his room with a wistful smile.

"Darling, I'm sorry I was so nasty this afternoon," she apologized. "I was upset and it was so dreadfully hot."

315

"It's all right, Tina." His face was cold.

"Have a glass of champagne with me and I'll go," she said softly. "I won't sleep if I think you're still angry with me."

"Tina, you don't give a damn about how I feel," he said callously, but his eyes lingered on the provocative thrust of her breasts beneath the diaphanous dressing gown, nipples taut in bas relief. Chad was right, Tina told herself with inner satisfaction. Eric had been long in the tropical jungles. "Pour me a glass of champagne and get out."

Tina put the glasses on the table by the window. Seth had uncorked the champagne so that it was ready to pour. She felt Eric's eyes on her as she filled each glass and turned to him. The last time he had made love to her was in Paris. The night before he caught her with that Hungarian diplomat in their hotel room. She had expected him to spend the evening at some reception given by the American Ambassador.

"You always like champagne, darling" she reminded, walking to him with the two glasses in hand.

"It's been a trying day." Warily he accepted a glass, sipped, his eyes averted from her now.

"Eric, don't be angry with me." She leaned toward him, one hand grazing his chest.

"Tina, drink your champagne and go." His eyes were cold as he drained his glass.

A faint smile touched her mouth. He might pretend to be disinterested, but his body was already betraying him. She took his glass, set it down on the table by the bed, finished her own champagne and turned to him again. Wordlessly she pulled off her dressing gown, dropped it to the floor, and walked to him.

"Were you terribly lonesome in Cuba?" she whispered, sliding her arms about his neck.

"Sometimes," he admitted, and pulled her arms away.

"Did you ever think of me in the jungle?" She reached a hand to caress his arm and he tensed.

"Never."

"Didn't you ever want a woman?" she challenged. He wanted one now. This minute.

"Often," he acknowledged.

316

"Eric, don't you want me? I want you. Terribly."

She drew his head toward her. Her mouth parted as it met his. Moments later he released her mouth.

"Take off that thing," he said, and began to strip.

She lifted the nightdress over her head, flexing her body seductively as she did so. With the white chiffon nightdress dropped across a chair, she moved to the bed and posed invitingly. It was working out exactly as Chad had predicted.

"You bitch!" Eric said hotly, lifting himself above her. "You rotten little bitch!"

Her arms reached to close in about his shoulders as he moved toward her. She felt so powerful, as though she owned the world, when he drove himself within her. Everything was going to be all right, she thought with satisfaction. Unexpectedly, she was aware of arousal. This was not a game anymore.

"Eric, again!" she demanded when he lay limp above her. "Please, Eric, again!"

Maybe she would lose the baby, she thought in the midst of their erotic lovemaking. *She hoped she would lose the baby.*

Finally he pulled himself away from her and rose to his feet.

"Go to your room, Tina."

"Eric, wasn't it good for you?" she pouted.

"Nothing's changed, Tina," he said with calculated brutality. "You're just a woman I took for the night."

Chapter Twenty-six

CAROLINE stood on the verandah at Hampton Court in the early morning fog and waved to Sophie and Andrew when they were settled in the carriage for the ride back to the city. The servants—except for Seth, Jason, and Lucinda—had returned to Atlanta last night. Seth would remain to manage the household at Hampton Court while the family was in residence during the hot weather. Lucinda remained to care for Tina. Sophie would come to Hampton Court again on Friday, to stay for the weekend.

Caroline watched the gleaming black carriage roll down the long private driveway. Sun was striving to break through the fog. She felt a fresh surge of grief as she stood alone in the morning silence. She was the mistress of Hampton Court, her long cherished dream; but she could not savor the pleasure with her grandfather dead. Let her be grateful for the weeks of closeness they shared, she exhorted herself.

Reluctant to go inside the house, she sat in a rocker and listened to the pleasing morning sounds. In a few days she must go into Atlanta and talk with Mr. Madison. She had acquired responsibilities with her inheritance. And she must remind Sophie of the promise she made in the General's name to the millworkers the day of the threatened strike. *She* must keep that promise now. The workers would understand a brief delay, but it must not be prolonged.

The next few days were strangely quiet in the imposing old house. She was grateful for Seth's presence, for Hallie, who remembered her father. Tina was constantly sleeping. Eric remained in his room much of each day, engrossed in writing the last of the articles he had been commissioned to do for the Detroit *Weekly Advocate*. He emerged at dinner, strained and withdrawn. With unnerving frequency, Caroline remembered his brief declaration to her on the telephone the day he paused in Atlanta en route to San Antonio. Had she imagined that?

Sophie came to Hampton Court on Friday afternoon, bringing the week's Atlanta newspapers with her. Caroline and Eric devoured their contents, anxious for news of Cuba and the Philippines.

Of the 4,200 sick American soldiers in Cuba, the newspapers reported, more than 3,000 of them had yellow fever. In the Philippines, five transports which had left San Francisco with General Merritt—who had been appointed Governor-General—had arrived with over 4,800 men, bringing the forces at Manila to nearly 11,000 men, with another 5,000 en route. General Merritt was entrenched within a thousand yards of the Spanish at Manila.

Caroline and Eric spent much of the weekend soberly discussing the war. Here was a subject she could discuss safely with Eric. Tina pouted because they stripped the war of all romanticism. Sophie barely heard them, Caroline guessed sympathetically. Sophie was mentally reliving the thirty years she had shared with the General.

On Sunday evening Eric went into Atlanta with Sophie. He would return the following evening. Caroline had restrained herself from talking about the mill situation with Sophie. Give Sophie a few more days to reconcile herself to the General's death, Caroline cautioned herself. She would be upset at having to cope with the workers at a time like this.

Monday was less oppressively hot than the previous days, due to an overcast sky and a welcome breeze from the Chattahoochee. Caroline took Eric's bicycle and rode about the acreage, pausing to talk with some of the tenant farmers who were picking corn. Toward the end of the month the cotton would be ready for first picking.

The tenant farmers expressed their condolences, yet she sensed a covert hostility on the part of some of them. Word had circulated that she was the new mistress of Hampton Court. They were concerned about the future operation of the plantation. She reassured them that Hampton Court would continue as it had under her grandfather's administration.

She asked directions to the fields rented to Cassius' family and bicycled there. Cassius sat on the front steps of the cottage, a sketch pad on his knee. He laid it aside and leapt to his feet at sight of her. He greeted her with delight.

"Miss Caroline, it's sure nice you take the trouble to come see what's happenin' to us. We listened to what Mist' Eric tol' us, and this year we put in peanuts 'steada cotton. They're comin' along real well. Come lemme show you."

Caroline left the bicycle against a tree and went with Cassius to inspect the rows of peanut plants in the family field.

"They grows in the ground," Cassius explained. "Underneath them green flower stalks. Mist' Eric say someday peanuts gonna make a lotta money for us."

Cassius walked back with her to where she had left the bicycle. Her eyes fastened on a pair of cotton curtains that graced one window.

"Cassius, did you paint the butterflies on those curtains?"

"Yes'm." He was suddenly shy. "I done it for my Mama's birthday las' month."

"When the finishing plant is operating at Hamptonville," Caroline promised, "we'll have you help us with our designs."

Cassius' face lighted up.

"Miss Caroline, I'd be the proudest man anywhere in this country!"

By the time Caroline returned to the house, Eric had arrived from Atlanta. Her eyes brightened as she listened to the sound of his typing up in his room. She felt so alone with both Sophie and him away. Tina was remaining most of each day in her room, complaining about exhaustion from the heat.

Tonight, again, Lucinda came downstairs to say that Tina was taking her dinner on a tray in her room. Caroline was simultaneously elated and fearful at the prospect of being alone with Eric.

"Was it terribly hot in Atlanta?" she asked Eric when they sat down to dinner.

"Like an oven. I couldn't wait to get back out here. At least the evenings are comfortable." His eyes were disconcertingly amorous.

"How's Jim doing with the new magazine?" She pretended to be involved in cutting the succulent roast beef Seth had served them.

"He's about ready to give up as a publisher," Eric told her. "His backers are reneging."

"But the magazine is fine," she protested in shock, knife and fork inactive in her hands. "It has a real purpose."

"It takes time and backing to establish a magazine," Eric said flatly. "Jim's running out of money."

"Eric, I don't truly know my financial situation." Color touched her cheekbones. She knew that everyone had expected Eric to inherit. "But couldn't I do something to help Jim keep the magazine running?"

"No, Caro," Eric said, and she stared at him in consternation. "It would be a waste," he explained. "Jim knows this. The Reform movement is dead for now. It'll surface again, but we can't know when. The magazine as Jim conceived it is doomed."

Caroline and Eric lingered at the table. It was impossible to sit on the verandah with the mosquitoes out in armies every evening, though the outdoor coolness would have been welcome. They could hear Tina screaming at Lucinda upstairs.

"That fish was awful!" she shrieked. "It's made me sick. You go downstairs and tell Seth!"

The fish was perfect, Caroline thought with silent reproach. If Tina were feeling ill, it was probably from the heat.

"I must go up and see if I can do something for Tina." Caroline rose from the table. "Good-night, Eric."

"Good-night, Caro." His eyes held hers, telling her he loved her. Trembling, she hurried from the room and up the stairs.

She paused at Tina's door and knocked. Lucinda opened it slightly.

"Lucinda, can I bring up something for Miss Tina?"

"She sick to her stomach," Lucinda said stoically, and Caroline heard Tina being violently ill inside. "You better go, Miss Caroline." She closed the door.

Caroline went downstairs, sought out Seth and asked for a

bowl of cracked ice. Perhaps she ought to send for the doctor, Caroline considered anxiously. With the bowl of ice, she returned to Tina's room and knocked again.

"I've brought some ice for Miss Tina," she called.

Lucinda opened the door and accepted the bowl.

"Thank you, ma'am." Lucinda was faintly sullen.

"Ask Miss Tina if I should send for the doctor," Caroline instructed.

"No!" Tina shrieked. "I don't want a doctor! Just go away and leave me alone."

ON THURSDAY Caroline had Jason drive her into Atlanta early in the morning before the sun reached its full intensity. She arrived at Cyrus Madison's office in the eight-story Equitable Building at Pryor Street and Edgewood Avenue as he himself arrived.

"How good to see you, Caroline," he welcomed her affectionately, but she sensed his curiosity at her appearance. "You're not remaining at the plantation for August?"

"I came in for the day," she explained. "I'd like to talk to you about what my inheritance entails." Caroline forced a deferential smile, but she was determined to be realistic.

"Of course, Caroline." He was startled at her request. "Come into the office and I'll try to be as clear as possible."

Cyrus Madison gestured her into a comfortable armchair before his desk, settled himself with an air of unease.

"Your grandfather's estate was quite extensive, Caroline," he began indulgently. "There're his shares in the mill, the house in Atlanta, the plantation, various stocks and bonds. You're a very wealthy young lady."

"It's a grave responsibility," Caroline said quietly. "I'd like to know in detail about the rentals to the farmers at Hampton Court. I'd like to know about the costs of building the finishing plant and how we're to pay for it—"

"Caroline, you don't need to worry your lovely head about such matters," Madison chuckled. "I'll handle everything for you. A gently reared young lady could hardly understand the financial workings of the plantation and the mill, as well as of your grandfather's other holdings. He was a director in several other mills, where he held stock and—"

"Mr. Madison," Caroline interrupted zealously, "my father taught me mathematics from the time I was five until he died. My mother continued this. When I was fourteen, she taught French to the son of a college mathematics professor in return for his teaching me calculus. I'll be able to understand."

Madison gazed keenly at her.

"The General told me you were an unusual young lady. I thought he was being a fatuous grandfather," he admitted humorously. "I'll go over all his holdings with you. If you have any questions, fire away."

An hour and a half later Caroline left Cyrus Madison's office. Financial arrangements had been set up for handling expenses of the house. As Josiah Hampton had done, she would cash a check each week to cover the expenses at the Atlanta house and Hampton Court and turn this over to Sophie for distribution. Mr. Madison would present quarterly figures on dividend and deposit checks to the various accounts Josiah had set up and which would now be legally transferred to her name with the filing of the will.

In two or three months, when Sophie was less distraught about the General's death, she would sit down with her and go over the mill figures. Mr. Madison had already shown her the plantation books. The rents that came in each year covered the expenses of maintaining the plantation; there was a small annual profit. Her grandfather's wealth came from mill stocks, bonds, and— largely—from profits earned at the Hampton Mill.

Caroline settled herself in the carriage. Impulsively she gave Jason instructions to take her to Decatur Street. She would stop off for a few minutes to visit with Noah Kahn.

"I'm going to New York tomorrow," he told her proudly. "To buy for the store."

"Then David will be all alone?" She knew that the Boltons were all at White Sulphur Springs for the hot months.

"He'll manage," Noah said philosophically. "I'll be away only a week."

"Tell David he's to stay at Hampton Court while you're away. Jason will come to the Bolton house tomorrow afternoon to pick him up."

"You're sure it'll be all right with the family?" Noah asked, but his face glowed at the prospect of David's being at Hampton Court in his absence.

"Of course," Caroline assured him with warmth. She could extend this invitation. Hampton Court was hers. "Tell David to be ready at four. Jason will pick him up at the Bolton house and then go to the mill for Miss Sophie. She comes out every Friday afternoon."

"It would be good to know he's with you," Noah acknowledged. "Thank you, Caroline."

In the carriage, Caroline sent Jason for a newspaper. When he returned, she told him to take her to the mill. Eagerly she read the newspaper headlines. Yesterday the Spanish government had accepted peace terms. The war was over.

At the mill Caroline walked into Sophie's office. She said nothing about her visit to Cyrus Madison. She told Sophie she wanted to come into the mill on a full-time basis in September.

"I want to learn everything about the business, Sophie. Not just the operation of the equipment, but the management and the selling."

"Josiah would be pleased at that," Sophie smiled, yet Caroline sensed her ambivalence. "When the weather is more bearable." Sophie dabbed at her forehead with her handkerchief. "Sometime in October," she stressed.

Caroline suppressed her impatience. She would return to Atlanta early in September. *Then* she would convince Sophie that she wished to come into the mill on a full-time basis immediately. She took a deep breath and geared herself for what must be said before she took her departure.

"Sophie, I made a promise to the workers that day when they were about to strike," she reminded. "I told them that the General would sit down with a committee they were forming and discuss their grievances."

"Caroline, I wish to God that was possible." Sophie's face was anguished.

"We have to do that for him, Sophie," Caroline pursued. "I made a promise in his name."

"There's no time," Sophie dismissed this. "We're running behind schedule on orders."

"Sophie, the three of us—Andrew, you and I—must sit down with their committee. Talk to Tom Coleman." Sophie's mouth tightened in distaste. "Arrange a definite meeting. I'll come into Atlanta."

"I'll speak with Coleman," Sophie capitulated. "But we can't sit down to a meeting this week. I'll set a time."

"I've invited David Kahn to spend a week at the plantation," Caroline told Sophie. "Noah is going to New York to buy for his store. David would have been all alone in the Bolton house. You don't mind, do you?"

"Why should I mind?" Sophie countered.

"Jason will pick you up at four-thirty. That's late enough for you to stay on Friday," she insisted tenderly.

"Be sure you talk to Andrew for a few minutes before you go back," Sophie ordered. "He would be disappointed if you left without seeing him."

"I'll look for him," Caroline promised.

CAROLINE SAT at the dinner table on Friday evening with gratitude for David's presence. His lively conversation was alleviating the sense of loss she felt each time she sat at the table and realized the General would never again be with them. Tina had come down to dinner for the first time in a week. She was unfamiliarly silent. Sophie seemed exhausted, distracted.

After dinner, Eric invited David for a walk along the river.

"Honey, you'll be eaten alive by the mosquitoes," Tina protested.

"We'll survive," Eric said coolly. "Come along, David."

Caroline moved to the parlor with Sophie and Tina. The curtains at the window fluttered in the welcome breeze from the river. She would have loved to walk with Eric and David, she thought wistfully, even with the battle against the mosquitoes.

"How long is that boy going to stay here, Caroline?" Tina asked curiously.

"Just a week," Caroline told her.

"It was so sweet of you to invite him." Tina abandoned her taciturnity. "He's probably never seen the inside of a house like this."

"He lives with the Boltons," Caroline reminded.

"I had forgotten," Tina apologized. "You told me how he's absolutely brilliant. Wasn't it wonderful of the General to leave money for his college education?"

Tina was going to chatter all evening, Caroline thought tiredly. Tonight she found it straining to listen to Tina's inane conversation. Sophie made no pretense of listening.

"Tina, why don't we go into the music room and have you play for us?" Caroline urged ingratiatingly.

"Why, honey, of course," Tina accepted with a gratified smile.

Eric and David returned from their walk while Tina continued to play. Caroline could hear them talking in the foyer. They were going directly upstairs to their bedrooms.

David was enchanted with life at Hampton Court, eager to explore the vast acreage. He sat down at mealtime with vivid reports of what he had seen. Tina seemed irritated by his presence, Caroline realized with silent reproach.

Sophie returned to Atlanta on Sunday evening. Caroline suspected she was relieved to return to the demands of the mill. On Monday Caroline slept late. Looking from her window at the gray, foreboding day, she spied David striding off into the woods. She was glad she had invited him to Hampton Court.

After breakfast Caroline settled herself on the verandah and tried to focus on the book she had chosen from the library. Unconsciously she listened for sounds of Eric's typewriter. After the weeks of worrying about him in the Cuban jungle, it was reassuring to hear him working. There were no sounds this morning.

After a half hour of desultory reading, Caroline abandoned the attempt. She leaned back and closed her eyes. In moments she was dozing.

"Caroline!" She awoke with a start. "Caroline!" David was charging frantically toward the verandah.

"David, what is it?" Instantly she was on her feet.

"I was walking out in the fields—" He was gasping after his

326

dash to the house. "I ran into a mob, Caroline. Some farmers—they've got a young black boy out there. They're going to lynch him!"

"Let's find Eric!" Caroline darted to the door. "I'll search downstairs. You go up to his room. And hurry, David!"

Eric was nowhere on the lower floor. There was no point in telling the servants what was happening, Caroline warned herself. They would only be in danger if they tried to help.

"David?" she called up the stairs.

"He's not here!" David descended with hazardous speed. "Caroline, what can we do?"

"Take me there," she ordered. "How far is it?"

"About a quarter of a mile. Can we take a carriage?"

"We'll go to the stable."

Giving Jason no inkling of the trouble, Caroline instructed him to bring out the buggy.

"Jason, hurry!" She called after him with an unfamiliar sharpness that earned an aggrieved over-the-shoulder glance.

"Caroline, what can we do?" David asked. "We ought to try to find Eric."

"There's no time," she dismissed this, her mind racing. *How was she to stop a lynching?* "Tell me what you know, David."

"There're maybe fifty white farmers, and this colored boy from one of the tenant families. He can't be any older than I am."

"What did they say he did?"

"They were yelling that he had just—just violated the daughter of one of the farmers." David stumbled in embarrassment over the word. "I know her, Caroline," he said with sudden distaste. "Sometimes she works in the mill down at Hamptonville. Sometimes she picks cotton. Mr. Roberts tried to talk to her a few times because she's always in some kind of trouble."

Jason brought out the buggy and Caroline and David climbed up. David took the reins. They rode recklessly over the path in the woods toward the fields.

"They're just ahead," David said. They could hear the infuriated voices of the would-be lynchers before they saw them.

"Stop the horse. We'll walk from here," Caroline told David. With the horse tied up to a tree, Caroline and David darted across an open field to the left. Now they could see the clusters of farmers gathered there in rage. Caroline spied a tall, slight, terrified boy, surely no more than fourteen. Two of the farmers were chaining him to a tree. Others were collecting small branches and piling them at his feet.

Caroline gazed in icy disbelief, realizing the intent of the man charging across the field with a can of gasoline in his hand. No! Dear God, no! She ran heedlessly, her breathing painful from the effort. Knowing she must stop this.

"Hang him by the ankles and burn him upside down!" a woman shrieked. Only now was Caroline aware of the pair of women in the crowd. "Burn him to a crisp!"

"Caroline!" David cried in alarm as she darted past the two men who had been chaining the boy to the tree.

"Stop this insanity!" Caroline commanded, while lightning crackled overhead. "There are laws in this state that forbid lynching!"

For a moment she had startled them into immobility, but she sensed immediately that they had no intention of releasing their quarry.

"Git away from that black boy, Miss," a sun-bronzed man ordered her guardedly, "before you git yourself hurt."

"Caroline!" David shoved his way to the front of the mob. "You've got to get out of here," he whispered fearfully.

"Find Eric." She mouthed the words to David, then focused her attention on the mob before her. "Listen to me!" she ordered. "I'm Caroline Hampton, the General's granddaughter. We'll have no lynching on our property!" She saw David pushing frenziedly through the mob. *Where was Eric?* "I want you all to disperse."

"Miss Hampton, you better move aside," another man said menacingly. "We ain't lettin' that boy live after what he done!"

"It's not for you to judge!" Caroline defied. "We have courts for that."

"He took my girl!" a woman yelled. "You burn that nigger, you hear?" she screeched.

"You won't take him," Caroline warned them. "Not unless you kill me first." Defiantly she positioned herself directly before the slight youth, the top of her head barely at his shoulders, her face flushed with her determination to stop the lynching.

"You jes' askin' for trouble. Now step aside and let us take him." Another farmer moved forward with deceptive softness.

"I won't!" Caroline lashed back at him and steeled herself for rough handling. "You're not touching him!"

"Take your hands off Miss Hampton!" Eric's voice cut through the noise of the mob. "Step away from her!"

The crowd parted to let him through. He strode to Caroline and stood beside her, his face taut with contempt as his eyes moved over the faces before him.

"We'll have no lynching on any land belonging to Hampton Court. Any man who lays a hand on this boy loses his fields."

"He raped a white girl!" a man yelled angrily. "You expect us to stand for that?"

"My land don't belong to the Hamptons!" a voice rose nastily from among the new arrivals. "You ain't scarin' me none!"

"I want a trial for him," Eric countered, and Caroline heard the fresh rumbling among the crowd. "We'll have a trial right here," Eric decided, tasting the rage of the onlookers.

"You gonna be the judge?" a woman snickered.

"We'll have a judge and a jury," Eric promised. "But first, where's the girl?" Eric was sparring for time, Caroline realized.

"Whatcha want her for?" somebody demanded, while Eric whispered to Caroline that he had sent David for the sheriff.

"Bring her here," Eric ordered forcefully. "Now."

He reached for Caroline's hand, squeezed it reassuringly for a moment while the others mumbled among themselves. Then a small, fair-haired girl of about twenty with a sulky mouth and suspicious eyes was led forward by a ruddy-faced, unshaven man who, Caroline realized, was her father.

"You're the girl who was violated?" Eric's voice was quiet, yet he managed to reach everyone present.

"He did it!" the girl said shrilly. "That black boy chained to the tree."

"Let's talk about it for a minute," Eric soothed. "We don't want the courts coming at you later saying you made a mistake," he chided. "Where did it happen?"

329

"Out there in the woods. I was just walkin' along and—and he grabbed me. He wouldn't let me yell. He put his big, black hands over my mouth—and then he threw me on the ground and he did it to me!" Her voice rose in triumph.

"When?" Eric probed.

"Just forty minutes ago—maybe a few minutes more."

"You're sure it was this boy?"

"I'm sure."

Eric turned to the trembling boy.

"What's your name?"

"Alfred," he whispered.

"Alfred, did you ever see this girl before?"

"Yessuh."

"When?"

"When she was pickin' cotton las' winter."

"You haven't seen her since?"

"No, suh. Not till jes this minute."

"He's lyin'!" somebody yelled.

"We don't know yet who's lying," Eric cautioned.

"You sayin' my girl's a liar?" her father demanded belligerently.

"He did it to me!" she shrieked. "It hurt somethin' awful! I never knowed it would hurt so much."

"Hey, Ellie Mae, not even a mule gonna hurt you," a voice from the rear jeered drunkenly, while lightning zigzagged across the sky. "You been doin' it since you was fourteen."

A heavy, startled silence fell over the mob.

"Maybe she wanted that big black boy to give it to her!" somebody called out in raucous humor. "Was that it, Ellie Mae? He wouldn't give it to you, and you got hoppin' mad at him?"

"I didn't touch her!" All at once Alfred was vocal. "I seen her in the woods, jes' fo' a minute. She asked me to do it to her, but I was scared. I don't want no trouble with white folks."

"Maybe he wasn't the one," Ellie backtracked. "They all look alike to me. I ain't sure it was him—"

"Go back in the woods, Ellie Mae," the drunk bellowed. "I'll put some of the black stuff on my face and give you a real good time."

"Maybe the fella was older than this one," Ellie Mae fabricated. "And I think he was fatter—"

"All right, everybody," Eric was calm. "Go on home. It's all over. And you, Ellie Mae," he said scathingly, "you try something like this again and you'll land in jail."

Caroline and Eric stood motionless while the crowd slowly began to disperse. Eric moved to unchain Alfred. A few huge drops of rain fell while he struggled to free the boy.

"Go on home, Alfred," Eric smiled reassuringly. "Forget this ever happened." Would he ever forget? Caroline asked herself compassionately. "Go," Eric reiterated with mock ferocity as Alfred stared at him, at a loss to express his gratitude, and he charged off across the left field.

All at once lightning struck a tree nearby. Eric put an arm protectively about Caroline, flinching at the sound of splintered wood. A moment later the rain began to hit the red clay earth in torrents. Eric scanned the area for a place where they might take refuge.

"There's a barn." He pointed across the field. "Let's run!"

Chapter Twenty-seven

B ELTED by the rain, with recurrent bolts of lightning lending an eerie brightness to the sky, Caroline and Eric darted hand in hand across a field tall with cotton. At the barn Eric pulled open the ramshackle door, and they hurried inside.

"You're soaked," Eric said solicitously, while thunder rumbled menacingly overhead, a night-darkness in the heavens.

"The storm will be over soon and we can go back to the house." Caroline managed a shaky smile. "The horse and buggy!" she remembered with alarm. "Eric, they're in the woods."

"David took the buggy to go for the sheriff," Eric soothed. "He's probably caught in this. But he'll take cover somewhere." With one hand he brushed Caroline's sodden hair from her face. "How did you dare stand up to that mob like that?" he rebuked. "You could have been badly hurt."

"I couldn't let them kill that boy." She shivered with recall. "I saw a man bringing a can of gasoline to ignite the leaves. I remembered what you told me, about that lynch mob when you were twelve. Eric, I had to try to stop them."

"David found me along the river. I'd heard the clamor. I was about to investigate."

"I don't know what would have happened if you hadn't come just then. They had no intention of allowing me to cheat them out of a lynching."

"They must be stopped." Eric's jaw tightened. "Lynchings are the disgrace of the South."

"I've read about lynchings, of course; but somehow, I never thought it could happen *here*."

"There was trouble close by less than a year ago." Eric squinted reflectively. "A white farmer refused to pay a Negro worker. They fought, and the farmer was killed. That night mobs roamed about murdering every Negro who had ever been remotely associated with him."

"Eric, how terrible!"

"The wife of one of the men vowed to swear out a warrant, but the lynch mob reached her first. She expected to give birth any day, but that didn't stop them." Eric's face was taut with fresh rage. "They tied her hands and feet and hung her upside down to a tree. Then they poured gasoline over her clothes and touched a lighted match to her skirts."

"And nobody stopped them?" Caroline asked in disbelief.

"Nobody. In moments her clothes were burned from her body. One of the men slashed her across the stomach with a knife. The baby fell to the ground. Another man stomped it to death."

"Eric, please." Caroline closed her eyes. "I don't want to hear this."

"Caro, I'm sorry." Only now did he realize how brutal he had been. He reached to draw her close. "Caro, forgive me."

"How can people behave that way?" Her voice broke. "Eric, they're human beings. They have families. They go to church. How can they behave like savage animals?"

"That's going to be changed." He cradled her in his arms while the rain beat upon the roof. "It's a crime now to be part of a lynch mob."

"But is that law being enforced?" She lifted her face to his in challenge. "Eric, you know it isn't!"

"It will be," he promised.

"If you hadn't arrived when you did, a lynch mob would have murdered an innocent young boy."

"You looked like a beautiful avenging angel standing there." He took her face between his hands. "I never loved you so much as at that moment. I would have killed any man who dared lay a hand on you."

All at once his mouth was on hers. Reason deserted her and

she responded with a hunger that matched his own.

"Caro," he whispered, his arms tightening about her. "The moment I saw you, I knew I was going to love you."

"These last months were awful." She lifted her face to his. "I was so afraid for you, down there in Cuba. You didn't even write when you were wounded." Reality had forsaken her. She was here in Eric's arms, and nothing else mattered.

"I knew you'd worry."

Lightning charged through an opening at the side of the barn, lending eerie brightness to their refuge. Caroline flinched.

"It's all right, Caro," he soothed.

She felt his heart pounding against her. She read the question in his eyes. She was dizzy with the new emotions that too often welled in her since Eric had become part of her life. She reached, without being conscious of the action, to bring his mouth to hers.

They clung together, his hands enfolding her. She felt the hard lean length of his body against her own, and she knew that today was destined to be.

"Not a night passed in Cuba that I didn't think of you, Caro."

"I thought of you every minute, too."

Eric swept her up into his arms and carried her to a corner of the barn where fresh-mown hay had been piled waist-high. Gently he put her down onto the fragrantly scented improvised bed. Her smile was tremulous. Her eyes shining.

She closed her arms about him in welcome when he lowered himself above her. His mouth sought hers again. Outdoors the storm was building to a Wagnerian crescendo. She would not think beyond this precious parcel of time, Caroline thought with reckless abandon. After all the lonely, wishful nights, Eric was teaching her to love.

THE STORM outdoors diminished. Caroline lay in Eric's arms, savoring his nearness, content now to be quiescent.

"Caro, I should not have allowed this to happen." Under his breath Eric cursed himself. "But after seeing you in danger that way, being away from you all these weeks—"

"Eric, no one will ever know." She had let this happen; she

334

had *wanted* it to happen. "No one will be hurt. I'll cherish the memory for always." For a little while she was fully a woman, giving herself to the one man she could ever love.

"Caro, I'll make Tina divorce me," Eric said with sudden resolution. "I'll insist."

"No!" Caroline recoiled. The perfect interlude was splintered. Reality intruded. She pulled free of Eric's arms. He meant to threaten Tina with exposure of her affairs. "Eric, you can't do that to Tina!" She struggled to her feet. "How could you put her through the scandal of a divorce?"

"There's no marriage between Tina and me." Eric rose to his feet. "I swear to you. We've had no marriage since our honeymoon. Surely you must have guessed, Caro. Tina was—"

"Eric, no," she interrupted anguishedly. "You mustn't tell me about Tina and you. You can't divorce her. We can never marry."

"Caro, listen to me." Eric's hands reached to draw her to him. She wrenched free.

"No! There can never be anything for us except today. No more, Eric." Caroline darted across the barn and out into the rain.

What happened today, she silently swore, would never happen again.

ERIC REMAINED in his room through dinner on the pretext of work. In the morning he left for Atlanta, telling Seth to explain to Tina and Caroline that he would remain in the city.

"I'll tell them, Mist' Eric," Seth promised worriedly. How much did Seth know about Tina's affairs? he asked himself bitterly.

Eric stirred restlessly in his seat on the long carriage ride back to Atlanta. Damn it, he knew Caro loved him. He had avoided a divorce before out of respect for the General, but there was no reason now to remain married to Tina. Why couldn't Caro understand that he had every reason to demand a divorce? Caro would suffer no disgrace if he divorced Tina and then married her. Only in the eyes of people who refused to recognize they were hovering on the brink of the twentieth century.

In Atlanta he had Jason leave him at Jim's office and take his luggage on to the house. In the office he found Jim and Mike packing cartons with a funereal air.

"I've given up the office," Jim reported.

Eric stared in disbelief.

"You can't practice law without an office."

"I can practice in an office that costs one-quarter of what this place sets me back." Jim grinned. "That'll help me pay Mike's salary. He's going to be my assistant."

"I'll make some coffee," Mike said sympathetically.

"I hate like hell to see you close down the magazine," Eric said somberly. "It's the end of an era for me, too."

"You've finished the series?" Jim questioned.

"The last of the articles is in the mails. I suppose I could do a follow-up. Roosevelt and the Rough Riders are up at Montauk Point."

Mike returned with coffee and resumed emptying a file drawer. Jim leaned back in his chair, inspecting Eric with quizzical appraisal.

"Right now I wish I was Josiah Hampton's grandson," he said with deceptive softness. "Instead of being a 'damn Yankee.' "

"In Atlanta that makes a difference?" Eric jeered, wary of where Jim was leading him. "You forget. This is the city that welcomed immigrants of all kinds after the War, as long as they were willing to help rebuild Atlanta. Even Northerners," he said with a grin. "You know about the immigration societies that were organized in the late 1860s and early 1870s."

"Eric, I love Atlanta," Jim said seriously. "It's not just a Southern city. It represents the best of everything in every section of this nation. Atlanta is a fine, beautiful lady, richly endowed with guts," he pursued with a rare touch of romanticism. "She's never been afraid to roll up her sleeves and work, yet everybody has to admit she has class."

"Hear, hear," Eric said with gentle derision.

"I want to spend the rest of my life right here," Jim pursued, "working to make Atlanta a great city. If I were native-born, I'd be out there fighting this minute to replace Joe Kelly in the primaries coming up in October."

"Kelly's not running for Councilman?" Eric asked in surprise.

"He announced this morning that he's withdrawing for reasons of health," Jim reported. "There's going to be a wild scramble for a replacement."

"You could try for it," Eric suggested. "You're a lawyer. That's a strong asset."

"No more." Jim reached for his cup of coffee. "A hundred to one Woodward will make it in as Mayor. No lawyer this time. Not even a capitalist. We're entering a new period of politics in this city, Eric. You could make it into the Councilman's seat. The General's memory is very fresh right now. You were wounded in Cuba."

"As an onlooker," Eric reminded with a lifted eyebrow.

"With a gun in your hand," Jim corrected, leaning forward earnestly. "You worked in the Red Cross hospital and in the yellow fever camp. Eric, if we handle this right, you can replace Kelly."

"No," Eric rejected. "I don't want to become involved in politics. Henry Grady—"

"Don't give me that story about Henry Grady, the journalist," Jim brushed this aside. "We're in another period, Eric. If you want to help to build this city to its real destiny, you're going to have to do it within the framework of politics."

"No," Eric resisted stubbornly. "I don't want to replace Kelly in the primaries, even if this were possible. I don't believe I have a chance of winning," he said candidly.

"Eric, we can bring this off. Let me talk to the right people," Jim coaxed.

"No, Jim." Eric was aware that Mike was shamelessly eavesdropping. Jim and Mike had been plotting this before he arrived.

"Where do you go from here?" Jim questioned in frustration. "Are you going to try for a job on the *Constitution* or the *Journal*?"

"After the stories I've written for you attacking some of the stands they've taken?" Eric mocked.

"Where then?" Jim demanded.

"I don't have to write for a newspaper. I could go to the Klondike," Eric said with an effort at humor. "There's plenty happening up there. A man can make himself rich in weeks if he's lucky."

"Do one thing for me, Eric," Jim said slowly. "Think about this for a week or so. Then let's talk again."

"You'll stay off my back if I do?"

"I'll stay off your back," Jim promised.

"I'll think about it," Eric agreed. "Now tell me, what the hell is happening in Cuba and the Philippines?"

HAMPTON COURT seemed desolate without Eric's presence. Caroline was glad for David's company. He was distressed by the near-lynching, which brought back the ghastly memories of pogroms in Europe. Caroline listened while he talked with pained intensity about the village where he had lived with his family.

"David, that can't happen here," she soothed.

"But it almost happened, Caroline," he pointed out realistically. "Not just in the South do people act in this terrible way. Noah writes to cousins in New York. They tell him that there are streets in that city now where a Jew dares not walk for fear of being mobbed and beaten by Irishmen. In New York a colored man is not welcome in a white church, nor his children in a white school."

Unexpectedly, Chad arrived at Hampton Court to spend the day. Caroline was pleased. When he left late in the evening, after a sumptuous dinner, Tina seemed immeasurably cheered. She remained downstairs with Caroline when David went up to bed, and Caroline sensed that Tina was in a conversational mood.

"It was sweet of Chad to ride out in all this heat to spend the day with me, wasn't it?" Tina said with a vivacity that had been in eclipse for weeks.

"He should have stayed overnight."

Tina sighed.

"I can't imagine why Eric went running back to Atlanta in all this heat. He told Seth he wasn't coming up for the rest of the summer."

"It'll soon be September. We'll go back early," Caroline soothed.

"I know I may be jumping to conclusions because I'm so hopeful. I mean, it's really too early to tell. But, Caroline—" She leaned forward with a confiding smile. "I think I'm pregnant."

For one agonized moment—too brief for Tina to notice—Caroline stared at her in shock.

"Tina, how wonderful!" She forced herself to appear delighted. "Eric will be so pleased." Eric had lied to her. *I swear to you. There's no marriage between Tina and me. We've had no marriage since our honeymoon.* Her pulse was racing. Her throat tight. He was playing a game with her, and she had been naïve enough to believe him. Another of Eric's camp followers, she taunted herself. Just another conquest.

"I hope Eric is as excited as I am about the baby." Tina smiled wistfully. "I just wish Grandpa could be alive to know. He would have been so happy."

"I'm sure Eric will be happy." Caroline summoned all her strength to conceal her shock, her hurt. Suppose she had allowed Eric to talk to Tina about a divorce? Or had he said that, convinced she would not allow it? "Tina, let's have a glass of champagne to celebrate." Her air of conviviality was strained, but Tina was unaware. *How could Eric have lied to her that way?*

"It seems dreadfully wicked for us to celebrate before I've told Eric. But he isn't here and you are," Tina declared ebulliently. "We'll have champagne."

Caroline was relieved when she was able to escape to the refuge of her room. She threw herself across the bed, trying to cope with the realization that Eric had lied to her. It would have been better if he had said nothing after they had made love.

She knew about Eric's affairs with women. How could she have been so stupid—so cheap—as to delude herself into believing there was something special between them? Something he had never shared with Tina. But Tina was carrying his child. *How she wished it were she.*

Chapter Twenty-eight

ERIC left the streetcar at the end of the line and walked toward the house. In today's mail at Jim's office he had received a copy of the Detroit *Weekly Advocate* carrying his article about the alarming spread of yellow fever among the American troops in Cuba. Charlie Freeman had edited every word of thoroughly deserved praise he had written about the Twenty-Fourth Infantry's nursing care at the fever camp. Damn, that infuriated him!

"Charlie probably was pushed into it." Jim's explanation repeated itself in his mind. "His backing comes from Republicans with heavy investments in North Carolina."

The Detroit *Weekly Advocate* had some minor Southern circulation. Charlie Freeman's backers wanted to do nothing to increase Negro power in North Carolina.

Approaching the house, Eric stopped dead in astonishment.

"Lucinda, you didn't iron my green voile. I told you I wanted to wear it down to dinner tonight." Tina's voice, faintly shrill, filtered through her bedroom window.

"Miss Tina, it ain't dry yet," Lucinda soothed. "I jes' washed it an hour ago, when you tole me."

Had Caro come home with Tina? Unwary anticipation surged through him as he swiftly went up the stairs to the verandah and crossed to the front door. In the house he mounted the stairs with a burst of speed, his mind resolute. No matter what Caro said, he would tell Tina he wanted a divorce. Tina could sue for the divorce; that was the gentlemanly way to handle it, he thought with a flicker of humor. But damn it, he would not be tied to her any longer than was legally necessary.

Earlier than usual Eric went downstairs to the parlor to await the summons to dinner. Sophie arrived from the mill and was surprised when he told her that Caroline and Tina had returned.

He talked with Sophie, all the while waiting for the moment when Caroline would walk through the door. Lord, he had missed her! But he couldn't have stayed at Hampton Court another day, knowing her adamant rejection of the divorce. *Had she changed her mind?* Was this the reason for their early return?

When Caroline arrived, she was impersonal in her greeting, contriving to avoid even a cousinly kiss on the cheek.

"Sophie, have you set up the meeting with Coleman and the committee yet?" she asked.

"I didn't expect you in town so soon," Sophie protested.

"But you'll set up a meeting now?" Caroline pursued, her smile persuasive. It was as though he were not in the room, Eric thought. She had refused to talk about a divorce, but he had not expected this hostility.

"As soon as possible," Sophie said shortly. "We're still running behind schedule."

"Eric, darling!" Tina floated into the room with outstretched arms.

"Why did you come back in this heat?" Sophie chided.

"I was just dying of loneliness at Hampton Court. For my sake Caroline agreed to come back early." She turned to Eric again. "Eric, will we have a Peace Jubilee in Atlanta? Caroline said there was an article about it in this morning's *Constitution.*"

"Atlanta would be a logical choice," he agreed, his mind struggling to cope with Caroline's attitude.

"It would be poetic to have a Peace Jubilee in the South." Caroline's face lit up. "In this war a Southern general led both Southern and Northern soldiers, and Southern and Northern soldiers fought beneath a Northern general. In Cuba the War Between the States was laid to rest."

"There's talk about inviting President McKinley," Eric contributed.

"Why not?" Tina asked, her smile dreamy. "President Cleveland, Vice-President Adlai Stevenson and six members of the cabinet came here for the Exposition in '95."

"We'll hold a reception," Caroline decided.

"Caroline, with your grandfather dead only a few weeks?" Sophie recoiled in shock.

"*For Grandpa,*" Caroline declared, her face wearing an incandescent glow. "He'll be part of the Peace Jubilee. Sophie, you know he would be pleased."

"I'm sure he would," Sophie said grudgingly. "But I don't think I could participate, Caroline."

"You'll participate, Sophie," Caroline insisted. "The family will participate. If the Peace Jubilee comes off." For a moment her eyes met Eric's. For that involuntary moment they were alone. Eric was assaulted by the memory of the scent of hay in a rain-pelted barn, with Caroline in his arms. His instinct was to take her by the hand and run with her to a future that was theirs alone.

They sat in the parlor after dinner while Tina played for them. Caroline foiled his every effort to speak to her alone. He excused himself and went up to his room. He would tell Jim tomorrow that Tina was divorcing him. Jim would represent her. Tina could hardly refuse him. He'd threaten her with total exposure. That wouldn't be difficult, considering her carelessness with Marshall Shepard. Yet how the hell could he expose Dolly Shepard to scandal? He would have to frighten Tina into going along with a divorce.

He listened for sounds from downstairs that would tell him the others were retiring for the night. He waited a few minutes after he heard the bedroom doors close behind each of the three, then left his own room to go to Tina's.

He paused before Tina's door, gearing himself for a nasty scene.

"It's Eric," he said as he knocked.

"Come in," Tina called. He walked into the bedroom. Lucinda was turning down the bed. "Lucinda, you can go now."

"Tina, I have to talk to you," he began when the door closed behind Lucinda.

"Eric, honey, I was coming to your room in a minute," she said with girlish sweetness, moving toward him. "I have the most exciting news." She slid her arms about his neck. He stiffened in

342

rejection; but Tina, caught up in her revelation, was unaware. "That's why I was so impatient to come home. I just couldn't wait another day to tell you. Eric, darling, I'm pregnant."

He stared at her in disbelief.

"What kind of crazy joke is that?"

"I was as surprised as you," she laughed, but he saw the glint of satisfaction in her eyes.

"That one night?"

"Honey, you'd been down in Cuba all those weeks," she reminded.

"Have you seen Dr. Ashley?" How could one night tie him forever to a marriage that was dead?

"I don't need to see Dr. Ashley yet. I know. Honey, aren't you pleased?" she pouted.

"No," he said bluntly. How could he ever be sure it was his child?

"How can you say that to me?" Tears welled in her eyes. "When I've been feeling so awful. If you didn't want a baby, why weren't you careful?"

Eric wheeled about and left the room without a word. All at once he understood Caro's coldness tonight. Tina had told her about the baby. After he had sworn to Caro there was no marriage between Tina and him. *Oh, God.*

In his room, Eric paced until dawn, cursing himself for being caught in an age-old trap. Was it his child that Tina was carrying? Every time he looked at that child he would be assailed by doubts.

At last, exhausted, he threw himself onto the bed and fell into a drugged sleep. He awoke early, lay in bed gazing at the ceiling while his mind wrestled with his approach to the future. How could he ask for a divorce with Tina pregnant?

Restless, rebellious, he rose and dressed. Without pausing for breakfast he strode from the house with an evasive good morning to Seth and hurried to the streetcar stop. Jim would still be at the old office for the next few days. Let him sit down and talk this out with Jim.

This morning the ride into the city seemed interminably long. Caroline's face haunted him. How could he expect her to be other than cold to him? She surely knew that Tina was pregnant. It would never occur to Caro that the father of Tina's child could be anybody else. But it *could* be he, he acknowledged.

At his destination Eric jumped from the streetcar with relief and hurried to Jim's office. Jim was clear-headed and calm. He needed that this morning.

"Where's Jim?" he asked Mike, while he gazed about the deserted floor with a sense of loss. He had come here to work for Jim after a period of depressing uncertainty. Jim had solidified his thinking. "He's usually here at the crack of dawn."

"He's got himself a case already," Mike explained blithely. "Some poor old guy who's supposed to have murdered his wife. He'll never see a cent in fees," Mike predicted.

Eric crossed to his old desk and sat down. He had no destination. His assignment with the Detroit weekly was over. Jim's magazine had published its last issue. Jim was right; where the hell did he go from here?

"Do you have the morning paper, Mike?"

"Sure." Mike pulled a newspaper from out of his top desk drawer and carried it over to Eric. "Feels funny knowing we won't be here next week—" His eyes were nostalgic.

Eric was halfway through the article on Kelly's withdrawal from the race for Councilman when Jim returned.

"I hear you have a case," Eric greeted him with a grin.

"I've got a few things going." Jim dropped into a chair. "Been feeling folks out about this Councilman opening."

"You going to try for it?" Eric asked.

"I'm not," Jim said briskly. "I want a candidate with a chance." He leaned forward. "You, Eric. Have you taken a look at the new slates? We're going to see some real reforms in this city."

"Jim," Eric interrupted. "I've got problems of my own. Tina told me last night that she's pregnant."

Jim knew about Tina's long-standing affair with Marshall Shepard. He knew about the other men who filled in between Tina's bouts with Marshall.

"Your baby?"

"How the hell do I know? I hadn't been near her since our honeymoon." He never discussed Tina with anybody except Jim.

344

"Then the night we buried the General, Tina came to my room at Hampton Court. After all those weeks in Cuba I was susceptible. It could have been that night." He shrugged. Or it could be Marshall's child, or the man who taught her to drive that damn loco-steamer.

"A child could be a political asset," Jim said calmly. "Folks like to vote for a family man. He seems more substantial."

"Jim—"

"Now shut up and listen to me," Jim ordered. "I've been feeling out some people about the possibility of your running. I didn't say you would," he said appeasingly. "I said the thought was running through my mind that you ought to be approached. The reactions were what I expected. You'll have heavy support."

"Because of the General," Eric pinpointed. "They expect to use his name."

"That's part of it," Jim acknowledged. "But you're a colorful character in this city. You do the unexpected. You could have been groomed to run the Hampton Mill. Instead, you worked for a struggling Populist newspaper. You went to Cuba, got yourself wounded. Your articles in the *Weekly Advocate* placed you at Kettle Hill, the Red Cross hospital, the yellow fever camps. That's colorful, Eric," he reiterated. "And then you stopped that lynching at Hampton Court."

"How did that get into the newspapers?" Eric demanded. It was all there, making him sound like a folk hero.

"I accidentally mentioned it in the right places." Jim grinned. "You can't stop an old newspaperman."

"I swore I would never become involved in politics. I swore I'd stay clear of law." But Jim was opening a law office in Atlanta, and increasingly he thought about reading law in Jim's office.

"You were rebelling against your grandfather. You were two strong men, and he leaned too heavily on you. Politics is your natural arena. That's where things happen, Eric." He leaned forward earnestly. "Every day counts now. Let me set it up for you to try for Kelly's spot."

The room was heavy with silence as Eric debated inwardly. Jim's eyes were galvanized to his face. Mike stood motionless at a file cabinet, waiting for him to speak.

"All right, Jim. You try. I'll be your man. And if you want me, I'll come into the law office with you." He chuckled. "I come cheap. Just coach me to pass the bar examinations."

Jim leaned forward and smacked him jubilantly across the shoulder.

"Finally you're talking sense."

It was ironic, Eric thought, that he should be running for public office only a few weeks after the General's death. Why couldn't he have made this decision while the old man was alive? It would have been a glorious victory for him.

He needed a direction. Caro would never trust him again; there was no way of explaining his way out of Tina's trap. If he was elected, he would have a job that would keep him too busy to think about the muddle he had made of his life.

CAROLINE COULD not bring herself to go to the mill until Sophie, Andrew and she had sat down at a meeting with Coleman and his committee. She waited restlessly for Sophie to give her a definite date.

She was sleeping badly, constantly faced with Tina's pregnancy. How could Eric have lied that way? How could she have been so naïve? Long ago she had warned herself against being drawn into the circle of his charm.

There was no place in her life for a man like Eric. Yet she felt so drawn to his strength, to his compassion, to his way of thinking that was so like her own. She remembered him standing before that lynch mob and compelling them to face the truth. Here was a man she could love forever if she was not aware of his philandering, his dreadful treatment of Tina.

The Peace Jubilee was announced for mid-December. Caroline drew Tina into plans for an elaborate reception on the first evening of the Jubilee. Four days after Tina and she returned from Hampton Court, Eric—with elaborate casualness—told Sophie, Tina and her over dinner that he was replacing Kelly in the primaries.

"Tomorrow morning's *Constitution* will carry the story." His smile was ironic. "I'm finally taking the General's advice."

"Eric, how marvelous!" Tina glowed. "You're certain to win."

"We'll know that after the primaries next month," Eric shrugged. "There's not much time for campaigning."

"I'm glad you decided to do this, Eric," Sophie said with quiet satisfaction.

Caroline forced herself to meet Eric's gaze.

"I'm sure you'll win." He had vowed he could never run for office. What had changed his mind? The prospect of being a father? He gave Tina no indication that he looked forward to this role. "Tina, you'll be the Councilman's wife by the time we entertain during the Peace Jubilee," Caroline predicted, contriving an air of levity.

"I won't be able to be there. I'll look terrible," Tina sulked. "I'm showing already."

"Not at all," Caroline lied, her color high. Why did Eric keep staring at her that way? "You never looked more beautiful. We'll give a dinner to launch Eric's campaign. Right away, before anybody guesses about the baby."

"When, Caroline?" Tina was ambivalent.

"A week from today," Caroline said, and Tina brightened. "We can manage everything by then." She compelled herself to consult Eric. "Give us a list of people important to your campaign. They'll be invited."

"I'll discuss it with Jim and let you know tomorrow," Eric said with sardonic politeness. He was furious with her.

"Where will we have the dinner?" Tina was intrigued. "At the Kimball House?"

"Here." Caroline ignored Eric's obvious displeasure. "We'll be able to entertain forty in the formal dining room," she estimated. "Won't we, Sophie?"

"Caroline, it seems so callous," Sophie objected. "With your grandfather dead less than two months."

"He would want it this way," Caroline insisted. "Nothing would make the General happier than to know that Eric was on the Council."

"Caroline, you can be as persuasive as Josiah," Sophie smiled. "Of course, he would want us to do anything to help Eric."

Caroline recalled the elaborate menus of dinners given by Lord

347

Englewood. His two daughters would describe each course to her on the morning after each dinner party, which was an effective way of delaying their lessons. The Hamptons would give a dinner, Caroline vowed, that would long be remembered in Atlanta.

Sensitive to Mattie's feelings, Caroline—seemingly on impulse—arranged for Mattie to leave on Thursday for a long weekend with her daughter in Decatur. She phoned Marian Bolton and asked for advice about hiring a gourmet chef on very short notice.

"Caroline, you're in luck," Marian said warmly. "There is a man here from New Orleans on a visit to his wife's family. He's one of the finest French chefs in Louisiana. Try to hire him for your dinner," she urged. "It'll be a feast."

After raising her offer for his services to a figure that she knew would scandalize Sophie, who handled the household accounts, Caroline persuaded the Frenchman to capitulate. He would come to the Hampton house early Friday morning. The dinner on Saturday evening would be a masterpiece.

Tina was constantly at the dressmaker's establishment, eager for her dinner gown to conceal her condition. Caroline knew that to Tina the imminent loss of her figure was a torment.

"Every day I'm bigger, Caroline," she wailed. "I'm so small-boned everything shows on me!"

Caroline was aware that Eric was striving for some private moments with her. She avoided this until the night before the dinner. Tina was closeted in her room with the dressmaker. Sophie was going back to the mill to go over some sales figures with Andrew.

"Don't work too late, Sophie," she urged, seeing her to the door.

When she closed the door behind Sophie and started across the foyer, Eric stalked toward her, his face stubborn.

"Caro, I have to talk to you."

"I told Tina I'd be right upstairs to look at her dress," she fabricated, making no effort—now that they were alone—to conceal her hostility.

"To the devil with Tina!" he said, and reached out to bring her to him. "Caro, you've got to listen to me!"

"You listen to me!" she shot back. "You are Tina's husband. The father of her child. Start behaving that way!"

"You don't know, Caro," he began, and she pushed him from her.

"No more of your lies, Eric. Please."

"Caro, you don't understand." He moved forward and pulled her to him. His mouth came down on hers.

For one anguished instant she went limp in his arms. Then she was stiff with anger, thrusting him from her.

"Don't you ever touch me again!" Her eyes blazed with reproach, hurt, and an unwary passion.

"This whole situation is insane, Caro."

"I agree. Please remember who you are, Eric. I'm your cousin. Nothing more."

"I know you, Caro." His voice was suddenly tender. "You're no marble statue in a museum. You're a woman. The woman I love."

"Good-night, Eric." She spun away from him and darted up the stairs. *How dare he behave this way.*

THE DINNER was an acknowledged success. It was assumed that Tina was responsible for the arrangements, and she gloried in the compliments showered on her in the course of the evening. At Caroline's instigation, Tina delicately confided to several of the wives of party leaders that the future Councilman would be a father in the spring. As Caroline had anticipated, this confidence was received approvingly.

A scheduled meeting with the millworkers was postponed for the following Saturday. Caroline suspected that Sophie had contrived for Andrew to go out of town to purchase repair parts for equipment. Sophie insisted that Andrew be at the meeting. Caroline knew she was right. The workers had great respect for him.

Caroline talked with Grace and Henry Roberts about the needs of the workers.

"I want to see a ten-hour workday, and a half day of work on Saturdays. I want an adequate school for the children up to the age of fourteen. The houses should be less drab, more comfortable."

"This will all take time," Henry cautioned. "But let them know that you mean to help them toward a better life."

"I worry about their health," Caroline said, her eyes disturbed. "Andrew says absenteeism is terribly high, and I know they're not shirking."

"They are susceptible to pellagra," Grace said with rare bluntness, "because they can't afford a proper diet. The prisoners in the Atlanta jails eat better."

"Wages will increase," Caroline said with determination. "I promise you that."

On Saturday, Caroline, Sophie and Andrew sat down in Josiah's office with Tom Coleman and his committee of seven. Caroline knew that Sophie would have preferred that she not be present, but she had initiated this meeting and she was determined to be present.

"We must have a wage increase," Tom Coleman said, brushing aside preliminaries. "We can't exist on what little we earn—"

"That's out of the question," Sophie broke in angrily. "In Augusta the mills are cutting wages."

The meeting erupted into a screaming match between Sophie and Tom Coleman and his committee. Futilely, Caroline tried to intercede. Andrew seemed helpless.

"Andrew, tell them we'll meet again on Monday," Caroline whispered. "They'll listen to you. Tell them we need time to check our mill operating costs."

After a moment of indecision Andrew took charge.

"All right, everybody, quiet. Quiet!" he said with greater strength, and the sounds of battle ebbed away. "We'll meet again on Monday," he decreed. "We need time to check our operating costs. We'll see if we can continue to operate with a wage increase."

Consternation glowed in the eyes of the committee members, except for Tom Coleman's.

"You shouldn't be stooping to scare us, Mr. Andrew," he said coldly. "Maybe we don't have much book learning, but we know enough to count up what it costs to make a product. You can pay us more and keep the mill running at a handsome profit. You're buying cotton at less than five cents a pound. You're paying piddling wages. And you're selling high."

"We'll discuss it on Monday," Andrew said briskly. "We'll have our figures. You'll come here at this same time."

Andrew stood up. The meeting was over. Sophie remained seated behind Josiah's desk. She was furious.

"Andrew, how could you let them believe we'll raise their wages? Have you lost your senses?"

"I asked Andrew to say what he did, Sophie," Caroline interjected, and Sophie gazed at her in shock. Sophie was remembering that she—Caroline—held the largest interest in the mill. Except for the twelve percent of shares willed to Sophie and Andrew, she stood in her grandfather's position. "We don't want a strike. That's bad for everybody. We'll go over the books," Caroline said with quiet strength. "Let's find out exactly where we stand." She was trembling from the effort to retain her composure.

"We pay the highest wages in the state!" Sophie reminded, her voice unnaturally high.

"We're behind on orders," Andrew reminded worriedly. "We can't afford a strike."

"We can't afford a raise," Sophie snapped.

"Let's look at the books now," Caroline pushed. "Let's see where we stand."

Sophie's eyes clashed for a moment with Caroline's. She seemed to be appraising Caroline's strength.

"We'll go over the books," she acquiesced.

For almost three hours they compared figures. Sophie put forth endless arguments against raising wages. Andrew watched, silent and unhappy, while Caroline and Sophie added figures, made evaluations.

"Sophie, you must see the facts." Caroline struggled against impatience. "It's all here in front of us. We can maintain the profits of what the General considered good years and still raise wages."

"That isn't progress," Sophie objected. "Our profits should match the best years."

"Our income will rise when the finishing plant is completed and in operation. But we can afford a raise now," Caroline said with conviction. "Andrew, you see it, don't you?"

"I think we can manage a pay raise," Andrew agreed.

Caroline turned to Sophie, who frowned in indecision. Andrew suggested a figure.

"Cut it in half," Sophie ordered tersely. "You can tell the committee on Monday morning, Andrew."

It was a small victory, but Caroline was jubilant. This was the beginning of change at Hampton Mill. With Andrew on her side, Caroline decided with soaring confidence, she would transform the Hampton Mill into a glorious model for the South to follow.

Chapter Twenty-nine

C AROLINE sat over a restaurant luncheon with Jim Russell—which she herself had arranged—listening intently to his assessment of Eric's position in the primary.

"We have a fighting chance, Caroline," Jim told her. "We've picked up a lot of support, but there's a lot of resistance in some areas because of Eric's Populist views."

"We must do every thing possible in these final two weeks." Her mind was reaching out for ways to improve the odds for Eric. She told herself she hated Eric, yet perversely she yearned to see him win. "Jim, could we—" She faltered. "I know so little about politics, but I was thinking—"

"Go ahead, Caroline," Jim encouraged.

"Eric might pick up votes if we arranged some teas for the Atlanta ladies," she began, and Jim laughed.

"I know what you're thinking, but unfortunately those ladies can't vote."

"They might convince their husbands to vote for Eric," Caroline pointed out. "Eric could come and speak to them. Tina could appear with him." She took a deep breath. "Eric and Tina make a handsome couple. The ladies will be charmed."

"Quite possibly." Jim nodded contemplatively. "But our funds won't stretch to anything that fancy, Caroline."

"I'll raise the funds," Caroline promised, her color high, "on the condition you swear that Eric will never know." She stammered. "He would never allow it." Eric never gave any indication that he was upset that she had been willed most of the General's estate, but she knew instinctively that he would object to being financially beholden to her. If she had not come to Atlanta, she thought soberly, Eric could afford the most expensive campaign in the city's history.

"Eric doesn't have to know who's footing campaign expenses," Jim assured her. "But there's the time element to consider—"

"We can hold the teas at the Kimball House," she told him. "Every afternoon until primary day."

"Have you any idea what this is going to cost?" Jim asked. "It'll be expensive."

"I know exactly what it'll cost." She saw his surprise that she was prepared with this information. "Without giving my name or any details I checked it out with the hotel. They can arrange for the first tea to be held within two days of our committing ourselves. We'll have to extend invitations by areas, won't we? But I'm sure you'll know how to manage that." Her words were tumbling over one another, as always happened when she was emotionally involved. "I'll pay all the expenses if you can handle the invitation end of it." She waited for his reply.

"I can handle it," he said after a moment's cogitation. "I was wondering about Eric's wife. Do you suppose she could be rehearsed to say a few words to each group of ladies?" He smiled humorously. "We don't expect her to be a Tom Watson. Just an appealing plea to convince their husbands that Eric belongs on the Council."

"I'll work with her," Caroline promised.

Caroline maintained an unmovable wall between Eric and herself, though she labored to make the teas a success. Seemingly Jim Russell had enlisted her help. She propelled Tina, despite complaints, to the Kimball House each afternoon.

Tina presented the brief speech prepared by Caroline in a breathy, young girl fashion that was appealing. Once in the Kimball House ballroom Tina always rallied, relishing the role of the beautiful wife of the candidate.

Caroline kept to herself the realization that, despite the adroit tailoring of Tina's dresses, the ladies surely suspected her pregnancy and felt a kinship. They would urge their husbands to vote for Eric.

Caroline awoke on primary morning to a perfect day. She dressed with haste, intent on arriving at the breakfast table before Eric left for last-minute campaigning and to vote. It was ridiculous, she upbraided herself, but she wanted to be standing on the verandah this morning when he left for downtown. He would return tonight, she promised herself, the party's candidate for Councilman in the December municipal election.

Eric and Sophie were at the table.

"Good morning." Caroline's eyes grazed Eric to dwell on Sophie. "Isn't it dreadful, Sophie, that *we* can't go out to vote?"

"I would vote for Eric," Sophie admitted, "but I doubt that I would bother for anyone else." Her face tensed. "I have enough to cope with at the mill."

"Problems?" Caroline was alert.

"I hear Tom Coleman is talking to the men about another wage increase."

"We gave them a tiny raise, Sophie," Caroline pointed out. "Andrew had considered double that figure."

"Andrew can be emotional on occasion," Sophie dismissed this. "We have to look ahead. We must have a reserve for bad years."

"The Depression is behind us, Sophie," Eric reminded. "We're moving into a period of expansion."

"You young people refuse to look ahead," Sophie admonished. "You only think for today."

"Perhaps we're afraid to look ahead," Eric said with sudden irony, his eyes holding Caroline's for an unguarded moment. "I have to go." He pushed back his chair.

"When will we know the results?" Caroline asked.

"It could be three or four in the morning. Don't stay awake. You'll know by breakfast."

"I'll go with you to the door." Sophie rose to her feet. Only the brightness of her eyes betrayed her avid interest in this primary. "I'm going to the mill now. I should have been there an hour ago." She reached out with one hand to fleetingly touch Eric's face. "Josiah would be so proud of you today." Sophie had delayed going to the mill so she could see Eric off this morning.

Caroline lingered at the table for a few moments, conscious of

Eric and Sophie's voices fading away. All at once she was on her feet and hurrying down the hall and out onto the verandah. Sophie was walking toward the mill, Eric striding toward the streetcar stop. He should be taking the carriage today, she thought.

"Eric," she called out, and he swung around with an air of anticipation. "Good luck at the polls."

His eyes searched her face for a poignant moment.

"Thank you, Caro."

Caroline climbed the stairs to her room. She ought to go into the mill. There was so much she had to learn. But how could she think about anything except the primary today? She would not go to sleep until she knew the results.

"Caroline?" Tina's voice called petulantly from behind her door.

Caroline opened the door and walked into Tina's bedroom. Tina was still in bed, propped up against a mound of pillows.

"How're you feeling?" she asked affectionately.

"Awful," Tina complained. "I can't get comfortable enough to sleep. Thank God, I won't have to show up at any more of those teas."

"Tina, when are you going to stop stalling and go to see Dr. Ashley?"

"I'm not going to see him," Tina said with faint defiance. "I've talked about it with Mama, and we've decided that Lucinda will deliver my baby. She delivered me."

"Tina, in these modern times?" Caroline scolded.

"Having a baby is a normal function," Tina insisted. "I'll have my baby with Lucinda and Mama to help me." She shifted her position with a frown of impatience. "Caroline, I wish it was time already! I wish it was over! I hate being ugly like this!"

"We'll sit down this afternoon and start making our plans for the Jubilee reception," Caroline said coaxingly. "It has to be very grand."

"I won't dare appear," Tina reminded. "If I weren't pregnant, I'd be riding on one of the floats. I'm not missing just our reception. There'll be as many parties as there were during the Confederate Reunion, and I'll miss every one!" Her voice soared shrilly. "I don't want to have this baby! I never wanted it!"

Caroline paled.

"Tina, you're just upset. You don't mean that. You're going to adore the baby."

"I'm so tired," Tina whimpered. "I can't go anywhere, and I can't do anything, and Eric is so awful to me."

"He'll be different after tonight," Caroline promised. "When he wins the primary, he'll be as good as elected. Everybody in Atlanta knows that. Eric and you will do lots of entertaining after the baby is born."

"Caroline, I'd die without you." The phone jangled and Tina started. "That's Chad. He's getting up early to go out and vote." She reached for the phone.

"I'll talk to you later about the reception," Caroline said. Chad would cheer up Tina.

"CHAD, I don't want to hear about the marvelous time you had at the Capital City Club last night," Tina sulked. "I haven't been out of the house except to show up at those horrible teas Jim Russell set up for Eric's campaign. The way I'm popping out I can't go anywhere now until the baby's born."

"Do you know who's been paying for those teas?" Chad asked with a smugness that should have alerted her.

"The Party, I assume," Tina said irritably. "Eric can't afford that."

"Caroline paid," Chad murmured, and Tina's mouth opened in amazement. "She worked it out with Jim so that Eric doesn't know," he guessed.

"How did you find out?" Tina demanded.

"Darling, you know I have ways," Chad reminded. "Actually, one of the clerks at the hotel saw the checks."

"Why has Caroline kept it a secret?"

"Probably because she was afraid Eric wouldn't accept. Maybe she knows he's in love with her."

Tina grasped the phone so tightly her knuckles whitened.

357

"Chad, what are you talking about?"

"Haven't you seen the way Eric looks at her?" Chad needled.

"All he can do is look," Tina said coldly, but fury surged within her. He acted so high and mighty with her, but he was after Caroline. "Eric may pick up a woman for a night now and then, but he's not going to touch his cousin Caroline. He's a Southern gentleman."

"You're going to make sure he doesn't," Chad predicted. "Even though Caroline's mad about him. But she'll scream if he lays a hand on her."

"Chad, you're evil!" She was shaking with rage. "I'm lying here in bed feeling awful, and you're saying everything you can to make me feel worse."

"Darling, I thought you ought to know. Nothing's happening," he soothed. "And you'll make sure it doesn't. Eric doesn't have a chance with Caroline. She feels guilty just because she's crazy about him. That's why she pampers you all the time. Enjoy it, Tina."

Tina slammed a fist into the pillow.

"Sometimes I hate you, Chad."

"I'll take you to the theater tonight," Chad offered. "We'll sit in a box."

"I won't go to the theater looking like this!" she screeched as Lucinda came into the room with her breakfast tray. "Go away and leave me alone." She slammed down the receiver and began to cry.

"Miss Tina, you stop that," Lucinda crooned. "You have yourself some breakfas' and you'll feel better. You ain't been sick in the mornin' for a long time now."

Tina reached for a handkerchief and dabbed at her eyes.

"Lucinda, you go downstairs and tell Jason to be ready to take me for a drive in about an hour. I want to get out of this house for a while."

"Miss Tina, it's time you stopped ridin' all over in the carriage," Lucinda objected. "Far along as you is."

"Lucinda, stop telling me what to do. It's bad enough I've had to stop driving my loco-steamer. Go downstairs and find Jason. Then come up here and help me dress."

She waited until she heard Lucinda heading down the stairs before she lifted up the telephone to place her call. Marshall was not in his office. She might have known he would not be there on primary day. She called the house. Mr. Shepard was home, a servant replied, and asked her to wait.

"Marshall, are you voting for Eric?" Tina drawled, masking her excitement at the sound of his voice.

"Is this a campaign call?" Marshall mocked. Immediately Tina realized that Dolly was not home.

"This is a lonesome call," Tina murmured. "I want to see the father of my child."

"Tina, don't be absurd," Marshall snapped.

"Meet me somewhere," she ordered. She wanted to forget what Chad just told her about Eric and Caroline. "Meet me this afternoon."

"That's impossible," he rejected. "We can't be seen together."

"We'll arrive separately. Nobody has to know we're seeing each other." Marshall always had some place where they could be together. "Marshall, your son kicks me all the time. I'll bet he's going to be a hellion just like his father." Dolly would never give him a child. "Don't you want to feel him kick?" she asked with plotted wistfulness.

"My mother is away," Marshall said after a moment. "I have the keys to her house. There's nobody there."

"I can be there in an hour," Tina said. Would he hate her when he saw her big this way? Her breasts were marvelous in pregnancy. Marshall used to say she had the most beautiful breasts in the world. All at once she was arouned, visualizing his hands caressing them. Nobody had touched her since that night she pushed herself on Eric. "Give me the address, darling."

In exactly an hour, Tina stood with Marshall in his mother's busily Victorian parlor.

"Your baby, Marshall," she murmured and reached to bring his hand to her. "He's kicking this minute. Feel him."

"Damn it, Tina!" He scowled. "We shouldn't have let this happen."

"You shouldn't have married Dolly," she admonished. "We belong together."

"Tina, I need Dolly," he reminded. "I need her money. That's buying me a seat in the Legislature."

"Marshall, haven't you missed me?" She leaned toward him, her hands sliding about his shoulders. She saw his eyes fasten on the new fullness of her breasts.

"Tina, I can't take chances."

"You took a chance," she admonished. "And now I'm carrying your baby."

"Maybe," he said with brutal candor, and hot color flooded her face and throat.

"You bastard!" She pulled her hands away from him. "You know this is your baby! That last time when you were so stupidly careless."

"Tina, we shouldn't have come here." He frowned in irritation.

"Do you find me so repulsive?" she flared. He had brought her here and now he was sorry. "Did you expect me to be flat and beautiful?" Her voice rose to the edge of hysteria. "I hate you, Marshall! I hate every man alive!"

"Tina, stop that." He shook her by the shoulders. "Stop it!"

All at once his arms were about her. His mouth was on hers. She still made him passionate, Tina thought with pleasure.

"Marshall, love me," she pleaded when his mouth at last released her. His breathing was uneven, his eyes betrayed his desire. "It's been so long—"

"Tina, is it all right?" he asked nervously. "I mean, when you're like this?"

"Marshall, for us it's always all right." Confidence soared in her. He was remembering how it could be with them. "Let's go up to one of the bedrooms."

Silently, hand in hand, they left the parlor and climbed up the stairs to the first bedroom, walking slowly in deference to Tina's awkwardness in late pregnancy.

"Tina, you're sure it's all right for the baby?" Marshall reiterated when they were inside the large, square, obviously feminine bedroom.

"Damn the baby, Marshall!" she said fretfully, and saw his shock. "I mean, there are ways," she said with deceptive sweetness. "Undress, darling, and come to me." She was already un-hooking the back of her frock, not waiting for his help today.

She saw the way his eyes focused on the lushness of her breasts as she pulled the bodice of her dress and the top of her chemise to her waist. She stood with shoulders thrust backward, hands lifting her breasts in a provocative offering. Her nipples were twice their normal size, she thought, and could already feel Marshall's teeth and tongue tasting them.

"Lie on the bed, Marshall," she ordered, pleased when he was stripped to skin and hard with excitement.

With a provoking slowness he crossed to the bed and stretched along its length.

"Well?" His eyes were a challenge.

"It'll be as good as ever," she promised.

In moments, divested of her undergarments but swathed from waist to toes in the skirt of her dress to conceal the hated belly, she was positioning herself above him. His hands moved forward to clutch at the spill of her breasts. She heard the sound that rose in his throat as her hand found him and guided him to her.

"Tina, you wonderful bitch!" he muttered as they moved to-gether and her inner muscles drew him into her. "Oh, God!"

Chapter Thirty

C AROLINE and Sophie were alone in the parlor. Tina remained in her room. Eric would be downtown all evening.

"It'll be good for Eric to be on the Council," Sophie said. "And he'll be good for the Council." She gazed with disconcerting keenness at Caroline. "But I worry about you."

Caroline felt herself grow hot.

"Why do you worry about me?" she strived for lightness.

"You have so little social life." Sophie's eyes were troubled. "That one incident at the UDC meeting should not color your whole life here in Atlanta."

"Sophie, we just gave the dinner for Eric," Caroline reminded. "We're having the reception in December. I've been going to all the teas—"

"You're talking about politics," Sophie dismissed this. "At your age you should be involved in all kinds of social activities. Tina could talk to her mother about getting you on some committees. That would be a beginning."

"I'd hate that, Sophie," Caroline rejected. "Now that the primaries are over, I'll be coming into the mill regularly."

"That's not a social life," Sophie said tersely. "And you keep putting Andrew off when he invites you to the theater or the opera."

"It didn't seem right to go out when the war was hanging over our heads. And then when the General was sick—" Her voice ebbed away.

"Caroline, don't be like me," Sophie exhorted with rare intensity. "Don't give your life to the mill. Don't find yourself at forty-six with nothing to show for the years."

"Sophie, you have a lot to show! How many women are at the head of a mill? Every worker there has the greatest respect for you."

"The mill was my marriage, Eric my child. Thank God for the General and him," she said honestly. "But it wasn't enough. A woman needs a man of her own. She needs to carry his child."

"I don't want to think about marriage for a long time," Caroline said unevenly. *She would never marry.*

"Don't wait too long," Sophie warned. "Don't close your mind."

Sophie was thinking about Andrew, Caroline guessed. But she could not marry Andrew. She could not marry anyone, feeling this way about Eric.

"How late do you suppose it'll be before they know about the primaries?" she asked.

"Long after I've gone to bed," Sophie guessed. "I told Eric if there was any news by ten, to phone us; but it'll probably be far into the morning."

Promptly at ten Sophie rose from her chair in the parlor.

"I'm going to bed," she said, stifling a yawn. "Eric isn't going to call."

"Shouldn't there be news by now?" Caroline was wistful.

"Not likely."

"I'll go up in a little while, too." Caroline made a point of never being alone with Eric, but tonight was special. She could not go to her room without knowing the outcome of the primary.

She gazed without seeing into the cheerful blaze Seth had started against the evening chill. She had allowed Eric to make love to her. She had wished for that. But she would never forgive him for lying to her. With merciless repetition his voice echoed through her mind. *"There's no marriage between Tina and me. I swear to you."* But Tina was pregnant, and Eric made no denials.

At midnight Seth brought her a pot of tea.

"Seth, go to bed," Caroline chided affectionately. "You're up so early in the morning."

"I'll go now, Miss Caroline. I was just hopin' we'd know how

363

Mist' Eric made out before I went to sleep."

"He's going to win." Caroline forced herself to sound confident. Jim had warned it would be a close race.

"I 'spect he will."

Caroline alternately read and dozed. She sat up with a start when she heard the front door open. *It must be Eric.* She jumped to her feet and darted into the hall. He had closed the door and was crossing to the stairs.

"Eric," she called and hurried forward, her eyes questioning.

He smiled sardonically, one eyebrow lifted.

"It seems likely there'll be a Councilman in the family."

"Eric, congratulations." Caroline's heart was pounding. She realized that she was here alone with Eric. Sophie and Tina had long been asleep. The servants were in their quarters above the stables.

"Caro, have a glass of wine with me to celebrate," Eric persuaded.

All at once the atmosphere was electric. She knew Eric was remembering, as she was, that afternoon in the barn.

"No thank you, no." She felt the color flooding her face. "It's late." Too late for them. Why did he look at her that way? It was a lie. "Good-night, Eric."

She hurried up the stairs, conscious of his eyes following her to the door of her room. She walked inside, closed the door behind her. Trembling. She had not trusted herself to remain another moment alone with Eric.

CAROLINE SPENT much of each day at the mill, involving herself in every phase of its activity, yet her mind was constantly focused on the coming municipal election. Eric and Jim campaigned with religious zeal, determined that election day would prove Eric the new Councilman from his district. Noah, too, dedicated every free hour he could take from the store—when David covered for him—to working for Eric's election.

Tina was increasingly difficult as she grew more awkward, screaming at Lucinda, shrieking at Caroline at the slightest provocation. Caroline forced herself to be patient with Tina, ever conscious that she was carrying Eric's child. Eric used his campaigning as an excuse to be away from the house for most of his waking hours.

The night before the state elections—which preceded the municipal elections by a month—Caroline and Sophie sat in the parlor before a crackling fire and discussed the candidates.

"The *Constitution* expects Van Wyck to be the next Governor of New York," Caroline said, "but I'm sure Roosevelt will win. He has all that Cuban glory on his side."

Sophie straightened up in her chair at sounds in the foyer.

"There's Eric."

In a few moments Eric and Jim came into the parlor. Both of them looked exhausted, Caroline thought.

"It's all up to the voters now." Eric crossed to warm himself before the fire. For an instant his eyes rested on Caroline. She averted her own.

"Has there been any news about the situation in North Carolina?" Caroline asked Jim. She was horrified by the "White Supremacy Jubilees" being staged in North Carolina, with hundreds of armed red-shirted men parading to build up race hatred.

"You know about last night?" Jim's face was taut with distaste. Caroline nodded. Her eyes reflecting his feelings.

"What happened, Jim?" Sophie demanded. "I haven't read a newspaper in three days. We've had some machinery breakdowns at the mill."

"All last night colored mobs were parading in the suburbs of Wilmington, protesting the Red Shirt parades. The Wilmington Light Infantry and Naval Reserves are standing by."

"Charles Aycock knows the only way he can win the Governorship is to disenfranchise the Negro majority," Eric picked up tersely. "He's got Ben Tillman up from South Carolina to help him. There's a rumor folks in Richmond sent fifty thousand rounds of ammunition and a carload of firearms a few days ago."

"They've brought enough small arms into North Carolina in the last month to equip a whole U.S. Army division," Jim told them. "And ex-Congressman Waddell, who should damn well know better, is inciting whites to violence."

"With the Peace Jubilee five weeks away, they're trying to resurrect the War Between the States." Caroline shook her head in frustration.

Seth came into the parlor with coffee. Sophie poured for them. Caroline made an effort to relieve the tension in the room.

"How are you enjoying being an attorney again?" she asked Jim.

"I'd rather be a newspaperman," Jim conceded, "but I always do well financially in law. And now that I've got Eric to prepare for the bar exams, I keep busy enough to stay out of trouble."

"Eric!" Sophie glowed. "You said nothing to us about that."

"Wait till I'm accepted by the Georgia bar," Eric shrugged.

The following evening, at Andrew's urging, Caroline went downtown with Eric and him to the *Constitution* building. Wedged between the two men in the bitter cold that had not discouraged a crowd from gathering, she watched the state election returns being flashed by the newspaper. It was an excruciating blend of torture and delight to stand here this way so close to Eric. Now and then the crowd jostled them, and Eric or Andrew put a protective arm about her waist.

"It'll be tomorrow night before all the votes are counted," Andrew reminded at eleven. "Let's go home."

As ERIC and Jim had predicted, Teddy Roosevelt won the gubernatorial race in New York. Allen Chandler, who had been Georgia's Secretary of State—and who boasted that he had returned home after Confederate service with "one wife, one baby, one dollar, and one eye"—was elected Governor of Georgia.

In Phoenix, South Carolina, four Negroes were lynched as an aftermath of election race riots. In Wilmington, where the whites won over an intimidated black majority, the ex-Congressman who had been inciting violence led a mob of four hundred in shooting up the Negro district. Eleven Negroes died; more were wounded. Caroline prayed that next month's municipal elections in Atlanta would evoke no violence.

The family would not go to Hampton Court for Thanksgiving; the traveling would be too difficult for Tina. However, in mid-

November Caroline went up alone for a day. She placed roses on the General's grave, a cluster of violets on the grave of her grandmother. She sat on a granite bench on this cold, gray day and remembered with gratitude the beautiful closeness that had developed between her grandfather and her in those final days of his life.

After lunch at the house, with Hallie fussing over her with proprietary affection, Caroline climbed into the carriage again for the trip back to Atlanta. Her thoughts were monopolized by the frenetic days of the Reunion. Grandpa enjoyed their reception. Tears welled in her eyes as she remembered his pride when he introduced her to their guests. How she wished he could be here for their reception during the Peace Jubilee!

No, not a reception, she decided in a burst of exhilaration. A magnificent ball, with supper prepared by the New Orleans chef. A fine orchestra, masses of orchids and roses and lilies. They would open the ballroom that Sophie had described to her in rich detail, but which she had never seen. It would easily accommodate a hundred guests. For Papa she would give this ball. Let Atlanta know that Francis Hampton's daughter had come home.

Caroline threw herself into the arrangements for the ball. She made a secret trip to Hampton Court to enlist Cassius' talents in designing her gown. The New Orleans chef was cajoled into returning to Atlanta. Under Jim's manipulations a printer had been prodded into delivering invitations with unprecedented speed.

Again, unknowing to Eric, Caroline siphoned funds into the final frenzied weeks of his campaign. There must be no slipup. Eric must win. She told herself she was doing this out of respect for the General's memory.

Caroline slept little the night before the early December day when Atlantans were to go to the polls to vote for municipal officers. The strain of maintaining an outward appearance of cousinly interest in Eric's campaign had torn at her nerves. In truth, Eric monopolized her thoughts.

She awoke on this election morning with an instant realization of its importance to Eric's life. If he won today, he would move onward and upward in politics. Of necessity, he must carry Tina with him. She was never in a room with him that she was not conscious of her love for him. She always felt Eric's silent rebuke that she refused to allow him to talk to her on a personal level.

She stared at the ribbon of sunlight that lay across the rug. Eric would win the election. Tina would give him a child. *She* would move out of his life, except as the wealthy cousin who could be useful in furthering his political career. Everybody would admire the handsome Councilman and his beautiful wife. The mill would be *her* life, Caroline reminded herself.

She dressed and went downstairs. Sophie was going to the mill as though this were any ordinary day, but she could not bring herself to leave the house. How absurd that women couldn't vote!

At an unprecedented hour, Tina came downstairs and sought her out.

"Lucinda said you were here in the library."

"I was too excited about the election to go to the mill," Caroline acknowledged. "How're you feeling?"

"I can't sleep," Tina sighed. "I'm so tired of being stuck in the house." She lowered herself into a chair. She was so big; she could be carrying twins, Caroline thought. Why did she still resist seeing Dr. Ashley? It was absurd, on the brink of the twentieth century, for a woman to be delivered by a family servant and her mother.

"Caroline, do you think Eric's going to win?" Tina was emerging from her constant sulkiness in the excitement of the day.

"Unless there's some kind of upset," Caroline assured her.

"What kind of upset?" Tina frowned.

"Tina, unexpected switches in voting occur occasionally." *Don't let it happen today.*

"Chad thinks Eric will win." Tina sighed. "If the baby was born already, we could have a victory party."

"There'll be other victory parties," Caroline soothed, torturing herself. "Years of them."

The day dragged. Tina remained downstairs, keeping Lucinda running back and forth between her bedroom and the library. Caroline's head ached from Tina's incessant chatter.

Earlier than usual, Sophie returned from the mill.

"Have you heard anything about the election?" she asked immediately.

"Chad called. He said folks are saying that a lot of voters are going to the polls," Tina reported. "I wish we knew what was happening," she said querulously.

After dinner the three women settled themselves in the parlor. There had been no word from Eric all day. It was late in the evening when they heard him arrive. He was talking in the foyer with Seth.

Unable to restrain her excitement, Caroline leapt to her feet and darted to the door.

"How was the turnout?" she called to Eric.

"Good," he said, walking to the door. "We can't claim victory until the votes are counted, but the feeling downtown is that I'm in."

"Darling, how wonderful!" Tina bubbled. "You'll be in office when the baby is born."

As ANTICIPATED, Eric was voted in as Councilman from his district. By now all of Atlanta was emotionally and physically involved in the coming Peace Jubilee. It was to be the most splendid occasion ever experienced in the city. Generals Wheeler, Shafter, Young, Henry and Lawton would attend. President McKinley and Mrs. McKinley, along with five members of the Cabinet and their wives, were coming.

The night before the Jubilee, high winds whistled eerily through the pines and rattled the shuttered windows of the Hampton house. For three days the New Orleans chef had been busy in the kitchen. Mattie had been shipped off to visit a son and his family down in Plains, Georgia. Tomorrow a man would arrive to supervise in the floral decorations in preparation for the ball. Two orchestras had been hired, and Chad—chosen by Caroline to lead the pre-supper cotillion—was in consultation with the conductors on his choice of music.

Tonight Eric arrived from downtown with news of preparations for the Jubilee.

"They've finished the big Peace Jubilee arch at Peachtree and Edgecomb. The decorators at the stores are having a devil of a time tacking up their miles of bunting in this wind."

"Do you suppose it's going to be this cold and windy tomorrow?" Sophie asked worriedly.

"The weatherman says it's going to be cold and clear," Caroline said. "And the wind won't be so biting."

"Are you all going to the Union Depot when the President arrives in the morning?" Though she sulked about not being able to participate in the social events, Tina was curious about every small detail of the Jubilee.

"The Presidential train is scheduled to come in at eight," Caroline said, her smile whimsical. "I don't think any of us will be there."

"The President and his party will be met by an Executive Committee and a Reception Committee. And undoubtably hundreds of others," Eric said dryly. "There'll be sufficient without us."

"The ladies of the Jubilee Committee will meet them at the depot," Tina's voice was aggrieved. "I don't know why Mama wasn't invited to be on that committee."

"I have four tickets for the public reception at the Capitol tomorrow afternoon at two. Sophie, would you like to go with me? Caro?" Eric asked casually.

"You didn't ask me!" Tina was enraged.

"Do you want to go, Tina?" Eric asked with exaggerated politeness.

"You know I can't!"

"Exactly," Eric acknowledged. "So why ask?"

"I'd like to go to the Capitol reception." Sophie surprised Caroline with her acceptance of Eric's invitation. "You'll come with us, Caroline. And I'll tell Andrew to join us. You said you have four tickets, Eric."

"Sophie, there's so much to do for the dinner," Caroline hedged, though she longed to attend the reception.

"You can be away from the house for two hours," Sophie said briskly. "We'll go with you, Eric."

"Stay in town for the Floral Parade," Tina commanded. "I

want to know what each carriage looked like and what everybody wore." Her face tightened. "I'd be riding in the parade if it wasn't for the baby."

"We'll see the parade," Caroline promised.

As they climbed into the carriage the next day, en route to the Capitol reception, they heard the sound of artillery in the distance.

"What was that?" Caroline inquired.

"A twenty-one-gun salute for the President," Andrew told her. "He must be arriving at the Capitol."

Eric was taciturn, pretending to be interested in the display of flags flying from the verandahs of the houses they were passing. Caroline knew that Andrew's attentiveness to her annoyed him.

At the Capitol they discovered that the arrangements for admission to the building to be by ticket only had been swept aside by the inability of the guards to hold back the enthusiastic hordes that pushed through the doors. They joined the crowd on the lower floor of the Capitol. There the guards managed to hold the visitors in check, waiting for word to allow an orderly procession to cross the rotunda to the foot of the marble staircase, where President McKinley would personally greet them.

"General Wheeler is with the President!" a radiant young woman confided to them. "And General Young and General Lawton!"

Uneasily conscious of Eric's arm about her waist as the crowd jostled them into closer proximity, Caroline focused on inspecting their surroundings.

The entire first floor was vivid with red, white and blue bunting. Long streamers dropped from the galleries. Flags were entwined about the pillars. Everywhere were pictures of the heroes of the recent war, with the President's portrait occupying the place of honor.

They followed the procession into the rotunda, spent their brief moment with the President and left by the Mitchell Street entrance to join the convivial throngs waiting on Peachtree for the Floral Parade. Hordes of policemen good-humoredly held back the crowds on the sidewalks.

"You should be riding in one of the carriages," Andrew told

Caroline, a hand at her elbow.

"I should be home right now attending to the details of our ball," Caroline laughed.

Shouts went up and down the street when, with the Presidential party on the reviewing stand, the procession began. First came the mounted police, and behind them the Fifth Regiment band. The first display was from the Atlanta Fire Department. The yellow rose-draped wagon, drawn by four handsome horses, was covered by a canopy of roses of the same golden hue, from which hung a huge firebell made of red roses. Two small boys garbed in "fire laddies" suits sat under the bell. The crowd cheered lustily.

Caroline made mental notes for Tina as victorias, tea carts, and other equipages appeared in view, all beautifully decorated with flowers that sometimes concealed the entire vehicle. Roses, orchids, chrysanthemums, violets and lilies were on lavish display.

Caroline and Sophie agreed that they would leave rather than wait for the return of the procession and the selection of the prize-winners. Caroline was anxious to return home for a final inspection of the floral decorations for the ball.

After complimenting the florist and consulting with Seth about the arrangements of the tables, Caroline went upstairs to report to Tina on the parade. Sulkily, Tina listened to every detail that Caroline could recall.

"You haven't even shown me your dress," Tina chided. "I know it was delivered yesterday."

"I'll stop in your room on my way downstairs tonight," Caroline promised. Only Andrew and Cassius knew what she would wear tonight.

Had she chosen her gown capriciously? She had shocked one of Atlanta's finest tailors. But that gown was meant to be an announcement to Atlanta.

Caroline went to her room. Patience, too often sad-eyed and listless these last months, was ironing the new gown.

"Miss Caroline, this is so pretty," she said with more vivacity than she had displayed since Zeke's death. "You is gonna be the most beautiful young lady at the party."

At Patience's insistence she took a nap, sleeping until Patience awoke her. Sophie had ordered trays sent up, since supper would not be served until after the cotillion.

Caroline ate, then dressed in deliberate leisureliness. She heard Chad arrive and expected he would come up to visit with Tina. Instead he went into the ballroom where the musicians were tuning up for the evening. Chad was delighted to have been chosen leader for the cotillion.

Twenty minutes later, Sophie simultaneously knocked at the door and called to her.

"Caroline, we should be downstairs in the receiving line in a few moments."

"Sophie, I may be a little late," she apologized. "But Eric and you will be there."

"Caroline, it's your ball," Sophie reproved.

"It's the family's ball," Caroline laughed. "I'll be down shortly."

"Are you all right?" All at once Sophie was solicitous.

"I'm fine, Sophie," she reassured, her voice affectionate.

She sat in the slipper chair before the fireplace so that Patience could brush her hair. Nobody had rejected her invitation. Tonight Francis Hampton's daughter was entertaining some of Atlanta's finest citizens. Tonight was a triumph for Papa.

Again there was a knock at the door. When Patience made a move to respond, Caroline halted her with a silent gesture.

"Who is it?" she asked.

"Lucinda. Miss Tina say, please stop by her room before you goes downstairs."

"I'll be there, Lucinda."

In a few minutes Caroline heard the first carriage arrive before the house. Music—the lilting "Blue Danube"—was circulating through the lower floor. Caroline rose from her chair to go to the chest-on-chest across the room. She pulled open a drawer. She had taken her grandmother's exquisite stone cameo, set in a frame of tiny pearls and diamonds, from the library safe last night. She would wear it on a slender black velvet ribbon.

"Lemme fix that, Miss Caroline."

Patience moved forward with an admiring smile. Caroline

373

stood immobile while Patience slid the ribbon through the loop at the back of the cameo and then adjusted it about her throat. She could hear carriages pulling up before the house now, one after another. Festive sounds filtered up the stairs and into her room.

"Don't sit up for me, Patience," Caroline ordered. "And pray that I don't disgrace the General."

"You'll do him proud." Patience glowed.

Caroline left her bedroom and knocked at Tina's door.

"Come in." Tina's voice was sulky.

Caroline opened the door and walked inside, closing the door behind her. Tina sat in an armchair before the fireplace, her feet propped on a petit-point footstool.

"Is my gown all right, Tina?" She anticipated reproach, and an explanation hovered on her lips.

"It's beautiful," Tina surprised her. She was shocked by the glint of malicious pleasure she saw in Tina's eyes.

"Thank you, Tina." She bent forward to kiss Tina on one cheek. "Seth has instructions to send up a tray with exactly what we're having for dinner, and a bottle of the best champagne."

Caroline left Tina's room and walked to the head of the wide, curving staircase. Eric and Sophie stood at the entrance to the ballroom, welcoming their guests. Seth was opening the door to fresh arrivals, Annie Mae and Jason relieving others of their wraps. A half dozen guests talked animatedly to Eric and Sophie in the brilliant illumination of the foyer's gilt and crystal chandelier. Others had gone inside the ballroom.

Caroline geared herself to descend to the foyer. *She was Francis Hampton's daughter and these were her guests.* The gentlemen wore tuxedos with black vests, and some wore pleated shirt-fronts rather than the conventional stiffly starched fronts. The ladies were elegantly attired in gowns of silk, velvet and satin in the delicate pinks and brilliant blues so fashionable this season.

Holding above her ankles her multi-layered yellow organdy skirts, splashed with hand-painted butterflies executed by Cassius, Caroline walked down the stairs. The yellow skirt was an attractive overlay for the peach skirt beneath. The heart-shaped neckline displayed the splendor of her shoulders and was a becoming setting for Louisa Hampton's cameo. The gown had been meticulously copied from the French original.

Caroline observed rather than heard the gasps of the ladies when they became aware of her approach. They were shocked that the General's granddaughter could be so ignorant of fashion, so gauche, as to wear lowly cotton on such a formal occasion.

Eric excused himself to come forward to take her hand. Caroline's smile was dazzling, giving the others no indication that she was aware of the furor her gown created. Silently Eric escorted her to the receiving line.

"Is this beautiful young lady the General's granddaughter?" An elderly gentleman beamed at her.

"Caroline, may I present Dr. Otis." Eric was amused by the startled stares her gown was evoking. "Dr. Otis, Miss Caroline Hampton."

"What a lovely gown, Miss Hampton," Dr. Otis said gallantly.

"Thank you, Dr. Otis." Caroline's voice was soft yet sufficiently vibrant to carry into the ballroom. "I chose cotton, though my tailor was shocked," she admitted, "because I knew it would have pleased my grandfather." Aware of the undercurrent of drama in the foyer, the guests in the ballroom ceased to chatter. "The cotton for my gown was grown at Hampton Court. It was woven at the Hampton Mill. It had to be finished by hand because our finishing plant is still being built. It's a product of Georgia."

"Hear, hear," a portly gentleman moved forward approvingly.

"It's time for the ladies of the Cotton Kingdom to promote our native product." Caroline's gaze encompassed her guests. "We must show the rest of the world that cotton can be beautiful."

"Hear, hear!" more male voices approved.

Sophie reached to squeeze her hand. Eric's eyes rested on her with a proprietary pride that was not his right, she thought, while he introduced her to the next guests in line.

When all their guests had been received, Caroline retired with Sophie and Eric to the ballroom. She paused a moment at the entrance to admire the magnificence before her. White damask walls, elegant red velvet drapes at the tall, narrow windows that marched like proud sentinels on three sides. Masses of red roses, white lilies of the valley and blue hyacinths vied in fragrance and carried out the patriotic colors of the Jubilee. Three crystal chandeliers, ordered from Vienna by Josiah Hampton twenty-five years ago, lent a dazzling brilliance to the colorful assemblage.

Chad had arranged for the seating of the couples on three sides of the room. Andrew, who was to be Caroline's partner, stood beside their gilt chairs at the head of the cotillion. She sensed his elation that she had chosen him. Chad had rehearsed them for their position as first couple.

Sophie went to take her pre-arranged place at the ladies' favors table. Tina's mother was performing this duty at the gentlemen's favors table. Caroline crossed the ballroom to sit at Andrew's right. It was understood that, out of respect for Tina's condition, Eric would not dance this evening.

There was an air of drama as Chad gave the signal to one of the orchestras to play. He took his position on the floor to announce the first figure. At his instructions, Caroline and Andrew and the second couple rose from their chairs and began to waltz about the room. The cotillion had begun.

Chad was a fine leader, Caroline decided as the cotillion continued. She had chosen him to placate Tina, but he was at his best in a role such as this. His eyes sparkling, his voice ebullient, he called out a variety of figures, never allowing the dancing to become monotonous for the couples who watched.

Chad had been helpful, too, in choosing the favors. There were fans, jeweled matchboxes, jeweled perfume bottles, tiny boxes of candies and cigarettes, a collection of amusing toys, all to be set up on the favors tables as they became needed. Chad had arranged every detail with meticulous care.

Caroline was startled when Eric appeared before her, favor in hand, eyebrow lifted in sardonic amusement.

"Eric, you were not to dance," she reproached under her breath.

"I couldn't resist the chance to hold you in my arms," he whispered. "Caroline, you can't refuse," he tantalized. "No young lady refuses a gentleman in the cotillion."

"You're outrageous!" Her eyes blazed, though she forced herself to smile lest the others be aware of her fury.

"You're beautiful." Eric's voice was a caress. "I watched you coming down that stairway tonight, knowing you were going to shock the devil out of those proper ladies below, and I was proud that I love you."

"You are never to say that to me again!" she warned.

"Smile for our guests," he ordered, "or I'll kiss you right here on the dance floor."

"How dare you behave this way when Tina's closeted up there in her room, carrying your child!" Her color was high, her heart pounding.

"Maybe it's my child," he said, his eyes cold.

Chad clapped his hands for the dancing to cease.

Trembling, Caroline sat down to wait for the beginning of the next figure. She was unnerved when Eric contrived to dance with her again, no more than ten minutes later.

"Eric, you are supposed to ask young ladies who are without partners to dance," Caroline said through clenched teeth. "If you must dance." Tina's mother was watching them with unconcealed disapproval.

"I'd like to waltz all night in a room alone with you," Eric told her. His eyes held hers in amorous declaration.

She wished their guests would disappear. She wished they were alone here with the music and the scent of flowers. She wished she were lying in Eric's arms and he was making love to her, *When would she stop feeling this way?*

A clap of Chad's hands and the spell was splintered. She was relieved to be able to return to her chair and watch the others for a while, yet fearful that Eric would again contrive to have her as his partner.

At last the cotillion was over and they retired to the formal dining room for supper. The guests were vocally delighted with the favors they discovered at each place setting. For the men there were elegantly crafted silver cufflinks depicting the olive branch of peace; and for the ladies exquisitely designed silver pins representing doves of peace. Red roses, lilies of the valley and blue Chinese forget-me-nots carried out the patriotic color scheme.

The supper began with oyster cocktails and green turtle soup, after which was served a superbly sauced filet of sole, *veau à la*

377

portugaise, diamondback terrapin, along with two hothouse vegetables and a fruit salad and sherbet. For dessert there was *baba au rhum* and a chocolate mousse. A fine sherry, two rare wines and two champagnes accompanied the various courses.

Caroline contrived to appear delighted with the obvious pleasure of her guests, yet every moment of the sumptuous supper she was conscious of Eric's presence, his recurrent glances in her direction. When the guests returned to the ballroom after supper to waltz to the continuous music, she arranged not to dance with Eric.

At last good-nights had been said, and Caroline went out to the kitchen to express her gratitude to the chef and the staff he had brought with him from New Orleans. The evening was a triumph. Returning from the kitchen, she heard Tina's mother in agitated conversation with Chad on the stairs. They had gone up to say good-night to Tina, Caroline realized, while Mr. Kendrick lingered in the library for a last drink with Eric.

"I don't care what you say, Chad," Mrs. Kendrick was insisting. "I saw how Eric flaunted himself with Caroline. Tina has to hide herself away upstairs, miserable and sick, and he and Caroline danced together twice. He couldn't keep his eyes off her tonight. Just wait till after the baby's born. Then he's going to hear about this!"

Chapter Thirty-one

S HORTLY before noon on the following day, Eric hurried Caroline and Sophie into the carriage that was waiting to take them downtown for the Jubilee parade. After- ward they would go to the Agricultural Building at Piedmont Park to hear the President speak before a huge public meeting.

"I don't know why you're rushing us so," Sophie complained. "The parade won't start before one. It's cold to be standing there so long."

"Sophie, you want to be able to see something besides the backs of their heads," Eric joshed.

Caroline gazed out the window, unable to share in the conviviality that seemed to be embracing Sophie and Eric. She was exhausted; sleep had been elusive last night. She was disturbed that Tina's mother suspected that the relationship between Eric and her was more than cousinly.

No one else had noticed, Caroline consoled herself. She had made a point of being attentive to several of the young gentlemen among their guests who seemed to be fascinated by General Hampton's granddaughter. Part of that fascination was evoked by her inheritance, Caroline guessed realistically.

Why had Tina pretended to be asleep when she stopped by her room after the last guests had gone? Ten minutes later, Caroline remembered, she could hear Tina in heated conversation on the telephone. Mrs. Kendrick hadn't told Tina about her suspicions? Caroline recoiled from the prospect of an ugly confrontation.

Jason drove them as close to the parade route as was feasible

379

today, and then they left the carriage to walk. Despite the cold, Whitehall Street was one mass of humanity, Peachtree and Marietta jammed from curb to doors.

"Look at the schoolchildren!" Sophie said in amazement. Blocks of children, every one clutching a flag, waited eagerly for the parade to begin.

"Ten thousand of them," Eric reported, while they pushed themselves to a good vantage point on Peachtree. "All here to welcome the President at his request."

"They're expecting a hundred thousand to be lining the parade route," a man beside them said. "This cold weather won't stop anybody."

Caroline sought to reflect the festive mood around her; but her mind, like Sophie's, focused on the Reunion parade five months ago when they watched the General ride in the downpour that had cost his life. Confederate veterans would march again today. At last the sounds beyond told them the parade was beginning. The crowds waited expectantly. Cheers broke out as a squad of mounted police appeared to open the way. Directly behind them came Governor Candler's staff and the Grand Marshal and his staff. Tumultuous cheers filled the air when President McKinley appeared in the following carriage, along with the Governor and President Hemphill of the Jubilee Association.

Caroline watched through misty eyes as 4,000 soldiers marched with admirable precision, sunlight glistening on their guns and bayonets. The Third Tennessee Band followed, playing exuberantly, and behind them came the Atlanta Artillery and the Governor's Horse Guards with sixty mounted men. The fife and drum corps played "Auld Lang Syne" and "The Girl I Left Behind."

The crowd swelled into one prolonged yell of homage when General Wheeler and his escort of one hundred mounted veterans who had served with him during the Civil War rode into view. Every man present saluted.

Tears rolled unheeded down Sophie's cheeks. Caroline fumbled for a handkerchief. The General should be here, mounted on his horse, riding with General Wheeler. He was here in spirit while the blue and the gray united to honor the President of the United States and the Confederate General who had fought so valiantly in the War Between the States.

"If we leave now," Eric said softly, "we'll get good seats out at the Agricultural Building."

They managed to push their way through the crowds and left the parade route to seek out Jason, who waited with the carriage. In communal silence they rode to Piedmont Park. Although the Presidential party was not due at the auditorium until three o'clock, after a luncheon at the Piedmont Driving Club, people had begun to gather in the building since one o'clock. Caroline was relieved that Eric had suggested their coming early; very soon there would be no seats available.

The Fifth Regiment Band played a steady procession of appropriate music to stem the restlessness of the waiting crowd. At last the President and his party arrived. The auditorium was packed to capacity within minutes. Each member of the party was greeted with cheers as he ascended the platform. The audience was on its feet as the President, with Mrs. McKinley leaning on his arm, and beaming with pleasure, arrived at the front of the platform.

The meeting was called to order by Colonel Hemphill, who introduced Dr. Landrum. At the close of the prayer, the band struck up "America." When the band completed the national anthem, Secretary of War Alger leapt up unexpectedly and advanced to the front of the platform.

"Let everyone in the hall join in singing 'America'!" he urged.

The band began to play again, and with Secretary Alger leading, the huge audience sang. President McKinley stepped forward to the front of the platform, along with the others of his party, to join in the chorus. The hall rang with the voices of 8,000 joyously singing "America."

Colonel Hemphill arose to introduce the President of the United States. A hush fell over the audience while McKinley stepped to the front of the platform. Eric leaned forward to whisper to Caroline that McKinley, who had risen from a commissary sergeant to brevet major in the Union Army in the War

Between the States, wore a Confederate badge pinned on him by one of the veterans.

All at once the hush became a burst of cheers, compelling the President to wait before beginning his speech. He spoke with a strength that claimed and held the crowd's attention. Many were astonished that he spoke to them of the policy of his administration toward the foreign territories of the nation. There had been no word of this when he addressed the Assembly.

"I would like to hear him repeat what he said at the Capitol yesterday," Eric whispered to Caroline, and she turned to him with misty-eyed acknowledgment. *The time has come,*" McKinley had said, *"for the Federal government to unite with the South in caring for the graves of the Confederate dead."* This was the ultimate tribute to the South.

Now President McKinley was paying tribute to the South for its part in the war with Spain. With uplifted hand, his voice rich with emotion, he said, "That flag has been planted in the two hemispheres and there it remains the symbol of liberty and law, of peace and progress. Who will withdraw from the people over whom it floats its protecting folds? Will the people of the South help to haul it down?"

"No! No!" a thousand voices echoed through the auditorium. The audience was on its feet, cheering wildly.

Caroline sensed Eric's unhappiness as the President spoke of expansion, with the crowd—still on its feet—seemingly in approval. When McKinley finished speaking, the band struck up "Dixie." The President joined in the loud applause.

Now the audience called for General Wheeler; and the diminutive veteran of two wars, in full uniform and with one hand on the hilt of his sword, stepped to the front. The cheering was so prolonged the General was about to return uncomfortably to his seat, but Secretary of the Treasury Gage laughingly stopped him.

The General—Georgia's own—spoke briefly, to be followed by Lieutenant Hobson and General Shafter, all to loud and prolonged cheers. Generals Young, Henry and Lawton were presented to the audience, to more cheering. At last, with much emotion, the ceremonies were over, and the huge audience moved out of the auditorium.

Caroline clung to Sophie's hand when, flanked by Eric and Andrew, they made their way to the waiting Hampton carriage. Like Sophie, she was poignantly aware of the General's absence on this day which would have meant so much to him. In her mind echoed General Wheeler's voice as he spoke from the platform this afternoon:

"I wish to say that all during the day telegrams have been pouring to President McKinley from Grand Army posts in the North, thanking him for the expressions he made at the Capitol yesterday regarding the graves of Confederate soldiers."

At last they had laid the War Between the States to rest. Before the joint session of the General Assembly at the Capitol yesterday, President McKinley had read the epitaph.

Caroline and Sophie dined alone. As incoming Councilman, Eric had been included among the three hundred Atlantans and visitors invited to the banquet at the Kimball House in honor of President McKinley and his party. Earlier Andrew had asked Caroline to go with him to the Grand Theatre tonight, when the ladies of the Social Events Committee of the Peace Jubilee would be entertaining Mrs. McKinley and the Cabinet wives at a theater party. She had gently rejected this with the excuse that she would not like to leave Sophie alone on this final night of the Jubilee. Today they were all painfully conscious of the General's death.

Caroline wished that it was possible for the family to go to Hampton Court for the Christmas holidays. Tina's increasingly difficult pregnancy obviated this. Tina continued to refuse Caroline's urging to have Dr. Ashley attend her. Sophie was impatient with Tina's constant crying spells, though she was also unhappy that Eric displayed only perfunctory solicitude toward Tina.

"Tina's just going into her sixth month," Sophie said to Caroline tiredly three evenings before Christmas, when Tina's wails of unhappiness—filtering to the lower floor of the house—were punctuated by a screeching fit at Lucinda. "How are *we* to survive?"

"She's having a difficult pregnancy. And she's carrying such a big baby." The delivery was going to be hard, Caroline worried. Dr. Ashley should be in attendance.

"She's behaving stupidly," Sophie said bluntly. "Expecting to be delivered by Lucinda."

"Tina's a romantic."

"Tina has never had a truly romantic notion in her life," Sophie denied. "She has ridiculous fantasies about what her life should be like. She's been spoiled shockingly by her mother and Chad. Tina worships Tina."

"She'll change after the baby is born," Caroline soothed. "You'll see."

Caroline was troubled by the covert hostility toward her that she sensed in Tina. That hostility had surfaced the first night of the Peace Jubilee. This was part of Tina's pregnancy, she told herself. It, too, would disappear, when the baby was born.

Caroline was painfully cognizant of the difference between this Christmas and the previous one. The General and Zeke had both been alive then. The family had gone to Hampton Court.

Christmas Eve passed quietly. On Christmas Day, Caroline persuaded Sophie to go with Andrew and her to attend the children's party in the mill village. She had worked with the Robertses to assure the party would be a success. Beneath the tall pine tree set up in the church were gifts for each child. Caroline had bought books of Joel Chandler Harris' *Uncle Remus* stories, tops, kites, dolls, tea sets.

When they arrived at the party, Caroline was aware of a silent resentment toward them on the part of the parents who had come to help. Even the children lost their exuberance.

"We won't stay long," Caroline whispered to Grace and Henry after a few minutes. "We just wanted to see the tree. It's beautiful."

At Grace's insistence they drank hot chocolate and listened to the children sing "Silent Night" before they left the village. Jason dropped Andrew at his cottage and then continued to the Hampton house. Alighting from the carriage, Caroline and Sophie felt the first wet flurries of snow.

"I'd like some tea," Sophie said with a frown. "It's so raw outside."

"I'll have some with you," Caroline offered. She sensed that Sophie was reluctant to be alone.

They went to the library, where Seth had kept a roaring fire going all day. Eric looked up from his chair, where he sat reading.

"You didn't stay long."

"The children didn't seem comfortable with us," Caroline said candidly.

"The mill folks are becoming increasingly aware that they're at the bottom of the social ladder," Eric reminded, "and they're resentful. The children feel this."

All at once a frenzied scream rent the quietness of the house, and then another.

"Lucinda!" Tina shrieked. "Lucinda!"

"I'll go up to her." Caroline sprang to her feet.

"Lucinda will go," Sophie said, but Caroline was hurrying from the room.

"Lucinda!" Tina screamed again a minute later.

Darting up the stairs, Caroline spied Lucinda rushing into Tina's room. Without bothering to knock, Caroline pushed open the door and went inside. Lucinda hovered over Tina, a hand on her swollen belly.

"Lucinda, what is it?" Caroline asked in alarm.

"She havin' pains," Lucinda said unsteadily. "She—she losin' the baby."

"I'll call for Dr. Ashley." Caroline was pale with concern.

"No!" Tina shrieked.

"Miss Tina, I gotta go downstairs to git some things," Lucinda soothed. "Them pains comin' awful close together."

"Caroline, stay with me." Tina's eyes were glazed with terror.

"I'll stay." Caroline hurried beside the bed.

"Miss Tina, you hold on to this," Lucinda ordered, putting a towel in her hand. "When the pains start again, you hold tight."

Before Lucinda had closed the door behind her, Tina was screaming again.

"Why are they coming so fast?" Tina complained when the pain subsided. "I never wanted this baby! I hate it! I hate it!"

"Tina, you're going to be all right." Caroline sat beside her at the edge of the bed. She reached to smooth Tina's hair away from her face as she writhed with the next pain. Caroline was in a private torment of her own. It was Tina—not she—who was losing Eric's baby, but in a strange fashion she felt guilty because she had wished so desperately that it was she who carried Eric's child.

Lucinda returned with fresh sheets and towels. Water was on the stove downstairs, she reported.

"Miss Caroline, you better go now. I'll take care of Miss Tina."

"I'll stay," Caroline said quietly.

"Miss Caroline, it ain't right," Lucinda objected. "A young lady what ain't married."

"I want her to stay," Tina gasped and reached out for Caroline's hand.

"Miss Tina," Lucinda was distraught. "I can take care of you."

For two hours Caroline sat beside Tina, her arms bruised by the grip of Tina's hands, her body exhausted. Tina was just going into her sixth month. Why was it this bad for her?

"Lucinda, can't we do something to help her?" Caroline asked anguishedly.

"She narrow," Lucinda said sullenly. "It ain't gonna be easy."

Tina screamed again. A wild animal scream. She released Caroline's wrist in her agony.

"I'm sending for Dr. Ashley," Caroline said. "He can do something to help."

Caroline hurried down the stairs. Eric was at a window in the library, staring out at the steadily falling snow.

"She's losing the baby?" Sophie asked.

"Yes. Eric, I think you ought to call Dr. Ashley."

"I'll call right now." He strode to the telephone.

Caroline hurried upstairs to Tina's bedroom. Lucinda had thrust aside the covers. She hovered above Tina.

"It ain't gonna be long, Miss Tina," Lucinda encouraged. "You keep pushin'."

"Dr. Ashley's coming," Caroline told Lucinda. It was Christmas Day. Would Eric be able to reach him?

The pains were coming one on top of another. Tina flailed about the bed, pounding with her fists.

"Come on, honey," Lucinda urged. "You gotta push."

"I hate it! I hate it!" Tina screamed.

"It's comin'!" Lucinda said finally. "I kin see the head. Sure fast for a first baby. Now you push real hard, Miss Tina. Harder!"

With a surge of compassion Caroline went to stand beside Tina. With a towel, she wiped away the perspiration that beaded Tina's forehead.

"I hate this baby!" Tina screamed, and with one furious push, ejected the tiny body.

Lucinda leaned forward to sever the umbilical cord. She lifted the baby from Tina and deposited it in Caroline's arms.

"I gotta take care of Miss Tina."

Plaintive wails echoed through the room. Arms and legs flailed weakly. Caroline cradled the tiny, perfectly formed infant in her arms. *Eric's son.* Tenderness suffused her. But all at once the wails ceased. The infant lay limp in her arms. *Eric's baby was dead.* He had come three months too soon.

"Miss Caroline, you go tell Annie Mae we wants some hot water up here," Lucinda ordered. "You jes' rest, Miss Tina. You is gonna be fine in a lil' bit."

Caroline wrapped the infant in a towel and laid him on a chair. Now she left the room to hurry down to the kitchen to deliver Lucinda's message. Eric came to the door of the dining room.

"Is it over?"

"She lost the baby," Caroline said tautly.

"Poor little thing," he whispered with compassion.

"It was a boy." Did he want to see his son?

They both started at the sound of the carriage pulling up before the house. Dr. Ashley was arriving. Eric charged to the door to admit him.

"I'll show you to Tina's room," Caroline said, while Eric relieved Dr. Ashley of his coat.

She led Dr. Ashley to Tina's room, and then went to her own. She could not bring herself to face Eric just yet. She sat in a chair by the fireplace, listening to the muted sounds from Tina's room next door. Silently she grieved for the dead infant.

At last Dr. Ashley emerged from Tina's room. She heard him go down the stairs. He was talking to Eric in the foyer. Caroline opened her door and eavesdropped. Tina would be all right, wouldn't she?

"She was delivered of a son, who lived only a few moments," Dr. Ashley said briskly. "She'll be fine."

"A miscarriage," Eric said with odd emphasis.

"Not a miscarriage," Dr. Ashley corrected with unexpected brusqueness. "She had carried through the entire seventh month. The infant was fully developed." *Not Eric's child. He was in Cuba when this baby was conceived.*

While Eric stared at the doctor, his mind absorbing the facts, Caroline hurled herself down the stairs.

"Dr. Ashley," she called. "Please wait."

"You were with Tina when the baby was born," he said gently. "Lucinda told me."

"Dr. Ashley, the General would have preferred to have this known as a miscarriage," Caroline said with wistful sweetness. "You'll see to that, won't you?"

"I have to report every birth," Dr. Ashley reminded, but his eyes were troubled.

"Dr. Ashley, forget this one," she pleaded. "Out of respect for the General's memory."

Her eyes clung to his. He sighed.

"It was a miscarriage."

THE FOLLOWING morning in a cold, dreary sleet, Caroline and Eric set out in a carriage to bury the dead infant in the family cemetery at Hampton Court. Eric was taciturn on the drive to the plantation, his gaze focused out the window. But as they approached the private road to the house, he turned to Caroline.

"You were wonderful with Dr. Ashley yesterday. I didn't think what it would mean to the family if the truth were known. I knew, of course," he said bitterly, "that Tina was having an affair with—"

"How dare you be so sanctimonious!" Caroline lashed at him. *He* had driven Tina into affairs with his callous disregard for her feelings. And what about his affairs? "But for the grace of God, I could have been pregnant. This could be our baby we're burying this morning."

"Caroline, listen to me." He reached to pull her close, but she pushed him away. "What we shared was right. We love each other. There was no love between Tina and me. She came to me that night we buried the General. I was upset and exhausted—and overheated," he acknowledged. "I wanted to hold you in my arms. But Tina was there. She threw herself at me," he said with contempt.

"I don't want to hear this!" Caroline said hotly. "I don't want to hear another word!"

"You *will* listen some day," he vowed. "There'll be a time for us. I refuse to believe there won't be."

The carriage turned in at the plantation road. Caroline stared out the window, her body taut. The sky was gray and forbidding, the ground cold and wet. She shivered in the depressing, dank chill.

Eric leaned from the window.

"Jason, let us off here and go on to the stable."

Eric jumped down from the carriage, extended a hand to Caroline. Avoiding his eyes, she allowed him to help her down. Solemnly Jason lifted the little white box that had been nailed together in the privacy of the stable last night, and lowered it into Eric's arms. Cradling the casket, Eric walked with Caroline to the family cemetery.

A message had been sent to Hampton Court and a freshly dug grave at one side of the cemetery waited to receive Tina's baby. While Caroline stood by, fighting tears—for herself, for Eric, for the tiny dead infant—Eric lowered the casket, covered it, and said a few words for the child who could not be his.

Silently Eric and Caroline walked to the stable, where Jason waited for them. Without going into the house, they left Hampton Court. They were halfway back to Atlanta when Eric broke the heavy silence.

"Tina and I will move out of the house," he said tersely.

"No!" Caroline was involuntarily vehement. How could she survive without seeing Eric each day? She kept a wall between them, but she knew Eric was there. "It would be unrealistic," she stammered, because he was gazing at her with unnerving intensity. "You need the Hampton background if you decide to run for the Legislature. Living in the General's house is a constant reminder. I know how you feel about achieving on your own, but *getting there* is important. You have something to contribute, but you can't do that without public office."

"I'm the Councilman," he reminded. "I take office right after the first of the year."

"With the right campaign you'll be running for the Legislature next year," Caroline shot back. "You'll be in a position to fight for reforms. Tina and you will stay at the house," Caroline insisted, "because it was Grandpa's dream that you bring honor to the Hampton name." Her eyes held his, daring him to refuse.

"We'll stay," Eric said shortly.

Chapter Thirty-two

NEW Year's Eve passed with little outward acknowledgment in the Hampton household, though most of the nation was aware that they were on the threshold of the last year of the century. On January 2nd, Eric began his term as Councilman. At the house he was somber and uncommunicative, despite Sophie's efforts to draw him out each night. Tina remained in her room, refusing to see anyone except Lucinda and Chad, who came daily.

"Tina's scared to face Eric," Sophie said bluntly when she sat alone in the library with Caroline toward the end of the second week in January. "But she has to come out of that room."

"I'll talk to Chad tomorrow," Caroline decided. "We can't let her go on this way. She could be headed for a breakdown."

"I don't like Chad," Sophie admitted. "But if anybody can handle Tina, it's her brother."

Caroline left the mill next morning at eleven, knowing Chad would be arriving. She reached the house as he was emerging from his carriage.

"Caroline, how nice to see you," he said ingratiatingly. Normally when he arrived, she had been at the mill for hours already. Yet Caroline sensed he was guarded. Chad, like Tina, was nervous about what actions Eric might take in regard to his marriage. He knew the family recognized that Tina had not miscarried, that the baby she bore could not have been Eric's.

"I came home especially to talk to you, Chad," she told him. "I'm worried about Tina. Dr. Ashley says she's fine. There's no reason for her to cling to her bed the way she does. Take her out to the theater or to a concert, Chad. Make her understand we're concerned for her." Caroline's eyes held his, transmitting silent reassurances. She saw the relief that welled in him.

"I'll make her take me for a drive in the loco-steamer," Chad promised. "She was furious when I insisted she stop driving it back in September."

Two hours later, standing at the window in the mill office Sophie had assigned to her, Caroline saw Tina and Chad walk from the house and to the stable, where the loco-steamer was kept. In another few minutes she saw the car moving down the driveway. Chad had been successful.

Caroline was impatient with the slow progress on the finishing plant. The General had allocated a specific percentage from each quarter's earnings to be spent on the plant. With additional funds, Caroline suspected, the work could be finished far more quickly. She discussed this in detail with Andrew, then with the building contractor.

On a bitterly cold January morning Caroline ordered a carriage to drive her to downtown Atlanta. She had phoned Cyrus Madison at home last night and asked if she might see him as soon as possible.

"Miss Caroline," Seth appeared at the library entrance, "Jason's out front with the carriage."

"Thank you, Seth."

In the residential section the lawns were picturesque with blankets of an earlier snow, roofs white, trees hung with icicles. Caroline was hardly aware of the winter splendor. She was gearing herself for a battle with Cyrus Madison.

The lawyer greeted her affectionately, yet she sensed a wariness in him.

"You're looking lovely, Caroline," he said.

Without preliminaries Caroline explained her mission. She wished him to sell a substantial amount of her stocks so that the work on the finishing plant could be accelerated. As she had expected, he argued against this.

"Mr. Madison, I've gone over figures with Andrew at the mill. We know that we can earn far more by finishing our own cloth than those stocks will earn. I'm sure if the General were alive I could convince him of this. I have figures right here."

She pulled sheets of paper from her handbag, indicated what anticipated profits would be on finishing.

"Once we're finishing cloth, we'll be able to move into manufacturing clothes as well. Atlanta is perfectly situated for this. With the railroads and—"

"Caroline," Cyrus interrupted, "you're envisioning a dynasty. Josiah lives again, in you."

"You'll arrange to sell the stocks?" Caroline's eyes searched his.

"I'll make all the arrangements," he promised. "You'll have the funds within ten days. It'll be a loan to the Hampton Mill," he stipulated. "To be repaid out of future profits."

"We'll begin working on two shifts." Caroline was enthusiastic. "I hope by the end of July the finishing plant can be in operation." Let them open on the anniversary of the General's death.

Caroline returned to the house, buoyed by her meeting with Cyrus Madison. She would have lunch with Tina, she decided, then go over to the mill village to visit with Grace and Henry. She knocked at Tina's door.

"Who is it?" Tina asked querulously.

"Caroline. I thought we might have lunch together." Tina's earlier hostility toward her had evaporated, yet she suspected that Tina resented her position in the household. "I have an idea about birthday parties for the mill children. I want your reaction to it," she coaxed.

The door swung open. Tina stood there, coldly beautiful in an emerald green dressing gown.

"I'm going to Mary Lee Harrison's party for her cousin who's down from New York, and Mary Lee always has such lavish refreshments I shouldn't eat a thing. But I'll eat a little to keep you company," Tina said sweetly. "You're not going to Mary Lee's party?"

"I don't know Mary Lee Harrison." Tina was needling her for not being invited. "The Harrisons were not at either of our dinners, were they?"

"No," Tina admitted.

Seth was at the front door as they reached the bottom of the stairs. Bart Menlow stood there, his arms laden with a huge parcel. Caroline loathed Menlow. He was loud-mouthed and arrogant, though Sophie said he was a good foreman. "Miss Sophie said to please put these books in the library," he ordered Seth condescendingly. "She wants to go over them away from the noise in the mill." Bart's eyes strayed past Seth to linger brazenly on Tina.

"Is there anything else?" Caroline was infuriated.

"That's all," he said sullenly. "Miss Sophie wants the books in the library," he reiterated.

"They'll be there. You can return to the mill now."

Over lunch Caroline explained to Tina that she wanted to talk to the Robertses about providing a group birthday party each month for the children of Hamptonville.

"The party will be in honor of all the children whose birthdays fall in that month. Mattie can make up a huge birthday cake, and we'll serve hot chocolate with it," Caroline explained.

"Caroline, how thoughtful of you," Tina murmured. "I'm sure the children will love it."

Caroline was delighted with this unexpected interest on Tina's part.

"Would you like to help?"

"I'd adore to help," Tina said with appealing spontaneity. "I suppose you'll have it in the church?" Caroline nodded. "Then I'll help you with the decorations," Tina promised. "I'm good at that."

Caroline left the house to walk to the village. This morning's sunshine had fled behind clusters of dusky gray clouds. She walked with shoulders hunched against the cold, against the sharp wind that was just beginning to make itself felt.

"Lint head! Lint head! Cotton mill trash!"

Caroline was startled by the chanting jeers of a cluster of children at the edge of the village.

"Cotton tails! Cotton tails!" they chanted now and laughed raucously.

They could not be more than nine or ten, Caroline thought furiously as she charged toward the melee that had erupted. The town children had come to the edge of the mill village specifically to hurl invectives at the even younger mill children.

"Stop this! Stop it this minute!" She fought to separate the small fighters. "Stop it before I send for the police!"

"Get out of here!" Henry Roberts came running toward them, breathless from his efforts, trailed by two of the men who spent warmer days sitting in front of the company store. "Go on now," he ordered, pulling them apart. "Go back where you belong!"

The town children ran, yelling over their shoulders while the other children watched. The two fathers stared resentfully after them.

"Those awful children," Caroline apologized. The two fathers turned to her, in distrust. Everybody except those of the village were the enemy.

"Go to the church and warm up by the stove," Henry Roberts told the children. "John, come to the house and I'll have Grace give you a box of cookies to take to the church for them."

A few minutes later, with cookies dispatched as a hopeful panacea for the children, Grace and Henry Roberts sat down in their sitting room with Caroline.

"Nothing is going to change the attitude of others toward the mill folks until they've raised themselves economically," Henry told Caroline with worried eyes.

"They're going to have to get some education," Grace pointed out. "We've got the lowest of the rural population coming to the mills. And their children are learning no more than they have, going into the mills by the time they're ten," she said scathingly.

"We're going to change that," Caroline promised.

"You'll have to fight the parents, too," Henry warned.

"We'll do that. In time," Caroline stipulated.

When she left the Roberts house an hour later, the first birthday party was scheduled for the middle of February. She would have to fight for the children's friendship, but she was willing to fight. She remembered now the first Christmas party she attended at the mill village. How insensitive she had been then to their feelings.

She must make the mill her life. It had been the General's life in those painful years when her grandmother was like a small, sad child. And tonight, she reminded herself uneasily, she must tell Sophie about her plans for accelerating the building schedule for the finishing plant.

IT WAS almost eleven by the time Eric let himself into the house. A political dinner had demanded his presence downtown, and afterward he had talked with Jim about Prince Green's efforts in settling the mill strike in Augusta. The strikers had lost their main objective, but there had been some concessions plus tacit acceptance of the recently formed locals.

"Eric—" Sophie emerged into the hall from the library.

"Is something wrong?" He was immediately solicitous. Sophie made a point of being in bed by ten.

"I want to talk to you, Eric." She beckoned him to join her in the library.

"You look upset, Sophie." Eric lowered himself into a chair, his face concerned.

"Caroline told me tonight that she asked Cyrus Madison to sell a substantial amount of her grandfather's stocks," Sophie said agitatedly. "The money is to be deposited in the Hampton Mill account so that we can speed up the building of the finishing plant. It's a loan to the corporation."

"You don't think that's wise?"

"Of course I don't," Sophie snapped. "Josiah spent much thought and care in amassing his stocks. Caroline is capriciously selling them."

"To expand the mill," Eric pointed out. Sophie and Caroline were on a collision course, he surmised unhappily. "Caroline has the General's sharpness, Sophie. Remember that."

"She's too quick to spend," Sophie brushed this aside. "This is money that Josiah took a lifetime to earn."

"If Mr. Madison thought it was a bad move, he would have fought Caroline." It was a shrewd move, he thought with respect.

"Eric, the inheritance is Caroline's. Cyrus can only advise."

"Sophie, she's not throwing the money away on silly extravagances," he said reassuringly. "I suspect this could be a wise

396

move. I'll talk to Mr. Madison about it. Will that make you feel better?"

"Talk to him," Sophie said. "But I think we're reaching the point where Caroline will take nobody's advice. She's trying to do too much too fast."

"Have you talked to Andrew about this?" Eric asked.

"I just learned about it after dinner," Sophie shot back. "But I'll talk to him tomorrow. Maybe Andrew will have more influence with Caroline than I have." She inspected him quizzically. "I don't suppose you'd try to talk Caroline out of this ridiculous move?"

"Honey, I'm the last person Caro would listen to," he said ruefully. He rose to his feet. "It's late and you're up confoundedly early. Let's go up to our rooms."

CAROLINE WAS delighted when the financial arrangements were completed and a second shift began to work within the mill. She was pleased, too, that Tina was becoming involved in making arrangements for the first of the birthday parties, spending much time in the mill village. But these pleasures were overridden by the anguish of living within the same walls as Eric, yet keeping an invisible, unsurmountable wall between them.

On the Saturday evening before the party a startling drop in temperature hit Atlanta. Standing at her window long past midnight, unable to sleep because Eric haunted her thoughts, Caroline watched the steady fall of snow. Tomorrow everything would be frozen over. She was recurrently astonished by the severity of the weather in the United States.

Caroline bundled beneath the covers, grateful that Patience had insisted on bringing up an extra comforter tonight. Early in the morning the heat would come up from the furnace; and if that was not sufficient to warm the bedroom, Patience would prepare a fire in the grate.

Caroline awoke Sunday morning to discover the ground covered by an impressive blanket of snow. She stood at a bedroom window, coffee cup in hand, and admired the pristine whiteness that extended as far as the eye could see. Patience was piling a cluster of small logs onto the blaze she had started earlier.

"I'm going to dress and go for a walk," Caroline told Patience with an effervescent smile.

"No, ma'am," Patience rejected sternly. "They's four and a half inches of snow out there, Seth say, and it's so cold you can't walk. Annie Mae was goin' to visit her sister, like she do most Sunday mornin's, but she say she jes' turned around and come back home."

"I hear the children down in the village." Caroline listened intently. "They're out playing in the snow."

"They won't be long," Patience predicted. "Nobody's goin' no place today."

Caroline settled herself before the fireplace and read until it was time to go downstairs to the customary mid-afternoon Sunday dinner. When she arrived downstairs, Andrew—who had been invited for dinner—was in serious discussion with Sophie in the dining room about the probability of having to keep the mill closed the next day. The mill operated on waterpower.

"If it gets much colder, the water pipes will freeze," Andrew pointed out.

"I never remember weather like this in Atlanta," Sophie said with a faint shiver. "I told Seth to lay coal fires in here and in the parlor. There just isn't enough heat coming up from the furnace."

"It looks beautiful outdoors," Caroline said ebulliently.

"I nearly froze coming over. But that wasn't going to keep me from Sunday dinner here." Andrew's eyes were ardent as they rested on Caroline.

Within moments of each other, Eric and Tina arrived. The family sat down to dinner. The bad weather seemed to stimulate Tina.

"Chad says the streetcars are running only occasionally," she reported dramatically. "The streets are absolutely deserted. And the weatherman predicts it's going to be even colder tomorrow."

"Seth, how are we fixed for coal?" Sophie asked as he appeared in the dining room.

"I 'spect we'll be all right, Miss Sophie. Least for two or three days," he assured. "With this cold the furnace is takin' lots more than it do on most days."

"We may have to postpone the children's birthday party," Caroline said wistfully. "They'll be so disappointed."

"We'll have it a few days later," Tina brushed this aside. "I'll have more time to fuss with the decorations."

It amazed and pleased Caroline that Tina had become so involved in the birthday party arrangements. Had the death of her own baby affected Tina more than they realized? Was that why she reached out to make this party such a special occasion for the children? Involuntarily her eyes turned to Eric. He was staring at Tina with a thinly veiled hostility that unnerved Caroline.

Eric awoke on Monday morning immediately aware of the strong wind outdoors. A wood fire blazed in the grate, laid and lighted while he slept; and there were sounds of heat rising in the pipes. He reached for the dressing gown at the foot of his bed and crossed to a window.

He turned at the sound of his bedroom door being cautiously opened.

"I'm awake, Seth."

"Mist' Russell's on the phone downstairs. It's only six-thirty, but he say he has to talk to you," Seth apologized.

Eric hurried down to the library to the telephone.

"I don't know if you're aware yet of what's going on in this town," Jim began grimly. "This weather's breaking all records. We've had a drop of twenty degrees since yesterday morning."

"How low is it?" Eric sensed this was a crisis situation.

"Eight below zero. The city is immobilized. Nothing's being delivered. The police department and local charities are working hard, but they've got to have help. We must get coal and food to those without before nightfall. The weather's staying at zero."

"I'll dress and come right down to your office," Eric said immediately.

Eric left the stable in the trap because he knew this was his fastest conveyance to Jim's office. While the road into the city was almost deserted, the ground was treacherous, ice beneath the snow. The biting wind had piled up perilous snowdrifts. The trip required double the time it would have normally consumed.

Anxiety soared in Eric as he recognized the implications of the weather. Without coal, people would freeze. That, perhaps, was more essential at this moment than food.

THIS MORNING Caroline found Sophie still at the breakfast table when she came downstairs. Normally Sophie would have been at the mill for an hour by now.

"The weather's brutal," Sophie greeted her. "I doubt if we'll be operating for at least two days."

"I could hear the wind howling all through the night." Caroline seated herself at the table. "Twice I got up to look out at the snow. There was an eerie beauty outdoors." All at once Caroline's eyes were somber. "The children are going to be so disappointed that we can't have the party this afternoon." Impulsively she left the table to go to a window. "Do you suppose we could have the party?" She gazed speculatively out at the swirling whiteness.

"Impossible, Caroline," Sophie said flatly. "Nobody's stirring out of their houses today."

"Sophie—" Caroline stared into the distance with a premonition of trouble. "I don't see smoke coming from any of the village chimneys!"

"They're out of coal," Sophie surmised with a start. "They must have bought out the supply at the company store on Saturday. With this weather, coal goes quickly." Her eyes were troubled as they met Caroline's.

"I'm going to find out," Caroline said with sudden decision.

"Caroline, you can't go out in this weather," Sophie protested.

"I'll dress warmly and wear boots. I want to know what's happening in the village."

"Andrew will check," Sophie said firmly. "It's absurd for you to go out in this weather."

"Andrew may sleep all morning," Caroline pointed out, heading for the door. "He knew the mill would be closed today."

"Caroline, wait and talk to Eric," Sophie expostulated.

"Mist' Eric went down to the city." Seth came into the dining room with a pot of coffee. "Mist' Russell called him at six-thirty."

"I'll be all right, Sophie," Caroline said as she darted from the dining room.

Wrapped well against the elements, Caroline left the house and struggled through the snow, a scarf held about her face against the biting wind. Her eyes searched the chimneys of the village. Nowhere did she see the familiar spirals of smoke. If Jim had called Eric into the city, the situation must be desperate.

Panting from exertion, her eyes tearing from the wind, Caroline knocked sharply at the first house she reached. The door was opened barely an inch, just wide enough for an eye to view the intruder.

"May I come in, please?" Caroline asked gently.

With a look of reproach, because she brought bitter coldness into the room with her, the stooped man at the door pulled it wide enough for her to enter, then slammed it tight. Half a dozen bleak faces stared at her from positions on a sagging bed covered with a multi-colored patchwork quilt and from decrepit, split-bottomed chairs. Each of the inhabitants of the room sat draped in coats, blankets, whatever might be utilized to give warmth. The grate was empty, long-dead ashes beneath it.

"Are you out of coal?" Caroline asked, while her eyes took in the meanness of the room. A shaky table sat at one side and on it were several cracked plates and cups. On the walls hung a string of red peppers, bellows, a gourd dipper.

"We ain't had no coal since yesterday mornin'," the man told her stoically. "There ain't no more in the company store. We're most out of food, too. Monday everybody goes to the store to buy."

"There's no food in the company store?" Caroline asked.

"It's closed," he explained.

"I'm going to talk to Mr. Roberts," Caroline told them. "We'll get coal and we'll have the company store opened."

"We'd be most obliged," his wife said.

Caroline discovered that the Robertses, too, were out of coal. They sat in their sitting room sipping hot tea against the frigid weather.

"I came to the big house before six," Henry explained, "to ask to use the phone to order coal. But the coal yards won't accept an order on my word. Nor will they deliver this far out. I was waiting for a more respectable hour to come to the house and ask what we could do." His worry for the well-being of the villagers seeped through his calm exterior.

"I saw there was no smoke coming from the chimneys. I suspected there was no more coal or wood." Her mind was darting about for a solution. "We'll have to take wagons into Atlanta to the coal yards and bring back the coal ourselves. Can you round up a crew of men?"

"Right away." Henry was on his feet. "But you'll have to arrange for payment."

"I'm driving in with you," Caroline told him. "But first let's stop at Andrew's cottage. He'll arrange to open the company store so food can be distributed."

At Andrew's cottage they were admitted by his housekeeper.

"Mist' Andrew still sleepin'," Aunt Frannie told them. "But I'll git him up. You come inside and set."

A few moments later Andrew was striding into the room.

"What's happening?" His eyes moved from Caroline to Henry Roberts.

Caroline explained the situation.

"I'll see that every family gets food," he promised. "The store should have been open."

At Andrew's insistence, Caroline remained at his cottage while Henry and he left to arouse the storekeeper and to round up men and wagons. Aunt Frannie brought Caroline coffee while she waited. In less than ten minutes Henry was at the cottage door.

"I have a closed carriage to take you into Atlanta and two wagons with four men to load," he reported to Caroline.

"We'll need enough coal to keep every house in fuel for at least two days." She viewed the two wagons through a sitting room window. They seemed pitifully inadequate.

"Caroline, we'll make as many trips as necessary," he said with conviction. "When you've made the financial arrangements, I'll bring you back here in the carriage."

In the coal yard patronized by the Hamptons, Caroline identified herself. Before the owner could complete his apologies about being unable to deliver, Caroline explained she had brought wagons and men. Around them other wagons were being loaded by their owners.

The coal yard owner told them about the heroic measures being organized since dawn to prevent Atlantans from freezing to death or starving. The *Journal* had two relief wagons moving about the city with provisions. The police and the Atlanta Charitable Association were becoming commissaries for receiving and distributing coal, warm clothing and food.

"Let's just pray to God this weather breaks," the coal yard owner said seriously. "Water pipes are bursting. Stoves are exploding. I don't have to tell you how hard it is to move about the city."

For the rest of the day, under Henry's supervision, the men from the mill village made repeated trips to the coal yard until every house had fuel. Caroline worked with Andrew in delivering food from the company store to the various families, along with blankets and warm clothing. She encouraged them to nail coverings over the windows to keep out the biting wind.

Caroline stood before the company store while Andrew emerged with a box of provisions. She smiled when she saw the smoke that rose from the village chimneys.

"They won't be cold tonight. Not as cold as they have been," she amended. The houses were inadequate in extreme cold. Something must be done about them.

ERIC CLIMBED into the trap and Jim joined him on the seat.

"If tomorrow morning remains bad, I'll pick you up at your house at six," Eric promised.

They rode in contemplative silence until Eric pulled the horses to a stop before Jim's modest house.

"You'd better soak in a hot tub or you'll be useless tomorrow," Eric taunted affectionately.

At the house, Sophie astonished him with her report that Caroline has been at the village since morning.

"I'll go over and bring her home. It'll be night soon."

Eric drove slowly. Drifts were everywhere. He heard Caroline and Andrew before he spied them.

"Andrew, you must take care of that cough," Caroline scolded. "You should not have been rushing around in this awful weather."

"I'm fine, Caroline," Andrew insisted, but a fit of coughing belied this.

"Caro!" Eric called brusquely and moved slowly toward them. "Get in the trap," he ordered. "It's growing dark already. You can't stay out any longer in this."

"We've finished for the day." Caroline allowed Andrew to help her up. "Everybody has coal and food."

"Come on up, Andrew," Eric told him. "We'll take you to your cottage."

Eric deposited Andrew at his door. Caroline called after him to take care of his cough. Then Caroline and he drove away with night settling darkly about them.

"Do you suppose the cold will let up tomorrow?" Caroline strived to be casual alone with Eric.

"If not, we'll be delivering food and coal again in Atlanta," he said. How could Caroline sit beside him this way and behave as though nothing had ever happened between them? Abruptly he drew the horses to a halt. He heard Caroline's quick intake of breath.

"Caro, I have to talk to you—" His voice was harsh with urgency.

"Eric, I'm tired. I'd like to go home." She gazed sternly ahead.

"You have to listen to me. You have to know the truth about Tina. Half of Atlanta knew about her affairs before our marriage. The half that had not included me."

"I don't want to hear," she objected tersely.

"Four days after our marriage, our second night on board ship," Eric charged ahead, "I came to our cabin to find her with the purser. She had expected me to play poker all evening with the captain. I let her convince me that she had drunk too much champagne." *Darling, I'll never drink another drop of champagne as long as I live.* She had wept and flung herself into his arms. "But then she was indiscreet in London and Paris and Vienna. You must know about Marshall Shepard—"

"Eric, I won't listen!" Caroline lashed at him. "Stop talking this way or I'll walk to the house."

"Damn it, Caroline!" Eric exploded. "You're as stubborn as the General!"

Eric ordered the horses forward. They rode the rest of the way to the house in silence. At the house he wordlessly helped her down from the carriage and proceeded to the stable.

Eric made the trip into Atlanta again in the morning. However, by mid-afternoon the temperature had risen to twenty-eight degrees. The city came alive again. The crisis was over. Now his thoughts settled on his personal situation. How was he going to continue the farce that was his marriage?

Two days later Eric arrived at a decision. He sat down before Jim's desk and told him that Tina and he must arrange for a divorce. If Tina refused to sue herself, then he would take this action.

"Eric, if you divorce Tina, you're committing political suicide," Jim remonstrated. "And it'll be no better if she divorces you. The voting public won't accept a divorced man. Maybe someday they will, but not in 1899."

"Jim, I have a right to a life of my own." Eric leaned forward, his face etched with determination. "This is a shabby masquerade I'm playing with Tina. It's got to end."

"Eric, use your head. You've got a tremendous future ahead of you in this state. Don't throw it away in an impulsive moment."

"I've been thinking about this since the day I returned from my honeymoon," Eric said. "I delayed while the General was alive because I knew how he felt about divorce. To him it was the ultimate scandal. But he's gone, and I won't be tied any longer to Tina."

"At the cost of your political future?" Jim challenged.

"What happens in my bedroom does not concern the voters."

He rose to his feet. "If you won't handle the case, I'll find a lawyer who will."

"Stop being a hot-head," Jim chided. "Let me figure how we can handle this."

CAROLINE WAS about to leave the house for the mill when Seth came to tell her that Jim Russell was on the phone. She rushed into the library to take the call.

"I wanted to reach you before you left for the mill," Jim said. "Can you come into the city this morning?"

"I can be there in an hour."

"I'll tell Mike to put up the coffee."

This morning Caroline drove herself into Atlanta in the phaeton. She drove without awareness of the winter beauty about her, haunted by what Eric had confided to her about Tina. Her sleep had been disturbed by the memory of those heated moments in the trap with Eric when he had been determined to make her listen to him.

Almost since her arrival in Atlanta, she had been convinced that Eric drove Tina into her affairs by his brutal neglect. But all at once veiled, barbed remarks that Chad had made to Tina from time to time in her presence acquired fresh meaning. Chad knew about Tina. He knew about the affairs before and after her marriage. *Poor Eric.*

Not until she was seated in Jim's office and sipping pungent hot coffee brought to them by Mike did she have any inkling of what he wished to discuss with her.

"Caroline, you must talk to Eric." He leaned forward, elbows on his desk. "I know he's in love with you. If anyone can influence him, it's you."

"What's happening?" Caroline asked, making no effort to deny Jim's assertion.

"Eric insists he wants a divorce."

"He mustn't." Caroline was pale. "Has he talked to Tina about it?"

"Not yet. I've tried to make him understand it would be political suicide, but he refuses to listen. He told me if I won't handle the divorce, he'll go to another lawyer."

"He's not threatening divorce because of me," Caroline forced herself to say. "I've told him how I feel about that. I won't change my mind."

"Within the next few weeks we have to lay the groundwork for his running for the Legislature. But he can forget about it if there's a divorce. No man in this district is going to the polls to vote for a divorced man. It's absurd, but it's a fact of life."

"I don't know how much good it will do, but I'll talk to Eric," Caroline agreed, her eyes troubled.

"It's important that Eric run for the Legislature. We need him there."

"I'll talk to him," Caroline reiterated.

She left Jim's office and returned to the house, much disturbed by what he had told her. Yet if Eric divorced Tina—or forced her to divorce him, the road would be open for *them*. No! She could not allow herself to become Eric's wife at the cost of his career.

In the afternoon, Caroline was busy with the delayed birthday party. Caroline remained to help Grace with the cleaning up, glancing at the clock at regular intervals. How few clocks and watches existed in Hamptonville! The villagers' lives were ruled by the sun and the factory bell.

Guessing that Eric would soon be home, Caroline left the village. She would wait in the library and waylay Eric before he went upstairs to his room. Her heart pounded at the imminent confrontation. Only a few days ago she had refused to listen to Eric. How did she expect to make him listen to her today?

She sat in the library before the fire, leaning toward the blaze more for comfort than warmth. She heard a sound at the door. Eric was arriving. She leapt to her feet and darted into the hall. He was in the foyer.

"Eric, may I please talk to you?" Without waiting for his assent she went back into the library and sat before the fireplace.

"What do you want to talk about, Caro?" Eric asked tentatively from the library door.

"I spoke to Jim today," she said quickly, lest he think she wished to talk about themselves.

"About what?" Eric sat in a chair across from her.

"About you, Eric." Involuntarily her eyes softened. "He's afraid you'll make a terrible mistake."

"In divorcing Tina?" His voice was mocking. "I should have arranged that the moment we returned from Europe."

"Eric, no! You mustn't. Not because of Tina," she said, and she saw hope leap into his eyes. "For yourself."

"I have a right to live." His jaw tightened.

"Eric, you can do so much for the South if you stay in politics. Grandpa was a powerful man in the Old South. You can be as powerful in the New South."

"I'm not power hungry," Eric retaliated. "I want to—"

"Eric, listen to me," she insisted. "I'm thinking what good that power can do. You have a gift for making people believe the way you believe. You can help Atlanta—and the South—to achieve its true destiny."

"I could do that with you, Caro." He rose to his feet, moved to her. "We can do it together."

"If you divorce Tina, you'll never be elected to another office. Some people are born to serve, Eric. You and I are like that. And in a special way we'll always be together. Building Atlanta. Building the state. My father may have gone to England to avoid fighting in the War Between the States, but his daughter has come home to help build a great city. Your Atlanta and my Atlanta. It has to be that way, Eric."

Her eyes held his. She trembled with the effort not to allow him to take her in his arms. He reached for her hand and brought it to his mouth.

"I'll never love another woman, Caro."

Chapter Thirty-three

TINA walked distastefully over the winter earth, still brick-hard in early March though narcissus bloomed in fragrant, colorful display as if spring had truly arrived. She was going to the mill ostensibly to ask Caroline if she would like to go with her to a whist and luncheon party later in the week. The invitation had been called in this morning.

Caroline would politely turn down the invitation. She occasionally was accepting evening invitations, with Andrew as her escort; but during the day Caroline went to the mill as religiously as Sophie did.

Tina smiled secretively while she climbed the stairs to the mill entrance. Bart Menlow was absolutely mad about her. Before the birthday party she had deliberately lingered at the church, working on the decorations, on the chance she might encounter him on his way home when the mill closed. He wasn't married; he lived alone in a mill village house. Twice she saw him. He couldn't take his eyes off her.

She was repelled by the look of flagrant poverty that marked the mill folk, but Bart Menlow was different. He was a foreman, she soothed her pride. He was a handsome, coarse animal, she thought, who would drive her out of her mind in bed.

She opened the door to the mill and walked inside. Lord, this noise was awful. And how could anybody stay all day in this heat? She strolled down the empty corridor toward Caroline's office, her eyes searching at each open door for sight of Bart.

She spied him in the weaving room. She paused there, as though interested in the operation of the machinery. He looked up under the pressure of her gaze. She smiled and moved on down the corridor.

"What are you doing here?" Bart's voice stopped her a few feet down the corridor. She turned to him with provocative grace.

"I came to talk to Miss Caroline." Her voice was cool, but her eyes carried on a silent, heated conversation with him.

"I don't like that one." His tone was contemptuous. He moved closer, his eyes on her breasts. How tall he was, Tina thought. Strong as a bull. "She's not like you." His voice was suddenly amorous. He lifted one muscular arm to rest his hand against the wall, in effect imprisoning her. She wished they were alone somewhere this minute. She wanted his hands on her. She wanted him in her.

"What am I like?" She pretended to be amused.

"You're like me," he grinned. His eyes moved brazenly down the length of her and returned to rest on the low neckline of her dress beneath her open coat. "You go after what you want." He moved closer to her. He was dying to make love to her; he couldn't deny that if he tried. "And we want the same thing."

"You're taking a lot for granted." But her voice was uneven. Why couldn't they go somewhere right now?

"I'll show you," he promised. "I live in the first cottage on the right side when you come straight from the mill. I'll expect you tonight."

"What makes you think I'll be there?" But she knew she would. She had never been with anybody like Bart Menlow. No gentleman, this one. He would push her around until he had his way. *It would be marvelous.*

·"You'll be there," he said smugly.

Tina stiffened. Caroline was walking toward them.

"Thank you, Bart." Her voice was polite but detached. "But here comes Miss Caroline now."

Bart dropped his arm and moved away, his face thunderous. Tina walked toward Caroline, determined to carry off this situation. So Caroline had seen them together that way. What could she tell Eric? Bart didn't lay a finger on her. Caroline could not have heard what he said.

"Honey, I came to ask you if you'd like to go to a whist party and luncheon at Kathy Collier's house next Tuesday. Kathy wants to know right away so the tables will be even."

"I'll be at the mill, Tina," Caroline said politely, her eyes avoiding Tina's. "Thank Kathy for me, please, but explain I won't be free."

Tina left the mill and returned to the house. Caroline wondered why she had not just phoned, Tina surmised. But it didn't matter. Caroline couldn't say a word to Eric.

What could Eric do if he found out she was going to Bart's cottage? Beat her? He was too much the Southern gentleman for that. And Chad said Eric would not dare divorce her. Not when he was hoping to go to the Legislature.

Why shouldn't she go to Bart's cottage? Eric never touched her. Marshall wouldn't come near her since that time before the baby was born. He was scared of losing Dolly. It was disgusting the way Eric kept looking at Caroline. *It made her sick.*

She telephoned Kathy Collier to say she would come to the whist party and Caroline would not. For the rest of the afternoon she alternately sulked and plotted what she would wear when she sneaked away from the house tonight to go to Bart's cottage. Why had the old man left everything to Caroline? It wasn't fair.

If Eric had all that money, she would make him let her spend three or four months of every year in Paris. The French knew how to appreciate beautiful women. Her mind dwelt extravagantly on images of herself in a luxurious house in Paris, with a salon that included all the famous men of Europe.

Late in the afternoon, Tina heard Eric arrive from the city. He was talking with Seth in the foyer. She waited at her door until she heard him at the head of the stairs. Now she emerged from her room.

"Is it cold out?" She smiled winsomely.

"It's brisk," he told her.

"Eric, has Caroline said anything to you?" she asked with an impulsive air, then paused as though in confusion. "I mean—" She lowered her eyes before the glow of inquiry in his.

"Did Caroline say anything to me about what?" he asked impatiently.

"I saw Caroline come out of Andrew's cottage this afternoon."

He didn't like to hear that, she thought smugly. Especially when he knew that Aunt Frannie was down in Americus for a week. "I know Andrew just adores her, and I was wondering—do you suppose they're about to announce their engagement?"

"Ask Caroline," Eric said coldly. "She doesn't confide in me."

Tina chattered gaily all through dinner, covertly watching Eric's frequent glances at Caroline. He believed that Caroline had been in Andrew's cottage. Maybe Caroline was going to marry Andrew, though why she should settle for somebody like Andrew when she was so rich was difficult to comprehend. With all the money the General had left her, Caroline could marry anybody she wanted. Except Eric, Tina reminded herself complacently. Eric belonged to her.

After dinner Tina played a Chopin sonata, and then pleaded fatigue and went to her room. With Lucinda fluttering about as usual, she changed into one of her sheer Paris nightdresses and her favorite emerald green velvet dressing gown.

"You is gonna freeze in the nightgown," Lucinda warned. "It's for summer."

"I'll be fine," Tina insisted. "Go on to bed, Lucinda. You look tired."

"That fire's gonna need fixin' in a little bit," Lucinda hedged and Tina frowned. Sometimes she suspected Lucinda could read her mind.

"I'm going to lie in bed and read the new issue of the *Ladies' Home Journal*," Tina soothed. "It'll be warm enough under the comforters."

Tina sat before the fire, turning the pages of the magazine, inspecting the fashions on display. She listened for the sounds of the others coming up to their rooms. At last the closing doors told her that everyone had retired for the night. Seth would go now to his room in the servants' quarters over the stable.

Tina went to a bedroom window. The sky was splashed with stars. A bright moon illuminated the earth. She could walk to Bart's cottage without a lantern.

Tina changed her slippers for gilt leather shoes with very high French heels and pulled a long cashmere cape from the closet and draped it over her dressing gown. She opened her bedroom door and cautiously walked down the hall, descended the stairs, and let herself out of the house.

The mill village was dark. The workers went to bed immediately after their suppers. Only one house was lighted. Bart Menlow's. Holding her skirts clear of the ground, she walked as swiftly as her high heels allowed. A faint smile on her face, she knocked lightly at Bart's door. He pulled it wide instantly.

"You took long enough," he admonished, standing before her in trousers and undershirt, though the small, sparsely furnished room was chilly.

"I had to wait until everybody was asleep." She enjoyed the look of passion on his face. With a secretive little smile she removed her cape and dropped it on the one chair in the room. "It's cold in here," she complained, walking to the fireplace. A small log smoldered in the grate.

"Want some coffee?" He moved toward her.

She swung about to face him.

"No."

Bart grinned.

"I know what you want." He reached to pull her to him.

She stood motionless while his hands moved about her back, closed in about her rump with a roughness that brought a glint of reproach to her eyes. He maneuvered with one leg to separate her thighs.

"Do we have to stand here like a pair of animals?" she mocked. She didn't need Marshall. Not with this handsome, overheated bull panting to push himself into her. Her eyes moved to the iron bedstead, a rumpled quilt thrown carelessly over the mattress.

"You gonna get what you want, honey," he promised with an air of braggadocio. "Every way you want."

"You talk a lot." Her smile was a challenge. But her teeth were on edge when he pinched a nipple with a roughness that was new to her.

"That hurt!" she objected, but she was aroused.

"You love it," he said, bringing his mouth down to hers.

His mouth was bruising hard, the stubble of his beard irritating. She parted her lips and his tongue thrust forward. She felt the hardness of him pushing between her thighs. Her hands

413

tightened on his shoulders. *He was as good as Marshall.* She wanted him inside her, this minute.

"Bart—" she said, her breathing uneven, when he released her. "Stop bragging and show me."

Unexpectedly he laughed and released her.

"Go over by the fire while I show you." His smile smug, he began to pull off his clothes. Despite the chill in the room he was perspiring.

Tina stood before the meager heat in the grate. Feet wide apart he planted his massive, muscular body before her. Her mouth went dry.

"Take off that thing," he ordered.

Without a word she pulled off the green velvet dressing gown and let it drop to the floor. Waiting for him to take her.

"On your knees, honey," he told her.

"No!" She wouldn't let him take command.

"You do what I say!" His hand swung out and slapped her across the face. She swayed for a moment before she dropped to her knees. The muscles low within her pelvis were convulsive. Why did he make her wait this way?

"You be good to old Bart," he crooned, "and he'll be good to you."

When she made a move to withdraw, he pulled her head to him again, grunting in passion. His hands released her. She rose to her feet and spat into the fire.

"Damn you!"

"Take that thing off." He gestured to her nightdress.

"Why?" Her eyes were hostile, yet she was conscious of her soaring arousal.

With one gesture he ripped her nightdress down the front, his eyes daring her to object. They stared at each other like a pair of gladiators in the arena. He grabbed at her shoulders, brought his mouth to one breast. She closed her eyes, threw back her head, giving herself up to feeling while his tongue moved about the nipple and his hand fondled.

She forgot that the room was cold while his mouth moved in moist heat down her writhing torso. She cried out in animal

414

pleasure when his hands parted her thighs and his mouth filled her. Her hands closed in about his unruly hair, urging him to stay with her.

With a sudden gesture he pulled himself from her and smacked her hard across the rump.

"Get down on all fours," he told her, his voice hoarse, his eyes bright. "Like a pretty little pussycat."

"Bart, let's go to the bed," she pleaded.

"Later," he soothed. "Don't worry, honey, I can do this all night. I won't send you home cheated."

He hovered above her, hard and impatient. She cried out in pain. His hands moved about to squeeze her breasts.

"Bart, you're hurting me!" Yet there was a joyousness in her voice.

"You love it, you little bitch!" he crowed.

He lifted himself from her, helped her to her feet. They swayed together, his hands rough on her. She would be black and blue tomorrow, she thought.

"Bart, please," she whispered. "Now!"

"Tell me what you want," he told her.

"Bart," she objected, yet already the words welled in her throat.

Only now did he lift her off her feet and carry her to the bed. Now she felt in command. He lifted himself above her. Her hands reached to bring him to her.

"You bastard!" she swore. "Making me wait like this!"

She lifted her hips to his. They moved together. The muscles within her drew him deeper within the cavern of her pelvis.

"Honey, you'd be the queen of any whorehouse in this goddam state!" he swore.

He was crazy about her. He wanted to devour her, she thought in triumph.

APRIL SUN shone brilliantly on Caroline as she sat behind her plain, utilitarian desk and listened to the complaints that Tom Coleman reeled off about conditions here at the mill. Basically the committee and he were concerned about another wage increase. Prices were high at the company store, though admittedly not as high as at the country stores. Their wages bought frustratingly little.

"I'll talk with Miss Sophie and Mr. Andrew," Caroline promised. "We'll see what can be done."

Caroline sat at her desk, gearing herself to approach Sophie. Sophie was going to balk, but the request for an increase was justified. She was going to have to do something about raising the age level of the children working in the mill, also; and that was going to launch a battle on two fronts. Night after night, when she lay sleepless, she forced herself to concentrate on mill problems.

She left her small office and went to the other end of the floor to Sophie's cluttered office. Andrew stood beside the desk, going over shipping figures with Sophie.

"Could I talk to you for a few minutes?" she asked. "To both of you," she added.

"Sit down, Caroline." Sophie was wary.

"Tom Coleman just left my office—" Caroline began and Sophie interrupted.

"Why doesn't he stay on the job, where he belongs?"

"He's head of the committee," Caroline reminded, and took a deep breath. "The workers are asking for another increase."

"They're out of their minds!" Sophie exploded.

"Sophie, the Northern mills are paying wages that are thirty-seven percent higher than ours, and they show a profit." Caroline strived for calm.

"The Northern mills are moving South to cut wages," Sophie reminded.

"At a time when the country has emerged from the Depression and conditions are prosperous!" Caroline was scornful. "They're greedy!"

"The unions are pushing workers to demand a larger share of the profits," Andrew pointed out. "We—"

"The strike of the weavers at the Fulton Bag and Cotton Mills back in February was settled in less than a week," Sophie interrupted. "The unions have no power in the South."

"But they will have," Caroline said strongly. "If our workers are

416

satisfied, we'll be able to cope."

"I think we ought to agree to a small increase," Andrew said, and Sophie stared at him in astonishment.

"You're being indulgent, Andrew."

"I'm being practical. We're working at full capacity. We can't afford even a week's strike if we're to keep orders rolling. And we can afford it. Profits for the first quarter of '99 are at a record level, even with the latest increases."

"Let's think about it for a week," Sophie hedged. "I'll go over the figures again."

"There's something else I want to talk about," Caroline pushed ahead. "It's time we led the way in the textile industry with a regulation against employing children under fourteen. They belong in school."

"Caroline, I understand how you feel," Sophie said with unexpected gentleness. "But a regulation like that would close half the mills in the South. It's economically impossible."

"It's a humanitarian necessity," Caroline contradicted. "We could replace the children with migrant workers. There are always workers looking for jobs at the mill."

"The workers won't have it," Sophie objected. "They need the children's wages to survive."

"Let's call a meeting of the committee and present it to them," Caroline insisted, her cheekbones edged with color. "Give them a chance to consider educating their children."

"That sounds fair," Andrew approved.

Sophie looked from one to the other.

"All right, call a meeting," she agreed.

Sophie was convinced the workers would reject the age regulation, Caroline realized. She figured this suggestion would shake them up to the point where they would forget about an increase.

Andrew arranged a meeting with the committee. Sophie sat back and allowed Caroline to explain the proposal.

"We want to petition the county for a school for Hamptonville," Caroline began confidently. "A school that will be able to educate the children up to the age of fourteen—"

"We don't send our children to no schools when they get that old!" a worker objected.

"They belong in school." Caroline's eyes were bright with determination. "They need an education."

"How are we gonna eat if the children are gonna sit on their backsides in school?" another worker demanded, and others joined in the outcry.

"Wait a minute!" Tom Coleman shouted above the melee. "Now you listen to me. Too many of us are ignorant and illiterate. It's time to raise our young'uns to live better than we do. In Atlanta Afro-Americans are going to school while little white Anglo-Saxons are working in the mills. I tell you, that's not right!" Caroline disapproved of his reasoning but welcomed support.

"What good is school gonna do if the family starves to death tryin' to keep them there?" a worker derided.

"I know you need money to feed your families," Caroline interceded. "That'll come from another Hamptonville project." Sophie stared sharply at her, but she continued. "We'll employ many of the idle men—the ones who are unable to operate mill equipment because of their years at farm labor. They'll work repairing the mill village houses. Those must be made to withstand the elements. The blizzard in February taught us that."

Sophie turned to Andrew in consternation. He was gazing transfixedly at Caroline. She would have taken them into her confidence, Caroline thought guiltily, except for fear of Sophie's open rebellion. But she would advance the funds for repairing the houses from what remained of her stocks. She had battled with Cyrus Madison over this; he disliked her putting everything into the mill.

"How long will this building work last?" somebody asked skeptically.

"At least six months," Caroline promised. She had questioned the construction boss at the finishing plant. "By then the finishing plant will be in full operation. We can provide jobs for men who haven't been able to work the mill equipment. We are a family," Caroline said earnestly. "Let's work together and live better. *Let the children go to school.*" Her eyes swung from one member of the committee to another.

Tom Coleman rose to his feet.

"You get a school at Hamptonville," he said, "and we'll send our children to them until they're fourteen years old."

The following afternoon Caroline was in Jim's office, asking him to draw up a petition for a school, which they could present to the county.

"It's going to be a long, drawn-out affair," he warned. "And you must make some offer to show Hampton participation."

"What kind of offer?"

"The best thing would be to donate three acres of Hamptonville land for the school," he told her.

"Of course," she acquiesced. "I can do that, can't I?"

"I don't know," he surprised her. "Are you Chairman of the Board?"

"The General was," Caroline said uncertainly. "He won't be replaced until the annual stockholders' meeting next month. Jim, isn't there another way to handle this?" She chafed at the possibility of more delay.

"You own the house," Jim deliberated. "Donate three acres at the edge of the property. That's close enough for the children and far enough from the house not to cause objectionable noise."

"How long before we'll have a school?" Caroline asked.

"It'll be two years, even with the gift of the land," Jim admitted, "before the country begins to build."

"Jim, that's outrageous!" Her eyes blazed. "Why must those children wait another two years?"

"No matter how much you battle, it won't be any sooner." His smile was rueful. "Bureaucracy."

"It *has* to be sooner." If they delayed, the workers would change their minds. "Jim, there has to be some way I can get that school built."

"Only if you build it yourself." He squinted in thought. "The county has to provide teachers and books if there's a school."

Caroline's face was stubbornly set.

"We'll build." Her mind was racing. Most of the General's stocks had been allocated to finishing the plant. The rest must go to repair the houses. "What will it cost? For a modest school just large enough for Hamptonville," she emphasized.

"You should be able to do it on two thousand," Jim decided.

"I'm going to have to scrounge for the money," she acknowledged, and explained about the stocks.

"Hampton Court is a huge plantation. You could sell some acreage."

"No," Caroline rejected. Like the General, she would not sell one acre, nor would she sell one share of mill stock. "But there's my grandmother's jewelry. I'm sure it's quite valuable." *She knew how to raise the money.* "Jim, will you draw up the papers to notify the county that the Hampton family will build the school? We'll start immediately. It won't take long to sell the jewelry."

"I'll help you get appraisals," Jim offered. "You're not accepting the first offer."

"You're sure the county will supply teachers and books?" She sought reassurance.

"By law they must."

"Then Hamptonville will have its school. No children will work in the mill before they're fourteen."

In the evening Caroline left the parlor to go to the library safe to withdraw the velvet-lined black leather box that held her grandmother's jewelry. When Tina and she returned from Hampton Court last September, she had opened the safe and inspected the exquisite jewelry that the General had given Louisa through the years. Then she had replaced it for safekeeping.

With the box cradled in her hands, Caroline returned to the parlor. Sophie was absorbed in needlepoint, Tina sullenly flipped the pages of a fashion magazine. Eric was in the city again tonight, working with Jim on a case that had just come into the office.

Caroline paused at the door, gearing herself to face the shock she knew she would elicit from Sophie and Tina.

"I thought you might like to look at Grandma's jewelry." She forced a smile. "Before I put it up for sale." Sophie and Tina were staring at her as though she had lost her mind. "I'll keep one necklace," she stipulated. "Out of sentiment."

"Why are you selling the jewelry?" Tina was horrified.

"I need the money to build a school at Hamptonville. Unless we're willing to wait two years for the county to approve the funds."

"Why can't we wait?" Sophie abandoned her needlepoint.

"Sophie, we can't deny those children for another two years."

"But Caroline, all your beautiful jewelry just to build a school?" Tina frowned in distaste. "Chad says if you educate the millworkers' children, they'll never want to work in the mills."

"Tina, it's important that they have some education," Caroline insisted. "Jim will advise me about selling these pieces. When I have two thousand in cash, I'll stop selling."

"I don't understand how you can talk so calmly about selling your grandmother's jewelry." Sophie's face was taut with disapproval.

"Caroline's right," Eric said from the doorway. "Let the school be a living memorial to Aunt Louisa. The Louisa Hampton School. The General would approve."

ERIC STOOD at his bedroom window, gazing out into the night. How was he going to continue living in this house without ever touching Caroline? She was determined to keep that damn wall forever between them.

He started at the knock on the door.

"Yes?"

"Sophie." Her voice was unnaturally high-pitched.

Eric crossed to open the door. Sophie walked inside.

"Eric, I have to talk to you." She was distraught.

"Of course, Sophie." Gently he showed her to a chair. She was furious because Caroline was selling the jewelry. She was frightened of Caroline's strength.

"Eric, we must stop Caroline's rampage. She's moving without authority into Josiah's position. She is not the Chairman of the Board!"

"Did something happen at the mill today?"

"It's everything. The way she insisted on fighting for wage increases. Now this business of not hiring children under fourteen. The school. I never expected the workers to go along with that, but Tom Coleman sided with her," she said bitterly. "Eric, everything's happening too fast for me."

"Sophie, Caroline knows what she's doing." Jim had briefed

him on the school business. He had suspected Sophie would be upset. "It's going to have to happen all through the South."

"I'm going to fight Caroline," Sophie said with fresh strength. "Late next month we hold the annual stockholders' meeting. I'll make sure every small stockholder is present. I'll fight her for the Chairmanship of the Board. I won't allow Caroline to wreck what Josiah took a lifetime to build."

Chapter Thirty-four

IN Hamptonville the sounds of hammering broke through the early morning May air. Repair crews worked on roofs or were putting up siding. The sounds carried to the edge of the Hampton house acreage, where workmen ripped into the just-cleared ground. Caroline watched with elation. How quickly the school was coming into being! The Louisa Hampton School.

A cluster of children from the village watched while the crew prepared for the day's work. They were accepting her at last, Caroline thought, though they seemed to be slightly in awe of Tina.

Had she made a mistake in involving Tina in the birthday parties? Was Tina using her participation to cover an affair with Bart Menlow? Increasingly this suspicion troubled her. Bart was an animal, Caroline thought with distaste. Recurrently she remembered the intimacy that had radiated from them the day she spied them together at the mill. Twice since that day she had encountered Tina in conversation with Bart, each time in front of the company store. She was discomforted by the way the men who sat there before the store had looked at them.

"Caro—" She whirled around as Eric called to her.

"I came to see them break ground for the school," she said self-consciously.

"I suspected you would."

"Everything's going well." She pulled her eyes away from his. Even outdoors this way, amidst the children and the workmen, she felt disconcertingly alone with him.

"I've been worrying, Caro—" Eric said with sudden seriousness.

"About what?" Immediately she was concerned.

"Sophie and you."

"She's unhappy," Caroline acknowledged. "I can't make her understand that we have to move ahead."

"She's convinced you're going after the Chairmanship of the Board."

"I am." Caroline turned to face him. "I thought everyone understood that."

"Caro, you're so young."

"What does that matter? I know what needs to be done! I'm the major stockholder. I thought I could count on becoming Chairman on the strength of that. With Sophie as Secretary and Andrew as Treasurer, as they have been for years."

"Sophie and Andrew own twelve percent of the shares that once belonged to the General," Eric reminded. "He was in control with his fifty-five percent."

"And I'm not," Caroline said. "Unless Andrew and Sophie vote with me. But what I've done at the mill since Grandpa died was with Sophie's approval. She fought Andrew and me, but in the end she agreed."

"She went along with the raises. She's against not hiring children from ten to fourteen."

"Do you think we should?" Caroline challenged.

"Damn it, no!" Eric scowled. "But you're pushing Sophie into a corner too fast."

"The mill committee agreed not to send their children to work once the school opens. It was their decision."

"You talked them into it," Eric said bluntly. "You manipulated."

"With Tom Coleman's help." Her color was high.

"There's a stockholders' meeting in three days," Eric reminded.

"I know."

"Sophie's going to fight for the Chairmanship."

"With six percent of the shares?"

"She's contacting every small shareholder to be present or to give her their proxy. If she can carry all of those votes, along with hers and Andrew's, she's in."

"I didn't know." Caroline fought against panic. "Sophie always grumbles, but I thought that Andrew and she and I would vote together. The three of us carrying on for the General."

"It'll break Sophie's heart if she doesn't win." Eric's eyes were troubled. "I had no right to tell you she's going out to all the stockholders, but I was hoping you'd understand then how much it means to her."

"Eric, I have to fight her. You know that. We're moving into the twentieth century. *Things must change in the mills!*"

"You're trying to move too fast," he insisted. "I'm talking to you this way because I love Sophie and I love you."

"We're cousins, of course." Her face became a polite, impersonal mask.

"Caro, stop this cousin absurdity!" He spoke with an intensity that threatened to shatter her composure.

"Eric, you are not to talk to me this way!" She forced herself to ignore the pounding of her heart, the traitorous desire in her to' run somewhere private with Eric. To be loved by him again, as on that stormy afternoon at Hampton Court. "I won't go to the stockholders, of course." She kept her voice even, her eyes avoiding his. "It's too late. But I'm going to do everything in my power to win the Chairmanship of the Board. I have to do this."

"Thank God I have no shares!" Eric's face was pained.

"There are things that must be changed at the mill," Caroline reiterated, "and I intend to see that they are changed."

"Sophie loves you, Caro. Remember that." Eric swung about and stalked away from her.

One of the children shyly approached Caroline to ask a question about the school. Caroline responded, but her mind was struggling to cope with the coming stockholders' meeting.

The few days before the meeting were steeped with tension. Caroline was conscious of Sophie's inner rage. Sophie's hurt. She had given most of her life to the General and the mill, and here came the long-absent granddaughter to demand control.

Caroline recoiled from the prospect of public conflict with Sophie. Andrew worried about a confrontation between Sophie and her. In the eyes of the small investors, Sophie must seem the logical choice to replace the General. She remembered how her grandfather had told her about the hundreds of small investors who had rallied to the support of the mills after the War Between the States.

" 'Bring the factories to the fields' was the rallying cry in those days," Josiah had said with rich satisfaction. "The cotton mills were our road to salvation."

But this was the New South and Sophie tried to live the Old. She must guide the mill as *she* saw fit, Caroline realized, or she could not survive in Atlanta.

TWO HOURS before they were to go to the house for the meeting, which would be held in the ballroom, Andrew came into Caroline's office. He looked as though he had not slept much the night before.

"Caroline, Sophie's going to ask for the Chairmanship today." His voice was strained. "She's recommending that you replace her as Secretary."

"Andrew, I'm fighting for the Chairmanship."

"Caroline, be patient. In time we can persuade Sophie to see what has to be done."

"We have run out of time, Andrew!" She took a deep breath. "I have to ask you something. I told myself I wouldn't, that it wasn't fair. But I must know. If I make a try for the Chairmanship—and I will," she reinforced, "will you vote with me?"

"You'll have forty-nine percent with my shares, but that's not enough," Andrew pointed out.

"Will you vote with me?" she cornered him. "I know how you feel about Sophie. It's asking a lot."

"I'll vote with you, Caroline," he promised. "But Sophie will be elected."

"We'll see." Caroline's smile was enigmatic.

At two-thirty Sophie left the mill. A few minutes later Caroline and Andrew followed her to the house. The meeting was scheduled for three o'clock. Caroline waited until the last moment to come down from her bedroom to join the meeting in the ballroom.

426

Caroline was conscious of an air of drama as she walked into the ballroom. A hundred chairs had been assembled and set up for the annual meeting. Caroline sensed that most of the stockholders rarely appeared. Sophie had summoned them.

They appeared to be people of modest means, seeming not entirely comfortable in the opulence of the Hampton home. Surely they could understand the deprived lives of the millworkers. The need to make those lives more endurable.

Following tradition, Sophie called the meeting to order. She spoke with restrained emotion about their need to elect a new Chairman of the Board.

"I would like to place my name in nomination for that position." There was a flurry of applause. Her eyes were guarded. "Is there anyone else among our stockholders who wishes to place his—or her—name in nomination?"

"I'm Caroline Hampton, the General's granddaughter," Caroline said clearly, meaning to be heard by everyone present. "I would like to place my name in nomination."

She started at the murmur of hostility that rumbled through the room. But comprehension was swift. Sophie had warned them that the General's granddaughter was out to ruin the mill. They were worried about their investments. Sophie rapped on the table with the gavel.

"We'll have quiet," she ordered. "Let's hear what Miss Hampton has to say."

Caroline rose to her feet, her color high. She spoke from where she stood. Words she had carefully rehearsed in her bedroom.

"The mill operates profitably. When the finishing plant is completed, our profits will increase further. But the time has come to look within the mill. Not just the Hampton Mill, but mills throughout the South. Unless conditions of the workers are improved, we face an era of crippling strikes—"

"Unions won't come in and ruin our mills!" a man interrupted in anger. "They better stay up North!"

"The workers deserve higher wages." Caroline's voice was impassioned. "They deserve a shorter workday. Their children belong in school. Prisoners in the jails have better food than what the millworker can put on his table! We're standing on the threshold of the twentieth century! Let us lead the way with reforms!"

The meeting erupted into chaos, one stockholder after another calling out in rage. They were little people, with anxieties and hopes not so different from those of the millworkers. Where was their compassion? Why were they fighting her?

Sophie banged with the gavel until the uproar diminished to a low rumble of indignation.

"We'll vote now," Sophie said, when Caroline, shaken but defiant, relinquished the floor and sat down. "Andrew—" She sat with pencil poised in hand.

"I vote six percent of Hampton Mill stock . . ." Andrew began and hesitated. "I vote six percent," he proceeded, "for Miss Caroline Hampton."

Sophie gazed at him in disbelief. Her hand trembled as she entered the vote.

"I vote six percent for myself," Sophie announced, "plus nine percent for which I hold proxies."

Then, one by one, Sophie called out the names of the stockholders present. Without exception they cast their votes for her. A total of forty-nine percent. All at once Sophie seemed disconcerted.

"I vote forty-three percent for myself," Caroline said distinctly. With Andrew's six this added up to forty-nine. Sophie was suddenly pale. The atmosphere in the room was heavy. "Plus two percent for which I hold proxy." She held up a sheet of paper. "Stock owned by Mrs. Laurette Bolton."

There was a stunned silence in the room for a moment.

"The majority votes have been cast for Miss Caroline Hampton," Sophie said with painful slowness. "Miss Hampton is now the Chairman of the Board."

"Miss Caroline, it's almost time to go downstairs for dinner," Patience woke her apologetically.

"Thank you, Patience." She managed a smile. "I only meant to nap for a few minutes."

428

"You been sleepin' about an hour," Patience said affectionately. "I 'spect it was because it go so hot this afternoon. You
wanna change into somethin' cool for dinner?"

"I should." Caroline rose from the bed. "The white voile, I
think."

Wearing the white voile, Caroline left her room and went
down to the parlor. She was the first to arrive. A few moments
later Tina joined her.

Tonight Caroline found it difficult to be indulgent toward
Tina. Last night she had stood at her window and had seen Tina
leave the house. She knew she should turn away, but compul-
sively she had watched until Bart Menlow emerged from a grove
of pecans and pulled Tina into his arms.

"That must be Eric now," Caroline guessed as they heard a
carriage pull up before the house.

A few minutes later Eric appeared in the doorway.

"What happened this afternoon?"

"I was elected Chairman of the Board." Caroline heard Tina's
swift intake of breath.

"How did you manage that?" Eric lifted an eyebrow.

"Andrew voted with me." She saw the flicker of annoyance in
Eric's eyes. "And I persuaded Congressman Bolton's mother to
give me her proxy for her two percent. Eric, I had to do it."

"Where's Sophie?" he asked.

"She hasn't come down yet."

"She's upset." Eric looked unhappy.

"I'm sure of that," Caroline conceded. "But she's still running
the mill. It'll be the way it always was."

"Except that you make the big decisions," Tina pointed out.
"Like the General did."

Seth appeared in the doorway.

"Mattie say she's ready to serve dinner now."

"Seth, please have someone call Miss Sophie," Caroline told
him. "She may have dozed off in this heat."

"Miss Sophie said to tell you-all to please excuse her. She's
tired. She's havin' dinner in her room."

Caroline subdued her instinct to run upstairs to Sophie's room.

"Thank you, Seth. And please tell Mattie we're going right into the dining room."

Over dinner Tina chattered vivaciously about the play she had seen earlier in the week with Chad. Tina and Eric must be together socially, Caroline thought, lest people begin to talk. The young Councilman could not *always* be involved in civic duties.

Eric interrupted Tina's monologue about what the ladies had worn to the theater.

"I hear the Young Men's Library Association is forming a merger with the new free library." He ignored Tina's glare of outrage.

"Wasn't it wonderful of Andrew Carnegie to give Atlanta a hundred thousand dollars for a public library?" Caroline said enthusiastically.

"The YMLA has let folks come into their reading rooms whenever they liked," Tina said arrogantly. "I don't know why everybody's making such a fuss about Mr. Carnegie's gift."

"This will be a *public* library," Caroline emphasized. "People can borrow books and take them home. People who work don't have time to visit reading rooms."

"Oh, honey, you're always so concerned about working people," Tina said distastefully. "Chad says the more you educate the lower classes, the more they're going to demand."

"Eric, what's happening about the Legislature?" Caroline asked quickly to forestall a scathing rejoinder from him. "If you're going to be involved in the October primaries, won't you have to begin campaigning now?" She felt safe in talking with Eric in the presence of Tina or Sophie. There was no danger of any emotional exchange.

"Jim's already laying the groundwork," Eric told her, and Tina's face brightened. "Noah's forming a young people's group to campaign for me. I'm going back downtown tonight to talk with them."

"Noah Kahn?" Tina asked contemptuously. "He's a foreigner. He can't even vote!"

"He's a little too young to vote in this year's election," Eric agreed, "but in December he'll become a naturalized citizen.

Noah's articulate and eloquent. He'll enlist voters," Eric prophesied.

"How wonderful that Noah's becoming a citizen!" Caroline glowed. "We'll have David and him to dinner to celebrate."

At uncomfortably frequent intervals through dinner, Caroline was unhappily conscious of Sophie's empty chair at the table. Had she forever alienated Sophie? She was troubled, too, that she had persuaded Andrew to line himself up with her against Sophie.

When they rose from the table, Eric reminded Caroline and Tina that he was going downtown for the evening.

"Caro, you'll have to go up to Sophie," he said quietly.

"I know," she said. Her heart pounded at the imminent confrontation. "I'll go up now."

"Are you coming downstairs again?" Tina asked aggrievedly. "I'll be all alone."

"I'll be down shortly," Caroline promised.

As she mounted the stairs, she encountered Mattie coming down from Sophie's room with a tray. Sophie had scarcely touched her dinner, she thought involuntarily. She paused before Sophie's door, then knocked.

"Yes?" Sophie's voice was raspy.

"It's Caroline. May I come in?"

The door swung open. Sophie stood there, pale and aloof.

"Come in, Caroline. I have something I must tell you." Sophie closed the door and turned to her. "I'm moving out of the house in the morning. I'll remain at the mill for two or three weeks, until Andrew and you can—"

"Sophie, no! The Hampton Mill can't run without you!"

"You're the Chairman of the Board," Sophie reminded. "You've won. That's the way you wanted it."

"Only because I need that power behind me to put through reforms, Sophie. But I can't accomplish what I mean to bring about unless you're there running that mill! Sophie, I want to see the Hampton Mill and Hamptonville the pride of Atlanta, jewels of the South. Together, Andrew, you and I can make them a monument to the General. We're moving into a new century,

431

Sophie. Let us lead the way, in the General's name!"

Her eyes clung to Sophie's. She saw love for Josiah Hampton and for her and for the mill battle with the old doubts.

"I think you're wrong in these reforms, Caroline. All this expensive expansion." Sophie gestured in disapproval. "But you're every inch Josiah's granddaughter. I can't walk out on either of you."

Chapter Thirty-five

C AROLINE threw all her energies into the mill activities. Work was proceeding on schedule on the school. Men who had not worked for fifteen years were earning wages repairing the houses. The finishing plant was fast approaching completion.

On a hot, sultry afternoon just before the first anniversary of Josiah's death, the contractor came to her office and declared the finishing plant completed. Andrew could begin the installation of machinery on the following day. Jubilant, Caroline left the office to seek out Andrew and Sophie. She found them together in Sophie's office, going over bills of lading for newly arrived machinery.

"Andrew, you can start installing the equipment tomorrow," Caroline announced. "The finishing plant is ready."

"I thought it would be at least another two or three days." He was elated.

"I pushed them to have it ready for tomorrow," she confided, and saw comprehension in Sophie's eyes.

When Andrew came to the house in the evening, talk about the new finishing plant dominated the conversation until Caroline inquired about the progress of Noah's group of young campaigners.

"They're distinguishing themselves. David may be the mathematical genius, but Noah has the makings of a statesman." He smiled faintly. "It appears likely that I'm going to win in the October primary."

"You'll win the election," Andrew predicted. "Congratulations, Eric."

Despite this optimism about his campaign, Eric seemed restless and unhappy, Caroline thought.

"It's so awfully hot tonight," she said. "Why don't we all go for a carriage ride through Piedmont Park?"

"That's a fine idea," Sophie approved. "You four young people go. I'm going to sit out in that screened area on the verandah and watch the fireflies."

"Sophie, come with us," Caroline encouraged. Sophie was deliberately throwing her with Andrew again.

"You four go, and by the time you come back I'll see that Mattie has a freezer of ice cream ready for you," Sophie promised. "And scat. No sense sitting around the house in all this heat."

Jason brought the attractive light wood wagonette that comfortably seated six to the front of the house. Andrew helped Caroline up and then extended a hand to Tina. Eric was instructing Jason the route they wished to follow, including Atlanta's favorite "nine-mile circle."

On this hot end-of-July night they encountered many other carriages bearing residents seeking relief from the heat. Eric was taciturn, Andrew content to sit closely beside Caroline as they rode through the night. Tina repeated gossip she had absorbed at various parties during the past two weeks, though Caroline suspected that neither of the two men heard a word that she said.

They returned to the house to sit on the screened area of the verandah with Sophie. Seth brought them freshly churned chocolate ice cream laced with pecans from Hampton Court.

"I remember reading what Stendhal said when he first tasted ice cream," Andrew said reminiscently. " 'What a pity this isn't a sin!' "

"Meaning that anything pleasurable must be a sin?" Eric challenged. "What a stupid man!"

"Hardly," Andrew objected. "Stendhal was one of the great novelists of his time."

"I've been spared that pleasure," Eric said coldly.

"Eric, you're being rude," Sophie rebuked. "That isn't like you."

"Excuse me." Eric rose to his feet, his ice cream half-eaten. "I have an early appointment in the morning."

CAROLINE AWOKE at six as usual, but this morning she did not join Sophie for breakfast. Instead, she went to the stable and took out the phaeton. On the anniversary of the General's death she meant to drive herself to Hampton Court.

The early morning air was pleasant, the sky a brilliant blue, in sharp contrast to the dreary drizzle of the day on which they had carried the General's body to rest beside those of his wife and two younger sons. On the long drive to Hampton Court, Caroline's mind lingered on the sweetness of the last weeks with her grandfather.

At last she approached the private roadway to the house. She fought back the tears that threatened to spill over. Two-thirds up the long approach to the house, she reined in the horses and leapt down from the phaeton. With the horses secured to a tall white birch, she began the walk to the family cemetery.

She stopped at the turn in the road to pick a handful of red roses to place on her grandfather's grave. She hesitated, then snapped off a few white rosebuds for the grave of Tina's baby.

As she walked up the slight incline to the cemetery, Caroline was startled to discover that someone had preceded her. Eric sat on a granite bench, his eyes fastened to the General's grave. She half-turned to flee, but Eric spied her.

"Caro—" His voice was infinitely gentle.

"I should have known you would be here."

"I hate myself for not getting back in time to see him alive," Eric said. "I should have been with him."

"He was so proud of you, Eric."

"I'm glad you were with him, Caro. He loved you."

"I loved him."

With a tremulous smile, she bent to place the red roses before the simple marker. Then she walked in silence to the tiny grave at the side of the cemetery and stooped to lay the white rosebuds on a bed of lush, green grass. A marker had been set there. "Baby Hampton." Involuntarily, Caroline lifted her face to Eric.

"I brought the marker here," Eric said.

His eyes held hers. He was remembering—as she was—the drive to Hampton Court with the tiny white coffin. He was remembering his avowal of love, his futile efforts to convince her that there would be a time for them.

Caroline rose to her feet. Her throat was tight. *She must not allow herself to feel this way toward Eric.* He moved toward her. All at once she was in his arms.

"Caro. Oh, Caro!"

He kissed her with a hunger that matched her own. For a moment she responded, her arms closed in about his shoulders. Then reality intruded.

"Eric, no." She forced herself to pull her mouth from his, ignoring the pain of denial. "Eric, let me go." She struggled to release herself from his embrace.

"It's wrong for us to live a lie, Caro," he protested.

"Don't talk to me about lies!" she said in sudden fury and saw him flinch. "We'll go up to the house and we'll have breakfast." Her voice was uneven despite her efforts to regain her composure. "They'll be expecting us today. Then we'll return to Atlanta. Separately."

ERIC SMOLDERED with frustration on the solitary ride back to Atlanta. He had been rude to Andrew last night because he was jealous. Tina's whispered remark, when they walked from the house to the carriage, had burnt itself into his brain. *"Eric, do you suppose Caroline and Andrew will announce their engagement now that her year of mourning is over? She's in and out of his cottage constantly."*

How did he dare to be jealous? To hope to see Caroline doomed to a lifetime without love when she was capable of such passion? She would never permit him to divorce Tina to marry her. But it was unconscionable of Andrew to expose her to gossip. Knowing Andrew and Caroline, he would not believe there was an affair between them; yet others would surely believe otherwise.

Eric knew that Andrew always went to his cottage for lunch.

He would be there today when Andrew arrived. Aunt Frannie greeted him graciously but with surprise when he knocked at the cottage door.

"Has Mr. Andrew come home for lunch yet?" he asked politely. He knew Andrew had not come home.

"No, sir, but he'll be here directly," Aunt Frannie assured. "Come in, Mist' Eric, and let me give you some lemonade while you waits for him."

A few minutes later, Andrew walked into his small, charming sitting room.

"Andrew, I want to talk to you." Eric rose to his feet.

"Of course," Andrew acquiesced. His eyes were curious.

"Caroline's year of mourning is over," he said abruptly. "When the devil are you going to ask her to marry you?"

"Eric, nothing would make me happier than to marry Caroline," Andrew said quietly, "but she's made it painfully clear she considers me as a brother. I've never so much as held her hand."

Eric stared hard at him for a moment.

"Forgive me for being such a fool." Eric fought to contain his rage at Tina. She had been lying; he should have realized that. "I was concerned for Caroline."

"Stay for lunch," Andrew invited.

"Thank you, no," Eric said quickly.

"Mist' Eric, you ain't goin' no place." Aunt Frannie's voice halted him at the door. "I set two places at the table, and you is gonna be at one of 'em." She grinned delightedly. "We got brook trout caught jes' this mornin'. And you know you ain't gonna walk out on that."

CAROLINE FINISHED her lunch at her desk, drained the tall glass of iced tea. The mill was beautifully quiet for the brief lunch period, most of the workers outdoors. Sophie had asked her to total up several pages of figures, a task Sophie loathed. Only one column remained to be done, and this was swiftly accomplished.

Caroline gathered together the pages of figures and headed

down the long, deserted corridor that led to Sophie's office. A dozen yards down the corridor she halted, aware of frightened sounds of protests. She swung off the corridor to the left. Bart Menlow was with a frightened thirteen-year-old who worked at the looms. He had ripped the bodice of her dress to the waist.

"Take your hands off Betsy!" Caroline ordered furiously.

Bart turned to her, his face etched in rage; but he released Betsy. Clutching at her torn dress, she fled.

"Come into my office," Caroline ordered, and strode ahead of him. Inside her office, Caroline faced him with perilously controlled anger. "Bart, I know you're supposed to be an efficient foreman, but if you dare to lay a finger on any girl in this mill, I'll see that you're discharged!"

"She threw herself at me," Bart swaggered. "She's been givin' me the eye for weeks."

"Betsy is a child!" Caroline's eyes blazed. "You ought to be horse-whipped."

"*You* ain't a child," he grinned, moving toward her. "You're a real woman. Lots of fire. That's the kind I like."

"Get out of here!"

Bart reached to pull her to him.

"You need a man like me to make you know you're a woman."

Caroline slapped him across his face. He laughed and drew her against him. She kicked him hard on a shinbone. He howled and released her.

"You're fired!" she said breathlessly. "Get your things together and get out of this mill!"

Trembling, Caroline hurried from the room and off to the rarely used side exit. She did not trust herself to face anyone. Her only thought was to escape to the privacy of her room at home. She felt soiled from the touch of Bart Menlow's hands.

Tina, who had been eavesdropping from behind some piled-up bales of cotton in the corridor, charged into Caroline's office.

"You animal!" she shrieked at Bart, her eyes green coals of fire. "Do you chase after every woman in sight?"

Bart's laugh was derisive.

"What's the matter? You think you're bein' cheated?"

"I hate you!" Tina shrieked. "You told me you loathed her. And I come here looking for you, and you're trying to make love to her!"

"That's none of your business, Tina. I take any woman I want. What makes you think you're special?"

"I'll kill you, Bart!" Tina was white with rage. "No man treats me like this!" Her eyes darted about the room, lighted on a paperweight on Caroline's desk. She picked it up and threw it at Bart. "I hate you! I hate you!" All at once she was silent, staring in shock. The paperweight had caught Bart on the temple. He lay on the floor, unconscious.

Tina was aware that the workers were returning to the mill. The lunch period was over. In panic, she ran. *Go out the side way, her mind exhorted. Nobody must see me.*

SOPHIE LOOKED up from her work with a frown. Why had the machines stopped? What was going on? She rose to her feet and hurried out onto the floor. A woman was screaming hysterically at the far end of the corridor. There was a jumble of excited voices.

"Andrew, what's happened?" she called as she strode in the direction of the uproar.

"All right, everybody, back to the machines," Andrew ordered. "Back to the machines," he reiterated strongly.

"Andrew, what is it?" Her eyes moved past him to Caroline's office, where someone was trying to cope with the hysterical woman.

"Bart Menlow," Andrew said slowly. "He's dead on the floor of Caroline's office. He's been murdered."

"What happened?" Sophie's face was drained of color. "Where's Caroline?"

"Stay out here, Sophie." Inside the office the hysterical woman was sobbing quietly now. "I'll phone for the police."

"First call the house to see if Caroline is there," Sophie told him.

The sobbing woman was led from the office. Sophie stood out-

439

side the door, avoiding the sight of Bart Menlow's body.

"Seth, is Miss Caroline at the house?" Andrew asked. After a moment he quietly thanked Seth and hung up.

"She's not there?" Sophie's eyes searched his.

"No." Andrew reached for the phone again.

Had Bart tried to attack Caroline and she ran? *But who killed him?* Sophie asked herself. Struggling to regain her composure, Sophie stood by while Andrew phoned the police and reported Bart's murder.

"They'll be here in a few minutes," Andrew told her, putting down the phone. "They'll want to question the workers."

"Andrew, *where's Caroline?*" Sophie's voice was strained.

"She may not have been here when it happened," Andrew soothed, but his eyes lingered on the lunch tray that sat at one side of Caroline's desk.

"She had lunch only a little while ago," Sophie reasoned. "Our trays came from the house at the same time. Andrew, *where is she?* The police will want to know."

The police arrived. They questioned Andrew and Sophie, then circulated among the workers, Andrew and Sophie in attendance. A man remembered being en route to a storage area when he heard Bart and Caroline arguing. Sophie's throat tightened. What had happened in Caroline's office?

"Where is Miss Hampton?" one of the pair of policeman inquired.

"She went home for a nap," Sophie fabricated. "It's so hot here in the mill."

"It's as hot as hades," the policeman agreed. "Now where would the house be?"

"General Hampton's home," Sophie reared. "Everybody in Atlanta knows where that is. She's his granddaughter."

Bart's body was removed. The two policemen left. Andrew turned to Sophie in consternation.

"Why did you tell them she went home?"

"Sparring for time," Sophie admitted. "We must get hold of Eric. He'll know what to do."

Andrew phoned Jim's office. Eric was out making calls. Jim

440

was at court. Andrew left word that this was an emergency. One of them must be reached immediately and be told to phone the Hampton Mill.

STANDING AT a window of her bedroom, Caroline saw a pair of policemen walking up to the verandah. Terror gripped her. Had something happened to Eric in the city? She rushed into the hall. Seth had opened the door to the policemen.

"I'm sorry, sir, but Miss Caroline ain't here. She's at the mill."

"They told us at the mill that she had come home," one of the policemen said. "Tell her we have to talk to her."

"Seth, I'm here," she called, hurrying down the stairs. "Has something happened to Mr. Eric?" She was pale with alarm.

"No, ma'am," one of the policemen answered politely before Seth could reply. "We came here to talk to you. He said you weren't here." He gestured toward Seth.

"He didn't know," Caroline explained. "I came in through a side door. What is it?"

"We have to take you to the station house to answer some questions, Miss Hampton." The policeman appeared uncomfortable. "I'm sorry, ma'am, but a man named Bart Menlow was just found dead in your office. We have to take you in on suspicion of murder."

Caroline reached for the post of the bannister to steady herself. Bart Menlow dead? But how could they suspect her of his murder?

"Seth, please call Mr. Russell," she said unevenly. "Tell him what's happened." She forced a smile. "Don't look so stricken, Seth. This is some ghastly mistake."

441

Chapter Thirty-six

ERIC tiredly mounted the stairs to the verandah. The afternoon had been fruitful, yet he felt none of the jubilation that was his right. He approached the door and Seth pulled it wide, as though he had been watching for his return.

"Thank the Lord you is home, Mist' Eric!" he said fervently.

"Seth, *what's happened?*"

His voice uneven, Seth reported the events at the mill and at the house. Eric listened, enveloped in incredulity.

"Mist' Eric, the policemen took Miss Caroline to the station house." Seth's eyes glowed in indignation. "They oughta know Miss Caroline wouldn't hurt even a ant crawlin' on the ground."

"When did this happen, Seth?"

"It musta been more'n three hours ago. She still down there. Mist' Russell phoned and said for you to call his office soon as you get home if he didn't reach you before."

Eric pushed past Seth and charged to the library. He picked up the phone and called Jim's office, pounding on the desk with one fist as he waited for a response. Finally Jim's voice came through to him.

"Jim, what the hell's going on? Seth told me the police had taken Caroline into custody."

"It's crazy, Eric. I just returned from the station house. I couldn't arrange for Caroline's release. I—"

"What kind of evidence can they have?" Eric interrupted explosively. "How can they hold her?"

"She was arguing with Menlow minutes before he was found murdered. A millworker heard them. Caroline ran away from the scene. Of course she's innocent," Jim said calmly. "You know and I know, but the police don't. Eric, down here I'm still a 'damn Yankee,' " he reminded. "Maybe it would be better for Caroline to be represented by a Southern attorney."

"No, she'll want you," Eric said with certainty.

"You know Judge Renfrow personally?" Jim inquired.

"He went to law school with Cyrus Madison," Eric pulled from his memory. "I'll meet you at the office in forty minutes. I'll phone Madison and then we'll call on Judge Renfrow. We'll ask for Caroline to be released in my custody."

"You'll need a court order," Jim reminded.

"Caroline will not stay in that jail overnight," Eric swore. "Wait for me at the office."

In the library Eric cursed under his breath as he had difficulty locating Cyrus Madison. He had left the office but had not yet arrived at his house. Damn, he needed Madison to intervene with the Judge!

Silently Seth came into the room and placed a tall glass of lemonade beside Eric. The house was torpid with the day-long heat of the sun. Again and again Eric phoned Cyrus Madison's house, ignoring the Madison servant's promise to have Mr. Madison call as soon as he arrived.

At last Eric reached Madison and succinctly briefed him.

"Good Lord, Eric, I can't believe this! I'll call Renfrow immediately. How dare they consider holding Caroline overnight in the jail! You go straight to Renfrow's house, Eric. I promise you he'll give you an order for Caroline's release."

Eric phoned Jim, reported his success.

"I'll meet you at the station house," Jim said. "Go get that release, Eric."

Within an hour, Eric walked into the station house. Jim was striding restlessly about the small waiting room. He stopped dead at sight of Eric, his eyes questioning. Silently, Eric extended the court order.

Within minutes arrangements for Caroline's release into Eric's custody were consummated. Pale but composed, Caroline was brought into the waiting room.

"Caro—" Eric reached to pull her to him for a moment. "It's

going to be all right. I'm taking you home."

"I knew you'd come, Eric," she whispered.

"I have a carriage outside." He kept a hand protectively at her elbow while Jim, smiling encouragingly, moved ahead to open the door.

Eric and Jim sat with Caroline in the library, shooting question after question at her. Jim brought up the possibility that Betsy might have returned to kill Bart.

"No," Caroline rejected this. "Not that sweet little girl. She's barely thirteen. A child. And she was terrified of Bart."

Sophie appeared at the library door to insist they come to dinner. Tina was staying in her room with a headache.

"The heat, I suppose," Sophie shrugged. "Andrew is here. He's as anxious as we are."

Over dinner Jim and Eric both questioned Andrew and Sophie, hoping for some lead to whoever had killed Bart Menlow. They came up with nothing. After dinner Eric and Jim left the house, intent on asking questions at the mill village. They stopped first at the Roberts cottage.

"Eric, what an awful thing to happen!" Grace was distraught. "How could the police suspect Caroline?"

"The man was found dead in her office," Jim explained. "They were heard arguing. Caroline had caught Menlow molesting a young girl."

"Who was it?" Henry demanded. "Nobody told us about that."

"Betsy Jackson," Eric said. "Do you know her?"

"A dear, fearful child." Henry's face tightened. "Her mother was here just a few minutes ago. She was distressed that Betsy hadn't come home, though the factory whistle blew almost two hours ago."

"Her father's a religious fanatic," Grace said, grimacing in distaste. "He's sure she's run off with some man. He's sitting sanctimoniously in his house reviling her. I suspect she was terrified to go home after being manhandled by Menlow."

"Why?" Jim asked.

"Her father would blame Betsy for leading him on." Grace shook her head. "That poor little girl."

"We've got to find her. She may be able to help clear Caro.

Betsy didn't kill Bart," Eric reassured as Grace was about to protest, "but she may *know* something."

Jim and Eric agreed with the Robertses that it would be futile to waste time questioning Betsy's parents. They left the mill village and went to the house for a carriage. For hours they roamed about Atlanta, explored the length of Decatur Street, asking questions, learning nothing.

By midnight they conceded further search was futile.

"She could have gone into the woods," Jim said reflectively. "But it's useless to attempt to search there in the dark. I'll meet you at dawn," he told Eric. "We'll go through every inch of woods adjacent to the mill village."

Eric returned home. Caroline was on the verandah with Sophie and Andrew. He dropped tiredly into a rocker beside Sophie.

"Did you learn anything?" Sophie asked hopefully.

"Nothing, but we will," he promised, masking his alarm. "Betsy's disappeared."

"Eric, she could not have killed Bart Menlow," Caroline reiterated. "But it worries me that she's missing. What could it mean?"

"That she's afraid of her father," Andrew supplied dryly. "He doesn't work. His wife and children work. He stays home and prays for their souls."

"Eric, what happens now?" Caroline was making a major effort to be calm, he realized.

"We're searching in the woods in the morning for Betsy. I have this feeling that she'll help us find out who killed Bart Menlow."

"Let me come with you," Caroline pleaded.

"You stay here at home," Eric ordered. He managed a weak facsimile of a smile. "You're still a suspect, Caro."

"Eric, the police have no real evidence against Caroline," Sophie strived to be realistic. "Even if she goes on trial, they'll have to free her." She hesitated. "Won't they?"

"Of course," Eric reassured her. But at this point it was impossible to know how a jury would react, he thought uneasily. "I have to be up at dawn." Eric rose to his feet. "I'll need some sleep to be of any use tomorrow."

Eric paced about his room, knowing he could not sleep until Caroline was cleared. He had not trusted himself to remain on the verandah with her. The compulsion to take her in his arms and comfort her had been overwhelming. At last, exhausted, he stretched across the bed to wait for dawn.

With the first streaks of dawn lightening the sky, Eric left his room and went down to the verandah to wait for Jim. In moments, Jim rode up in the buggy. Last night's heat had disappeared. The morning was cool and clammy, with fog settling low over the trees in the distance.

For almost three hours Eric and Jim searched the fog-draped woods, discovering no trace of Betsy.

"Let's go to the mill and ask more questions." Jim refused to show anxiety. He smothered a yawn. "Maybe we can get some coffee somewhere."

"Let's go to the house for breakfast. Then to the mill." Eric was aware of hunger and a gnawing headache.

At the house, Eric was pleased to learn that Caroline was sleeping, yet he was disappointed not to see her. Her life had become infinitely precious to him. After breakfast Jim and he went to Sophie's office.

"Close the door, Eric," Sophie ordered when Jim and he entered the room. "Did you find Betsy Jackson?"

"We went through every inch of the woods," Jim said in exasperation. "She wasn't there. Let's go over this whole situation again. Who at the mill hated Bart Menlow enough to kill him?"

"Few of the workers liked him," Sophie admitted. "He did his job well, and we closed our eyes to his surliness. But we wouldn't have tolerated anything like what happened with Betsy." Her face was stern with recall.

They were engrossed in dissecting Bart's background when a light knock on the door intruded.

"We're not to be disturbed," Sophie called out in annoyance. "Go talk to Mr. Andrew."

But instinct propelled Eric to his feet. He went to open the door. A small, slight girl, her shoulders hunched tensely, was walking away.

446

"Betsy?" he called, and the girl swung around with a frightened stare.

"I just wanted to talk to Miss Sophie," she stammered.

"Come in, Betsy," Sophie invited.

Her small face fearful, Betsy walked into the office. Eric closed the door again.

"Are you all right, Betsy?" Eric asked with solicitude. "We were worried about you."

"I was scared to go home when Mr. Bart tore my dress," Betsy confessed. "I got a needle and sewed it, but Pa would still be mad."

"Sit down, Betsy," Eric coaxed, easing her into a chair. "Tell us where you were."

"I hid in the finishing plant all night. Then Mr. Andrew came with the men to start putting up the machinery, and I sneaked out." She took a deep breath. "I heard somebody talking about Miss Caroline being arrested, and I had to come and tell you, Miss Sophie. Miss Caroline couldn't have killed Bart."

"How do you know that, Betsy?" Sophie inquired gently.

"I was worried about Miss Caroline being alone with him. Everybody was outside eating their lunch. I went back to see if Miss Caroline was all right. She was leaving. A minute later another lady walked into the office. She yelled at Mr. Bart something fierce."

"Did you know the lady?" Jim asked. "The one who came in after Miss Caroline left."

"Yes, sir," Betsy admitted uncomfortably. Her eyes moved apologetically to Eric. "It was Miss Tina."

With Jim in tow, Eric rushed back to the house. He left Jim in the parlor to charge upstairs to confront Tina.

"Who is it?" Tina asked when he knocked sharply at her door.

"Eric. I have to talk to you."

She pulled the door wide.

"Eric, please don't talk too loud. I have a fearful headache."

"Tina, Bart Menlow is dead," Eric told her.

The color drained from Tina's face.

"I thought he was only stunned," she stammered, without

447

realizing for a moment that this was an admission of guilt. "I went to the office to talk to Caroline and he tried to attack me," she improvised frantically. "I fought him off. I hit him with a paperweight, and then I ran. That's why I have this terrible headache. He was going to rape me, Eric. Right there in the mill. The workers were all outside. We were alone."

"I don't believe you," Eric said contemptuously, "but I'm sure the court will when you claim to be defending your honor. You'll stand trial, but you'll be released." She was staring at him as though mesmerized. "I have to go downstairs to discuss your defense with Jim Russell. I'll give you fifteen minutes to dress. Then we'll go down to the police station and you'll turn yourself in. You'll be released in my custody."

Tina stared blankly for a few seconds as Eric stalked from the room, closing the door behind him. *She couldn't go through a trial. She wouldn't.* She felt sick as she envisioned the headlines. *Beautiful Society Matron Attacked by Mill Foreman.* A stupid millworker!

Suppose they found out she was having an affair with Bart? Then she couldn't say he tried to rape her. Folks in the mill village had seen them together. Those men at the company store, always leering at them.

She flung herself across the bed and reached for the telephone. Her voice was shrill with panic when she gave the operator the number she wished. Chad and she would run away. She wouldn't let them take her to trial!

"Chad, what took you so long?" she shrieked when he picked up the phone.

"I was painting." He was irritated at this interruption.

"Chad, listen to me!" She was fighting against hysteria. "This is terribly important. You've got to get lots of money. We have to leave Atlanta right away. I'll get the loco-steamer out of the stable and drive to the edge of Inman Park. Bring the phaeton and we'll take it to—"

"Tina, are you drunk?"

"Chad, I killed Bart Menlow." She heard the gasp at the other end of the line. "Papa has at least ten thousand dollars in the safe. He always keeps that much there. Chad, I won't let them put me through a trial!" Her voice soared thinly. "They'll find out about Bart and me!"

"Tina, get hold of yourself," Chad ordered. "I'll get the money and meet you by the lake at Inman Park. We'll leave the loco-steamer there and take the phaeton to Athens. We can get a train there. Tina, it's going to be all right," he calmed her. "I'll get the money. We'll go to Paris. We can live for a long time on that money. You'll have a salon," he promised. To Chad, Tina knew, this was the ultimate adventure. To flee Atlanta with his beautiful sister. "Now do exactly what I tell you—"

"TINA ADMITTED picking up a paperweight and throwing it at Menlow. When he fell, she thought he was only stunned," Eric finished his account. "Then I said he was dead, and she came up with the rape story."

"Why did she throw a paperweight at him?" Jim was curious.

"He must have said something that displeased her." Eric's smile was ironic. "You know Princess Tina."

"There'll be no question of a conviction," Jim said. "Tina was in Caroline's office, waiting for her. The foreman came in and tried to attack her."

"I told Tina she has to go immediately to the police station to turn herself in. You'll come with us, Jim?"

"Certainly," Jim said with a wry smile. "I'm the lady's attorney."

Impatient at Tina's delay, Eric went upstairs and knocked at her door. Lucinda emerged, her eyes frightened. She closed the door behind her.

"Mist' Eric, Miss Tina taken terrible sick. You best go call the doctor quick."

"What's the matter with her?" Eric was skeptical.

"She got awful pains in her stomach and she been real sick. Please, Mist' Eric. You call the doctor!"

Caroline came into the hallway.

"What is it?"

"Tina's been taken ill," Eric said without emotion. "Lucinda thinks the doctor should be called."

"I'll go to Tina—"

"No, ma'am," Lucinda rejected. "She don't want nobody but the doctor, she say."

"All right, Lucinda," Eric acquiesced. "I'll phone for Dr. Ashley. Caroline, come down to the library with me."

"Has there been any word of Betsy?" Caroline asked while they hurried down the stairs.

"Betsy's all right. She cleared you, Caro."

"Betsy?" She stared at him in disbelief. "I don't believe that."

"She didn't kill Bart. It was Tina," Eric explained. "Betsy saw her go into your office after you left. Tina confessed to me. She's concocted some story of an attack. She'll probably be cleared." He frowned. "But I don't like her using this excuse of being ill. She ought to go directly to the police and turn herself in."

"Where's Tina?" Jim rose to his feet as they walked into the library.

"She claims she's ill. I'm calling Dr. Ashley. I think she's stalling on turning herself in." Eric moved toward the telephone.

"Eric, wait!" Caroline was staring out the window.

Jim followed her gaze.

"Tina isn't here," he told Eric. "She just drove away in the loco-steamer."

"I'll have to notify the police." Eric reached for the phone. He should not have left Tina alone!

"Hold it, Eric," Jim ordered. "It'll look bad if the police find out she's running. We have to stop her. Where would she run?"

"To Chad," Caroline guessed. "He said she always comes to him when she's in trouble."

"Let's go there," Jim decided. "Fast."

The three of them left for the Kendrick house in Jim's buggy. En route, Jim embellished on his line of defense.

"No jury in the country will convict Tina for defending her honor," he concluded.

"The rape story might not take hold," Caroline seemed to be forcing herself to speak. "She was having an affair with Bart. Some of the mill villagers know."

"If the police go digging, they'll find out more." Eric frowned because Caroline looked so reproachful. *She still didn't believe what he had told her about their honeymoon.* "Tina was expelled from boarding school at fifteen when she was caught *flagrante delicto* with a student from a neighboring military school. Two years later it cost her father a fortune to pay off the wife of a postman who caught Tina in her husband's bed. I know this," he said, his eyes holding Caroline's, "because Chad drank too much at a dinner party at the house right after we returned from Europe, and he told me in colorful detail. He thought it was a colossal joke on me." He saw the realization of truth well in Caroline. He felt her vindication of him. For a moment it was as though they were alone in the world. For this precious moment Caroline made no effort to deny their love.

Jim was engrossed in the problem that faced him, unaware of the poignant exchange between Eric and Caroline.

"This will complicate Tina's defense," he sighed. "The police are sure to find out. But we can reduce the charge to manslaughter."

They were approaching the Kendrick house.

"Tina's not here!" Caroline was alarmed. "Her loco-steamer isn't out front."

"She may have put it in the stable," Jim pointed out, while Eric leapt down and extended a hand to Caroline.

"No," Caroline was convinced. "Her father wouldn't allow it. The loco-steamer frightens their pair of bays."

Walking up the steps to the Kendrick verandah, they were assaulted by a strident feminine voice that carried clearly through the windows.

"Yes, I've called the police! But you've got to come home immediately!" Mrs. Kendrick was near hysteria. "The safe's been opened and all the cash and stocks are gone! Even my jewelry!"

Eric rang the bell. A frightened maid opened the door.

"Miz Kendrick ain't seeing nobody this mornin'," the maid said agitatedly.

"She'll see us," Eric insisted and led Caroline and Jim into the foyer. "Has Miss Tina been here?"

"No, suh," the maid told him.

"Is Mr. Chad here?" Caroline asked.

"He went chasin' off in the phaeton a little while ago. Miz

Kendrick here by herself and she ain't feelin' like company."

"Ellie Mae!" Mrs. Kendrick screamed. "Come here this instant."

"Tina's run off with Chad," Eric gave voice to Caroline's thought. "He broke into the safe, cleared it out, and he's rushed off to meet her. Mrs. Kendrick hasn't caught on yet."

"Let's go," Jim ordered. "We have nothing to say to Mrs. Kendrick."

In silence they left the house and climbed into the buggy.

"We'll have to notify the police," Eric said. "Caroline must be cleared."

"The police will go after Tina." Caroline's eyes were pained. "She shouldn't have run away. It's going to be ugly now."

"We'll go to the police after we've had lunch," Jim stipulated with cool deliberation. Caroline and Eric stared at him. "By the time we leave the Kimball House restaurant, Tina and Chad will be on a train bound for God knows where. They'll never return to Atlanta."

They lingered over luncheon in the charming restaurant, each conscious of the urgency for delay. Each convinced that this was not a circumvention of justice. Tina would pay for the rest of her life for that moment of rage. The police would never catch up with Tina, Eric assured himself, when, at last, they rose from their seats and left the restaurant.

Fifteen minutes later, Caroline, Jim and he sat in the office of the Captain of Detectives. The detective listened gravely to Jim's recital of events.

"I understand your anxiety to clear your client of the murder charge," he said with a slight smile of compassion for Caroline, "but the word of a thirteen-year-old child is questionable. Particularly in these circumstances."

"The charge will surely be changed to manslaughter," Jim reminded, his tone deferential. "A paperweight was thrown in the heat of anger. Not by my client, but by Mrs. Tina Hampton. And we have not only the word of Betsy Jackson, but that of Councilman Hampton."

"My wife confessed to me," Eric said tersely. "She's headstrong and impatient. She was furious with the man, and she threw the

452

paperweight in a fit of rage." If Tina had remained in Atlanta to be tried, she would have received a sentence of no more than a year, Eric guessed. It was likely that she would not serve a day. But life under such circumstances would be impossible for her and her family. "I'll give a statement to that effect."

"Why isn't your wife here to give the statement herself?" the detective inquired, deceptively attached. His eyes moved from Eric to Caroline. He was arriving at a conclusion that infuriated Eric, but this was a moment for diplomacy.

"I expected that she would turn herself in," Eric explained. "But while Mr. Russell and I waited in the library of our home, she took off. We assumed she was going to the home of her parents, Mr. and Mrs. Kendrick. We went there, hoping to catch up with her and persuade her to come here; but she had not been seen at her parents' house."

"To be blunt, Captain," Jim intervened, "Mrs. Hampton has bolted. Probably in the company of her brother."

"We had a report of a robbery at the Kendrick house about two hours ago." The detective's mind was adding up facts. He rose to his feet, crossed to the door in rapid strides, pulled it wide. "Sergeant Culpepper, what have you got on a robbery this morning at the Kendrick residence?"

"That was kind of funny—" The desk sergeant ambled toward the detective. "The men got over there and found out it was all a mistake. The son had taken the contents of the safe and carried them over to the family bank vault. His mother said the maid had forgotten to give her the note he'd left. Wouldn't you think they would have talked about it first?"

"Thank you, Sergeant Culpepper." The detective closed the door. "We'll send a man back to the Kendrick house. We'll try to locate Mrs. Hampton." He paused. "I'd like you to make a statement, Councilman, and sign it. Under the circumstances, we'll withdraw the charges against Miss Hampton."

CAROLINE LEFT the police station, flanked by Eric and Jim. She was shaken by the confrontation with the police, relieved that it was over. The police would make a perfunctory effort to apprehend Tina, then abandon it. The case would be closed.

"We're going to read some unpleasant newspaper accounts," Jim warned. "But they won't harm your campaign, Eric." Caroline was startled. For a little while she had forgotten what this might mean to Eric politically. "Don't look so stricken, Caroline," Jim soothed. "Voters will sympathize with the wronged husband."

"I mean to divorce Tina," Eric told him.

"No one expects you to do otherwise." Jim leaned forward to kiss Caroline on one cheek. "Take my buggy," he told Eric. "You can bring it in tomorrow. I'll hop a streetcar home from the office."

Caroline and Eric went to the carriage. Eric helped her up and seated himself beside her. He reached for her hand and brought it to his mouth, his eyes making love to her.

"When my divorce from Tina is final, we'll be married. At Hampton Court. Unless you're afraid to scandalize Atlanta by marrying a divorced man?" he challenged tenderly.

"We'll be marrying in the twentieth century," Caroline reminded, her smile incandescent. "I defy anybody in Atlanta to be shocked."

The nightmare was over. Together Eric and she would bury the ugliness of his marriage to Tina. They would work together to help Atlanta toward its great destiny. They would carry on the General's dream.

ACKNOWLEDGMENTS

I would like to thank Mr. Franklin M. Garrett, Historian of the Atlanta Historical Society, for having written his wonderfully informative book, *Atlanta and Environs*, and for his courteous assistance and that of the staff of the Atlanta Historical Society during my research in Atlanta. Among those on the staff I wish particularly to thank Archivists D. Louise Cook and Richard Eltzroth, with special gratitude to Librarian H. Eugene Craig, who was tireless and gracious despite the abundance of my requests. My thanks, also, to Ms. Janice Coleman of the Special Collections Department of the Atlanta Public Library, who so promptly and efficiently responded to my repeated requests for information, to Mr. Billy Townsend of the Department of Natural Resources in Atlanta, and to the ladies of Swan House and the Tullie Smith House Restoration of the Atlanta Historical Society.

For the Columbus, Georgia, chapters I was graciously helped by Ms. Dae Lane and the volunteer ladies of the Springer Opera House Restoration; by Ms. Emily Woodruff; and Ms. Loretto Chappell, who so delightfully and vividly recalled her childhood memories of a Columbus long past for me. My thanks, also, to the staff of the Bradley Library, including Mr. Edge Reid and Ms. Virginia Story, and most particularly to Reference Librarian Jeanne Hollis, who searched endlessly for material for me and drove me to all the historical spots to refresh my memories of Columbus.

My thanks, also, to Mr. Donald Kloster of the Smithsonian Institution in Washington, D.C., and to Mr. Frank Bradley and Ms. Natalie Seweryn and the staff of the Genealogy Room of the New York Public Library.

To my daughter Susie, who has learned to type, my gratitude for providing me with typed copies of the myriad negative photocopies that came to me from the Atlanta Public Library.

—JULIE ELLIS